FIRESTORM

FIRESTORM

William Coyle

William Morrow and Company, Inc. • New York

Library of Congress Cataloging-in-Publication Data

Coyle, William.
  Firestorm.

  1. World War, 1939–1945—Fiction. I. Title.
PS3553.0956F57 1988   813′.54   88-12814
ISBN 0-688-07363-8

Printed in the United States of America

First U.S. Edition

1 2 3 4 5 6 7 8 9 10

BOOK DESIGN BY LINEY LI

FIRESTORM

1

Shrove Tuesday

AT an airfield on the edge of the fenland village of Starkley, it was hours after dark on Shrove Tuesday, 1945, a day of such showers and low clouds that crews were hoping the long mission they had been briefed for would be scrubbed because of weather. Reardon waved good-bye to the rest of his crew, who were going forward along the fuselage of the Lancaster bomber and—in the technical language of Pathfinder Force—Visual Centerer called D-Dog, and went forward to his turret. He liked this parting of the ways, the other seven going forward to the more spacious end of that tube of aluminum. He even liked to see Challenor's hulking back. And this was strange, since Challenor was not only his brother Australian, but also the other gunner in the crew. Reardon was bound to him by tribal and professional links.

Even now, very tired, cramped with terror at the idea of the flak over Dresden, he felt some of his old professional excitement. When he pulled the doors behind him and closed off his turret, he would become Arse-End Charlie at his mighty Wurlitzer. Electric wiring would carry his instructions in a fragment of a second to the pilot, and the pilot, a journalist from Maidstone, would obey them without wavering. Because at this stage of his career and his struggle, he knew that there were too many English pilots who had disregarded the orders of colonial or low-class tail gunners and burned alive for it.

It always seemed to Reardon a long walk from the hatch to the turret—longer than the living room in Rose Bay. He carried a flashlight in his ungloved hand, saw at every step along the fuselage the multicolored strands of intercommunication and oxygen cables, and close to his knees, the alloy ammunition racks which would carry, if needed, fourteen thousand rounds of belted ammunition to his guns. They would be useless, though, against well-directed flak.

When he first entered this trade, the figure fourteen thousand nad filled him with excitement. But there was a falsity to it. You couldn't fire the guns for more than three seconds at a time without causing either a jamming in the breech or a telescoping of rounds. All this fire that had been packed into the bomber for him had limits.

He got to the turret without trembling—so that was one test he no longer had to worry about. He stepped through the swing doors, perched himself on the barely padded seat, and dragged the doors closed behind him with the leather straps provided by a kind War Cabinet to prevent gunners from dislocating their elbows. He locked the doors with the wire lever he could reach with his left hand, then immediately plugged in his oxygen mask. He had found himself doing this very early, even before takeoffs, even though Inch wouldn't be turning on the sweet oxygen until they reached twelve thousand feet. He never put the mask on until his doors were locked, though. There was a slight, masturbation-like guilt attached to getting ready so early to suck in the sweet oxygen the engineer would soon turn on. Yet everybody, especially experienced crews with drinking habits, sweated on their oxygen, stayed on oxygen all the time. It was said to be good for the senses, and therefore particularly good for gunners' vision. It was certainly good for the soul, Reardon knew.

A rain squall threw itself against the red-brick squadron buildings across the airstrip. Everyone in every bomber was looking for the red flare that would be fired from the control tower to cancel the operation. But that would happen only if Bomber Command at High Wycombe had the same foul weather as Starkley.

*   *   *

In the esteemed, or at least self-esteemed, town of Rossclare—
a world away, on the dairy farming north coast of New South
Wales in Australia—it was already late into a breathless summer
night. Dairy farmers were turning over for the last time before
their alarm clocks rang. The Brisbane mail train, laden with some
Australian militiamen and some USAF postal personnel who had
found the Rossclare Refreshment Room closed, hauled itself out
of Rossclare station, hooting like a being afflicted with extreme
spiritual or animal want.

On the second floor of a building separated by a high gate from
St. John Vianney's Hospital, Sister Mary Perpetua Reardon—sister
by blood to the far-off gunner—slept in a light nightgown with the
bedclothes kicked down. One rim of the gown rose nearly to her
right knee, and the legs this accident displayed to Rossclare's steamy
moon were elegantly shaped. The limbs of other nuns which might
be here and there visible to the stars throughout this convent of the
Sisters of Compassion, would not have shone so perfectly. Sister
Timothy, Perpetua knew, had chunky country legs. Sister Francis
came from the freckled Irish, and her freckles—originally said to be
brought on by the Australian sun—shone all the more redly now
that her body was hidden from the sun most of the day by the
proudly worn, medieval habit of the Sisters of Compassion. As for
Mother Felice's legs, only God and the moon had ever seen them.
She never bared them except on rare picnics to Brunswick Heads
and during the week she had recently spent at Mr. Brosnan's
secluded house at the beach. But simply in terms of years on the
clock, there was no chance that they could match the unconscious
perfection of Sister Perpetua Reardon's.

Perpetua's sleep had been disturbed, full of dreams of surgical
emergencies involving Father Proud, or of the Bishop's dapper
little secretary, Father Lawlor, chastising both her and Father
Murphy in front of the entire community of St. John Vianney's. In
these dream sessions before Father Lawlor she was never fully
dressed in her habit—generally her veil and headgear were missing. She was conscious of her spiky dark brown hair, cropped to fit
under the hood of her order, sticking up unprettily, indecently.
Proud lay wounded on the refectory table. Her warmth for him,
her desire—if that was what it was—was still there, but blunted,
thwarted. And in these dreams he became confused with a timber
worker from up the river, at Rossclare.

The man, a remote cousin of Father Murphy's, had been brought in to St. John Vianney's earlier in the summer. He had been cutting down a tall mahogany which, in falling, had snapped off a sapling at its base and sent it catapulting toward him. The tree, rendered by velocity into a terrible weapon, had struck him just below the chest. When he reached St. John Vianney's, there had still been twigs and pieces of foliage mixed in with his exposed viscera. It was understandable that in Perpetua's dreams the timber worker and Father Proud should be somehow combined. There was horror, too, as dapper Father Lawlor—the Bishop's little, thin-lipped zealot of a church lawyer—accused her in front of the entire community of St. John Vianney's of endangering her brother in the turret through her particular friendship with Sister Timothy, and even with Father Proud.

Fortunately missing was that dream of a crashed bomber of the kind Sister Perpetua had seen only in the motion pictures Father Murphy borrowed from his friend Mr. Brosnan, owner of the Astoria Theater, and showed for the benefit of all the nuns and brothers in Rossclare in the woodwork room of the brothers' school.

This was an irony of Sister Perpetua's existence. She knew nothing of Naxos 2, the German night-fighter radar. She knew nothing of the patterns of flak around the German cities, nor of H2S radar which flew in the bellies of the Lancasters, nor of *Schrägemusik*, the terrible 30-millimeter cannons pointing up at an angle of fifteen degrees and sitting in the nose of the Messerschmitt 110's. She knew nothing, either, of the coning of searchlights, the terrible incandescent threat they were. Or what she did know was derived from Father Murphy's film evenings. Nor did she understand, nor would she know for another four or five years, that jet-propelled Messerschmitt 262's were sometimes bent on contesting the same air space as her brother's Lancaster. She was an honest, New World girl living a thirteenth-century life in a distant and prosperous town in the New World. This life had been now influenced a little by a most moderate war, but she still carried a tribal instinct that her brother's survival would be more influenced by her worthiness as a nun than by the dazzling technology of the failing Reich or the imperfect stratagems of Bomber Command.

Perpetua groaned in her dreams as, in the cell next to hers, the retired and elderly Mother Catherine awoke with a grunt, the fact that she was still alive always taking the old nun by surprise.

A green flare had appeared, arching above the Starkley control tower. On the limits of the perimeter the engines of Reardon's Lancaster ARH D-Dog, and then of twelve other bombers, began to grind and rage. With two of ARH's engines running, the sound seemed intolerable. But when all four were churning, it became somehow bearable, though little splashes of slick water were swept backward to streak the perspex of his turret.

The Lancaster rolled forward onto the perimeter track. He spun the turret away from the plane behind—the whole mechanism and his view of the night turned with that smooth, hydraulic purr, itself a sort of technical reassurance in the face of the odds. Through the cutaway section of perspex he saw darkly over the turret controls the flat fenland of England. He and Challenor often discussed why the Poms—the British—were willing to die for such country. Reardon and Challenor weren't willing to die for it. They were here instead to show what they were made of—or at least that had been the original intention.

Between their first airfield station, Parsfield, and the road into York—on the way to catch trains to London or Scotland while on leave—Reardon and Challenor had often had pointed out to them a hill on the Wolds where Lancastrians had been slaughtered during the War of the Roses.

"So," said big Challenor, winking at Reardon, "Lancastrians got done like a dinner there during the War of the Roses? Shit a brick, eh?"

They had long ago concluded that storied Britain—the Britain they had heard about in Australian classrooms, the England of Wordsworth and Treasure Island, the England of Kings and Crusades—did not exist anymore, if it ever had. He and Challenor had spent a war on boggy airfields and had never spotted that England, had—with happy exceptions like Enid Hadgraft—spotted little but meanness, rationed food and rationed souls, in the villages around the remote airfields from which they had been flying over Europe's complicated skies for nearly two years now.

Somewhere out there beyond the turret in the eastern fenland of Huntingdonshire, somewhere out there under the eternal mist,

Alf Hater's bicycle was rusting in a bog. Alf, a little pointy-nosed terrier of a man, had abandoned it one night when a bull had charged him on the way back from the pub in Great Starkley, and the mist had not lifted enough in three months for Alf to go back looking for it. Everyone knew the bull had not really charged. Alf had a phobia about cattle. Once on leave in Dorset with Challenor and Reardon, he had walked an extra two miles to a village pub rather than cross a paddock filled with tranquil dairy cows. One fixed stare from a cow could panic him. The fear Alf had once limited to his relationship with cows had spread to flying operations now that his father had thrown his mother out. Old man Hater, true to his name, had written to Alf and as much as boasted of the bonfire he had made of Mrs. Hater's memory, burning her clothes and the wedding photographs in the backyard of the Hater house in St. Kilda in Melbourne.

"The Americans in Melbourne, who are in no way front-line soldiers," old Hater had written, "have corrupted most of the women, and your mother was not proof against them."

Mrs. Hater had written to Alf from a boardinghouse in Sydney and assured him that the friendship she had with a major in U.S. Intelligence—"a man with grown children," she said—was innocent, but that Mr. Hater was such a strict Methodist that there was no innocence in his world.

"My old man's a bastard, an utter bastard," Alf had said, before weeping in the Sergeants' mess one night. Since then his cow phobia had gotten worse.

"He bears watching," the large, portly Challenor said of Alf sagely. Alf had a redheaded girl of no great beauty up in Yorkshire, in Parsfield. She did not seem to Challenor or Reardon to be very reliable. If she let Aft down, too, then his world would be entirely denuded. Alf's problem was there wasn't much to keep him busy in the air between the brief half-hourly transmissions he had to handle.

So Challenor and Reardon had not forgiven old man Hater for increasing Alf's fear. Let the old bugger have his bonfire, but not at D-Dog's cost.

Over the intercom headphones Reardon began to hear George Winton, the journalist pilot, checking through the crew. The Ulster flight engineer answered him, a handsome boy called William Inch. There was no malice in him, he was always saying with a smile, "For Christ's sake don't say the Paddy Rosary back there, Reardon. I don't want God to finish us just because He thinks we're all Papists!"

Inch's style of teasing was more or less like Challenor's. "The bastard wouldn't make a bad Australian," Challenor used to say.

Next Winton called for a response from the navigator, the strange but brilliant Squadron Leader Stove seated at his H2S navigation set which, no matter how far the bomber went, continued to emit a cathode-tube image of the country below. Stove was the highest ranking member of the crew; bombers were not like ships—the skipper did not always carry the highest rank. Stove intended never to leave the RAF, having found within its informal wartime face the sort of society where he wanted to live in peace. He carried with him, even in the mess, a copy of the Articles of War and an immensely thicker commentary on the same. He knew, though, that a flight lieutenant like Winton could reprimand only airmen under the rank of sergeant, for instance, and so had once pointed out that he—not Winton—was the only one in the crew qualified to make formal reprimands.

Winton called in the bombardier, then Alf, then big, portly Challenor, packed into his mid-upper turret, then Reardon. There was already a crisp anxiety in Winton's voice, but that was normal. He talked anxious all the way to the target and back, and somehow it reassured Reardon. Talked clipped, too, as if there were already a threat, here on the edge of the misty fens. But he didn't talk like a panic merchant, as did their last pilot, Punch.

"Prepared to suck oxygen, Reardon?" he asked. He believed in oxygen, too, that it was good for the eyesight.

Reardon, half-ashamed, admitted he was.

"Suck it in, suck it in," Winton murmured. "Breach clear?"

"No worries, skipper."

"Give 'em a burst over the Channel," Winton advised. "You too, pop," he told Challenor.

He would order a beer with the same sort of urgency, but drink it slowly and in a very composed way. Yet, though losses to night fighters were rare now, at the end of this exhausting winter he was not composed about being raked from below by *Schrägemusik*, the uptilted cannon fire of the Messerschmitts.

Reardon heard over his earphones a technical discussion about fuel consumption and mileage, cross winds and deviations, between Squadron Leader Stove and William Inch, the engineer. Once he had listened hungrily to all such talk—he had desired an aeronautical education. Now his mind had lost its stretch. He rationed out his intellect. He did not listen to the conclusions Stove and Willie Inch were uttering.

He thought of his sister, Perpetua. It seemed to him that her just life guaranteed his own above blazing Europe. She had confessed once in a letter that she believed that, too, and it had given him courage.

2

Morning in the Convent

AS D-Dog rolled around from dispersal toward the runway end, twelve thousand miles away the broad-hipped Sister Roberta swung out of her bed at the demand of her alarm clock, kissed the floor, threw a towel over her head and a dressing gown over her shoulders and rushed off to the bathroom to wash herself quickly. She had only a quarter of an hour before she needed to rouse the others.

She was back in her cell within five minutes. The habit of the Sisters of Compassion looked to an outsider like one layer after another of complicated cloth. But there were ways of getting it on the body quickly. Roberta, like any other experienced Sister of Compassion, could manage the task in three minutes. Today, in her early morning daze, she took four. Then she sat on her bed and said part of the Rosary for the benefit of her mother, a constantly pale and ill woman in her early sixties. Some would say, and Roberta would have had to admit, that her mother was a professionally sick and exhausted woman. A hypochondriac. Roberta was aware of the seeds of hypochondria in her own body, but her crowded daily life had not given them any room to flourish. She did not have more than half an hour a day she could call her own. The fact pleased her.

She rose again, stared for an instant at some of the book titles in her shelf, picked up a small brass bell from her desk and went out into the corridor. She had time to look out of the eastern window. A slick of gold light was already on roofs, even though the sun had not risen yet. That light, stickier than honey, promised another hot and humid day in Rossclare. The pubs and Rendall's department store still slept under this first wash of light. It was too early for one of those jockey-like cellarmen to be hosing down the pavement in front of the Railway Hotel, the Commercial, the Hibernian. Sister Roberta believed she could see a wide-shouldered frock sitting on a model in Rendall's window.

At twenty seconds before a quarter past five by her watch, she moved into the corridor and began ringing the small brass bell. She hammered on Mother Superior's door. In Roberta's girlhood a Novice Mistress had taught her to hammer instead of tentatively knocking. This rousing of your fellow sisters was a work of emergency. You were waking them to the essential business of the day—the salvation of their immortal souls! She tinkled the bell and swung her freckled knuckles robustly against every door, from Mother Superior's to ancient Sister Catherine's, to Sister Perpetua's, the youngest in the community and still vaguely considered "skittish." Perpetua had the curse of good looks, too, so Roberta put a special, curative energy into the way she beat against her door.

At each door Roberta called out, *"Benedicamus Domino."* She was not supposed to move on until she heard the reply, *"Deo Gratias."* She was following the Jesuit Rule, devised in the sixteenth century by a redheaded mercenary called Ignatius Loyola. As every Sister of Compassion knew, Ignatius had his right leg fractured and his left damaged by a cannonball while defending the Spanish citadel of Pamplona against the French. That cannonball had been the voice of God for Loyola. A stint on a surgical table, unspeakable by the standards of these days of anesthesia, had changed him.

After long meditation, he founded the religious order that would become known as the Jesuits. He wrote a book of meditations, *The Spiritual Exercises*—an edition of which sat this morning in the choir stall of each of the fourteen Sisters of Compassion in Rossclare, in a continent that had not been discovered by Europeans at the time of Loyola's cannonball. He had also written a Rule for the priests who began to join him, and it was later amended by a Spaniard called Rodriguez, "for the use of Women Religious." On account of this Rule, Roberta now hammered on Perpetua's door and called, *"Benedicamus Domino!"*

As had happened a lot recently, Perpetua was raised from the deepest predawn sleep by Roberta. She yelled the *"Deo Gratias!"* automatically, before she knew she had. It was best to pretend you welcomed the day.

Perpetua did not welcome this one, however. It brought too many questions with it. Dazed, she put on a gown and flung a towel over her head. Then she moved into the corridor, knocked on old Catherine's door, and went in. She was grateful for this task of looking after the oldest nun in the community.

Catherine was wide awake, sitting up in her voluminous nightgown, her cap over head and ears. She was as fine and near-transparent as an elderly saint in a Renaissance painting. She had the sort of relaxed certainty that everyone wanted. And this morning—when Perpetua was so uncertain about Fathers Murphy and Proud of the diocese of Rossclare, and about their brother in the faith, Pilot Officer Reardon, Distinguished Flying Medal, high above Europe's dark night—it was a delight to see old Catherine, who had survived wars and turmoils as well as the Rule itself.

Catherine was very undemanding. She swung her own legs out of bed. Having kept the rule of silence since she was seventeen, she could see no further use for it.

"God's in a bad way," she would say, Irishly, "if he needs a poor old woman like me to keep her lips buttoned."

As Perpetua put a dressing gown over the nun's shoulders, she could smell a faint, sweet odor, both terrifying and fascinating. In devotional books and lives of saints you came across the term "the odor of sanctity," and perhaps that was what this was, mixed in with something that was growing inside Catherine and killing her in this, her eighty-second year. Perpetua held Catherine's table crucifix up to the old woman's lips. Catherine gave it a noisy kiss. Then she appraised Perpetua.

"You need building up with cocoa, girl!"

Perpetua smiled and did not answer.

"Listen," said the old nun, "there's just the one commandment. Happiness. For nun and man and dog, just the one rule. Happiness and happiness again." Because Catherine said this sort of thing, some of the other nuns considered her senile. "I didn't find that out until I was fifty years of age. I don't want you to wait as long as that, girl."

"She thinks she's back on an Irish farm," Roberta used to say. "Calling everyone *girl* like that!"

Catherine had robust, peasant bowels, which she generally exercised in the mornings. As Perpetua guided her down the corridor to the lavatory, she hoped the old nun would not be too long in the cubicle today. If Catherine was her normal brisk self, there was some chance that Perpetua could rush down the hospital to that front room reserved for priests and leading laymen, where Father Proud now lay in torment.

As Perpetua showed Mother Catherine into a cubicle, the old Irish woman clucked contentedly.

"Sure, the lovely porcelain," she said.

Sister Catherine had begun nursing in her early thirties in a hospital in Waterford, at a time when surgeons everywhere were just getting used to the idea of antisepsis and asepsis and where some of the older surgeons were still skeptical about wearing clean coats. She had been shipped out at the turn of the century to the order's hospital in Sydney, St. Brigid's, famous throughout that city as Bridie's. It had not been a very esteemed hospital in those days, "full of quacks and bluffers," as Catherine had once described it. This modern brick convent in Rossclare, a mere rural offshoot of Bridie's but fitted with internal plumbing, was a sign of how far the Sisters of Compassion had traveled in less than half a century. A sign, too, of God's approval of their work. The new hospital and convent, opened by Bishop Flannery in the war's first year, was to Catherine a sort of foreshadowing—in chrome and tile and brick—of paradise. Indeed, most of Rossclare's population still had only outhouses. But nothing had been too good for the good nuns, especially if the local Catholic population had to suffer the nagging and energetic fund-raising of a born businessman like His Lordship, Bishop Flannery.

While Catherine began her happy morning bowel movement, Perpetua moved through an archway to the washbasins. There was a vacant one beside Sister Francis, who was washing her face three times in honor of the Trinity. It seemed that there were few aspects of Francis's life that did not have some theologic meaning. When Perpetua first arrived at Rossclare, the delicate-featured Francis had been pointed out to her as an example to follow.

Francis was at that stage new to the community. These days she was not nearly as widely praised. Mother Felice the Superior was rightly worried about Francis's obsessiveness. Old Catherine had one morning described her as "an eed-jit." Many of the other nuns found her relentless, morbid perfection a little hard to take.

But they'd always backed Francis when she denounced Perpetua for careless behavior. This was an aspect of life as a nun that Perpetua had not gotten used to. In the outside world, people who ran you down in public were unquestionably the enemy. Here you had to consider them the voice of God, though their every gesture—to quote Catherine again—"gave you the creeps!"

Francis kept up the business of the Trinity even as she brushed her teeth—three to the right, three to the left, three up, three down. Whether or not this was enough to stop tooth decay, Francis wasn't going to break with the holy number. She also kept what the Rule described as "custody of the eyes." That is, she didn't look at anyone. It was only when you belonged to a silent community that you knew how eloquent the eyes could be, and how, therefore, if you were to be truly silent, the eyes had to be guarded. Perpetua, realizing she wasn't guarding her own, began to, looking straight ahead into the mirror for fear that at the next Chapter of Faults she might be accused of staring at people.

"Oh, God," Perpetua prayed desperately, "make me more generous-minded. Protect poor Father Proud. And do not judge my brother Bernard by his unworthy sister!" She was embittered, afraid and guilty, and she hated the feeling. Quickly finished at the washbasins, she rushed back to fetch Mother Catherine from her cubicle.

"My clan were blessed with bowels as sound as bellows," Catherine announced. Perpetua heard a slight gasp of laughter from one of the nuns at the basins. It was Timothy, the hefty daughter of a dairy farmer.

The old nun washed herself deftly, with a little help from Perpetua, who then helped her back to her cell. There she dismissed Perpetua jovially.

Back in her own cell, away from the eyes of Francis, Mother Superior Felice, and the others, Perpetua dressed with what was described in the Rule as "undue haste." She took the long white habit out of the cupboard and off its clothes hanger. She buckled the thick black belt with its great hardwood rosary around her waist—not too tightly, since once she had been accused in Chapter of Faults, down at St. Brigid's in Sydney, of accentuating her slimness by keeping her belt excessively tight. Onto her head she fitted the entire pinned-together assembly of the order's pre-scribed headgear. An inner cap of firm netting got sweaty in this weather and had to be changed every few days. To it was pinned an outer cap which fell down over the ears—the same one Cath-erine had been wearing in bed that morning. A band of highly starched linen called the bandeau was pinned around these two caps. Next Perpetua buttoned around her throat a cape—again the name for it was French: guimpe. Finally Perpetua fixed a gray veil over her head, pinning it in place with those long, white-knobbed pins which since childhood she had associated with nuns, with the mysteriously garbed Sisters of Compassion.

She took one look in the small seven-by-five-inch mirror each sister was permitted. She saw a pale, dark-eyed, full-lipped, un-happy girl masquerading as a nun. "Don't make the mistake of disliking yourself," Father Murphy had said to her. "Leave that to others. They'll line up to oblige you." And this morning Catherine had echoed him. "Save my brother, though," she said to her im-age. Then she put the mirror facedown, so that it would not reflect the day's heat, and left her cell. Again, to quote the heavily disap-proved-of Father Murphy: "They call them cells, but they're more comfortable and watertight than most of the farms upriver!"

The corridor was clear of anyone, and beyond Catherine's door was the stairwell. At the bottom Perpetua let herself out into the garden. Palms, ferns, frangipani, and much else that was luscious and subtropical grew here. Sometimes you felt, as you crossed the garden, that the Pacific islands where young soldiers were perish-ing in a decent cause were close indeed. She unlocked the garden gate with the key all the nuns needed in order to walk from the convent to the hospital and back again.

She entered the back door of the hospital. Halfway down the corridor Sister Calixta would be at her night station. Calixta did not wander around much during the night, leaving most of the footwork to an energetic girl called Bernadette Brady, a final-year nurse who liked night duty. Bernadette was a sort of ally, a cousin of Father Murphy's—like most of the Rossclare Irish. She wasn't visible at the moment either. Perpetua crossed the corridor like a ghost and entered the room where Father Proud lay.

She could not at first see the bed clearly. Something very like a mist of pain hit her and made her pause for a second. She was entering the awful territory of religious madness, of a madness more extreme than Francis's three to the right, three to the left. Yet Proud was amongst the best, the most sensitive. He had tried to get away into the army as a chaplain, possibly knowing that unless he escaped from the Diocese, he might destroy himself. But the army was already oversupplied with chaplains. Instead he had stayed in Rossclare, yearning for the University of Louvain in Belgium, an ancient center of learning from which the English Elizabethan priests had returned home to face the rack and the gibbet. Bishop Flannery had been going to send Proud there in 1940, but the war had prevented that. So Proud had become a mere curate in the Rossclare parish. And religion, or Proud's idea of religion, or Proud's idea of love and self-denial—or whatever it was that had done it—had given him a wound which, had he joined the army as a chaplain, even the Japanese would have been hard put to inflict on him.

Proud was asleep. Perpetua moved to the end of the bed and lifted the cloth cover over the catheter bottle, looking for traces of blood in the seepage from his bladder and wound. She was pleased to see that there was none—at least not enough to be perceived in this light. She covered the bottle again and turned to Proud's chart. He looked gloriously waxen lying there, sedated far beyond the reach of his own madness. The last time Bernadette Brady had looked and jotted it down, his blood pressure had been borderline—121 over 67. His pulse had been 110, his temperature 101.2 degrees. Bernadette Brady was, of course, waiting for him to improve or get worse by daylight before calling in the august Rossclare surgeon, Dr. Cormack.

Hauling out the large nurse's watch attached to her habit, Perpetua now took Father Proud's pulse, which was a fluty 112. Dr. Cormack may well have to be disturbed at his breakfast. She reached for the blood-pressure device and wrapped the bulb against the veins inside Father Proud's elbow. Pumping it up, she read on the mercury a sad result: 119 over 66. The reading promised all the worst things—internal bleeding, sepsis, shock.

Dr. Cormack wasn't the best surgeon Perpetua had seen. He was certainly good enough to have made himself a reputation in Sydney, if he'd chosen to. But not a great reputation. He was too rough with the tissues; he'd been taught by a "quick-in, quick-out" man in Edinburgh. Ten years ago his firm-handed though not incompetent techniques might not have been enough to save Father Proud. Now, combined with penicillin, they gave Father Proud's consecrated body a chance of some sort. The diocese of Rossclare would ensure that Michael Proud got the wonder drug, whether the fast-cutting Cormack had managed to remove all the infectious fragments of wood and graphite from the wound in the priest's peritoneum or not.

Perpetua knew Father Proud did not wish to live, though he had never said so to himself or anyone else. But he had inflicted on himself a berserk mutilation, one that left him barely alive and yet still fixed him in a state of unresolved torment. No doubt his comatose soul, still arguing with itself even under the weight of ether and opiates, would prefer to use the shock of the operation as an excuse to slip away. There was a story about the Irish Catholic convicts on Norfolk Island a hundred years past that reminded Perpetua of Proud's situation. Realizing that they could not enter heaven if they took their own lives, they would form a group and draw lots. The winner would be executed at once, usually with a shovel and by the man who drew the second longest straw. The killer would then be put on trial and would have time to prepare his soul for death and to repent of the murder of his friend. In this way two prisoners would be released from painful slavery without either of them being accused of suicide. The same death wish lay at the base of Proud's wound—a desire to die without being accused of suicide.

Perpetua was unwrapping the binding of the sphygmomanometer from Father Proud's arm and planning how to find Nurse Brady and persuade her to interrupt Dr. Cormack at the breakfast table, when Bernadette Brady herself and Father Murphy appeared in the doorway. At first she feared they might wonder what she was doing there, since she was not on duty and had obviously given up the silent time between the waking bell and chapel to visit a patient. Then she noticed that neither of them showed any shock at seeing her.

Murphy was large, genial, and strong-fisted. His dark hair was beginning to thin. His father was a hefty but gentle postmaster far up the valley, and Murphy was built on his father's mold.

"I'm a weak man mayself," he had confessed to Perpetua

once—the two were confidants. Murphy was her confessor and spiritual director. But he seemed to look for as much guidance from her as she did from him. "I like to hope there's a certain strength in knowing it."

"Sister Perpetua," he said now. "How is the poor, silly little bugger?" He meant Proud.

He drew Brady, his cousin, into the room beside him so that the door could be closed and Sister Calixta, if she did happen to walk down the corridor, would not necessarily hear them.

"Blood pressure not good," said Perpetua.

"I knew that, Sister," said Bernadette Brady defensively. "If it hadn't improved by seven, I was going to call Doctor."

The nurses had been trained to call Cormack Doctor in that way, as if he were the physician of all physicians.

"It was wise to wait, Bernadette," said Perpetua, to show she was not accusing this handsome farm girl, who had escaped the strenuousness of the milk shed only to take on the strenuousness of nursing. "But the pulse is 110 now, and I think Dr. Cormack should be called."

Perpetua suddenly felt too weary to cover her own tracks, to say to Bernadette Brady, "Don't tell him I ordered you to, because I'm not supposed to be here." She would have to trust the girl not to give her away.

There was a sense in which the three of them—Nurse Brady, Father Murphy, Sister Perpetua—were allies. In the community of the hospital their standing was not as high as that of others. Certain rumors about Father Murphy had led Mother Superior Felice to advise Sister Perpetua against having him as a spiritual adviser any longer, though she had not actually ordered it and for some reason had stopped short of telling Perpetua not to go to confession to Murphy. So Perpetua continued to confess to him, because it was not like confession at all. That is, there were none of the normal confessional terrors in it. It was more like an admission of mutual fears and doubts, in which Murphy seemed to edge toward the same frankness as Perpetua herself. Mother Felice would have approved more if Perpetua had chosen Father Proud as a confessor, but how could she have explained to Felice that she was frightened of Proud, of his romanticism and his good looks, of the sort of forced liveliness he showed when he was with most young people, especially the good-looking ones? Perpetua could not imagine being able to talk to any of the other priests in the diocese so freely, and the Bishop kept Murphy's best friend, Father Stone—another honest man, a sort of "know where you stand with him" man—two hundred miles away down the coast, in the parish of Orpenville, so that Murphy and Stone could only infrequently get together for booze and sedition.

Not that booze was considered a crime amongst the clergy of the diocese of Rossclare. The hard-drinking, no-nonsense pastor was one of the gifts of the Irish church to the Australian bush, and if the liquor ever went too far, then there was always prayer and drying out. But for religious sedition and the spirit of heretical humanism, Bishop Flannery could find less excuse and forgiveness.

With Nurse Bernadette Brady's upriver relatives, Father Murphy was far more a favorite than he was in the Bishop's residence in Rossclare. The Bradys, the Laceys, the Meaghers, the Rogans, and all the other poorer upriver dairy farmers and loggers were not all as affluent as Bernadette Brady's relatively well-off father, who had been able to afford to send his daughter to boarding school in Grafton. But Murphy—himself the son of a poor relative of the clan—would often turn up at the hospital door with any of his clan who had an injury, an enraged appendicitis, a fever, or a kidney stone. Many of them were bad payers—or what were called nonpaying L.O.G. cases (Love of God). It was obvious to Mother Felice, even though she was a great businesswoman, that the Sisters of Compassion must show compassion to the poor as well as to such wealthy farmers as Bernadette Brady's father. But it was generally considered that Father Murphy put moral pressure on her to take in more of the Meagher/Lacey/Brady/Rogan crowd than the economics of a private hospital should have to stand.

In this present emergency in Father Proud's sickroom, Bernadette Brady was loyal to Father Murphy both for clan reasons and because he flirted with her. She was loyal to Perpetua because Perpetua was her tutor. So both the priest and the nun, neither of whom should have been here anyhow, were safe to talk to.

"I'll go and tell Calixta," said Bernadette Brady with a wink to her priestly cousin, "that Doctor must be called."

"The blood pressure's 119 over 66," said Perpetua. "You can take my word for that, Bernadette."

Bernadette nodded and was gone. Murphy walked over and looked down at the fine-featured Proud.

"Poor little bugger. In the middle of an Aussie summer he looks like he's spent his life in a cave."

"His color isn't good," Perpetua agreed.

"You'd better make yourself scarce, Perpetua," he said, still staring down at the young priest. Then he looked up. "And I don't want any nonsense from you about not taking communion from me this morning. Mother Felix the Cat herself will think it's because you consider me a heretic or some such thing."

The morning before, the morning Proud had been found bleeding onto the good carpet of his room in the Bishop's residence, Perpetua had not taken communion from Murphy, whose week it was to say Mass in the convent. It was considered a little extraordinary for a nun in any community not to take communion, though no one was supposed to comment on it or ask any questions. "Hitler's probably going to communion this morning with a clear conscience," Murphy told her now, studying her face. "Hirohito would be, if he was a tyke. And let me tell you something else. There are people in Rossclare that have much more on their conscience than you do and still bowl up to the altar rails as if they'd paid for them!"

With that, either properly or improperly, he raised his hands and murmured the words of absolution at Perpetua. "In the front line," he said, "chaplains are allowed to give absolution straight off. And after what Mickey Proud did, we're all in the bloody front line, Sister. *Ego te absolvo ab omnibus peccatis tuis. In nomine Patris et Filii et Spiritus Sancti.*"

"Pray for my brother, Father Murphy," she murmured.

"I do. For what that's worth. Never mind, Perpetua. All that madness in Europe will be over before we know it."

"But there's still the madness in the Pacific."

"They won't make your brother double up for that?"

"He'll probably offer to."

"Clear out before Calixta finds you," he advised.

3

Quartering the Sky

TO the ears of Pilot Officer Reardon came the electronic hum of the radio wave from base. The bomber called D-Dog had broken the cloud cover over Cambridgeshire. Reardon could make out other Lancasters circling in the air above him, and in a break in cloud he picked up a glint of water and a village. "Can see the Ouse below us—that's Ely," said Squadron Leader Stove dreamily. "You can see the spire. Gone now, though. Cloud cover total."

Winton asked him with the normal anxiousness how long before they set course.

"Four minutes," said the squadron leader absently, as if at the moment he were studying military law rather than the chart.

Reardon began his quartering of the sky, for the Canadians had recently encountered jet aircraft nearly faster than the eye. As he moved the turret from left to right and back again, the doorways meant to connect him with the rest of the plane became for a time the outer fuselage. If ever he was to leave the plane, it was by these means, slipping the latch and falling backward into night air. Or dry air. For it had been in a daytime raid over Brest that he had once nearly left the plane, sure that the pilot and everyone else was dead, the plane screaming as it plunged at an aweseome angle, billows of black smoke entering the turret through its cut-out perspex. He'd had his hand on the latch when Punch, his pilot then, had yelled, "I've got it, I've got it," and the bomber had leveled out two thousand feet above the seven-towered castle of Brest.

There was a school of thought that said, Don't bail out under any circumstances these days. If the plane was on fire, some said, it was best to jump without a parachute, since airmen who landed safely were being hung from lamp posts by ordinary German citizens.

Again there was some more patter between the navigator and Winton, Winton being told to set course 115 degrees magnetic in a minute's time; Winton asking in return, like a distressed accountant, that the squadron leader check the deviation. Reardon kept quartering the night sky, moving the turret on its smooth hydraulics, grateful to be busy and alone. The cold, which he now took as part of his life, barely worth mentioning, was probably somewhere between ten to fifteen degrees below freezing tonight. From other gunners, Challenor, for example—the ones who lasted—he got the impression that they welcomed it as he did—as a kind of anesthetic. And spring was rumored to be coming, though winter was dying hard. The night he now quartered was sharper than a knife, the turret veering in the wondrous hydraulic track. Still no substitute had been found for his smarting eyes, and Challenor's. D-Dog and all the complicated lives of the seven others lived by the eyes of Reardon and Challenor; and of these four eyes, Reardon's two were the more important.

For it was from the rear and beneath that the jets, or any other night fighters the Reich possessed, would approach. Reardon had lived to be disappointed in every item of science offered him in the past two years for the detection of night-fighter infiltration. The fact that the sky was at some stages so full of clever young Germans in shaped metal platforms capable of high speed and cunning deceleration seemed to cry out in a scientific age for a solution along electric or radio pulse lines. But there was no adequate one.

At the start of Challenor's and Reardon's military careers, the night fighters of Germany had acquired a cunning radio called Lichtenstein. Perhaps the title was a joke on the small kingdom of the same name, since Lichtenstein radar gave the night fighters a visual range of only two and a half miles. But when the fighters so equipped were guided into bomber streams—which in those days included Reardon and Challenor aboard a Halifax dubbed J for Judy—Lichtenstein showed various murderous young fighter pilots precisely where the bombers were in the apparent vacancy of night.

Reardon remembered the joy with which a British black box called Monica was introduced to his bomber crew in the early winter of 1943. Monica would pick up pursuing fighters and feed a series of pip sounds into the intercom of J-Judy. Monica proved useless since it also picked up every other bomber in the squadron and the pack of hundreds of bombers in the bomber stream as well. It pipped away relentlessly all night, teasing the sanity and the vigilance of Challenor and Reardon and a thousand other gunners, creating too much urgent talk between the pilot and the turrets, causing swarms of bombers to swing from side to side in the sky to ensure that the space beneath them was clear, thus encouraging wing-tip collisions. Monica was a low farce rather than a softly voiced adviser, which was, of course, never admitted by station commanders. Monica caused novice gunners to shoot down bombers behind them in the stream and, excited by the great explosion they caused, to claim hits both over the intercom and during debriefing. This was a cruel thing to happen to a boy, in some ways crueler than the sudden ball of flame that instantly consumed the following bomber.

Monica was replaced by Fishpond. Planes in the air around the ship showed up as a blip on a cathode screen. A bomber blip was different from a fighter blip. The navigator told the gunner, the gunner instructed the pilot, and as the bomber corkscrewed, the gunner caught the Messerschmitt or Focke-Wulf in his sights and gave it a fast burst from the twin cannons.

But if Fishpond were ever an answer, it was a brief one. It was blocked by Naxos radio which the night fighters carried, like their cannon, in their noses. And not only blocked—Naxos actually homed in on Fishpond. So, after two years of technical wonders, the eyeballs of Challenor and Reardon were still the main protection.

D-Dog leveled, its nose due south in the direction of Reading, the coast, and pernicious Europe. "Dear Jesus, another great blaze," murmured Reardon, not loudly enough to be heard over the intercom, as the blast of northerly air entered the open perspex of his turret. "Permission to test fire?" he asked more loudly, making himself sound professional, an act he wondered how much longer he could bring off.

Winton said, "Okay."

Reardon swung his turret toward an empty quarter of sky and let off two seconds worth of .303 ammunition. "Same caliber our bloody grandfathers used on the Western front," Challenor used to say. "They stopped men with it. We're supposed to stop bloody 110's!" Reardon reported the guns in good order. Remotely he heard the brief stammer of Challenor's trial shoot.

"No gallstones in my system," Challenor reported to Winton.

"Okay," said Winton the journalist, inheritor of the full richness of the British language. "Okay. Everyone settle down." He didn't seem to like Challenor's imagery.

Even now it would not have surprised Reardon if Winton ever came to them—to Reardon and Challenor and Alf Hater after a briefing like this afternoon's, where everyone from the station commander to the bloody weatherman seemed to be at best temporizing and at worst lying—and said, "It isn't the right thing. We have to refuse to fly." As Callaghan's crew had done after Hamburg. They were still in the glasshouse in Scotland, being daily thrown against the wall, trodden on with hobnail boots and called perverts and cowards. But were they the saints?

Reardon had dreams like his sister Perpetua's. And Winton came to him in them and said, "We can't make these fires any longer. It isn't right. It isn't courage. It's bloody murder." Yet the Starkley squadrons, the one of Lancasters and Mosquitoes, did not look like murderers by daylight, and thank Christ, Winton never said it. And if there were any evil, both squadrons were truly punished for it in their dreams and their waking terrors. God knew there wasn't time to work it out anyhow; there was only time for courage, time for the dark hours and the turret. And it was a just cause, and the Polish priests, the Irish priests, the English priests, and the French, all had no doubt of it. There was a mass of theological backing for this Lancaster squadron of Starkley, Group Eight, Bomber Command.

At the time Callaghan's crew had pulled out after Hamburg, Reardon had not even been tempted to follow them. He'd known they were traitors who deserved the public humiliation and the glasshouse. Now all the old-timers, especially those who dropped the flares and target indicators and saw the burning cities from close up, had to ask themselves the question Callaghan and his crew had answered so emphatically after Hamburg. There were men everywhere who felt it was wrong to fly, but would rather die doing so than say it to anyone. And there were men everywhere like Bernard Reardon, who wondered what doubts they might be hit with later, when they visited at ground level the cities they now sighted from high above.

"That's the question," Reardon nearly said aloud into the intercom. There was always a point of the flight where he nearly said things aloud. With that stage past, a kind of peace came over him as he quartered the sky through his puffy eyelids. For though he had gunner's blight, bomber-crew conjunctivitis, his eyes were only twenty years old and still sharper than a rabbit shooter's.

Reardon heard Challenor's voice over the intercom. "Mid-upper to rear! Okay back there, tiger?"

Challenor had the art of saying something banal and wonderful when Reardon wanted him to. On film nights everyone laughed and whistled at the way American film heroes made speeches over the intercom. In fact, you could go for hours without hearing anything. But now Challenor repeated, as if knowing through instinct that he ought to, "Mid-upper to rear. Okay back there, tiger?"

Reardon, suddenly ecstatic, replied, "Rear to mid-upper. Positive peril to bloody shipping!"

Winton said without amusement, "You are a bloody peril! Shut up, you two Aussie perverts!"

And Challenor and Reardon smiled radiantly, each in his separate darkness.

4

Ashes

PERPETUA had now let herself back into the convent garden and up the steps. She steered the old nun outside into the corridor as the go-to-chapel bell was rung by Roberta.

At the head of the main stairs they met with Perpetua's plump friend, Sister Timothy, who winked and helped Perpetua edge Catherine down the stairs. "No stick," the old nun murmured. "I've not needed any stick or blackthorn and I never will."

Indeed she did need one, but used the young nuns instead. That was one of the comforts of community life. You did not die alone and without help.

"Anything of Michael Proud?" Timothy suddenly asked under cover of Catherine's deafness. Perpetua shook her head.

Timothy was a girl of twenty-seven, three years older than Perpetua. Perpetua remembered her warmly from the times they'd been punished together in the vast city hospital of St. Brigid's. Between shifts in the hospital, they had been regularly accused of rule breaking, and sometimes had to eat their meals off the floor. "Pretend it's a picnic," Timothy used to say.

Timothy came from a large farming clan who dominated a particular creek about a hundred miles south of Rossclare. They had turned up in numbers for Timothy's profession as a Sister of

Compassion in Sydney. Mrs. Mulcahey, Sister Timothy's mother, had begotten ten children, and though still robust, seemed a little worn down by the effort. Timothy herself would frankly tell anyone who asked that *she* didn't want to give birth to ten kids on some dairy farm. In her world there was only one way out—to take vows of poverty, chastity, and obedience as a nun. Normally girls like Timothy or Perpetua would go into one of the working-class teaching orders—the Sisters of St. Joseph, for example, who had educated half Australia, the half that belonged to the One True Faith, anyhow. Timothy considered herself very lucky to get into what she called a "flash order" like the Sisters of Compassion, and the war had done nothing to shake her rosy view of her good fortune. She did not seem to understand that girls now left their farms and country towns for the city, became welders and riveters and members of the army, navy, or air force, had unexpected freedom and their own wages. On the mountainous pastures of Tyler's Creek she had gotten the ancient idea other girls seemed to have outgrown by about 1900—that you could either marry a farmer and become a milch cow, or you could find a place in a local abbey and become a professed nun.

"Father Proud?" Timothy repeated, as if Perpetua hadn't heard her.

Perpetua shook her head once more. For some reason, she did not want to give news about the priest's vital signs. Though Timothy, too, had been part of the operating team on Father Proud, the team sworn to keep the great scandal of Father Proud away from those who might not understand it—Rossclare's atheists, agnostics, Freemasons, and Protestants; from those who could use it to attack the Church.

Dr. Cormack himself was a Protestant, but Sister Timothy and the others understood automatically that he was a particular kind, one who could be trusted. He had married a Catholic and promised—and fulfilled the promise—to raise his children as Catholics. To let a scandal like that of Father Proud out into the streets of Rossclare would be to cast doubt on the reasonableness of his generous marriage arrangement with his wife. He was the hospital's professional *good* non-Catholic. He seemed to take it as much for granted as Mother Felice did that he would "convert" when his time came, when he himself lay at the last of his strength in that fine front room Father Proud occupied at the moment.

Timothy turned to old Catherine. "She's pretty particular, this Perpetua, about keeping the great silence—as you and I were at the same age, Mother Catherine. But we learned, eh?"

Mother Catherine blinked and did not seem to hear. That's why Timothy said it. Timothy was bad at keeping silences. It seemed that in her big Tyler's Creek family people spoke when they felt like it, and pretty well continuously.

Perpetua led Catherine into the chapel, supported her while she bent her knee briefly in the direction of the altar, and put her into her seat beside that of the Mother Superior, Mother Felice. The nuns sat in strict order of seniority. This put Perpetua last, on the left-hand side of the chapel, facing Timothy. The chapel was arranged in the tradition of monasteries, so that two lines of nuns faced each other, and during the singing of Matins and Lauds or Vespers, the left side sang in response to the right.

Fourteen nuns graded exactly by seniority! And Perpetua's worry was that she could not imagine herself ever becoming Felice or Catherine, ever growing old enough in the Sisters of Compassion to earn one of those seats nearest the sanctuary.

Felice began the prayers. Perpetua answered automatically, wondering if her brother was over Europe now, if the unimaginable cold was getting at him, if some young German fighter pilot had him in sight. Some boy who also knew how to say, "Hail Mary, full of grace, the Lord is with thee, blessed art thou among women, and blessed is the fruit of thy womb, Jesus." Some boy from Bavaria or the Black Forest—which according to the convent library was a big Catholic area—who knew how to say, "I confess to Almighty God, to blessed Mary ever Virgin . . ."

The prayers ended and there was a silence. It would last half an hour. This was meditation time, the second at which the mystic touched the essence of God. The sisters were allowed to meditate sitting upright, and, not being born mystics, they could draw for inspiration on meditation books each of them had in her place in chapel. Without thinking about it, Perpetua tucked the cloth of her habit tight in under her hips as she sat, so that if by chance she fell asleep, her headgear would hold her upright and she would not loll. She had no plan to fall asleep, but sometimes, especially the morning after hard surgical procedures, fatigue would take you unawares. She did not know for what length of time her brother had to sit still during flight and scan the skies, but she sensed from what she knew that it was for long stretches. If she were watchful during meditation, it would somehow feed her brother's watchfulness.

She pulled out of the slot above her kneeler a book of meditations called *The Nun at Her Prie-Dieu*. Prie-dieu was just a fancy word for kneeler. She turned to the meditation notes for movable feasts—in this case Ash Wednesday. She knew that sometimes truth was revealed and consolations arose during these meditations, but she did not hope for any today. She wondered if Bernadette Brady had called Dr. Cormack yet.

"Ash Wednesday," she read. "Meditation point one: these are the last days of winter." The book was, of course, published in England. Beyond the chapel and in Rossclare, in the shunting yards and on the farms, men were already brushing sweat, not icicles, from their lashes. "These are the last days of winter, and ahead lie the daunting penances of Lent. But the good nun does not look forward with any regret to the rigors, the fastings, the penances of the period known as Lent. For in these hardships lie the certainty of that full summer of Christ's resurrection . . ."

The sentences seemed trite. But above all they filled her with an urgency for the war to end. I will fast for forty days, she thought, and the war will still not be over.

And what were German nuns thinking at their prie-dieux this morning about fasting through Lent and the glories of Easter? If the copies of *The Daily Telegraph* and the *Sydney Morning Herald* that Perpetua saw around the hospital were to be believed, the nuns of Bavaria and Württemberg and all other parts of Hitler's Germany would have little choice about whether or not to fast this Lent.

"Approaching Lent, the good nun sees in the coming pains of the season and the certainty of the Resurrection the especial rewards to which she can look forward on the day of her own resurrection from the dead . . ."

For some reason she could not understand, a small yelp of grief escaped her and her eyes filled with tears, which she instantly covered with her hand. Between her fingers she saw that no one seemed to have noticed—little involuntary yelps and even stomach rumblings were the commonplaces of this silent time, and happily, just then old Catherine uttered one of her strange pronouncements. "Grafton girls don't make good nurses," she said abruptly, loudly, toward the roof. "The Sisters of Mercy ruin them, and then they're no good for us!"

Perpetua heard Timothy chuckle, a few gasps of laughter from other nuns, and then silence reasserted itself. She found that her eyes were now dry.

There were orders in which people meditated for hours a day, and Perpetua was filled with a sincere wonder about how they managed it.

The second meditation point she referred to earlier than a serious meditator should have also mentioned late winter. The difference between the sun the Benedictine monk from Britain had written about and the actual Rossclare sun, which was already high over the glass behind Mother Felice's head, annoyed her. Then something in her, something divine or at least merciful, put her to sleep. As she had already planned, her tightly tucked-in garments kept her head upright, and all at once she was awake again and Father Murphy was entering the sanctuary, wearing the white vestments of Ash Wednesday and accompanied by two altar boys, one of them carrying a brass urn with the ashes of last Palm Sunday's palms lying darkly in it. Perpetua stood, her sisters also, and then knelt for the start of Mass.

It was clear that Mother Felice did not like Father Murphy. Felice was in her fifty-second year, a tall and strangely beautiful woman, and a very well-organized one, who had sat through thousands of Masses in her life. She did not like the way Father Murphy uttered the Offertory prayers as if he were talking in Latin to some fellow drinker. She had certainly approved of the way Father Proud said Mass. Father Proud uttered the Latin in the Italian manner and with a serious eloquence.

Perpetua herself had felt that Father Proud's Mass was a real Mass. But there was a rough mercy in the way Murphy said his, and mercy was what religion was meant to concern itself with. She had never quite believed the way Proud had uttered the great Latin liturgy. It had been like an acting performance in which you always remembered the real name of the actor and never lost sight of the fact that he *was* performing. Whereas from the first day she arrived in Rossclare, a young nun under a shadow, it had seemed

to Perpetua that Murphy had some genuine if rough-edged connection with the Mystery that lay at the heart of the ceremony of
offering which was thousands of years old, a Mystery superior
both to Father Proud's high sense of performance and to Murphy's rough treatment.

Mother Felice also may have had a low regard for Murphy
because of his drinking, which everyone knew about and treated
either as a mild weakness or a sure sign that he would never be
elevated to the rank of monsignor. Old Catherine let slip one
morning that she had known Felice's own father, now passed on,
who had been an estate agent with a notorious taste for liquor. He
had been a donor of St. Bridie's, and the cops would bring him
there in the early days of the century to sleep it off in a private
room, safe from the bewailings of his wife and the dangers of the
gutter. The young Felice probably judged her father hard, and
she now judged Murphy, another imperfect father, hard as well.

Certainly Murphy couldn't have survived as a Sister of Compassion had God or nature made him a woman. You could see his
frayed cuffs under the hem of his chasuble even from the choir
stalls. Felice despised that sort of thing, especially in a man who
could afford to keep his cuffs unfrayed, as most priests could in
this solidly Irish and Catholic part of the state of New South Wales.

Murphy murmured away over the urn of ashes. ". . . *Benedicat
et sanctificet hos cineres, ut sint remedium salubre . . .*" Soon, at the rate
Murphy did it, the ashes were ready. The nuns filed up in order of
seniority and Murphy marked their forehead with the ashes. "Remember, man," he addressed each of them in careless Latin, "that
you are dust, and to dust you will return." You had to admit that
the man who asked for your ticket on the North Coast ferry did it
with more sense of drama. Each nun went back to her place with
the smudge of vivid dirt on her scrubbed brow. As if, thought
Perpetua, the dust of cities wrecked by war had touched them this
Wednesday of ashes.

The Mass said by anyone was still the Mass, and Sister Perpetua
could not tell, by looking diagonally across the chapel as everyone
recited the Confiteor, whether Felice was taking a new and more
lenient attitude toward messy Father Murphy since yesterday. For
yesterday had disclosed to everyone what terrible mayhem could
lie beneath an orderly, a priestly, a well-mannered, an unfrayed
priest. Father Proud had certainly changed Perpetua's idea of

what a priest was. And Perpetua wondered if he had also changed Felice's. If I could come up to her and discuss that question, Perpetua thought, then I would be sure that the Sisters of Compassion were my home. Then I could talk with her about whether we should have done something about Proud after his strange behavior at Brosnan's beach house. Then I could live here, and die—during meditation—at the head of the chapel, muttering insults about the Sisters of Mercy and the way they spoiled girls in Grafton.

There were also stories about Murphy and his familiarity with one of the Lacey women upriver whose husband was on Bougainville fighting the Japanese. The idea was not that there was anything wrong between Murphy and this particular Mrs. Lacey on her dairy farm twenty miles away on a dirt road. It was that his familiarity with the woman was ill-considered. It led him, too, into arguing for the admission to St. John Vianney's of the sort of rough cases whom Felice would rather see sent to the casualty ward of Rossclare Base Hospital.

Felice was one of those women who, it was widely acknowledged, had made the order great in Australia. When old Catherine had first arrived from Ireland to become a nurse at St. Brigid's, Bridie's had been a hospital where even the proud poor had been embarrassed to present themselves—a hospital, that is, for syphilitics, drunks, and opium takers, with doctors to match. It was a slow business attracting the best surgeons, but by the end of the Great War Bridie's was a place in which not only the solid mass of Sydney's working class was proud to be treated, but even the wealthiest Australians.

Felice had entered the order about 1919 and worked enthusiastically for St. Bridie's prestige. Maybe she was more like her wealthy, inebriate father than she liked to admit, for she was a heroic fund-raiser in her own right. Father Murphy had his money on her to be head of St. Bridie's and then provincial of the entire order. But she would have to wait until Mother Wilhelmina, the present forceful head of Bridie's—whom Murphy referred to as "the Generalissimo"—died, retired, or was outmaneuvered.

In the meantime Felice, in exile in Rossclare, had shown what she was made of by expanding the old hospital and building a new convent. Her exile was a very constructive one, as Murphy liked to say with a smile. He knew more of the order's gossip than Perpetua did. Sometimes Perpetua thought he overdid it, actually helped generate gossip about himself and others. But she knew he never gossiped about the most important things. He behaved as if Felice's power games were not important, and were therefore a fair target for his palaver and jokes.

He seemed to think the Bishop, Thomas Flannery, was pretty irrelevant, too, and the Bishop returned the compliment. "If all God wanted was a mighty money collector," Murphy said once to Perpetua and Timothy, either about the Bishop or about Felice, "he could have ordained all the Rothschilds."

"But the Rothschilds are Jewish," said Timothy.

"Don't look now," said Murphy, "but so was Himself!"

Perpetua felt an urge to give him advice about his reputation for levity. But he was too good a friend, the only person she could speak to safely.

She had mentioned to him once her worries about the order's attitude to poor patients. There was compassion, certainly. But the rich got such generous treatment. She hadn't noticed that, she said, when as a child she had seen them coming and going outside Bernard's sickroom.

To which Murphy had said something greatly sensible. "Listen to me: Ask yourself if the reason you want to be up to your elbows in the poor is just so you'll feel more important. Just think about that, that's all I'm saying. Besides, while ever I'm 'round, I'll be injecting more poor people into this hospital than Mother Felice can stand—most of them relatives of mine."

Now, on Ash Wednesday morning, Father Murphy was reading the Gospel fast in Latin. He had merely skidded his thumb across his forehead, his lips, and his breast before launching himself into it. The exact crosses Father Proud made on his forehead, or his exact delivery, had not saved him from doing something frightful to himself.

Perpetua found herself wondering, as Murphy rattled through his reading from the Vulgate Latin version of the Gospel of St. Luke, whether Murphy performed better when he went upriver, home to the small timber town of Cudgerie where his father was the aging postmaster, mail sorter, and deliverer. From the way Murphy spoke, Perpetua had a sense that his parents, like hers, would forgive anything of their child, that he, too, was as strenuously loved as she was. They might even forgive the unutterable—the leaving of the priesthood; or the unthinkable—apostasy.

And what was apostasy? If you did the unutterable and left, there were ways of doing it and still keeping your peace with the Church. You might forever be a pariah in the four-square Catholic community. You would probably need to go and live in Western Australia, or find a battlefield to die on. But there *were* means. Dr. Lawlor, the Bishop's secretary, had studied canon law in Rome and was an expert in these means, though Perpetua was sure he would never make use of them himself. Because just as Felice was marked for greatness, so was Dr. Lawlor confidently predicted to be future bishop of Rossclare.

As Perpetua knew, there were means of exit open also to nuns, dependent on what order they belonged to. It was in some ways a little easier for nuns than for priests. There had to be something outstanding—the sort of thing Father Proud had done to himself—to make the Vatican relent and turn a priest into a layman, perhaps even allowing him to marry.

Apostasy was leaving without any of these permissions, walking away, leaving the vestments empty, proclaiming disbelief, marrying outside the Church.

And Murphy's parents would probably forgive even that, just as Perpetua was sure the senior Reardons would forgive her. This was one of the considerations that clearly chastened Murphy and stilled his doubts about being a priest. It would be a terrible thing to fail and to have to face that tolerance from your parents.

5

A History of the Reardons,
Remembered During Mass

THOMAS Reardon, ultimately to be father of Pilot Officer Reardon and Sister Perpetua, had arrived in Australia in 1917. He was born in the village of Glenlara in Cork and had spent two years working for a cousin who owned a grocery store in Oakland, California. He had found that as happened with many work-board-and-keep arrangements between members of the same clan, he was badly used by his Reardon cousins and lived about as well as an indentured laborer. As a result he had been attracted by an advertisement in the Oakland *Courant* in which an American gold-mining company offered young Californians free passage to the gold mines of Western Australia and good wages in return for a personal guarantee that short of death or personal injury, the employee would work in the company's mine for five years.

He applied, crossed the Pacific, traveled then by yet another ship to Western Australia and by truck to a place called Coolgardie, over three hundred miles out in the Western Australian desert, a town as desolate as any in the arid zones of America yet possessing a weird desert beauty.

The young Reardon did not understand that the arrangement the company was offering was not due to any lack of young Australians willing to work in the goldfields, but because the Australian miners had unionized and demanded certain minimum wages and levels of safety. There were frequent and vicious fights in pubs on the goldfields between the American scabs and "blacklegs" and the Australian miners. Tom Reardon often recounted these struggles during Perpetua's childhood. He never made any undue boasting about his part in them. He had been, he said, an amused observer.

One of the young Australians was crippled in such a brawl. A monument was erected to him, declaring him a "working-class martyr." Thomas Reardon considered this serious. With an Irish priest called D'Arcy and a young Australian unionist also of Irish connections, he formed a Committee of Public Reconciliation, which acted as informal mediators between the union and the gold mine. By 1920 peace had been achieved and all the Americans who stayed on joined the union. These negotiations were the high point of Reardon's life. He would never meet anyone like Father D'Arcy again, someone capable of calling forth such public nobility in him.

In 1919 he married a forceful Coolgardie girl called Teresa, a good Irish-Australian girl. Her parents had come to the West Australian goldfields at the turn of the century. Mrs. Teresa Reardon gave birth to a baby girl in a hut of timber, burlap, and corrugated iron on the Coolgardie goldfields at four o'clock in the afternoon of the hottest March day of 1920. It was a breech delivery and took some hours of anguish. Tom Reardon waited outside in the shade of a desert oak, where the temperature was 111 degrees. Union friends and their wives came all afternoon to comfort him and tell him it wasn't as bad as it sounded. But Tom Reardon kept replying to them that this was no place for a woman to bear children.

The new baby girl was quite healthy and was called Teresa too. It would not be until she had grown and had finished that six-month period of training called the postulancy that she would take the name Perpetua.

In 1922, when Tom Reardon had finished his five-year contract with the American gold-mining company, he took his wife and child to the West Australian port of Fremantle, where they boarded a ship for Sydney, the much-talked-about city on the other side of the continent, New York to Perth's Los Angeles. In their baggage was an Illuminated Address from Reardon's union brothers, testifying to his role as a peacemaker and his fraternal devotion to union principles. This address would hang in the lounge room of the house where the Reardons lived in Sydney. It was an item in Perpetua's earliest childhood memories, and in moments of adolescent boredom, she looked at it as if it were the symbol of an exciting goldfields childhood of which her parents had deprived her by coming to Sydney.

The Reardons lived in a small house in Rose Bay, not far from Sydney Harbor. Rose Bay was a safe, half-rustic suburb facing onto a long shore of sand and sheltered water. The harbor, this part of it especially, had a bad reputation for sharks, but there were net-protected areas where the Reardon children could acquire the Australian birthright—the ability to swim.

For there were Reardon *children*. In 1924 Mrs. Reardon gave birth to a boy in Sydney's St. Brigid's Hospital, on a cooler day than the one on which she had given birth to the future Sister Perpetua, and in better surroundings.

Tom Reardon was working in Sydney for a firm of Sydney importers of farming and industrial machinery. He achieved modest affluence and by 1928 had become chief clerk. The owner of the company would even have Teresa and Tom Reardon and their two small children over for Sunday-afternoon tea, and would allow them to use his beach house north of Sydney for two weeks every May and August, during school vacations. These, being autumn and spring, were not the best times to go surfing. But the water was still warm and the beaches nearly empty.

The Great Depression threw a meanness over everything. The importer fired nearly all his people and kept Tom Reardon on at half wages as a mercy. He was too shamefaced now to offer Tom Reardon afternoon teas and use of the beach house, and Tom would have been too shamefaced to accept it. The Reardons survived the Depression without Tom having to take up a pick or a shovel, or to travel from town to town to collect the dole. What did he have to complain about, then? But he felt betrayed. And, Perpetua guessed, he felt somehow shamed in front of his wife Teresa.

There was suddenly a closeness to their lives. Perpetua remembered how they would sit at the kitchen table on Saturday afternoons and run through all the grocery and butcher's bills, the electricity and the gas. They did it largely without any rancor toward each other, and there was never a loud argument. But Perpetua asked herself, Was this love? Was this the way all the glorious warmness, sweetness, and elegance you saw in the Saturday-afternoon pictures at the Wintergarden Theater ended? Did all that special wit and cunning and honey that went into a courtship have to end like this—Saturday afternoon, a kitchen table, a strong sun calling to her parents across the linoleum, while they, too intent on the milk bills for the past month, did not listen.

It was normal for every devout Catholic girl to ask herself if she should become a nun. A *vocation*, a calling, came only from God. But there were some human factors that helped—and one of them, as Perpetua the adult knew, had been the desire to escape the limits of suburban life. It was true, too, that if you put on the habit of the Sisters of Compassion, you escaped the twentieth century, you dressed as nuns had since the Middle Ages, you became a timeless woman. The price was that you must show compassion to people, particularly to students and to the sick. But this was a duty that appealed greatly to the adolescent Teresa Reardon.

Two human factors, above all, were powerful in cementing Teresa Reardon's sense of vocation to the Sisters of Compassion.

Tom Reardon, in more affluent days, had booked his daughter into the Sisters of Compassion's main convent on the foreshores of Sydney Harbor. By the time Perpetua was ready for her high schooling, however, the Reardon income had shrunk and she had to attend one of the order's lesser and cheaper schools in the working-class suburb of Darlinghurst.

There the head nun was a woman named Cecilia who may have been in her thirties, but seemed to young Teresa to be ageless. She was one of those handsome, milk-white Irish women, and taught both mathematics and English brilliantly and without using the cane lesser nuns had to resort to. Most of the girls she taught loved her in a suberotic sort of way, sought her approval, dreamed of her. Only the rival and dawning attraction of boys delivered them from the intention they all formed on meeting Cecilia their first day at the school—that of becoming a nun.

For Cecilia dominated the school, not just the classroom. She charmed the parents, made a winning football and cricket team out of the few boys who attended during the first three years, trained the girls in basketball and hockey. What a joy it was to hit a goal or net a ball for Cecilia!

The future Perpetua was as besotted with Sister Cecilia as were any of the other girls. At fifteen she was introduced to carnality by a boy named Grogan, who kissed her cheek and for a moment squeezed and caressed her left nipple. Then they both decided they were skirting an enormous and treacherous sea of eroticism and that they'd better stop for fear of not being able to explain in the confessional the scope of what it was they'd been doing.

In the same season as Grogan, the other determining event in Perpetua's vocation occurred.

By then Teresa and her twelve-year-old brother had the normal small regard for each other's company. Like most adolescent or preadolescent brothers and sisters, separated by two or three years, they looked upon each other vaguely as irritants, near strangers who showed unexplainable enthusiasms and behavior. One summer's night Bernard Reardon's irritability at the tea table was enough to make the gentle Tom Reardon yell at him and to cause the young Teresa to make blistering remarks. The more observant Mrs. Reardon noticed that her son's temperature was very high. She put him to bed, but he kept on getting up, arguing. His eyes were flickering, and sometimes he held his head between his hands and grunted. Mrs. Reardon put on a scarf and went to find Dr. Doyle, whose surgery was two blocks away.

Bernard Reardon was irrational and screaming with head pain by the time Dr. Doyle arrived. The doctor administered aspirin and broke the news to the Reardon parents: Bernard Reardon had meningitis. An ambulance would have to be called.

The boy was put in a darkened room with a ceiling fan at St. Bridie's. The nuns were, as Mrs. Reardon would always say, "wonderful to us."

The younger Teresa had to wait outside, and nuns came and went deftly in their leather boots, nuns of enormous piety and skill. While she waited, her young brother went into a fit at the height of his fever and then relaxed into a coma. The Reardon parents joined their daughter in the corridor. Dr. Doyle spoke at great length to the consultant physician, and then both of them asked to see Tom Reardon, and all three men conferred for a quarter of an hour at the end of the corridor. The consultant physician left. Tom Reardon looked ashen and gray around the mouth. At last he and Dr. Doyle moved toward Mrs. Teresa Reardon. You could tell from their faces what news they carried. Mrs. Reardon began to weep, and Teresa Reardon cried out in alarm and put her arms around her mother, burying her nose into the fold between her mother's shoulder and arm and sobbing savagely. As little as she'd spoken at any length or spent time with her brother recently, the world without him could not be imagined.

That night the young Teresa struck her cosmic deal—one that cost her very little, but a solemn one nonetheless. She would become a nun in return for her brother's survival. She would be as perfect, as all-knowing, as genial, as compassionate as Cecilia, as all the nuns who trod that corridor. She knew at once that the deal would be taken up, though she could not reassure her parents— for some reason, some totally obvious but unexplainable reason, the deal would be harmed if they were told too early. She kept her silence for a night and a day, and then during the second night, Bernard's temperature dropped and he woke. For the next week he was the wonder of St. Bridie's, showing total recovery and no signs of what was called "cerebral irritation."

Soon after his recovery, Cecilia left the small high school. The more senior nuns in the order said she was "transferred to New Zealand." She was a woman of such a range of talents that young Teresa and the Reardons could understand New Zealand might well need her. Only after Perpetua had become an adult and a Sister of Compassion herself did she begin to understand that "transferred to New Zealand" might have been a euphemism for leaving the order, becoming a lay person. Even for marrying.

The problem with becoming a Sister of Compassion was that you needed to take a dowry with you and give it to the convent— in that way the conventions of old-fashioned European marriage were preserved. Through the dowry the novice indicated her intention to become Christ's bride. You could, of course, enter the order without paying a dowry, but you might forever be conscious of the fact and embarrassed by it. Teresa Reardon left school at sixteen and worked for two years in a Sydney office, paying rent to her mother but saving her dowry sum. In the year Hitler met Chamberlain and invaded Czechoslovakia, Teresa reached her saving target of twenty pounds and made her approaches to the order's head house at Pott's Point, above Sydney Harbor. She was aware that her father had obviously been hoping the experience of work and her contacts with the right young men in the Catholic Youth Organization might have reduced her convent ambition, but in early 1939 she entered the novitiate of the order.

She said good-bye to her parents and her young brother in a parlor of the novitiate. She would always remember the young Bernard's brilliantined hair and his shining, scrubbed brow. This head of his was totally ignorant of the deal she had made while he suffered meningitis.

But now, eight years later, when he was a flier, perhaps he guessed that it existed. Perhaps, in Europe's dark, the suspicion strengthened him.

"Non veni pacem mittere, sed gladium," Murphy was reading negligently this morning. "I have not come to bring peace, but the sword."

Not peace, and something less than the sword, lay in the Reardons' kitchen during those Saturday afternoons.

Murphy finished and began to recite the Creed, again as if he were speaking in Latin on a public telephone and his money was about to run out. "I confess one Baptism in the remission of sins. And I expect the resurrection of the dead. And life in the time to come. Amen."

Then he swung around, parted his hands, and said, *"Dominus vobiscum,"* to the nuns.

He turned back to the altar to say the Offertory prayers over the bread and wine, and the nuns sat. *"Et cum spiritu tuo,"* they had said with an exactness that put his slapdash Latin to shame.

"I'm a scoundrel, but I'm a priest forever," Murphy had said to Perpetua once. "Fellers can get hung up on saying perfect Masses. If you read biographies of Martin Luther, you'll find that he was so taken up with getting the words of Consecration right, the words that change the bread and wine into the body and blood of Christ, in not muffing them in any sort of way, that he could barely get them out. You see, that's what the Reformation was. It grew out of *Father* Martin Luther, the Augustinian monk, trying to say a Mass that was too perfect. That sort of feller, he wants it to be his mystery, he wants to be as important as God is. Whereas I'm from up the river and all I know is that I can skate across the top, and I'm lucky to get from one side to the other."

So Murphy's rush could be read as a sort of reverence, but Felice and others seemed to give him little credit for that. *"Suscipe, sancte Pater . . . hanc immaculatam hostiam . . ."* "Accept, Holy Father, Almighty and Eternal God, this immaculate bread which I Your unworthy kinsman offer to You my Living and True God for my innumerable sins, offenses, and negligences."

Father Murphy cut across the middle of the little disk of immaculate unleavened bread with the edge of the ceremonial silver plate called the paten and then placed the host, so marked, on the cloth known as the corporal. The altar boys brought wine and water up from the side table, and Murphy poured a portion of each into the chalice. The ignorant thought that there was some "kick" in this mixture, but altar wine was such a sickly brew, as Perpetua knew from the few times she had risked sipping some, that it was no wonder that priests—who could not eat breakfast before they said Mass—suffered in such numbers from stomach ulcers.

Father Murphy, still muttering hasty Latin, made the sign of the cross over the mixture in the chalice.

6

The Glamour of the Black Troops

THE human substance of Pilot Officer Bernard Reardon now hung thirteen thousand feet above the South Coast and Selsey Bill. The cold front still raging up the Channel was slanting air at something like twenty degrees below freezing against his face, and his eyes were now puffed nearly closed. The pattern of his journey was established—the aching sight, the cramping of the spine from the barely padded seat and the parachute pack on which he sat, the electrical hot spot from his heated suit pooling heat unnecessarily under his buttocks and armpits, the coldness of the hips, the ice beginning to form beneath his oxygen mask and microphone; the elements so painful, but more familiar to him than his father's face.

Winton said suddenly with high schoolmasterly petulance, "Check that wind deviation, nav!" Somebody else blew the moisture from a mike. Below, the cloud was interminable, but across it the new enemy jets could move faster than perception.

There was a style Bernard Reardon lived by. It was what had put him in the turret, with seventy-one missions behind him. When Chaplain Wraith had gotten into trouble at Parsfield, he had re-

vealed before being marched away by the guards that Bomber
Command headquarters had it down on paper what the chances
were of a crew member lasting through a tour of thirty bombing
missions. It was one in three. One in three for the pilot. One in
three for the navigator, the wireless operator, the bombardier, the
engineer. It wasn't exactly news, but no one had bothered to state
the matter in these mathematical terms before, not in Reardon's
hearing. Wraith had not had time to say what odds headquarters
gave on mid-upper gunners, but they had to be somewhat longer.
And since the classic fighter attack developed from the rear, the
tail gunner was the outsider. The outsider in his little hydraulic
outhouse. The long shot.

Reardon had believed for the greater part of his career that
there were reasons of style why the odds did not apply to him. The
style came from Reardon's sense of the glamour of being Australian, though no one else in the Allied forces seemed to spot any
particular glamour in Australianness. Last Christmas his hostess
on a farm in Devon had asked him to leave for something he'd
said, something reflexive which she described as "typically Australian!" He hadn't meant to offend her. Maybe it was the gulf between the two cultures, though the English seemed to find the idea
of an Australian culture laughable.

When he and Challenor, centuries ago, perhaps even before
the English Civil War or the War of the Roses, crewed up together
and arrived in Parsfield, the whole crew, all flight sergeants, had
been sitting around drinking tea in the sergeant's mess when an
officer had peered into the room and said, "Well, here are the
black troops from the colonies!" Then he'd gone, as if no answer
to his statement were possible. The idea the officer had left hanging in the air was that the Australians were too barbarous even to
frame an answer. Challenor, who never lost his temper and was
always the conciliator, had stood up, enraged. "I'm going to job
that shiny-arse. Can't bloody speak to us like that!" But Punch the
pilot and Reardon held him back. They had done only one leaf-
let-dropping mission over St. Nazaire at that stage, and felt they
lacked the authority to ask for an apology.

But though the English were not likely to recognize the Australian style or put any value on it, it was there, it made its demand
on him.

In Reardon's case the style had something to do with stories his father had raised him on, about recent ancestors driven into exile in America or imprisoned in Australian penal colonies in Fremantle or Port Arthur. Great-uncle Reardon from Glenlara, for example, had been shipped to Western Australia in the 1860s for Fenian activities and pardoned by good Mr. Gladstone, Prime Minister of England, a few years later.

Then there was the idea of the goldfields and the Illuminated Address in the lounge room of the small Reardon house in Rose Bay. Until he was fifteen, Reardon used to lie awake at night envying his sister Teresa for having been born in the remote goldfields in Western Australia. He used to lie to other children at Christian Brothers, Rose Bay, about being born in Coolgardie. The idea was that the desert gave you glamour, too, and the desert gave you style.

The point of the war was that if you came from that enormous desert and had a Fenian great-uncle, then you were under no obligation to England. Anything you gave was an act of grace. That was clear from the start, when after they had finished their Australian training, an officer stood before them in an air-force camp in one of Sydney's leafy northern suburbs and said, "I know all you young blokes want to go and have a crack at the Nips. But the Poms are in trouble and need the sort of stuff only you blokes have got. So we're sending you to England first, and then you can come back and take a bash at the Greater Southeast Asian Co-Prosperity Sphere."

To the eighteen-year-olds to whom this nonsense was being spoken, it had seemed a reasonable enough proposal. You had to make some concessions for the privilege for having been born in a great southland, in the earth of plenty. For that is how—in spite of the Depression—these children-gunners saw their nation and the duty it imposed.

It was extraordinary to Reardon that Challenor, who came from South Australia, a state innocent of convictism and proud of its innocence, felt the same pressures of style. It must have been something in the air. In the air in Coolgardie, in the air in South Australia, in the air in Rose Bay on the edge of Sydney Harbor. He had gone on leave once with Challenor up to Northumberland, to stand in a drizzling churchyard and read the gravestone of Challenor's great-great-grandfather. So Challenor didn't have Fenianism to live up to or live down. Yet Challenor, too, lived under the onus of bush glamour.

Without the glamour and the style, Reardon could not have flown for more than thirty missions. If he had been English, with only the fens and the low hills to love, if he had not had a vision of Coolgardie, he couldn't have lasted more than one tour.

Distinctions of origin didn't count in this squadron, where everyone was so good at their work, everyone wore the gold eagle just under their left pocket lapel, everyone had seen everything, and you were therefore made—through what you'd seen—into members of the one race.

But the morality of the style and the glamour of Australia, of the wild colonial boy in his turret, still compelled him even here, where there was such mutual respect amongst the fliers, and even a kind of love. And if it were not for the love, and the style, Reardon knew, their work would be a crime. The benighted Germans, shooting back at them, by coning them in lights, by making them corkscrew to port, made fellow victims of the crew of D-Dog and their act of bombing a proper moral response. That, anyhow, was the moral sense Reardon clung to even tonight, as he faced with shrinking energy the long trip to Saxony.

. What fires he and Challenor had seen laid in their time in all the finest Gothic cities of Europe! Their eyes were bred to the straightforward Australian light, but they had learned to sift the dark above blazing cities and find a Junkers or a 110 there.

Tom Reardon had presumed his son Bernard would be a lawyer. His examination results in the 1941 Leaving Certificate had not been quite good enough to earn him a University Exhibition—a prize that paid for everything at Sydney University, down to your membership in the University Union. But the Reardons had always foreseen that he might not be talented enough to capture one of these rare Exhibitions. It was taken for granted that everyone would make sacrifices to make him a lawyer. For Tom Reardon had noticed that lawyers survived most of what history had to throw at them.

That summer of 1941–42 was a remarkable one in Australia. The women of Sydney looked more and more wan as it progressed. Mrs. Reardon feared for what might happen to her daughter Perpetua if the Japanese came. The newspapers indicated that the Japanese advance down the Malay Peninsula would run out of string like a yo-yo and rebound on itself. Just the same, no one except asthmatics and cripples was seriously contemplating spending 1942 studying law.

One February morning Bernard Reardon and two classmates swam far out into the harbor, reckless about sharks because the world had now changed. Treading water, they looked back at the spine of Dover Heights and the tranquil harborside suburbs, at the fishing wharf and the seaplane base where every day now the families of planters and administrators arrived from the tropics and began looking for flats and getting used to not being surrounded by native servants. They looked back at the golf course, the rugby field, and the great bulk of Sacré Coeur Convent. The three boys knew, without anyone saying anything, that Japanese would rape nuns and that Reardon's sister was a nun, though not of the Sacré Coeur order, and suddenly the shoreline and the heights behind it, though it had been known to the European eye for barely more than 150 years, seemed to appeal to them for defense. The paper the night before had said, JAPANESE ON SINGAPORE SUBJECTED TO TREMENDOUS BOMBARDMENT. Yet the accompanying map showed a battle line that left all the north and west of the island in the hands of the Japanese.

The three of them in their patch of deep water knew that there were three options open to them. They could begin university, join the Sydney University Regiment, and after a time move on to the volunteer Australian Army with a commission as second lieutenant. For some reason which Bernard Reardon could not remember, the three of them dismissed this option as dishonorable and unsuited to the urgency of the moment. The second option was to wait a few months and be conscripted into the militia, which by Australian law could not serve outside Australian territory—the Australians, particularly the labor government of the time, were passionate about the idea of not sending any youths unwillingly to die in foreign regions. The three swimmers dismissed the militia option too. It was totally out of spirit, like the first one, with the urgency of that particular day and with the preciousness of that particular harbor landscape.

The third choice was to join the Australian Army under an assumed name, fake one's age, and hope that since the Australians were about to lose some 25,000 men as prisoners of war to the Japanese in Singapore, and might very well lose many more in

Java and Sumatra, the checks on people's ages would not be too exact. It was immediately apparent to them—in fact it seemed the only terms on which they could honorably return to shore—that they needed to present themselves to the Showground, where the army was recruiting, that same day.

Four days later, wearing baggy winter-weight army uniforms and each carrying a kitbag, they debarked from a hot train onto a breathless railway station in the bush and were marched among the shrieking of insects to a barracks. They were two hundred miles inland and armed only with a bayonet each. Their webbing pouches were empty of ammunition. They had been promised rifles at some time in the future—the standard promise uttered to all young men who have ever rushed urgently to the colors. Their NCO's seemed to believe that the future of Australia depended on the state of their kit and how exactly they had mortised the corners of their sheets and blankets on their bunks.

At that same time, while Bernard Reardon learned how to make up army cots in the bush, more urgency prevailed at St. Bridie's. On February twentieth, three days after Singapore had fallen, the day after the northern Australian port of Darwin had been devastated by a series of Japanese air raids, the Mother Provincial Wilhelmina, head of the Sisters of Compassion in Australia, called all the nuns to the chapel of the order's so-called Mother House at Potts Point in Sydney. The air was full of the strange, mothering fragrances of an Australian summer—of eucalyptus sap bubbling in the groins of trees in the Botanic Gardens and along Victoria Street. It was the sort of day Perpetua had associated with Catholic Youth Organization picnics to Bondi, Bronte, Tamarama, Clovelly, the now threatened sea beaches of Sydney. Somewhere, she knew, boys were still using the excuse that the sand was scalding, to carry girls down to the tide mark. Then the eternal boy-girl joke!—carrying them farther still and dumping them boisterously in the first cool line of surf. But Perpetua had given all that up, for the reason that it only ended with dull marriage and discussions about meat bills over the kitchen table.

Wilhelmina had a strong, large-jawed face and was the first Australian to be provincial—though, of course, she was of the right stock, her family name being Devine and her parents coming from Kerry.

A table had been placed at the edge of the sanctuary, and behind it, a chair. Wilhelmina and the Mistress of Novices appeared in the doorway of the chapel. Wilhelmina blocked the sun with her big-boned body. Young novices and middle-aged nuns stood for her as she made her way alone up the center of the parquet floor, genuflected, and took the seat, crossing her large hands on the table. The Mistress of Novices had remained by the door, occasionally looking out as if for further visitors.

The novices had heard very little about the war, and the nuns hardly more. Mrs. Teresa Reardon had saved Perpetua from the news that Brian had illegally joined the army and that she was trying to retrieve him.

As for the Japanese, why were they doing so mysteriously well?

I'm not ready for this, Perpetua told herself. I'm not ready to be heroic.

"It is not often, dear sisters," said Wilhelmina in her matter-of-fact fund-raiser voice, "that those preparing themselves as brides of Christ in the tranquillity of the novitiate, or those living as professed nuns in our order, are forced to take notice of what is happening in the outside world, the world they have renounced. But one of those times has now arrived." With that she gave a very exact rundown of events in Asia, places such as the Celebes, Amboina, Moulmein in Burma, Manila and Bataan, the Lombok Strait and Palembang. Then Darwin and Broome, towns which, though thousands of miles away, somehow stung when their names were uttered, since they were part of Australia's mysterious wholeness. "We cannot expect the respect of the Japanese soldiers," said Wilhelmina. "Less than one percent of them are Catholics, and barely two percent are any form of Christian. Their religion is a form of ancestor worship! They have earlier in their history often shown their aversion for the One True Faith, and in the sixteenth century martyred many Jesuits and Japanese Catholics. Therefore, in the most solemn terms I can muster, I must call on you, my young sisters, to prepare yourselves for possible martyrdom."

Perpetua looked at once at her fellow novice, Sister Timothy, the hulking girl from Tyler's Creek, her face shining not with the prospect of martyrdom, but with rude country health. Then Sister Deidre, the light pattern of freckles around her nose, her features firm. She came from good Labour party stock, and her father was a member of the state legislature. Did she and Timothy look like martyrs? Do I look like a martyr? Perpetua would have liked to have asked them.

Of all those in chapel, only Sister Angela, who had severe lung problems and would eventually have to leave the order to go into the hospital for TB, looked like a credible version of a martyr.

"You should not panic, however," Wilhelmina continued. "Panic is an insult to God. You must know that if any agony does come, you will be helped through it sublimely by Our Savior and His Blessed Mother. You must be brave and unapologetic when you face the foe. You may wish to discuss with your spiritual director the circumstances under which a Christian woman—whether she be a novice, a postulant, or a nun—is permitted to take her own life. But I am sure that your spiritual director would confirm that it is totally contrary to the spirit of Christ to keep any means of self-destruction close at hand."

Timothy, across the chapel, made crossed eyes at Perpetua. The moment called for such lunacy and for hysterical laughter, Perpetua thought. But the Mother Provincial would not lightly spread a message like this. Did Mrs. Teresa Reardon have the "means of self-destruction" close at hand? Perpetua yearned for her mother, but would not be permitted to see her until Easter Sunday, the regular visiting day for postulants. Would both of them have faced the Japanese by then? Would both of them have found the strange grace Mother Wilhelmina promised?

It seemed that the Mother Superior of St. Bridie's, Mother Fredericka, didn't approve of Wilhelmina's warnings of coming martyrdom. She forbade all reference to them at evening recreation. "I won't have any morbid talk." So, returning to St. Bridie's, the nuns had to speak in lowered voices, over the checkerboards, chessboards, and various pieces of crocheting and needlework they were engaged on. Timothy, who had the normal farm girl's outspokenness, said, "I tell you what—it would be a good little Nip who could manage to rape me and not be torn to pieces!"

Tuberculous Sister Angela, an impressionable girl, murmured, "What if you became pregnant by a Jap and had to bear his little child?" It was very hard to fit such an eventuality into the present domestic arrangements of the Sisters of Compassion.

The Spiritual Director at St. Bridie's was a priest in his seventies, a former missionary chosen especially for his age and special ability never to say anything imaginative or exciting. But even he had something memorable to say these days. Sister Deidre confessed to Timothy and Perpetua one night at recreation that she had actually asked him about the circumstances in which a nun was permitted to take her life. The old man told her that there had been special meetings in the archdiocese of Sydney which priests had attended and at which moral theologians had spoken on the subject. For it appeared that many nuns and lay women wanted to know the answer to this question. And the answer seemed to be that if *proximately*, that is, *closely* threatened with violation, a nun might justifiably commit suicide, just as a lay woman might. But you were not justified in committing suicide just because the thing might happen tomorrow, or next week.

"Well, we needed all those clever fellows to tell us that?" said Timothy. "You know what it means? It means don't get your knickers in a twist!"

Not this message, but rather the message Mother Wilhelmina had given, dominated the prayers and imaginations of the novices for the next three months. It was the last thing they thought of before sleep—Japanese martyrdom. According to the Rule, they saw no newspaper and heard no radio, though Timothy extracted copies of *The Daily Telegraph* from patients and from a Post Office employee laying telephone cable into the convent.

The headlines gave them nothing for comfort—Sumatra was gone and the Japanese were all over New Guinea. Then, one morning before meditation, Mother Superior Fredericka announced to the nuns at St. Bridie's that a Japanese fleet had been turned back in the Coral Sea. This was in early May, and Australian winter was imminent, but through it the prospect of martyrdom and worse things diminished and the likelihood that they could remain normal nuns—except for Sister Angela with her incipient tuberculosis—became more likely.

By then Mrs. Teresa Reardon had shamed her son by arriving at an army camp near the country town of Wagga Wagga and reclaiming him as under age. But she knew it was a momentary triumph. Soon he would be eighteen and eligible for conscription, anyhow. They were sending the militia to fight the Japanese in New Guinea, which was considered Australian territory. And in any case, within a few weeks of being extracted from the army, he found out that the air force would take you if you were seventeen years and ten months. He was then one week shy of that. After a lot of arguments in the kitchen, a number of speeches from Tom Reardon that Bernard owed the British Empire nothing, and declarations by Bernard: "It's the Japanese! It's not the Empire!" his parents let him enlist. Because of the special times, he was permitted to visit his sister for half an hour at St. Bridie's one Sunday morning before he left by train for a flying school in that part of the state known as the Northern Tablelands. There he was surrounded by two hundred boys in blue overalls who all wanted to be fighter pilots.

By now he had the face he would take to war with him. Dark brown hair with a cowlick, green eyes, and Tom Reardon's thoughtful but crooked grin. He shared with his sister somewhat girlish features, more appropriate to her than to him. But no one drew attention to it, for he behaved well as a trainee warrior and had the sort of middle-height sturdiness that stopped others from using such terms as "pretty boy."

Everyone presumed that boys from the country who could drive trucks would do best. But they could not always manage the trigonometry, the navigational tables, or the formulae for the developing power of aircraft engines. They trained in cold, rocky country, and one morning when a frost lay on the ground and crackled under his boots, Bernard saw his first casualty. A Tiger Moth with an instructor and a student aboard stalled in a steep turn and simply tumbled from the sky. It struck him then that this business was not like treading water off Rose Bay. Here the sharks did indeed bite. Nor were the casualties long remembered. By mid-afternoon all trace of the instructor and the student had been removed from mess and dormitory. No last post was played at dusk, nor was there a minute's silence followed by a speech by the station commander at tea time. The choice was between getting out altogether, staying successfully up in the air, or being obliterated.

To his own surprise these absolute terms excited him. The pace was forced, and he liked that. Within eight hours you had to go solo and somehow get the thing up and down again. After ten hours, in goggles and old-fashioned flying helmet, wearing two sweaters under a pair of overalls, a map and a pencil strapped to his knee, he was flying night triangulation courses between rural towns like Tenterfield and Armidale and the flying school. He could not remember the boy he was a year ago, that boy in the Christian Brothers navy-blue uniform with the Celtic Cross on the breast pocket. He had become, to his own wonderment, a man of the air.

Then the most grotesque thing happened, the thing even worse than not being born on the West Australian goldfields. He became aware of a soreness on his left buttock. By the artful use of two small mirrors he discovered that he had a boil there. He suffered through another hour's flying. The thing had split, grown, re-closed, and spread the terrible purple of infection halfway down his hip. He went to the medical officer and begged for a quick cure. There was none. He found himself lying on his stomach in a hospital in the sheep town of Tenterfield, biting on a rubber plug as the doctors lanced and excoriated the carbuncle and packed it with sulfa.

When the carbuncle was cured, for some reason they made him return to Sydney to discuss where he would be posted next. It was a long, all-night journey, in a train that stopped at every milk stand along the way. And when he faced the postings officer back on the north shore of Sydney, where he had begun months before, he found that despite the national emergency, there would be no further courses for fighter pilots for another three months. "If you want to be a gunner, though," the postings officer said, "I can get you overseas within eight weeks."

Instantly, Reardon wanted to be a gunner. That was precisely how he was intended to answer the Japanese.

The gunnery school lay on the coastline, five hundred miles north of Sydney and not far from Rossclare; Perpetua had not yet made the acquaintance of that particular dairy and timber town, and was still at St. Bridie's. From the windows of the gunnery-school lecture hall, the Pacific looked just as vacant and unthreatening as ever. There was a different atmosphere here amongst the trainees—not the same fly-or-die urgency, but a calm excitement. Some of the gunners were very quiet. They were the sort of young men who had grown up in timber camps or working on cattle stations in Queensland, where to talk a lot was simply to let flies down your throat. Some of them were failures from the flying courses, though they took their failures lightly. Others were transfers from some other arm of the service which hadn't met their high hopes of being sent overseas. That's why there was such an air of exaltation in the place—everyone had been guaranteed a quick transfer into battle.

A few of the men were older than was usual. They carried themselves with a sort of wordly composure. One of these was a lawyer from Melbourne. His name was Cannon, and he must have been at least thirty-four or -five years. One night after they had all been on a leave bus to Brunswick Heads and had drunk particularly well in a back parlor—since Cannon seemed to know the owner—Cannon opened his cupboard and showed Reardon an RAAF uniform with the insignia of a Flying Officer on its shoulders. He had been working as a prosecutor and counsel for the accused in the RAAF Legal Section for nearly two years. "I was getting old there," he said.

Cannon was eloquent and a great boozer. All the eighteen-year-olds assumed he had powerful friends somewhere, and that as soon as he got his gunner's wings, they would turn him back into a commissioned officer. "Skipper of my plane will probably be a flight sergeant," Cannon said. "Just shows you how bloody grotesque the whole business of rank is. There are only two real ranks—fliers and nonfliers. What I've seen in the past two years makes me think that the nonfliers find it pretty hard to forgive themselves for not flying. Seems to sour them. Bloody well soured me, I can tell you."

Cannon was not the oldest—there was a man more than forty, though it did not say so on his records. He had fought on the Western front in 1918 when he was eighteen, the same age as the century. He had a twenty-year-old son who'd been taken prisoner in Singapore, and a remarkably young-looking but rather wan wife. Reardon saw her when she met their train at Sydney Central after they all came south on a last leave, wearing their gunner's half-wings and sergeant's stripes.

By then they knew how to strip a Browning air gun, had the contours of most of the major Japanese and German fighters in their heads, and on ten consecutive days had flown in an old Whitley bomber in groups and taken turns shooting at a drogue towed out over the sea by some other obsolete aircraft. The instructors tried to make you panic when your guns jammed because you'd fired too long and enthusiastic a burst. But you could only be failed for swinging the guns in a panic while trying to clear them, and accidentally letting off a burst at the drogue-towing plane itself. And there was no way that those who flew in the same plane as Cannon and the over-forty-year-old could do that. The composure of these older men spread like a lucky virus to the boys.

Bernard Reardon's last leave was as terrible as he'd feared. Mrs. Teresa Reardon had heard certain frightful stories about the chances of tail gunners. But the farewells were not too bad, for the gunners were leaving for England by way of the United States. The first part of their journey would be on the S.S. *Mariposa*, known in peacetime as a luxury Pacific cruiser. Reardon took care to introduce his mother to the two older men and to a calm and worldly South Australian of twenty-eight named Challenor. He and Challenor were to share a cabin.

Mercifully, Mrs. Reardon and her husband Tom were distracted from the vulnerable faces of the eighteen-year-olds, who looked too much like victims, by the faces of the three older men, who looked as if they could walk through any furnace without harm.

7

Felice and Chastisement

THE Mass ended. Murphy knelt at the edge of the sanctuary for a while, making a brief thanksgiving and murmuring his way through his Office. The Office was made up of the same seven so-called Hours as monks in the more cloistered orders spent most of their day chanting—Matins and Lauds, Prime, Terce, Sext, None, Vespers (called Evensong in the Anglican Church), and finally Compline.

Secular priests like Murphy had only to recite it rather than chant it, and were required to move their lips as they did so, as if to signal not a difficulty with reading but the fact that they were at their work. From their black Office books or Breviaries could be seen protruding all manner of cards—cards celebrating the ordination to the priesthood of this or that Murphy cousin, the taking of final vows by one of the Rogan or Brady girls in this or that order of nuns, and the black-lined memorial cards of members of the clan, or of friends' clans, who had passed beyond the Valley of Tears.

Tom Reardon told of desert Aboriginals in the days of Coolgardie who would massage certain desert stones, because if the stones were not spoken to and treated by touch, the world would stop, there would be no rain, no serpents, no kangaroos. The

Office was a little like that—priests uttered it to keep the world together. But Murphy did not spend too much time on it, again wanting to skate across the surface of mysteries which might devour him whole. He had once told Perpetua that he should brake back on the speed at which he said it, since he was now regularly shattering the forty-five-minute barrier.

Wednesday was usually Murphy's day to go to on pastoral calls upriver—that is, to visit his rough cousins for their spiritual welfare. But there would be no doubt that this particular day he would stay by the hospital. The Bishop would stay by the hospital, Father Lawlor would also, and during the day no doubt half the parish priests in the diocese would arrive and sit around in the front parlor of the hospital, smoking and speaking quietly and sometimes breaking into the lusty guffaws that were part of the style of the Irish-Australian clergy.

Meanwhile, at a guarded signal from Mother Felice, the nuns packed their missals away, rose, genuflected, and filed out of the convent in order of seniority. Except for the youngest and the oldest, Perpetua and Catherine, who left last because Catherine could not keep up a ceremonial pace.

But this morning, as Perpetua and Catherine reached the corridor, they found Felice waiting there with Sister Timothy. Felice said, "Sister Timothy will take Mother Catherine into breakfast. I would like a word with Sister Perpetua."

Timothy winked yet again at Perpetua and ran her arm through the crook of old Mother Catherine's elbow. Felice was the second Mother Superior to give up trying to curb Timothy's familiar farmyard manners. Perpetua stood by Felice and watched plump Timothy and tottering Catherine recede down the corridor.

"Sister Calixta," said Felice, "tells me that you have already visited Father Proud this morning." Calixta had obviously spotted her, though Perpetua had prided herself on not being seen by the night nun during the early visit to Father Proud. But Calixta must have seen her, or else got the news somehow out of Bernadette Brady.

"That's right, Mother," said Perpetua, flinching.

"Did you think there was any care you could give him which he was not receiving from Sister Calixta or Nurse Brady?"

It was a question that gave Perpetua an inevitable pause. "No,

Mother. I don't think there was any extra care I could give. Though I did take his pulse and blood pressure, and find them cause for a little concern."

"Ah, yes. And I believe that you influenced Nurse Brady into asking Calixta to call Dr. Cormack out of his bed?"

"The pulse and blood pressure both indicated that perhaps Dr. Cormack should be called for," said Perpetua. Her throat was utterly dry. "Since I was there, and since I had checked his pulse and blood pressure, I would be to blame as a nursing sister if I hadn't suggested they should soon call the surgeon in."

"Don't you think," Felice asked, "that within half an hour Nurse Brady would have checked Father Proud's condition and called Sister Calixta in? That's what I'm asking you. Do you have doubts about Nurse Brady's competence?"

"No, of course I don't, Mother!" She reflected how imperfect an instrument the English language was for talking to a Mother Superior.

Mother Felice inhaled and bunched her handsome mouth. "So this is what we have: a professed nun who breaks the rule first thing in the morning just to satisfy her curiosity. . . ."

"Not curiosity, Mother," Perpetua cried out too energetically. "Not curiosity. Really." She felt the tears she didn't want, the tears that would weaken her, prickling the corners of her eyes. But hadn't Felice and the others seen how Proud had crowded in on her? They noticed other small and negligible things about her. Why not that?

"Oh? Not curiosity? You can be a stupid woman, Perpetua! I mean, if it's not curiosity, then it's something worse, something that should be between yourself and your confessor. . . ."

"Concern, of course," Perpetua muttered. "It was concern."

Felice's voice became tiny, as it often did when she was genuinely—as distinct from merely officially—angry. "I don't believe it, Perpetua. Concern for yourself, maybe. For the vanity of your work. For the vanity of your friendships. But you have always had trouble with friendships. Particular friendship brought you to grief at St. Brigid's."

In the order, in fact in most orders, the term "particular friendship" had a definite and pejorative meaning. Particular friendships were intense and secretive friendships between two nuns, and were to be avoided. "P.F.," they called particular friends in the novitiate. They even had a verb for it. "Sister A is P.F.-ing with Sister B." It was a dangerous accusation to have aimed at you. It meant immaturity, unsuitability.

"Isn't that so?" Mother Felice persisted. "You had to leave St. Brigid's over a particular friendship."

Perpetua did not reply. It was an unanswerable question.

"Answer me," ordered Felice in her small voice.

"There was an accusation . . ." said Perpetua. She was straining for monastic obedience still, so she added, "If it appeared that way to others and through any fault of mine, then I'm grievously sorry for it."

"So you left St. Brigid's over a particular friendship," Felice reiterated for the third time, "and you were too familiar with that foolish young priest, Father Proud, whose temperament was too like yours. Too ardent, and far too emotional and reckless."

Perpetua burned now. It *had* been noticed. It was the first time Mother Felice had ever said anything critical of Father Proud, anything that indicated her admiration for him was not total. She must have always thought this way, for she was too strong a woman to change her mind just because of the disaster that had overtaken Proud.

"Now I know that there are many instances at St. Brigid's of your taking a vain personal interest in this case or that. It's no use being able to give out compassion if the giving out makes you so vain you can't then leave the patient."

The normal exchanges between young nuns and Mother Superiors did not include the words Perpetua wanted to say. Words such as, "Of course I'd want to feel his pulse! I feel through no fault of my own I *did* the damage to him." Perpetua remained silent.

"This is quite intolerable," said Felice. "This secret flitting between the convent and the hospital. It's part of the same disorder which produced this . . . this tragedy of ours. You'll not go mad and overdo things, Sister Perpetua. Not today. Not with the Bishop and all the clergy looking at us. You'll not make any decisions or recommendations concerning Father Proud or his condition. You'll keep yourself absolutely aside from it."

Felice reached her arm out and touched the cloth above Perpetua's wrist. "I'm telling you this for your own good, my dear sister. Not just as a Superior, I assure you. But as an older woman to a younger one."

Perpetua had begun to weep in spite of herself. She nodded. She wondered what Felice made of this—submission, obedience, repentance, an unwillingness to take advice?

"I want you to be a good woman today," said Felice. "And obey the Rule. And be humble."

She withdrew her hand now. When she spoke again, her voice was normal. "How am I supposed to punish you, to give you a penance? You're already pale. Already you don't get enough sleep."

Perpetua had an urge to say, "Punish me with scorpions, and it would not be enough!"

Felice said, "Come with me to breakfast. You know, what Father Proud did he did of his own accord. No one else did it to him. It is not part of the normal conversation, part of the *chat* between two reasonable people, to do what he did."

Felice was not touching her, but rather nudging her toward the refectory, where the breakfast table waited. "Come on. You must live an absolutely normal day and eat normally. Though it's Lent, your work is far too heavy for you to think of fasting. And let me say, leave everything to God. Especially while the Bishop is on our doorstep."

"I regret it all very much," said Perpetua.

Felice smiled. Her face was handsomest when she broadly smiled, though broad smiles, like broad anything, weren't much favored by the Rule of the Sisters of Compassion. "You mean you're sorry because you are going to embarrass us, or because we've had to waste time on this conversation?"

"It hasn't been a waste of time," said Perpetua.

"You argue with everything," said Felice. "And you have argued since the novitiate. With everything! Over stupid things, like what a word means."

"I'm sorry," said Perpetua.

They went into breakfast together, Perpetua and Felice. Everyone at the table knew what it meant—that Perpetua and Felice were having a policy meeting, or else Perpetua was in some disfavor. Everyone knew also that the latter was more likely. Sister Calixta, freshly off night duty, looked up, pointed a tight and embarrassed mouth in Perpetua's direction, and returned her eyes to her plate of porridge. Sister Roberta was reading poorly from Father Prat's *Life of Christ*, mispronouncing the names of obscure

Judaean hill towns. Old Mother Catherine would, throughout
Roberta's stumblings, occasionally make remarks about nuns long
dead. "Mother Mary Maeve was a glover before she entered." Or
else she would say, "Sister Renata is too impressed by wealthy
people."

No one took any notice, and it neither improved nor worsened
the quality of Roberta's reading.

Waiting for Felice to be seated, Perpetua bowed to her and
then took her own place beside Sister Timothy. Under cover of the
reading, Timothy murmured, "Father Proud hasn't died or
anything?"

"No," murmured Perpetua.

"What's his temperature like?"

Perpetua shook her head. Suddenly she thought, What am I
doing, a woman of twenty-three years, too frightened to speak up
at the breakfast table?

It was the sort of sudden thought, probably diabolical in origin,
Sisters of Compassion were meant to be able to suppress. Tepid
porridge on a hot Rossclare morning sat heavily on Perpetua's
power to resist the idea. Perhaps she clung to it because it was
better to think about leaving the order over a principle like that—
freedom of speech at the breakfast table—than because she had
killed a priest.

8

Hanging on by the D-Rings

THEY were following the estuary of the Seine in newly liberated France. Reardon's armpits were now overheated to the point of blistering while his knees froze. His Sydney childhood had led him to believe for most of his life that forty-five or fifty Fahrenheit was a cold day. Yet it seemed as if everything of meaning in his life had happened at the arctic temperatures of the high air currents over the North Sea and Europe; everything at this level was undue cold followed by the sudden burst of undue and unspeakable heat he knew he would encounter over Dresden.

He heard the navigator, Squadron Leader Stove, telling Winton on the intercom about the wind speed from the southwest— eighty miles an hour, according to the half-hourly broadcast from base. Wind speeds were discovered with varying accuracy by Windfinder bombers using measuring equipment, which then broadcast it to base. Base averaged the various speeds reported by the Windfinders and broadcast them to the planes.

Winton suggested that since they were a little ahead of track, he would fly a little dogleg over the North Sea. Otherwise, they'd be above the target too far ahead of the Master Bomber, whose prerogative and duty it was to direct them in their marking of the aiming point—the marshalling yards beside the old city, itself full of the sort of inflammably half-timbered medieval streets that contributed so much to Bomber Command's fire-raising successes. "Alter course four degrees starboard to two seven degrees true," Reardon heard Stove tell Winton. And then almost at once again, Stove said, "Getting fair picture of Le Havre on H2S."

Not that anyone could see the port through the clouds. The H2S screen gave Stove its radio-wave picture of the world.

"It stinks," murmured Reardon under his breath and behind his rubber mask, his transmission button safely turned off. He began to laugh. The story was that the head of the team of scientists developing H2S had given it this curious name—the formula for rotten-egg gas, hydrogen sulfide—after their chief had expressed disappointment in the early demonstrations of what the set could do. "It stinks," the great scientist had said. This story had—for reasons Reardon could not understand—become increasingly funny to him. He often muttered the little joke to himself. It was *his* joke, the way every seven-year-old has a joke. "It stinks," he murmured again.

His joke in the tail turret was somehow balanced by Challenor's invulnerability in the mid-upper.

What target was it of all the targets and all the coldnesses? Where had Challenor become immortal? It had been nearly two years before, Reardon knew that much. The spring of '43. Was it Kassel, Cologne, Dortmund, Münster? Reardon had heard these names in the classrooms of the Christian Brothers at Rose Bay. And now, without ever having looked at their medieval face, he had destroyed them. But it was over one of those places—no, not the Ruhr—somewhere deep in Germany, maybe Stettin, that Challenor had his great success.

This had all happened in the Halifax of 468 Squadron, before Challenor or he had earned the Golden Eagle of Pathfinders.

Yes, Stettin it had been! Radiator factories and sub-pens. They came in through a weather front, and the radiator factories, and only God knew what else, were blazing. When the Reverend Wraith got into his trouble in Parsfield, he claimed that there were Jewish prisoners in those radiator factories. The bombardier, since gone home to Australia, released the bombs fair into the furnace. The navigator had been lightly wounded in the thighs by flak, which had made a hole in the fuselage. Alf was comforting the man. Yet it was required that the bombardier usually with Alf's help, release a million-candle-power flash through the bomb doors and punch the button of the camera which would show them the level of destruction they had brought about. The photographs would be viewed the next day in the photo hut, and there was a stigma on any crew who failed to bring a snapshot home with them. So the bombardier asked Challenor to come down from the mid-upper turret and help him take the photograph. Challenor and the bombardier together kicked the flash package out of the bomb doors.

But, immediately below the fuselage, it exploded prematurely—exactly beneath where Challenor was standing. It enlarged the hole in the floor of the plane, and through it went Challenor. He had no parachute with him. His parachute lay on a shelf near the bomb bay. He should have fallen without interruption to the Baltic coast. But, though no one inside the plane knew it then, the D-rings of his parachute harness somehow caught in the sharp metal edges of the hole.

Challenor would later make light of this adventure of his, caught by the metal fragments of a damaged plane careering westward over Europe. But it was no light matter to Reardon. Afterward he always suspected that Challenor was one of those people who could imbue mute metal objects—in this case his parachute harness of webbing and metal—with amazing powers of cooperation.

In his rear turret at the time, he could hear the bombardier screaming into the intercom, "Challenor's gone!"

And Punch the pilot: "Where's he bloody well gone!"

"He's gone. There's a hole."

Alf Hater, the wireless operator, had finished dressing the navigator and begun screaming too. "His parachute's right here, skip."

"Oh Jesus!" said the pilot.

Challenor was gone, and in the rear turret Reardon was too busy to feel the shock of it. "Flak port abeam," he yelled. "Corkscrew port, go, go, go!" he called. There was even the joy, as the Halifax went into its corkscrew turn, to see the flak explode in three balls of yellow above him. Precisely where the Halifax would have been if he had not called.

Hater yelled as the plane gyrated. "The nav's vomiting!"

Meanwhile, outside the Halifax, all the way through that

wrenching corkscrew turn and dive and bank and climb, the D-rings on Challenor's harness held. In fact, the diving force that drove the navigator's instruments flying to the roof of the navigation booth jammed Challenor's harness more tightly still into the bent metal edges of the steel hull.

Challenor was big, a little over six feet. His parachute harness stretched and cut into his crotch, but he could raise his head without bumping the back of it against the fuselage or the knife-sharp edges of the hole. When he opened his mouth to yell, the wind that entered jammed the sound back down his throat. Scott, Amundsen, and few others had ever felt the force of wind he felt as the aircraft dragged him through its mad corkscrew. The wind gouged his eyes and froze his eyeballs. "Skip! Alf! " he was yelling, but no sound could get up his throat, and if it had, flak and engines and wind would have eaten it up.

For a while he hoped that the bombardier or someone else, looking out of the hole, would see him there, suspended from the plane. But then he realized that he was flying, with the plane, in the attitude of a cherub in a painting; he was streaming back from the hole. If he could be seen at all, he would resemble in the darkness a piece of debris.

Pummeled by the wind, he understood he had only two chances of release. One was to tear free from his harness and fall—and that, of course, might happen without his even trying. The other was to stick there and be shattered all over the Parsfield landing strip when the Halifax touched down. He knew that the pilot would be taking the Halifax J-Judy high as they sidestepped past the flak concentrations of the Ruhr and came up homebound toward the dangerous borders of Belgium and Holland. The flight surgeon said that you needed oxygen for consciousness above fifteen thousand feet, though everyone knew that was a sort of cautionary exaggeration. Because over Denmark once he had climbed down out of his turret to help the navigator with some job or other when the Halifax was at seventeen thousand feet and had felt fine without his oxygen mask.

But now he was half drowned with air—in fact he could gulp a breath only when the slipstream of J-Judy pushed him sideways. He had every hope that if the skipper took her to, say, seventeen thousand feet, he would mercifully pass out, like a recruit in a pressure chamber. He would not be alive, that is, by the time he was dangling over the North Sea. He would not see, from his weird position, the descent on Parsfield aerodrome.

He was most comfortable with his head bowed toward the wind. As the Hallie climbed, light flak burst green and yellow far beneath his feet. He first became aware of it through his closed eyes, and on opening them saw it a mile, two miles below him. They have their business to attend to, those gunners, he thought, and I have mine. That light flak would be Schwerin. Something precise must be happening down there—perhaps some Group 5 Mosquitoes bombing an optics lab, or some research place working on radar tubes.

He and the Halifax were aimed fair between Lübeck and Hamburg for the North Sea. By the time the heavy flak of Lübeck opens on the stragglers to the starboard, and that of Hamburg reaches up toward the stragglers on the port, I won't be feeling anything, he promised himself. He thought it would be wonderful not to feel the wind against his helmet and his skull, against the planes of his face.

The flak of Lübeck was reaching up on one side, the flak of Hamburg on the other. Punch, the pilot from Melbourne, had neatly threaded that needle.

He was dragged on through a bank of cloud, and when he next saw anything, it was the estuary of the Elbe. He could not breathe for cold and yet he saw the sea. He began the Lord's Prayer, partly to fill in time until he lost consciousness. No sound came forth, of course. He said it somehow in his diaphragm. He was not too worried about eternal salvation, whatever that was, for the Methodist minister had told them that those who died over Europe were Christian martyrs, and he was of sanguine temperament anyhow. He just wanted the wind to stop, and perhaps it would stop before he got to "Amen."

He got to "Amen" and came through more cloud, dragged by the scruff, to see moonlight on the ocean beneath him.

"Ah!" he muttered, deep down his throat, and then he was gone.

Next he knew, he was standing on his toes in ethereal light. On his toes even in death! he thought, and thought further that it might not make a bad gunner's epitaph.

When the Halifax had landed, dragging him under its belly, it had been at such speed that Challenor had remained flared backward. Only in the last yards, as the plane slowed, had his toes hit the tarmac, which had badly scuffed his flying boots and broken one or two minor bones. His face felt enormous as they unhooked his D-rings from the clasp of the jagged steel. The tower and the ground crew had spotted it first—a bomber landing with Challenor suspended from a hole in its waist. Then Alf Hater had noticed, in the growing light, and when the plane had nearly come to a halt, he saw Challenor's head beneath the hole in the fuselage. The disembarking crew watched as medical orderlies and ground crew loosened Challenor from his harness and laid him on the perimeter grass on a stretcher. Having prepared to accept the death of his friend, Reardon now had to get used to the mid-upper gunner's astounding survival.

Challenor had had windburn of the eyes and frostbite of the face, and would have died soon of hypothermia had the plane not landed. His face covered with lotions, he would spend less than two weeks in the hospital before rejoining his crew. This was because Challenor was older and more mature, Reardon understood, and realized the importance of continuity in the crew arrangements. And understood, too, how important it was to have a miraculous gunner amongst a crew, someone who had been dragged at strangling speed and heights, where oxygen wasn't supposed to be, fair across Germany, Denmark, the North Sea, and Norfolk.

Because of such adventures as had befallen Challenor, Bomber Command crews found it easy to believe in magic. If you didn't have magic, you had only the statistics, and the statistics were shitty. Now a lot of young fliers spent time debating within themselves questions they never uttered, about whether a miraculous survival like Challenor's meant that he and the others in his crew were absolutely doomed—on the grounds that their supply of good fortune had already been squandered, in one hit—or whether they were absolutely guaranteed a life beyond Bomber Command because their luck was unlimited. Reardon tended to the latter view. Again, the fact that his sister was a nun was accepted pretty uncritically by all members of all the crews he ever served on as an omen signifying unlimited good fortune. Even the Ulster engineer Inch believed it. For they were operating at heights of magic and balances of superstition unknown to ordinary beings of the modern age.

9

Theater Work

PERPETUA realized that Ash Wednesday was going to be a
hard day when, on entering the ground floor of the hospital
a few minutes after breakfast, she saw Bishop Flannery and his
Vicar General Monsignor Curran muttering together at the door
of Father Proud's sickroom. Both men carried on their broad Irish
foreheads the smudge of dust and ash meant to remind them that
they were mortal. They didn't look as though they were much
concerned with their mortality at the moment. They stood like a
wall between her and Father Proud's chart, by which she would be
able to discover at once whether Dr. Cormack had been there to
visit and what Father Proud's vital signs were. Within five minutes
she would be working in the operating room with Dr. Cormack,
but did not have the seniority to ask *him* about Proud.

If she were plainer and older, she'd be allowed to ask, but she
knew she should not desire either plainness or age. If you did that,
you ended up in the same corner as Father Proud. You did as
some of the more beautiful medieval saints did and rubbed pepper
into your features. Even if she had wanted to, she had the command of Father Murphy, her spiritual adviser, hanging over her.

For one evening during the once-weekly half-hour session each
sister was meant to have with her spiritual director, Murphy had

said, "I won't have you sulking because you're young and some of the other old chooks in your community aren't. And I tell you something else, too, as your spiritual director—that I forbid you even to think about some sort of self-defacement. There's enough of that going on out in the Pacific and in Europe!"

Astonishingly, this had been some weeks before what was now being referred to as "Father Proud's accident," so Father Murphy must have picked up some musk of self-loathing that was in the air. He didn't know, though, that it came from his friend, his sensitive cobber, his junior curate, Father Michael Proud.

Ten paces from Proud's door Perpetua nodded to His Lordship Bishop Flannery, a formal bow, which His Lordship recognized with a nod. Then she turned left and walked down the length of the hospital corridor to the operating room. After scrubbing her hands with disinfectant at the row of sinks just inside the operating-theater scrub room, she put on a clean surgical gown over her habit, stepped into the canvas surgical shoes, tied a mask around her face, and pulled on a pair of the modern rubber surgical gloves old Sister Catherine considered so heretical. "Didn't we run much better hospitals, and much better operating theaters, too, without a square inch of rubber on our hands?"

Through the swinging doors and in the theater itself she found the sharp-faced Sister McGowan. She was not a nun, but like Bernadette Brady, a lay nurse employed by the hospital. She was very good too—English by birth and training, she had followed her Australian husband to an ordnance depot outside Rossclare, where he was stationed. She would have been made the theater sister, except that that job always went to a nun. Perpetua had that over Sister McGowan—Perpetua was a member of the order, had qualified highly in the state nursing examinations, anyhow, and was herself good at the job. There were, of course, a few in the community who would have liked to have seen her bad at it, but Sister McGowan never gave them any comfort or intelligence on what went on in the theater. She was loyal, calm, more compassionate than her sharp face would indicate, and Perpetua had liked her instinctively.

Every night Sister McGowan would take special account of the ABC News, about bulletins concerning Bomber Command and Europe, and would write down the details for Perpetua. The Convent of the Sisters of Compassion did not contain a radio set.

Radio was—perhaps rightly—seen as a vanity, a limb of the World, and a distraction from the twin demands every nun faced—the pursuit of perfection and the care of patients.

When Sister McGowan had first discovered that Perpetua had a brother who flew in bombers over Europe, she had without asking kept her special ear out for news of that legendary bomber force that had now acquired a face for her, the crookedly smiling face of Bernard Reardon.

There were two other reasons why Sister McGowan slipped Perpetua pieces of paper with news of the air war, instead of communicating verbally. One was that Dr. Cormack dominated the operating-theater conversation, as surgeons were expected to, and as was quite right and proper. Since the surgeon set the agenda of talk, you could not always move the conversation around to bombing in order to let Perpetua know something of her brother's activities. To Cormack's credit, he sometimes remembered to make a vague reference to that particular area of the war, but he never spoke in detail about the news. He was not as exact as Sister McGowan.

The other reason was that if Sister McGowan had suddenly conveyed the latest news across the operating table to Perpetua, this would have been considered by Sister Francis and others as a breach of the Rule of Saint Ignatius Loyola as amended for Female Religious. The slips of paper Sister McGowan therefore slipped to Perpetua were themselves a breach of the letter of the Rule, but most successful nuns understood that you had to break the Rule in small areas if you were to keep it in spirit. Old Catherine certainly held this opinion. "You know," she confided once to Perpetua, "they think I chatter away like that because my mind's going. All they know! I chatter away because I've always been a windbag, a magger, a talker. It's my nature. I could have run a pub and attracted customers with my talk!"

This morning, although for the moment there was no one else in the theater, Sister McGowan operated from habit and passed Perpetua the normal slip of paper, on which she had written, "February 7th—Rostock on the Baltic Coast, over 650 bombers, oil tanks and refinery, 4 lost."

The slip of paper always said something like that. "Dusseldorf, 752 bombers, ball bearing and tank plants, 32 lost." Normal wisdom said that the "lost" figures were understated by the British

Ministry of Air, and that nuns in distant Rossclare who had brothers in Bomber Command had to take what comfort they could from the bluntly stated numbers.

One morning Sister McGowan brought in a slip of paper which, as well as saying, "Dortmund-Ems Canal attacked, 374 bombers, 3 lost," also said, "Increasing control of air and low casualties due to dominance over German fighters."

"After all that," Sister McGowan had said to her once, echoing Father Murphy, "they won't make him fight against the Japanese." Sister McGowan and her husband believed that the war against the Japanese would last at least another three years. Singapore must be recaptured—that was a symbol. And then there would be a fight in the islands of Japan. Sergeant McGowan, who was a reader, knew that it would not be a short one.

The plain in the midst of which Rossclare stood was plentiful. There were pineapples on some of the upper slopes, there was exactly the sort of timber the Australian and American armies needed for duckboards, and the local cooperative made cheese. Onto every northbound goods train, Sergeant McGowan loaded sawed timber from the local mills, cheese, pineapple, and powdered milk. Most of it was bound for Townsville, from which stoneships took it aboard and fed it directly into the war against the Japanese. He calmly foresaw three more years of such early morning and late afternoon meetings with expresses, mail, and goods trains. Sister McGowan, who sometimes got a fit of the laughs, and had once gotten such a fit with Sister Perpetua, might murmur, "The next best thing to being a soldier is to put a slice of pineapple in the hand of a soldier!" She would occasionally mock her husband in small ways.

While Perpetua had been meditating and suffering chastisement at the hands of Mother Felice, Sister McGowan had walked a mile to work and laid out the instruments for the day's surgery. She had the list as well—a gallbladder, two appendixes, three cases of tonsils, and, to Sister McGowan's amusement, the pilectomy of the Chairman of the Rossclare Shire Prickly Pear Eradication Board, Mr. Haylen.

In the anteroom Perpetua and Sister McGowan could hear Sister Timothy helping to robe Sister Francis, who brushed her teeth for the Trinity and who would be Perpetua's assistant during the series of operations.

Sister McGowan now presented Perpetua with the general tray of sterilized instruments which had been brought from the hospital's wet autoclave sterilizing system. She opened the outer toweling, ready for Perpetua to open the inner and set the instruments on a tray. Perpetua noticed that Sister McGowan asked no questions about yesterday's procedure on Father Proud. She had not been included in the operation team. She had not even been permitted in the anteroom. She had simply been told to report downstairs for general nursing duties. Timothy had been brought forward to act as scout nurse, and the operating list for the day, which was all postponable, was put off for twenty-four hours. There was no reason why this had to be, except that it had been impossible to predict how long the emergency surgery on Father Proud would take, and it was thought that separating it from all other surgical procedures would keep it secret.

Sister McGowan, who had "converted" to Catholicism when she married, didn't ask questions about or seem to object to the sudden reallocation of duties that had occurred yesterday. She was busily engaged in keeping the secret a secret too. She was doing it in the best way possible, by not asking for information. Maybe, Perpetua thought dismally, Sister McGowan would be a better nun than I am. She is comfortable with the idea of Father Proud's more or less guarded room downstairs. She is comfortable with Felice moving her about the hospital without warning. She could probably even see value to the idea of His Lordship Bishop Flannery informing Father Proud's parents by considerate but far from speedy means. Fortunately the Proud clan owned a hotel 150 miles south of Rossclare and forty miles up a valley by dirt road. His Lordship had called their parish priest by telephone, told him that Father Proud was very ill and that he should, at his first convenience, drive upriver and let the Prouds know that their brilliant son had had an accident of some sort. The telephone line did not reach inland to the Proud family's hotel in a small timber and dairy village. The telegraph did, but a blunt message on yellow telegram paper would be too alarming.

The lapse of time meant that Father Proud's true family, the clergy of the diocese of Rossclare, could close in around him. By the time the Proud family found its way to Rossclare, the emergency would—in one way or another—be over. They would witness either recuperation or a sincerely and solemnly performed Requiem Mass.

So, unwrapping the final cloth over the instrument tray, beholding the Moynaghan file duck clips, the tissue forceps, the aneurism needles, and the Fritsh retractors, Perpetua felt less a member of the Proud conspiracy than Sister McGowan was. She was pleased to be distracted by the arrival of Dr. Cormack and the pale young general practitioner who did the anesthetics for him.

10

The Hadgrafts and Blast Statistics

DURING high summer 1943, the leave before Challenor's strange survival outside the Halifax, Bernard Reardon met the remarkable Hadgraft family. The leave was a consolation not so much for the loss of two squadron bombers on the return from Hamburg, but for the subsequent mutiny of Callaghan's crew, about which no one talked, but, above all, no one would be able to talk about it at the Station itself if the flight crews were dispersed on leave.

An Australian airman on leave went to London, to Australia House, on the triangular corner in the Strand, where he would read the newspapers and even collect one or two half-year late Christmas greetings from those relatives and friends who did not know his exact service address. In the lobby and around the offices and notice boards, he would see old friends and hear the names of London clubs and nightclubs—"I know a bloke who can get us into *George Black's Revue*"; "Is that girl with the red hair still singing at the New Yorker?"

You could also go to a particular office where they set you up with a civilian household, often in the country. You could stay there for your leave if you did not want to spend too much time in high-priced London or suffer that peculiar spirituous, nauseous feeling that is a hangover.

A time in the country—a different sort of country from that around the bomber base at Parsfield—appealed simultaneously to Challenor and Reardon. Maybe they were still looking for that real England they'd been taught about in sizzling Australian classrooms. They found that a family called the Hadgrafts had room for "two British Commonwealth airmen" for five days. The Hadgrafts lived to the east of Cambridge, on a spur line. Australia House contacted Mrs. Hadgraft by telephone and issued rail warrants and food coupons for five days to the two flight sergeants.

During their few hours in Cambridge before the spur-line train arrived, Challenor and Reardon walked at a ferocious pace around the city, crossing the Bridge of Sighs, reading inscriptions in Great St. Mary's Church, with its funny pulpit on rails. A nineteenth-century locomotive with two passenger cars attached then dragged them out past an American military depot amongst gentle hills covered with ripening grain.

Half an hour later they were met at a siding by a distracted middle-aged woman who wore a scarf from which some lustrous brown hair escaped. She introduced herself as Mrs. Hadgraft. "We can ill afford the gas," she said dreamily, "but it's better than having you asking for directions in the village and getting confused." She seemed to presume that because they were from a far country their capacity for confusion was high.

"There's just my husband and myself," she said as she drove, her eyes darting from one side of the road to the other, "so it may be quiet for you. My husband, the professor, is rather over-worked." She gave a slightly hysterical little laugh. "I suppose everyone is now. But never mind, my daughter's coming home on leave on Wednesday—"

"Your daughter's in the Land Army?" asked Challenor.

"Oh no. She's not agricultural." Mrs. Hadgraft laughed again, her eyes darting. "She's a driver in the army. My son is a prisoner of war somewhere—picked up by the Germans in Crete." She made it sound like an arrest for being under the weather or for breaking a speed limit. "You young chaps must fly over his head occasionally, I suppose. . . ."

They came to a large, ugly house in front of what the English called a copse. The garden was overgrown, and seemed today to be pleasantly full of tiger moths and butterflies. "My son was the gardener," said Mrs. Hadgraft with a giggle.

Leaning over from the front seat which he shared with her, Challenor grimaced at Reardon.

It was a cold house. "Colder than winter in Quorn," Challenor muttered to Reardon. Quorn was in the interior of South Australia, an old Cornish copper-mining town, wide open on a windy plain, where Challenor had once served briefly as a bank clerk.

The Hadgraft fireplace had been bricked in and contained only a small, unlit coal fire. But an atmosphere of warmth was created by the arrival of a tea trolley, supervised from the flank by Mrs. Hadgraft and pushed by an elderly Welsh maid. "Thank God we still have Megan," said Mrs. Hadgraft. "We were allowed to keep her, our domestic help, because of my husband's contributions to the war effort." On the trolley was a Chelsea bun, a carrot cake, and a number of warm scones. The Hadgrafts lived well—perhaps they got special rations because of the professor's unnamed work.

"Plum jam for your scones," murmured Mrs. Hadgraft in her distrait manner, pushing her wispy but not unattractive hair back off her pale forehead. "We had some American boys from the depot here, and they call it jelly. Imagine! The word 'jam' exists in their vocabulary primarily as a verb."

The elderly maid, Megan, stayed, and after serving them, drank some tea herself. This equality between Mrs. Hadgraft and Megan appealed to the democrat in Challenor. Soon he and the maid were flirting together. "You're terrible boys, you Australians," said Megan. "I remember you from the First War. You're terrible boys, you are! You'll say anything!"

As if it had not really been her idea, as if in fact she didn't get many ideas herself at all, Mrs. Hadgraft said, "My husband *made a point* of listing us with the billeting office at Australia House. He thinks that since you've come so far, you deserve extra consideration. I don't know if you think in those terms or not? You see, he says that too many of the British expect that you would automatically come to our side given the peril to Britain and the Empire. But that is just our arrogance, he says. That really you had no need to come at all. I mean, Australia must be so different, I imagine."

They had both learned that it wasn't much use explaining how different Australia was. They muttered half-embarrassed speeches of appreciation for the Chelsea bun and, more or less, for being included in the great crusade against Nazism.

"I suppose it's unimaginable, isn't it?" Mrs. Hadgraft said, gesturing in the direction of the ceiling.

Challenor winked at Megan. "Only for me. They make me travel on the tail fin."

Mrs. Hadgraft looked at Challenor for a second with real concern, but good old Megan spotted it as a joke and guffawed.

After the tea, Mrs. Hadgraft showed them to their rooms. Reardon had the son's room. It featured a pile of Champion comic books, the customary collection of *Boys' Annuals*, and a photograph of a white-shirted rugby team of schoolboys, one of whom was labeled C. Hadgraft. C for Colin. He had the fine, thin, distracted features of his mother. He was slight in build, so he probably played scrum half.

Pending the return home of Professor Hadgraft, Reardon and Challenor went for a walk to a village church, where Challenor got his usual thrill out of reading gravestones of people who died well before the first settlement of Australia. They returned to the house to find a solidly built, shorter than average man with a bald head waiting to greet them.

"Come in, come in!" he said, taking them each in turn by the hand and giving them a strenuous shake. "Number 468 Squadron at Parsfield, isn't that right?"

They must have shown genuine astonishment.

"I work with the Ministry of Air," said the professor, beaming at them. "I could probably tell you what your last five missions have been, but that would be vainglorious even if the walls didn't have ears."

He went to and opened a liquor cabinet. It was crowded with bottles of gin and scotch. He pulled out a two-thirds full bottle of malt whiskey and insisted they have some with him. Reardon gagged a little on this vibrant liquor intended for Air Vice-Marshals and upward. The second one went down more easily, and before the third—by which time Mrs. Hadgraft had joined them and was drinking sherry—the professor raised his glass and said, "To all your brothers from far places, from Sydney and Auckland and Winnipeg, who perished in the recent Hamburg business."

Reardon found himself saying defensively, "We didn't have

such big losses, as a matter of fact." He was thinking of Callaghan and his mutinous crew in the Glasgow glasshouse. Did Professor Hadgraft know about them?

"Perhaps compared to other operations. You have certain 'special arrangements' to thank for that." The professor raised a finger to his lips then, as if he didn't want them to say what the special arrangements were. They were massed strips of tin foil, in fact, released through the hatches of the fuselage over the estuary of the Elbe at intervals of one minute. For reasons Reardon didn't understand, these completely foxed the big Wurzburg gun-laying radars on the ground. The tinfoil strips showed up on the screen as a snow of thousands upon thousands of planes, creating a window of safety through which the bombers could fly above the target. So the stuff was called Window. It did not rule out accidental hits by the flak crews or the peculiar sort of philosophic storm that had overtaken Callaghan's crew.

Then the professor lowered his voice. "Let me say that I believe, before long, half you boys will be transferred to Coastal Command and spend your nights protecting the Atlantic convoys, rather than the present dangerous business. But there! I've said too much already. A long and safe life!"

By the time they went to dinner, the room was no longer as cold as Quorn. Lit from within by Scottish malt, the two Australian gunners joined Professor and Mrs. Hadgraft, and the professor's assistant, a curly-haired young physicist racked with asthma, at the dinner table. Megan dished up to them what Challenor described later as "a not half-bad Beef Wellington."

The asthmatic assistant asked the professor offhandedly at some stage, "Are you going to High Wycombe tomorrow, sir?"

"Oh, yes," the professor answered. "It's the big clean-up tomorrow. I don't believe their figures, and they themselves will by now have seen Professor Franklin's figures to be erroneous to the very point of the criminal."

Challenor winked at Reardon in a way that said, "What in the hell is he talking about?" But they were impressed, too, since High Wycombe was the headquarters of Bomber Command.

Reardon and Challenor were both too disciplined by the nature of life on a Bomber Command station to open up any sort of discussion about details of the professor's research. But he seemed to know as much about bombing as any Wing Commander, and later in the evening, in the living room, he showed them a copy of *The Times* and a well-hidden report on a speech the Secretary of State for Air, Sir Archibald Sinclair, had made in answer to a Labor Party back bencher, Mr. R. Stokes, of Ipswich, in the Commons the day before. In an answer to the Labor Party member, Sir Archibald had stressed that Bomber Command was bombing only for military purposes, as he had already assured the House on March thirty-first, and that only Dr. Goebbels and the "incorrigible" Labor member had made any suggestion that the bombers were making deliberate attacks on working-class residential areas. He asserted that the Labor Party member was letting his working-class solidarity run away with his common sense, and his very question was an attack on the integrity of the gallant British, Commonwealth, Polish, and Czechoslovakian air crews.

Berlin, for example, was a center for twelve strategic railways, connected with the whole canal system of Europe, and the headquarters of Siemens, AEG, Daimler-Benz, Focke-Wulf, Heinkel, and Dornier. Was Mr. Stokes suggesting it wasn't fair game?

"Sir Archibald," said the professor with a wink when they had both finished reading, "knows how to stick to a line."

As the effects of dinner and of the malt whiskey began to abate and leave Reardon colder, he felt the onset of a sharp unease which he knew would keep him awake too long tonight. He was aware that 468 Squadron had sometimes dropped bombs on housing in Hamburg, the Ruhr, and other places, no matter what Sir Archibald Sinclair said. They were the houses of industrial workers, whose wives and children had—according to everyone except the Reverend Wraith at Parsfield—been moved to the country. Surely the front-line industrial worker was "fair game," the poor bastard.

The next morning Reardon slept late and was awakened after ten by the sound of a lawn mower in the garden. Below his window Challenor, sleeves rolled up, was pushing the freshly oiled mower and chattering to Megan the maid, who tottered along at his side, totally enchanted. Questions of bombing policy didn't seem to weigh so much on him, and watching Challenor, Reardon felt them drop away like a discarded weight.

The airmen spent the rest of the day pleasantly hiking and visiting rural pubs. Professor Hadgraft did not return from High Wycombe until after dark. Tonight he seemed even more distracted than his wife. He produced more malt whiskey. "You young fellows help yourselves to the whiskey while you can. That's it! Has my wife shown you where the volumes of the *Illustrated London News* are kept?" Having asked this question, he locked himself away in his study with his asthmatic assistant, signifying that they were to look after themselves for the evening.

"I reckon he'd be good," Challenor told Reardon, "at putting all those shiny-arses and deadbeats at High Wycombe in their places."

It wasn't that Bernard Reardon had lost the moral sensitivity Professor Hadgraft had raised in him the night before by showing him the report in *The Times*. It was rather that after a day in Challenor's company, he had again understood that there were Alf Hater and Punch the pilot, and the navigator and Challenor and himself, and then there was the rest of the race—and that the rest of the race either did not understand their peculiar existence or else confidently predicted, or actually plotted, their execution. Being in such a strange position, an airman could not ask for more than a just cause, loyalty in the air, and what Bernard saw as the Australian duty of proving himself brave. In fact everyone had begun using a new phrase that summer, a phrase to still moral doubt, of which, on balance, Reardon had very little and Challenor less still; a comforting formula nonetheless, in Reardon's opinion. "Fighting your own war." He had first heard it perhaps only a month before—he suspected that the Americans had brought it across the Atlantic with them. And the assertion couldn't have been truer of any body of people more than it was of the members of a bomber crew, who were linked to each other by mutual gravity like planets that shared the same solar system.

That was the trouble with civilians, with people who pushed stories in *The Times* at you. They made the war seem other than what it was. That was because they didn't know what it was, even if their sons *had* been captured in Crete.

The next morning Reardon and Challenor went to the railway station with Mrs. Hadgraft to collect Corporal Enid Hadgraft, army driver home on leave. She proved to be a beautiful auburn-haired girl who did not seem as overwhelmed by life and the demands of the war as her parents were.

*   *   *

She sat in the back with Reardon on the way from the station, achingly exquisite as she chatted away. She said things to her mother that Reardon could never imagine Perpetua (alias Teresa) saying to Mrs. Reardon. "Do you know that old goat Major French got me to stop in a lane in Surrey the other day so that he could tell me that his wife was cruel to him! If I were his wife, I'd be cruel to him too! I had to stage an engine failure on High Street in Guildford to get rid of him. Called depot and got someone else to come out and pick up the terrible old trout."

Mrs. Hadgraft tittered away as if she understood exactly the way men behaved with beautiful girls. Later in the journey Corporal Hadgraft turned to Reardon and said, "Daddy has a great admiration for you chaps, you know! He says that you have a rough vigor but that you're the New World, the world of the future. He does go on, doesn't he, Mummy, about how it's the end of *our* world? He keeps telling me I should go to Canada or New Zealand or Arizona or somewhere like that. I don't think you've got a rough vigor at all. You seem much nicer to me than Major French."

Challenor knew what to say: "We try to be nature's gentlemen, Miss Hadgraft. It seems to satisfy most of the people we meet."

"How's Daddy?" Corporal Hadgraft asked her mother, frowning.

"Oh, he doesn't like High Wycombe. Thinks they're on the wrong track, you see."

That was enough to reduce Challenor to silence. The Hadgraft vehicle moved forward through fields of grain that looked as if they had been producing maize, millet, and rye for centuries. As indeed they had.

Bernard Reardon wondered if he would ask Enid Hadgraft to marry him before or after dinner.

The professor seemed to revive with his daughter's return. Even the asthmatic assistant was livelier. At table the three of them—professor, daughter, assistant—played a game Reardon considered charming and as clever as hell. Enid, for example, would give her father the sort of clue you found in the *Times* crossword. "Sailor boy at home for a waterproof cover." The answer would be *tar*(sailor)*paul*(boy)*in*(at home)—*tarpaulin*. "Crumbs! Svengali has gone mad," the professor would say. To which the answer, which Enid got right, was *leavings*, an anagram of Svengali. The correct answers were heavily applauded around the table, while Challenor shook his head at such mental adroitness. Professor Hadgraft seemed to notice this. "I don't suppose you chaps play cryptic crosswords in the bush," he said. If anyone else had come out with that, it would have sounded patronizing, but from the professor it didn't. "Never mind. You'll play better games than this when the New World comes into its own!"

"Able to return where Napoleon suffered it," said the assistant with a smile, setting another puzzle for Enid and the professor.

"That would be Elba," said Challenor, to show he was no fool. The Hadgrafts laughed. "Sorry for butting in," Challenor said.

"No," the asthmatic wheezed. "Bravo!"

But soon the game languished.

Mrs. Hadgraft commented, "My dear professor husband is depressed."

"Oh dear," said Enid. "Are you still blowing up those poor little monkeys, Daddy?"

"Not monkeys," said Professor Hadgraft's assistant. "Gibbons."

"We use goats now," the professor told her. "Not that it matters. Fire is all the rage at High Wycombe now. Not blast." The professor turned to Challenor and Reardon. "I'm sorry, it's all an academic debate. Though I suppose it isn't so academic for you chaps."

"Nor for the goats!" said Enid.

"There are terrible developments," murmured the professor. "Really terrible. The chief chaplain at High Wycombe is very worried. And so am I!" His eyes flickered in the direction of Challenor and Reardon and he said no more.

The mysterious conversation about gibbons and goats which had prevailed at the Hadgraft's dinner table was resolved early next morning. Reardon was awakened by a knocking on the door, and opening it, found the asthmatic there, wearing a crooked tie and so strongly affected with a wheeze that Reardon thought he had come for assistance in getting to the hospital. "The professor sends his regards," the asthmatic gasped, "and says that if you would like to join him for this morning's blast test, he has cleared it with the commanding officer at the site. Flight Sergeant Challenor has accepted the invitation."

Suppressing the question about whether Corporal Enid Hadgraft had been invited as well, Reardon dressed and shaved as quickly as he could and joined Challenor downstairs in the hall-way. "What are we in for?" Reardon asked Challenor.

"Buggered if I know, Bernie," said Challenor, "But sounds more bloody intriguing than word games."

They were joined in the hallway by Professor Hadgraft, who carried a briefcase and a bundle of files, and by the asthmatic, laden with a much humbler burden of documents. Outside, amidst the long-neglected flowerbeds on which Challenor had so recently been working, a gray-blue RAF staff car, its engine running very quietly, waited for them. The asthmatic got into the front seat with the driver. The professor, preoccupied, indicated by nods that Challenor and Reardon were to get into the back with him.

"Could I ask where we're going, Professor?" Challenor in-quired.

"Up north near Ely," murmured the professor distractedly. "I know you'll find it of professional interest." As he climbed into the back of the car with them, he paused to dispose of the briefcase and the files on the floor. Then, as he found a place for his feet, he said, "You see, the only reason I'm troubling you like this is that I don't think chaps of your caliber should be too lightly used. Or abused, for that matter."

The car moved off. Along the roads of Cambridgeshire lines of farm girls, some of them riding on tractors, were going to work in the grain and potato fields. The professor and the asthmatic ex-cused themselves and began to read their files. Challenor leaned against the back of the front seat and tried to make conversation with the RAF driver, a young man about Reardon's age. But even Challenor couldn't kindle a conversation, since the young man had nothing to say either about the route or the scenery or the job or the war. Later Challenor would recall the journey and say, "We risk our lives, Reardo, to guarantee those little bastards have the right of being as dumb and suspicious as that."

As if the professor didn't want his academic brothers to know that he was on the road so early and so frantically committed, the vehicle skirted Cambridge. Very quickly after that the contours of the land dropped away into low wetlands, the sort of places where the Royal Air Force liked to situate its bomber airfields. Reardon's desires remained behind in the hilly country with Corporal Enid Hadgraft. But a bright day was rising out of the North Sea, and even the fens looked inviting.

When the car came to a barrier and a guard post on a road elevated above marshes, two RAF military policemen inspected them through the windows, recognized Professor Hadgraft and the asthmatic at once, and became very reverent, asking them how they were this morning.

"I've brought along two Australian friends from Bomber Command to witness the tests," the professor told the military policemen. "I spoke to the squadron leader."

"Of course, sir," said the more senior of the two guards, and waved the vehicle through.

A little farther they came to a nest of huts on their left which proclaimed itself to be ROYAL AIR FORCE WYCHFORD, NO. 2 VETERINARY UNIT. Still farther, they parked amongst a tangle of vehicles which included staff cars and trucks stacked with wire pens.

The professor packed up his files and his briefcase, extracting from it only a clipboard and a pencil, which he took with him when he left the car. The asthmatic secretary was similarly equipped.

Reardon and Challenor followed the two of them from the car down a slope and into a system of heavily sandbagged trenches. This opened on to a wider area, equally fortified with sandbags, where a number of Royal Air Force officers, flight lieutenants, and a squadron leader, stood with a few civilians whose suits gave them away as civil servants. None of the air-force officers was aircrew— none of them wore wings. Perhaps they were all from the veterinary station.

In the midst of this open, sandbagged depression, Reardon noticed, stood a small cement blockhouse about the size of a public toilet. He could not guess what that meant, except that it must be a place where the officers and civilians could retire when a planned explosion took place. For that was what all this looked like—a testing ground. He had seen similar places in training films.

Professor Hadgraft, whose arrival everyone had clearly awaited, introduced them. They were already aware of the power of the wings they wore, even though the officers outranked them. If you called an armed force "air force," the result was exactly as Cannon had told him it would be in the gunnery school in northern New South Wales: those energetic and essential people who did not actually *fly* sometimes gave off a sense of inferiority in the face of those who did. Reardon was immediately aware that his wings and Challenor's made them aristocracy in this bunkered area. They nonetheless saluted the officers, who returned the salutes with varying levels of welcome and hostility.

The squadron leader greeted the professor heartily. There seemed to be some fellow feeling between them. "The animals are ready, and the blast meters in place. But you'll want to check, of course."

The professor nodded in that distracted Hadgraft way and waved to his two guests. "You'll find this interesting," he said, implying they should follow.

The professor, the squadron leader behind him, walked toward a corner of the bunkered area where a sap just like a World War One trench ran away at an angle and followed a zigzag course. Duckboards lay along the bottom of this trench. A distant bleating of sheep or goats had been audible in the bunker, but as they filed through the zigzag trench, the sound became clearer and closer.

"They're goats, aren't they?" Challenor asked the asthmatic.

"That's right," said the asthmatic.

They emerged from the sap into what was a vast and curiously constructed area, an enormous pit in the ground. As far as Reardon could see, it was about the size of two football fields. It was divided up with walls of wood and plaster—mock houses, some of them with roofs, some without. A sort of lane ran down the length of the pit—it was clearly meant to simulate a main street. In many of the compartments of plaster and wood, as in the lane, bleating goats were tethered. Small black boxes stood by each goat and were screwed down to cement bases.

At last the party came to an open area amongst the fake buildings—a small square or park. Here, too, goats were tethered at various angles. And on a cradle at the edge of the square sat one of those new bombs they called "cookies," the two thousand pounders. The professor put his hand on it. The squadron leader laughed. "The armorers are somewhat nervous of these. They say they're slightly more volatile than the others."

The professor laughed too. "Well, if the damn thing went off now, I think High Wycombe would be delighted. Certain factions, anyhow."

"Come." The squadron leader smiled. "No despondency there."

The professor turned to the two flight sergeants. "This, believe it or not, is a fairly exact model to test the forces that operate when a two thousand pounder lands in a German street. I suppose intelligent fellows such as yourselves have already guessed as much. This is blast research—unfortunate, of course, but necessary. If only the damned figures were believed, that's all. There are chaps who don't like the figures and amend them upward. But there, I've said too much." This seemed to be his standard sentence and was uttered without any regret at all. "Let's go back."

Reardon noticed one of the goats in the square had his hindquarters to the bomb and was rooting in the dirt with apparent composure.

They walked back down the main road of this faked town of goats and back into the zigzag trench. An RAF handyman—an ordinary airman, what flight crew called "erks"—was working on some wiring running toward the bomb. He finished his work, stood aside to let the party pass, saluted the squadron leader, and joined the group. Back in the large bunkered area he reported to his officer. Everyone moved to the blockhouse in the middle, stooping to enter the low door. When all of them, even the erk they had passed in the zigzag sap, were in, the steel door was closed. There was a sudden smell of sweat in the air.

Beneath a narrow observation slit stood a table with a sort of portable electrical board on it. The wires, connected to the bomb, ended here and led to a red lever. The squadron leader, the professor, and the officer in charge of the electrical board consulted their watches and talked to each other, agreeing on what time it was and when the lever should be pulled. For some reason of bureaucratic or scientific neatness, it was clear that they had chosen 0800 hours—eight o'clock. The squadron leader's men, veterinary assistants, stood around in rubber boots with pistols strapped to their hips, muttering about how they were dying for a cigarette. Reardon noticed that Challenor seemed uneasy. "Suppose they know what they're doing, but there's a bugger of a lot of amatol in one of those two thousand pounders." At five minutes to eight someone went around handing out earplugs. The professor waved away the ones that had been offered to him. So, for some obscure reason he did not himself understand, did Reardon.

With thirty seconds to go, the electrical officer began to count. "Best to stand away from the walls, chaps," called out the squadron leader, and some of the erks took the plugs out of their ears to hear what he was saying. With five seconds to go, Reardon pulled down his forage cap tightly onto his head and put his thumbs into his ears. The sunlight coming through the observation slit jolted once. The sound was like one quick blow inside Reardon's head, and a pulse came up through the cement floor and hit his heart. Then someone opened the steel door.

As hearing returned, Reardon picked up the expected massed bleating of goats, and over it a layer of frightful screaming, the sort of sound that you knew at once, even if you'd never heard it before, as the universal cry of the beast in agony.

Now everyone had tasks to do. The electricians began retrieving their wiring and packing up their switchboard. The squadron leader, Professor Hadgraft, and the asthmatic moved off purposefully into the zigzag sap. Each of them carried a clipboard, with paper and pencils. Reardon and Challenor stood in the bright daylight outside the blockhouse, uncertain about what was required of them.

"If the professor won't be offended," said Challenor, "I don't think I want to go up there for a while. I'd rather take it all as a foregone conclusion."

Reardon therefore crept up the sap on his own. As he entered the mock town he was surprised to see that many of the walls were standing and that the goats farthest from the explosion seemed in robust health, though he saw one half buried in rubble and begging for release, and another lying still with a great splinter of wood through its head.

Of course, the damage was more noticeable toward the center of the explosion, which had altered the pit entirely. There was a crater surrounded by little but rubble. But the black boxes were still there, screwed to their cement bases, and a team of erks uncovered them with shovels.

Reardon was astonished at how many goats were still living not far from the edges of the crater. There was a comic scene when one of them, untethered by the blast, knocked down a rubber-booted assistant of the squadron leader. An occasional shot by one of the squadron leader's assistants would end the misery of this or that goat. One animal, tethered in a lane, seemingly unharmed, fixed Reardon with its eyes. "You ought to be dead, cobber,"

Reardon said to the goat, for it stood in line with where the two thousand pounder had been.

The sight of the live, bright-eyed goat did nothing to shake the morality he'd defined a few nights before—the morality of being a member of a bomber crew, the morality of mateship. He argued to himself that, unlike the goats, German cities did not lie passively beneath the threat of the cookies—the thin-cased, high-explosive drum bombs. German cities tried to catch you with low flak and high flak, to cone you in searchlights, while the night fighters, directed by radar, tried to tear you apart with the *Schrägemusik*. Reardon even began to feel a sort of anger at the professor for exposing them to this evidence of goats and high explosives, whatever it all meant.

Feeling superfluous at the bomb site, Reardon wandered back up the sap into the bunkered area. There, Challenor leaned alone against the blockhouse, smoking a Player's.

"Wish I'd brought a bloody book," he said. He stubbed out his cigarette against the concrete wall. "I suppose it's all goat meat up there, is it?" he asked.

"That's right," said Reardon. He did not know why he agreed, given that the scene up there had surprised him by displaying only half the mayhem he had expected. Instinct told him that Challenor might need to believe, as everyone in Bomber Command seemed to believe, in the power of the two thousand pound cookie—that that idea might help him hang on.

And in fact this suspicion would be verified within a few weeks, when the D-rings of Challenor's parachute harness would keep him attached to the fuselage during that endless journey home. Was it the power of belief in the two thousand pound cookie that would keep Challenor stuck there beneath J-Judy?

"It's a shambles," said Reardon, embroidering.

An hour passed before anyone else returned. The first one back was the squadron leader. He approached Reardon and Challenor.

"Listen, you chaps," he said confidentially. "When the professor asked me to play host to you, I had the idea that you had some special knowledge in the area. I mean, I didn't know that it was simply that you were guests of the Hadgrafts. What I'm trying to say is, I wouldn't talk too much about any of this when you get back to your squadron."

"Not much to talk about in my opinion, sir," said Challenor.
"Good chap," said the squadron leader.

On the way home the professor ordered the driver to stop at a
pub in a village somewhere north of Cambridge. He had till now
spoken little, and had even seemed to doze off in the back of the
car. He insisted, before they went inside to order, that the driver
lock all their notes of that morning in the trunk and remain with
the car. The bar was nearly empty, and the professor sent the
asthmatic to fetch four pints. Challenor went to help him carry
them. The professor used Challenor's absence to speak to Reardon. "I notice you had a look at the place afterward, but your
friend didn't."

Reardon said, "Yes."

"And what did you think?"

"Well . . . I've got to admit I was surprised more goats weren't
killed."

"Ah!" said the professor. "The data *does* support your observation. You understand? It *does* support your observation."

The asthmatic and Challenor came back with the beer. There
was an edge of polite hostility in Challenor as he raised his pint
toward the professor. "Your health, sir. I just can't stop myself
from wondering what all that rigmarole meant."

"It was a blast test. The Air Ministry and Bomber Command
employ me to make such tests. I began with the old five-
hundred-pounder general purpose and moved on to the cookies.
Humanity marches forward, Flight Sergeant."

"But I can't see why we . . . we're just gunners. I can't see why
we . . ." Challenor was both angry and painfully polite.

"You should ask your friend," said the professor. "He visited
the site. If I had my way, every member of every bomber crew
would." The professor took a deep drink of beer, then continued
in a lowered voice. "Because I'll tell you something, Flight Sergeant, which as a young man from the New World you should
know. And that is that no matter how thin the bomb casings
become, how large the percentage of explosive, and how large the
bomb, it still takes seventy pounds per square inch to cause any of
those goats even minor pulmonary disorder. And it still takes four

to five hundred pounds of pressure per square inch to kill them. And that means, expressed in another form, gentlemen, that even with these high efficiency, thin shell-casing cookies, it takes a ton to kill 0.8 of a German. . . ."

The asthmatic seemed alarmed by his superior's frankness.

"Unless you use incendiary bombs," said Challenor.

"Ah yes. Unless you use incendiaries."

The asthmatic began talking about other things, steering the conversation away, and gratefully Reardon helped him.

The car journey back to the Hadgraft's house from the pub seemed long, and the beer and the slaughter of goats sat heavily on Reardon's brain. Everyone appeared half somnolent, even the driver. There was no conversation of any interest.

The professor did not appear at dinner. A heavy pouring of malt whiskey before dinner might have incapacitated him. It served to render Enid Hadgraft increasingly lively and adept at interpreting the war news of that day, whether it derived from Burma, the Central Pacific, promising developments on the Eastern front, or stalemate at Anzio.

Conversation grew slacker toward bedtime. Reardon fell to sleep easily, a little stunned by all the messages people had been giving him that day.

He was awakened some time or other by a knock on his door. A little confused about what to do, he got up and opened it. A boy wearing pajamas stood in the doorway. It took a little time for him to understand that it was Enid Hadgraft, probably wearing an old pair of her captured brother's nightwear.

"Hello," she said. "I wanted to speak to you because we've probably given you a bad time here. I mean, we try to be nice. But my father's so totally taken up with the whole thing—"

"You've been very hospitable," said Reardon. For some reason he wished she'd go away.

"Listen, can I come in and just sit on the end of the bed?" she said. "My brother and I often used to talk late at night. Mummy and Daddy sleep very heavily. With Daddy it's malt, and with Mummy it's gin. Thank God! They deserve a good sleep."

"Yes," he said. "It's your room, when it's all said and done. I'm just a visitor."

"It's my brother's room," she replied, entering nonetheless.

Now that she was in, Reardon felt that it was one of the great adventures of his life, that he was about to be told extraordinary things.

She threw herself on the end of the bed and tucked her ankles in under her. "Hamburg's very big in this family at the moment. If you had met us last week, Hamburg wouldn't have been so large an issue. But it's destroyed Daddy, and after all, Daddy sets the tone, and so the tone's . . . well . . . strained."

"Why does Hamburg upset your father?" asked Reardon, sitting sideways on the bed.

She sighed. "Was it bad in your squadron?"

"You're not Mata Hari, are you?" asked Reardon.

"Come on," said Enid Hadgraft, groaning. "I know more about Bomber Command than you do. I would just have to ask Daddy in the morning, and he would tell me everything, squadron by squadron. He keeps account of all that."

"We didn't do so well, just our squadron," said Reardon. "We were over Hamburg twice, within a few nights of each other. The first time we lost only one to flak." It had been the first time they'd used Window, and the Germans were obviously thrown into chaos. But he didn't relay this information to Corporal Hadgraft. "The second visit, the night of the big fire, we lost one to flak over the target, and fighters jumped another one on the way home. And a third one cartwheeled on landing." He didn't mention the mutineers—Callaghan's crew, who had suffered the appalling bad luck of a kind of moral storm.

"That's why you got leave," said Enid Hadgraft learnedly. "Your casualties were higher than the average."

"If someone's weren't, there wouldn't be any average."

"That's a clever thing to say," said Enid, though it was impossible to tell if she really approved or not.

"Things even out," said Reardon, for something to say. He was seeing her more and more clearly in the darkness, seeing how magnificently her neck rose from her prisoner-brother's pajamas.

"Exactly," she said. "Do you know why my father took you to see the goats? In fact—as you heard—in the past they used monkeys, but there's a natural shortage of those in the countries of Britain. Anyhow, do you know why he took you to see them?"

"Not a clue, Miss Hadgraft," said Reardon, shrugging. "I mean,

I know he wasn't being a ghoul. It wasn't boasting or anything of that nature. I know that. He was dead serious."

Enid considered Reardon. He could now see the independent glitter of each brown eye regarding him. "Sergeant Challenor doesn't know why he was taken up there. Up into the fens to see goats tethered and blown up. I think he thinks the whole Hadgraft family is touched, you know, a little maniacal. Whereas, of course, my father is one of the sanest men in Europe. He likes to say 'in Europe' because he sees us all as one—England, France, Germany, the Low Countries, and all the rest. He's what you call a Pan-European. So he never calls himself the sanest man in England. It's always in Europe. And if a fellow does call himself the sanest man here or there, it only means one of two things. But you know that."

"No, I don't think I do know it."

"Come on, Flight, what could it possibly mean?"

"Either that he is the sanest man in the place, or else he's the maddest."

She leaned toward him and put a sisterly kiss on his cheek as a reward for being clever.

"And you're about to tell me my father's mad, are you, Flight?"

"No. I know he's not mad."

"So we come back, don't we, to the question of why he took you up into the fens so you could watch goats torn apart? What would you say to that?"

Reardon shook his head. She was making him a little desperate. "I don't know the answer to that one. That's why I probably wasn't much fun at the tea table. I don't know why he did. He was trying to teach us something."

"Ah!" murmured Corporal Enid Hadgraft.

"But like I said, what in the name of heaven it was, I don't have a clue."

"He was trying to save your lives, you see. He was even trying to save your souls."

"Souls?" Reardon asked, astonished.

"You believe in the existence of the soul, don't you?"

"Of course I do."

"I thought you did, because you're never profane. Flight Sergeant Challenor curses a lot."

Reardon laughed. "That's the way he goes about things. Most Australians speak pretty roughly, and sort of to the point. But they don't mean any harm."

Corporal Hadgraft nodded above her pajamas. "And if he thinks there's a woman who's overheard him, he always apologizes. That's what my father would call 'frontier good manners.' He says that manners have turned poisonous in the Old World, in Europe—that they don't mean anything anymore. That they only mean something in the New World. He should really go to Australia after the war, though I don't suppose there'll be many openings for blast physicists there."

"He was trying to save our *souls*?" asked Reardon, getting the discussion back on its tracks.

Corporal Hadgraft began to explain matters most corporal drivers did not have access to. There were three professors in the Extramural Section of the Air Ministry who were working on questions to do with blast. One was Professor Hadgraft, the other Professor Seppelt—these two were bitter rivals, she said—and the third was a quite pleasant man named Professor Bowman. Professor Bowman saw Bomber Command's task as rendering the German population, especially those who lived in industrial areas of cities, homeless. He had been working on the impact of blast and incendiaries on workers' estates and on the narrow-streeted, medieval centers of the major German towns. Professor Bowman was an honest enough fellow in the view of his colleague, Professor Hadgraft. But Professor Hadgraft believed that Bowman let his enthusiasm, his anti-Nazism (he had been a Communist in the thirties) influence his figures for homelessness per ton of bombs dropped by Bomber Command. Professor Bowman's desire to strike the Germans in their homes was based—so Professor Hadgraft believed—on a primary desire to give the Soviet Union support and comfort. So, perhaps without meaning to, he overstated his figures to keep Bomber Command and the Ministry of Air enthusiastic.

On the other hand, Professor Seppelt's overenthusiastic figures for deaths—as distinct from damage to homes—caused by blast were nearly four times Professor Hadgraft's estimate. Seppelt claimed, and produced figures in an attempt to prove it, that 3.4

Germans were killed per ton of high explosive. This was more than four times Professor Hadgraft's carefully arrived at figure of less than 0.8. Her father, Enid said, could not guess what Seppelt's motives in overstating the figures were. Since the introduction of the high explosive, thin-walled cookie bombs, Seppelt had actually upped his figures from 2.8, which he had attributed to the old thick-walled five hundred pounders. Professor Seppelt's figures made everyone at the Ministry of Air and at High Wycombe very happy, and so they looked at Professor Hadgraft's more accurate figures as the work of a killjoy. Professor Hadgraft himself believed that it was Seppelt's German name and background, as well as his desire to be awarded some Royal honor in the short term—before the war ended and his figures could be checked—that made him overanxious to please everyone from the chiefs-of-staff to senior men in Bomber Command.

Corporal Enid Hadgraft, lit by moonlight, encased in her brother's flannel, conveyed all this to Reardon deftly and with passion.

"My father's figures are the right ones," she said. "I know they're the right ones—it's not just that he's my father. He's been arguing with High Wycombe that the bombing has been the wrong way of doing business—please forgive me for saying this, it's simply his argument—and that everything should be thrown, most of Bomber Command's aircraft included, into the protection of the convoys in the Atlantic. You see, he claims that this would fulfill Bowman's hopes for the Soviet Union because it would mean that we could open a Second Front and invade Europe, as the Russians are always telling us to. But nobody wants to believe my father's figures."

Reardon covered his eyes a second, thinking of the public disgrace of Callaghan and his crew, feeling, as if by electric impulse, the gibes and blows and boots in the teeth they were suffering in the glasshouse.

"I have to be honest," said Reardon. "Neither do I really believe your father's figures. I've seen the cities burning. We came into Hamburg from the south and flew out up the Elbe estuary, and everytime I turned the turret, I saw Hamburg burning. I could still see it when we were right out in the North Sea."

"Ah yes," said Enid Hadgraft. "But that's the very point. Hamburg was a special case. It was the case that proved my father right.

And it proved Bowman right at the same time. For the first time in the war Bowman's casualty figures are exact. But that's not due to any merit on the part of Bowman and Seppelt. It wasn't blast. It was the fire and the fire alone that brought the results. And what results they were!"

Reardon found himself saying, "Yes, it was a terrible fire."

"I know," said Enid Hadgraft, almost impatiently. "Hamburg—according to Daddy—is unique. It created awful casualties amongst the Germans, but almost by accident, Daddy says."

He began to see that with a girl who kept saying "Daddy says," there might not be too good a chance of marriage.

But then, very cogently, she continued. "Look. If Professor Seppelt's figures were right, then by now one out of every three Germans would be homeless. You fly over Germany any old night of the week. Do you think the blighters are homeless? One third of them?"

"Maybe not a third."

"There you are. Seppelt is certain. And you're the one who flies, but you're not certain. Why should you die for Seppelt's predicted figures?" She was leaning forward, giving him a hard message. What should have been—according to the fantasies of boyhood—a soft exchange of bodies, had become a fierce exchange of souls.

"That's the message I've been getting all the time I've been with your family," said Reardon. "Join Coastal Command."

"Why not?" said Enid Hadgraft.

He had never met such a united family, a family that spoke with such a unified voice. "If I join Coastal Command, how could I fly with Challenor?"

"It's essential to fly with Challenor?"

"Yes," said Reardon without hesitation. "Besides, we don't choose where we're sent."

"You could apply for a transfer on moral grounds."

Reardon laughed. "You're in the services. You know how they operate. Besides, my conscience isn't appalled, or anything like it."

She reached forward with her index finger and drew it down the line of his nose. It was a very familial gesture, as if he were the wayward son of the Hadgrafts. "I know there are mysteries that happen up in the air which none of us understands, but for God's sake, Flight, Challenor's a very ordinary fellow. I mean, he's not part of the actual physical equation of flight? I mean, it's possible for a plane to get off the ground without Challenor's help, isn't it?"

Reardon shrugged. He really wondered if it were possible.

"But you're so young."

Without knowing he had said it, Reardon murmured, "I am a hundred years old."

"And determined to die!" said Enid Hadgraft.

"No," he said, and was certain about this. "Determined to live."

"Ah! You believe that's what Challenor does for you?"

"Yes."

"That makes you two rather special goats, doesn't it? This is the way governments work on people. On the other side of things, on the German side, God knows what statistics children your age are being fed."

"I suppose they just try to stick by their friends and do the best they can," said Reardon.

"And in the name of all that," Enid replied, "all the worst crimes of humankind are forgiven."

"Coastal Command is nothing," said Reardon.

"I wonder if you'll think that the next time you're over Hamburg," murmured Enid Hadgraft with a perception that frightened Reardon.

She got up from the bed. She knew she was fighting a lost cause—matching twentieth-century statistics against the force of nineteenth-century mateship. Reardon himself was astonished at the way mateship triumphed.

"By God in his heaven," said Corporal Enid Hadgraft, "I hope you prevail through all this."

She moved to the door. He could barely see her when she turned back and said, "Just remember the goats, though, and the buildings for that matter. Remember your surprise."

11

Nursing and Compassion

PERPETUA saw Dr. Cormack arrive and said good morning to him. Then Councillor Heffernan, sedated and apparently happy, was wheeled in by Sister Francis and one of the young lay nurses. Francis and the nurse rolled the councillor from the trolley onto the operating table, so that he lay on his side. He waved a hand slackly toward his friend, Dr. Cormack. "Don't worry about anything, Frank," said the doctor. "Within two weeks you'll be running around with the Magpies."

The Magpies were the Rossclare Rugby League team, to whom Dr. Cormack was honorary physician.

Councillor Heffernan was soon etherized and rolled forward onto his stomach, exposing large white buttocks, slightly freckled, which had been shaven. Even the slightest exploratory parting of the buttocks by Dr. Cormack showed some of the most engorged, purple, soft tissue Perpetua had ever seen. Cormack asked Perpetua for a scalpel and a swab and began.

"Poor Frank Heffernan," said Cormack, almost under his breath. "These are real raspberries."

But about Father Proud he volunteered no information at all. "Did you all see His Lordship downstairs?" he asked offhandedly at one stage.

"Yes, Doctor," said Perpetua and Sister McGowan in well-trained unison. Timothy, the scout nurse, laughed.

"Have to be on our best behavior, eh?" Cormack observed. But still he did not say if Bishop Flannery was downstairs to attend a deathbed or celebrate a recovery.

As the day of her profession as a nun in the Sisters of Compassion had drawn near, the young Perpetua presumed she would be a teacher. That was how she had pictured herself—surrounded by children in crisp uniforms of subtle blue. She had that vanity, in those days: a preference for the unique blue of the Sisters of Compassion girls instead of the heavy, cheap, navy-blue tunic that she and other not-so-well-off children had worn at the Sisters of St. Joseph's School. Was this snobbery? In fact, she realized later, it was probably something worse—her childhood had made her desire the immaculate, the unstained: polished mahogany on the floor, sparkling windows, crisply starched uniforms.

The Sisters of Compassion had all that. They had come a long way in this young country. If an order of nuns could be fashionable, then the Sisters of Compassion were fashionable, far beyond the Catholic community, and it was reasonable that a young woman who did not want to get older and have to argue over gas bills at a kitchen table on Saturday afternoons should be drawn to them.

The most visible face of the Sisters of Compassion was, of course, St. Bridie's, built on a slab of land nicely placed to catch the wealthy ill of Sydney's eastern suburbs and—through its outpatient department—the beaten whores and scabby drifters of King's Cross. But though Perpetua/Teresa might daydream about soothing brows and the relatives of the ill in Bridie's, she knew that when she took her vows as a nun, she and the other postulants would be sent to one of the order's schools, and that she would not be considered for nursing training at Bridie's until she was in her mid-thirties.

She supposed she had the war to thank for what really happened. The government could not estimate how many casualties might arise from the war in the Pacific, but seemed to believe that since Singapore and the islands of Japan would one day have to be captured, Australia should have many nurses, whether they were nurses who had taken vows in orders founded in the seventeenth century or were just ordinary Australian women.

The day before her profession—when she would enter the chapel dressed as a bride, prostrate herself before the Archbishop of Sydney, utter her vows, and then be robed in the habit, the apparently complicated veils and guimpes and capes of the order, while her father and mother, formally of the Coolgardie gold-fields, watched from the body of the chapel, their faces half stricken with fulfillment and loss—the day before the great event, the Mistress of Novices called Perpetua to her office.

"Well," the Mistress sighed. It was her job, Perpetua understood, to make it seem as if all her efforts at perfecting the novices had been ineffectual. But she was not by nature a severe woman—the provincial of the order, Mother Wilhelmina, knew that you didn't appoint to a post like Mistress of Novices people who wanted to be severe, who enjoyed it, who couldn't wait to flog the young into shape. You appointed a sensible woman who knew, nonetheless, how to make harsh decisions.

The Mistress of Novices' face fell away into a smile. "Everyone says you're impetuous. Some of the older nuns here complain that you walk too fast, and even run. Perhaps you don't trust God enough—you have to get to where you're going quickly so that you can find out whether He can manage the situation or not. That's the impression. It's a mental habit of yours which, I can tell you now, will attract a lot of complaints from older nuns, who have seen your sort of impulsiveness before, in a number of young nuns."

Perpetua was in a happy frame of mind. It was the last day of silence, prayer, and reflection before the profession day, and the party afterward to which all the parents could come, marking her full-fledged admission to the perfections of sisterhood. She had few doubts that with help, divine and order-ly, she could become an acceptible Sister of Compassion. What the Mistress of Novices was saying she had heard before from a number of people, so she nodded and nodded, hoping the Mistress would get to the point.

The Mistress of Novices' upper lip folded down quite nicely over her lower, creating a neat dimple on either side of her mouth. She must have been a handsome girl, and it was known that she was one of the crop of World War One nuns. They were the ones who had been galvanized into entering the Sisters of Compassion by some war death or other—a fiancé killed at Gallipoli, a brother at Passchendaele.

"We're sending three of you to train as nurses at St. Brigid's. We think you have the practical skills for it. You will just have to rein yourself in and not become overexcitable when you see the sick and the maimed, that's all."

She said that she was sure that with God's help, Perpetua could manage it.

Perpetua was excited by the way her career had taken a new direction in a few minutes. She found that the ambition to teach the young evaporated before she had left the office of the Mistress of Novices. She wished to sing, felt an enormous gratitude to the order and the Deity.

She could not tell anyone since she was still in what they called "retreat," the eight-day period of meditation before profession. A Jesuit gave the postulants three conferences a day in the chapel; they sat there while he talked to them from a table placed in front of the altar and urged them to so fill their hearts with love for the crucified Christ that it would overflow, touch, vivify all the people they dealt with—the children they taught, the parents of children, Australia, the world, the universe. He was a fashionable and eloquent Jesuit, known to be an expert on religious art. He did not overdo the hellfire or the stuff about clods of earth dropping on the lid of your coffin, and what did it profit a man or woman, et cetera, et cetera? You were entitled to one or two private sessions with him, where you talked about particular fears you harbored about yourself, which you might be taking with you into your career as a professed nun. But otherwise you could not speak, and Perpetua had already had her private conference, and doubted in any case whether the Jesuit would be much excited by the news that she was being entrusted, at such a young age, with nursing duties.

She walked around the gardens of the novitiate, amongst the gum trees shrilling with cicadas. The gravel crunched beneath her hardy shoes. She could not pray or think straight. In an ecstasy, she raised her face to the sun—the sun the rest of her body had renounced; except for the two-week vacation every year, she remembered, when the nuns were permitted to go to Shell Harbor, south of Sydney, to a house the order owned. There they were allowed to wear a swimming suit appropriate to the age, though they were to wear bathrobes while out of the water and avoid the vanity of suntanning.

The problem of not being able to tell anyone was fairly quickly solved. Filing down the corridor of polished mahogany toward the refectory for a Spartan lunch, she heard Timothy mutter behind her, "I'm going to St. Bridie's. And so is Deidre."

Perpetua felt suddenly cheated. Deidre's record was good, but Timothy was considered a little crude by the order's standards, and was a notorious breaker of silences. Being sent to St. Brigid's was all at once not as astounding an event as it had appeared to be an hour before. But then Perpetua understood what a vain and mean thought this was. Especially since she could not imagine life in the novitiate without the occasional, ordinary sanity of Timothy's mutterings. And so, as Timothy passed her to take up a seat at the table, Perpetua muttered, "Me too. St. Bridie's." Timothy exchanged one glance of wide-eyed joy.

And then they had sat in joy to eat.

12

St. Bridie's

IN late 1941, as the Pacific war began, she was given a cell on the
top floor of St. Bridie's. From its window she could see on one
side the terraces of Darlinghurst and, on a corner, a two-story
hotel enhanced on three sides with a wrought-iron balcony whose
best days were past. Lots of sailors went there—American, Australian. They were always loud, and there were never officers
around to inhibit them, which was probably what they liked about
the place. There were also lots of loud women with hennaed or
peroxided hair, whom Perpetua would sometimes see during her
study hour leaving the hotel with soldiers and sailors at six o'clock
at night. Sydney hotels closed at six P.M. and therefore encouraged
people to get drunk quickly.

The women would often stand back bowlegged from the sailors
and argue with them. Perpetua felt a sisterly feeling for these
women, ached to treat them better than the sailors obviously did,
and to talk to them. For they were the ones who, it was known,
turned up regularly in the outpatient clinic with broken noses and
split eyebrows, with hard-to-get-at wounds under their dyed hair,
with torn knees from being hit and collapsing on gravel, or with
cuts from gashing themselves on the sharp, cement edges of pave-
ments. But not until the end of the second year of training would

she be permitted in the outpatient clinic. It would not be until the end of the second year that she would be able to talk to these particular sisters of hers.

"You find," said a ward nun to her one night, "that a great number of those women who come to outpatient to be stitched are Catholics. They have everything a Catholic should—rosary beads in their handbag, along with other things." (Perpetua herself would discover later, when the time passed and she was working in the outpatient clinic, that the other things included condoms.) "And they wear St. Christopher and Miraculous medals. And those poor sailors who might die in the Pacific islands with those girls on their consciences!"

Perpetua was happy. In the morning there were lectures supervised by the director of nursing, a tall, elegant woman—what the nuns called "a secular"—that is, a non-nun. She was probably the best respected non-nun in the entire, massive hospital.

After the lunchtime prayers and devotions, which included the Examination of Conscience—a period in which each nun was to reflect and pray for her faults—the newly arrived nuns, like the lay or secular nurses, were at first assigned to routine tasks, and then, later, to more adventurous ones. She and Timothy and Deidre, for example, sterilized rubber sheeting or stored rubber air cushions and pillows, lightly powdering them with French chalk and leaving them slightly inflated. They cleaned the ward sterilizers with steel wool and sandsoap, and polished the outsides. They stacked the bedpan sterilizers with the narrower-necked bedpans for males and the more open-necked ones for females. "Which just shows you," whispered Timothy, "that men piss neater than women do."

The quiet and genial Deidre had a father who was a high official in the Department of Health. Sometimes, when her father was visiting the hospital on business, she would be called from her routine tasks to spend a few minutes chatting with him, in the presence of the Mother Superior or one of the other convent officials in the polished parlor downstairs.

Sister Deidre's father did not overdo this privilege. He was a good Catholic. He was a sign that the Knights of the Southern Cross had control of the Department of Health, and therefore of the fact that the Sisters of Compassion would ride higher than they had in the 1890s, when the government departments had been dominated by Masons.

In her routine duties around St. Bridie's, collecting trays or bedpans, Perpetua continually saw headlines. They were always hopeful ones, but despite her lack of worldliness, she could sense what was at best a stalemate, at worst, a disaster. The Australians had been capturing Italian prisoners in the Middle East by the ten thousands, but that was over now that the Germans had arrived. There had been a disaster in Crete too. While sponging this or that patient, elderly males or females, she would clear away the dangerous maps of the war the newspapers printed daily. She knew that soon those maps would claim her brother, who was in his last year at school, and she sensed that then there would be only a painful, vacant sunshine in the house in Rose Bay.

Timothy said that the reason they had not had any young nun-nurses before was the fear that sponging the male genitals would drive young nuns crazy. Timothy, having grown up on a farm, thought this a fatuous idea. And Perpetua agreed. The tired male limbs and manhoods that Perpetua sponged and talcumed in her long days of training seemed no more or less worthy of compassion than the armpits or the genitalia of elderly women. The war had not yet begun in the Pacific, and few of its casualties turned up in the wards of St. Bridie's. It was still pilectomies of Knights of the Southern Cross, or gallbladders of devout Catholic women. Yet she knew that her brother Bernard was never safe, yet might be rendered safe by her devotion, by her constancy.

Every Saturday, after the noon lunch, there would be the Chapter of Faults. It was then that her week of decent service seemed to be denied. She and Timothy, in particular, attracted the accusations of a number of the nuns of St. Bridie's. "It seems to me, dear Sister, that you move at too fast a pace between the pulmonary and the ENT ward." "It seems to me, dear Sister, that you spend too great a period of time studying the front pages of newspapers which may be at the side of patients' beds."

The Mother Superior Fredericka, a severe, large, broad-faced woman who did not lack in that compassion meant to be the order's stock-in-trade, would impose on them token punishments for these lapses. At the beginning these penalties consisted largely of polishing candlesticks in the chapel, or bringing the marble of the altar stairs to an even higher shine than all the devotion of the Sisters of Compassion had so far managed.

Then, one Thursday night after a class, Timothy and Perpetua

got the message to report to Sister Consalva. Consalva was a
woman who had no great future in the order and was considered
lucky to have gotten into St. Bridie's in the first place. It was she
who looked after the dead.

They walked down the steps and entered the dissecting room.
Across a floor of cold tiles Consalva, gray and middle-aged, was
behind a screen, where a dead woman, red-haired, lay naked on a
table. There was a knife wound below her ribs, and from the lips
of the wound it was not hard to imagine that the knife had reached
up toward her heart. Consalva was already washing the woman,
whose terribly artificial red hair quivered under this scrubbing.

Perpetua, in all her career as a nurse, would never meet anyone
more efficient. Consalva taught Timothy and her how to plug the
ears of the dead. Rolling the red-haired, stabbed woman over, she
showed them how to insert a plug with forceps into the rectum.
Then she did the same with the woman's vagina, slowly, so that
both Timothy and Perpetua understood the process. Perpetua felt
as she did when she watched the women at the hotel far below her
cell window. Sisterly. They were doing a sister honor. And Consalva did this sister the greatest honor possible. The ears and
nostrils were plugged, and some cotton wool placed between teeth
and lips. The wound was given its final dressing—a gauze covering
was strapped firmly over it. The knees and then the ankles were
bound together, but Consalva used cotton wool between the bandage and the flesh, as if there might be bruising or resistance.

A jaw bandage, such as Perpetua had only seen in the film *A
Christmas Carol*, was tied around the woman's jaw and knotted
above her red-haired skull. Then a sheet was thrown over her and
Consalva, Timothy, and Perpetua wheeled her to the elevator at
the end of the corridor. It was a renowned elevator, used only by
nuns traveling from floor to floor, or by those escorting corpses.

During a week on night duty Perpetua discovered that people
died in the small hours, when the fight seemed least worthwhile.
In the small hours, too, most babies began to fight their way out of
their mother's womb, as if to replace the losses from the ranks.

It was also during night duty, working with the ward sister in
the orthopedic ward, that Perpetua encountered the legend of the
Brown Lady.

At three A.M. Perpetua and a lay nurse wheeled the loveless
blue corpse of an old man without relatives or children down to

the elevator at the end of the corridor. They delivered it to Mr. Brosnan, another old man, a devout sayer of the Rosary, blessed with many grandchildren, and Consalva's aide.

They then returned to their ward to do the normal night duties, to look for signs of restlessness, to administer a sedative to those in distress or a glass of water to the dehydrated. Good work. Work you could see the effect of, the easing of fear in the patient's eyes. "Could I bring you a glass of water, Major?" Perpetua asked the patient who had undergone an operation for a bone tumor the afternoon before and who had seemed parched all day. The major's eyes flickered. He was one of those elderly soldiers, probably a veteran of the Great War, which people now had begun to call World War I. These days he ran remote training camps for young soldiers, or organized the disinfection of blankets somewhere in the bush for the next intake of recruits whom—following the terminology of American films—people had begun to call "rookies."

"I'm very comfortable, Sister," the major told her. "The Brown Lady just brought me a glass."

A peculiar tremor went through Perpetua. She had heard something of this brown nun, but she had presumed it just an item of gossip circulated around the hospital by lay nurses and talk during recreation hours in the convent. It was an axiom of convent life that the periods of silence a nun had to endure encouraged the natural gossip in every human being. Although a nun was meant to resist the impulse to give way to the mere vanities of idle chat, Perpetua had observed that a lot of idle chat occurred, and sometimes it was idle chat dressed up as serious.

The gossip about the Brown Lady concerned a nun who had died before World War One. She had been a nun from a different order than the Sisters of Compassion, a small French order that dressed in brown and since those days might have become extinct. She had apparently perished of septicemia when a scalpel she was handling—one that had been used in an operation on an infected wound—nicked the knuckle of her right hand. According to the story, her arm had ballooned and soon her whole body had grown distorted and purple with the poison. Her death was a sort of cautionary tale about the dangers of handling instruments too loosely, dangers that had been diminished recently by the new drugs, the sulfas and penicillins. The Brown Lady was a martyr to sepsis. She knew in her terrible death, so far from France, what thirst and consuming fever were.

Older nuns swore that postoperative patients for the last thirty years had mentioned her, the Brown Lady with the glass of water in hand. Her touch to the forehead quelled fevers. But the question Perpetua had always asked herself, and most skeptics uttered, was whether these people had already heard of the Brown Lady legend before they went for their operations, and were therefore already prepared to visualize her during their postoperative fevers. Had the major heard of the legend? Perpetua was filled with an urgency to know.

"The Brown Lady?" Perpetua asked.

"The nun," said the major, "in brown."

"Did you know there were Brown Ladies here, Major? Before you came?"

There was a stutter of laughter from the major. "She spoke with a foreign accent," said the major.

"But had you heard of her before?" asked Perpetua straight out. She felt ashamed of herself. The major—having been comforted by whatever hand—should have been permitted to drift away into sleep.

"Heard of her? No," said the major, still laughing quietly.

He seemed very excited, and Perpetua guiltily knew she was partly the reason for that, with her interrogations.

"My daughters went to the Sisters of Compassion, you know," said the major a little distractedly. It was a distinction parents often boasted about. "At Potts Point. But I've never seen one who wore brown before."

She ceased to harry him. She took his pulse and told him he should sleep. And to her amazement, though he was a major and she was a barely professed nun, he obeyed her, closing his eyes and slipping away from pain.

The ward sister in the major's ward was a nun called Sister Brendan. She was a woman in her early forties, Perpetua guessed, and her face was uncreased. She had a fine complexion which she had inherited from Irish forebears. There were the spotty Irish and the translucent ones and the dark ones. Brendan was of the translucent breed. Perpetua could tell that she was a good-looking woman—they used terms like "striking" or "handsome" for women like Brendan in the outside world. Though you were not supposed to bring those terms with you into the order, they were part of an inevitable baggage. Brendan's mouth seemed to be in constant subtle movement, though the rest of her was pure composure. But these little muscular movements of Brendan's mouth warned Perpetua that Brendan did not approve of her. Perhaps she did not approve of all the young, newly professed nuns being admitted as nurses, perhaps she did not approve of Perpetua herself, or perhaps there were forces in Brendan that made universal disapproval all too easy. Perpetua did not know the answer, as much as the question caused her grief.

Brendan was a model and competent nun and was expected to reach a middling eminence in the order. Perpetua was sure of one thing: that the way Brendan's mouth moved had nothing to do with meanness or a desire to punish either her, Timothy, or Deidre.

The Chapter of Faults, as a spiritual exercise, began soon after lunchtime on a Saturday. The Mother Superior, in this case Fredericka, sat on a highly carved wooden chair in the chapel, with the sister porter, whose duty was to run the business of the convent, kneeling on her left on a hassock, and her deputy kneeling on the right. Facing her and also kneeling, except for those who were aged or ill, was the entire community of St. Bridie's, more than fifty nuns.

Neither the Jesuits, from whose Rule that of the Sisters of Compassion was derived, nor Mother Fredericka were ignorant enough of human nature to know that there was great opportunity for the Chapter of Faults to be used for settling scores and jealousies. The idea was not meant to be petty vengeance, but rather that the sisters would, in a spirit of charity, draw the visible faults of this or that nun to the attention both of the nun concerned and of the Mother Superior.

Fredericka had once warned the community that sometimes the announcement by one sister of a fault in another said as much or even more about the faultfinder than it did about the nun who was the target. The exercise therefore began with a decade—that is, one fifth of a Rosary—to protect the community against backbiting and petty jealousy.

After that it was a brave or certain nun who rose to accuse any of her fellow sisters of faults.

At the Saturday sessions in the chapel the newly professed sisters and trainee nurses attracted most of the accusations of imperfection. The community had until now been middle-aged, and it was not used to the flippancy of girls in their twenties. At one Saturday evening recreation Sister Timothy, that husky farm girl, said to Perpetua, "Wonder how they filled in their time at Chapter of Faults before we came?"

On the Saturday after Perpetua's conversation with the major on the matter of the Brown Lady, an elderly Irish nun accused Sister Deidre, the quietest and most composed of the three new sisters, of having her sleeves rolled up too high during the task of scrubbing bedpans. Another elderly nun had a grievance against Timothy. "It seems to me, dear Sister Timothy," the older nun accused, "that on at least three days this week you spent an undue period of time reading the newspapers of various patients in the Ear, Nose, and Throat ward, especially in reading the *Daily Telegraph* and evening *Sun*."

These two were considered particularly pagan journals, more so than the sedate *Sydney Morning Herald*.

The pale and beautiful Sister Brendan also rose. "It seems to me, dear Sister Perpetua, that you engaged a patient in conversation about ghosts late at night in the orthopedic ward for your own vanity and to no benefit of his."

Seated in her place in chapel, Perpetua was grateful for the cover her veil and starched hood gave to her burning face. It was justice, she knew. She had behaved like a child. She felt fury at Brendan too. Why hadn't Brendan taken her aside at recreation and said, "Don't have long conversations with the patients at night." Wouldn't that be better than humiliation before the community, advice given in this punishing way and a penance soon to be imposed by Mother Fredericka?

Deidre's penance this time turned out to be fairly light, as could be expected of such a minor infringement as the length to which your sleeves were rolled. She was required to spend her recreation time polishing brass in the sacristy, the sort of punishment Timothy and Perpetua had already suffered. Timothy and Perpetua themselves were excluded from the nuns' table for three days.

They were to kneel on the floor of the refectory and eat their meals in that posture.

If such humiliations helped sustain her parents in the face of her brother's recently announced intention to go to war, she did not complain. The floor of the refectory was stone, however, and hard and icy to the knees. On the second evening of their eating on their knees, side by side, inside the U of tables that accommodated the rest of the community of nuns, Timothy murmured under cover of the strident reading of a devotional book by one of the nuns, "Pretend it's a picnic." Perpetua felt a surge of sisterly feeling toward Timothy. She had thought that such simple feelings of sisterhood would arise easily in a community, but it was only while eating with Timothy on the stone floor that she felt them. The rest of her days, and even her nights—including her dreams—seemed plagued by faultfinding and the stress of learning the practical crafts of being both a nurse and a nun.

A seventeen-year-old boy from a farm on the south coast was rushed to St. Bridie's by ambulance. In a world where the young were taking heroic wounds, he had suffered a very ordinary one— he had trodden on a nail in the cow shed in the half light before dawn and had not had the time to do anything about it. Now he was suffering all the classic symptoms of tetanus. His jaw was locked so tight that his local doctor had had to punch a tracheotomy hole in his throat. It fluttered bloodily and emitted occasional rasps of air. But the boy was close to respiratory failure. A specialist anesthetist kept him alive with a mixture of muscle relaxants and stimulants. Such relaxants as megamide and daptozole entered the boy's arm from a drip above his bed. The boy's case was so severe that the anesthetist even used a drug considered slightly unorthodox by older surgeons—curare—synthesized from poisons Amazonian Indians used on the tips of their arrows. It barely allowed the boy's jaw to slacken.

He was a very ordinary-looking Australian boy. Tall, the lantern jaw of the Scots or the dark Irish, and a scatter of freckles over a flesh gone pallid blue. Once while Perpetua was taking his pulse, his eyes snapped open in alarm. "Bail that big brindly one," he instructed her.

She knew it was farm talk. "All right," she told him.

"The big heifer," he reiterated.

"Yes," she said. "Don't worry about it. It's already been done."

He never spoke to her again, but this simple conversation seemed to bind her to him. She had a feeling that she was somehow related. She could imagine the white, wide-verandaed, corrugated-iron-roofed farmhouse on a green hill from which he had stumbled in the dark to go off to the milking shed for that fatal puncture of the foot. No doubt he had elder brothers who were away in military camps somewhere, perhaps flying in bombers. If his father were alive, Perpetua never saw him at the bedside. And so, a widow's boy. And the widow thinking, What will I do next year, when he's old enough for the army? In the two days it took the boy to die, Perpetua was moved to the Ear, Nose, and Throat ward, but absented herself every chance she got so that she could run along the corridors of St. Bridie's to the Chest ward, where the boy lay behind screens.

On the final evening she found at the boy's bedside the young priest from the parish church on the corner next to St. Bridie's. He was giving the boy a last anointing. Oil across the fluttering eyelids, the nostrils, the ears, the lips. *"Per hanc unctionem,"* said the priest. "Through this anointing . . ."

It seemed pitiable, just the near-dead boy and the young priest. And so, without a word, Perpetua dropped to her knees and stayed till the ceremony was over. Even after the priest put the lid on the little silver container of chrism, of oil blessed with great ceremony by the Archbishop of Sydney the previous Easter, Perpetua stayed. She stayed even after the priest left. She did not know what to do. She was stuck there, immobile. She adjusted the useless drip bag then, and took the boy's barely noticeable pulse. It was the arrival of one of the young doctors, his inspection of the boy, his shrug, his own offhand playing with the drip tube, that released her from the boy's bedside.

She arrived in chapel fifteen minutes late for evening prayers. That is, when they were virtually over.

Next Saturday at Chapter of Faults, Brendan again rose. Her lips moving in a way that, even to Perpetua, still signified no malice, Brendan uttered the formula which by now was so familiar to Perpetua—the formula of humiliation she had been hearing all her grown life. "It seems to me, dear Sister, that you have become so taken up with concern for particular patients, particularly a young male patient, that you have been unable to reach chapel in time for your appointed duties. It seems to me also, dear Sister, that you have absented yourself from your rostered ward to attend the bedside of such patients."

Mother Superior Fredericka seemed to be familiar with all the details of Perpetua's actions. "When are you going to stop embarrassing us and embarrassing God by being mentioned every week, Sister Perpetua?" she asked. "You run around the hospital too much, like a disordered child. When is that going to stop? Would you mind telling me? Do you think that I like to sit at table and watch you eat your meal off the floor? You are a penance on me as well as to yourself."

Deidre and Timothy, who had once more been accused of delinquencies—Timothy was still reading patients' *Daily Telegraphs* and carrying on long conversations with lay nurses, mere employees of St. Bridie's, women with a life beyond the hospital. But there was the implication in Brendan's manner and Mother Fredericka's that Perpetua's crimes were the most serious. "You are a professed nun, but you are still not fully and finally professed in our order," Fredericka warned her as she knelt amongst the other nuns. "Please do not think for a moment that you will be permitted to take the final vows of our order as a matter of course. It is precisely at this stage of their vocations that many a young woman of our order has found her future destroyed by vanity."

Perpetua knew that it was not Fredericka the individual nun speaking. Superiors in religious orders were required to speak this way, with the awesomeness of a divine voice. Perpetua was filled with a churning sense of shame.

There came a phase during which Sister Brendan accused her less often at Chapter of Faults, in fact seemed to grow tired of mentioning her imperfections. But the accusations were taken up by a dark young nun called Sister Paul, who managed the admissions office and was a notoriously fast typist. *That* sort of speed, however, did not seem to cause offense to the Sisters of Compassion. Paul accused Perpetua of having her sleeves rolled up to a vain height—the accusation earlier brought down on Deidre's neck. A young doctor called McGuire, recently discharged from the army after persistent malaria and now doing an internship at Bridie's, had fallen into a savage malarial fever one evening just before prayer time. He had gone to lie down in one of the staff rooms, and a young secular nurse, even less senior than Perpetua, had come along the corridor begging her to help. Dr. McGuire, the young nurse said, was raving, shivering, and sweating like a tap.

Perpetua entered a vacant private room and found the young doctor shuddering on a bed he had pushed, for some delirious reason, to the middle of the room. He lay there wrapped in a sheet that was uniformly wet with sweat.

She sent the lay nurse to find one of the senior physicians and stayed with McGuire until the man arrived. Dosages of Atebrin and Paludrine were ordered by the senior doctor. Perpetua and the young nurse kept watch until the fever began to abate. By then, yet again, she was late for the evening prayers and even for dinner. The young, dark-complexioned Paul accused her of it in the next Chapter of Faults. Paul, about thirty years old, her features sharp and neat as her typing, and Brendan—with her pale, handsome features, and her strange judgmental lips—became objects of fear to Perpetua in the landscape of St. Bridie's, beings to whom no satisfactory answer could be made.

One Saturday after the lunchtime reading of the martyrology, the list of canonized saints and martyrs for that day, Fredericka waited in the corridor as the nuns marched past, bound for chapel and the Chapter of Faults, in exact order of seniority. The long bone of Fredericka's nose gleamed with authority, but there was a halfway indulgent smile on her lips. She took Perpetua by the elbow as she passed and pulled her gently out of the procession. "I suppose you're dreading this by now, child," she said matter-of-factly.

Perpetua's palms were sweating. "No, Mother," she lied. "It confuses me. But I believe it's supposed to."

"I am sick of hearing you harried and scourged in the Chapter of Faults," said Fredericka. "I am sick of watching you kneeling before me as I eat my meals. I have asked Sisters Brendan and Paul to forgive you in their hearts and not verbally. There is an embargo—that's what I'm telling you. An embargo on mentioning you during Chapter of Faults. I am appealing to you, sister to sister, and I am praying to you. So are Brendan and Paul. We will not state your faults in front of the community, but in return I want you to find them in your own heart. And to seek God's help in expunging them."

Together with a flash of gratitude, Perpetua felt a surmise overtake her: would she ever be able to speak in such grand, finished sentences of the type that only superiors seemed capable of? Did a sort of gift of tongues, sonorous and solemn, enter such women as Fredericka, and would it one day enter her? Then she found that she was weeping.

"Now don't be a silly girl, Perpetua. You chose to be one of us. Now act like one of us."

That afternoon, though even Deidre was mentioned by one of the older nuns for having laughed inordinately during recreation, Perpetua was not named. Glowing with her new immunity and her resolution to be worthy of it, she returned to the Ear, Nose, and Throat ward, resisting the childlike temptation to stop in the orthopedic ward and thank Brendan for the new understanding she'd shown. Above all, Perpetua thought, there *is* sisterhood here, after all.

13

Aiming Points

FLIGHT Lieutenant Wraith was an Anglican priest of the
diocese of Chichester. A hook-nosed man in his early thirties,
he was already chaplain at Parsfield station when Reardon arrived
there and began operations with Flight Sergeant Punch, Challenor, and the other members of J-Judy. Wraith had an excellent
reputation with "the boys," and drank in all the messes—both the
officers' and, with the immunity that extended only to chaplains,
the sergeants'. He ran a Christian fellowship open to airmen of all
religions—it even attracted the occasional Pole. He was always
there to say good-bye to the crews at their last meal before operations, and in the debriefing room in the small hours or first gray
light on their return.

Whenever ops were scrubbed, especially if airmen returned
back to the warmth of the buildings after sitting in their bombers
for an hour or two—waiting for takeoff instructions, waiting for
the weather to clear over Parsfield or else over some distant European target—he would pass amongst them in the mess with a
crooked, tentative smile on his face, apparently as delighted as
they were to have been spared for another night. The rumor was
that he had once sat down beside one bomber crew and said,
"Well, it's off!" and a little stutter escaped his lips and tears en-

tered his eyes. It was presumed from this event that Flight Lieutenant Wraith needed protection from the realities of war.

Not long after Reardon's first mission at Parsfield, Wraith became aware of some streak of religious devotion in Reardon and
asked him after some debriefing or other if he would like to attend
the fellowship. Reardon had politely said that he would if he
could. At which Wraith smiled crookedly. "I know you chaps have
to get permission from one of your own," he said. "A Catholic
priest, I mean. Although I like to think of myself as a Catholic too.
Anyhow, I'm sure you'll get it without too much difficulty. After
all, we're all together in this great enterprise. This war must signal
the end—I would imagine—of the divisions which began with the
Reformation."

Reardon quickly got permission, as Wraith had said he would,
from a visiting Catholic chaplain, a Benedictine monk, a remote
Englishman so like Wraith himself that he seemed to bear out
Wraith's opinion about divisions wearing thin.

Reardon found the first fellowship meeting he attended sur-
prisingly crowded. Few of the flight crew were among the throng,
however. Catering, pay, medical, educational, meteorological, and
other officers; a number of ground crew warrant officers, mechanics, and ordnance men made up the bulk of the crowd. And there
were about a dozen young WAAF's, air-force servicewomen, pale
from all-night operational vigils, from the strangeness of sleeping
by day, of fitting the casualty rates into God's great plan. Wraith
gave a short talk/sermon which was listened to hungrily by all the
people in the room.

He spoke of how it was possible to find God through the gaps
in the savagery of the war. God was almost crowded out of the sky
by the extraordinary science of the bombers, of their destructive
force, of their extraordinary navigational aids, at whose sophisti-
cation the layman could but guess. In the spaces between these
wonders and the destructive horrors of the war, said Wraith, we
must reach forward, particularly now, to touch the face of God
which lies behind everything, all plans, all wonders, all horrors.

Afterward tea and biscuits were served from a long trestle
table. Reardon was surrounded by the people Challenor called
"shiny-arses." Challenor would also have been contemptuous of
any spiritual doubts and anguish they might suffer. No matter how
many bombers they saw take off at dusk, they knew that *they* had

every chance of being a breathing human being at dawn. Their concern about a sky crowded with terrors was superfluous to Challenor.

But Reardon was enjoying this close sight of so many of these other people of Parsfield, and, he had to admit, even the way the eyes of men much older than himself flickered to his gunners wings and wavered aside. He talked politely to a WAAF in the photographic section, asking questions about her work. She came from Cumberland. She had a boyfriend who was in Tunisia. There was little to distinguish her from a million other English girls you could meet that year.

Flight Lieutenant Wraith came up to them and chatted to the girl for a moment, who then excused herself. It was as if she wanted to give Wraith a chance to work on Reardon.

"Good to see you here," said Wraith. Immediately he raised a question that had been on Reardon's mind. "You notice we don't get many air crew. There are a number of reasons for that. You see, in a way, it's those who sit and wait here every night while you chaps are over Europe who have the most questions to answer. I mean, at least you chaps are dealing with reality. But they have to deal with imagination, and the gaps at table in the mess. Not that they eat with you, but they're aware of these things, these undeniable absences. Whereas you chaps are dealing with the absolute as well as the real. Absolute danger. And, of course, absolute damage when you are successful."

"Absolute damage is the aim," Reardon said. "Not always achieved." He knew he wasn't giving away state secrets. He had noticed that as well as attending debriefings, the Reverend Wraith hung around the photographic hut a lot, looking fixedly at the day-after-the-raid photographic record of the target.

The conversation had not gone far when they were joined by a young flight-sergeant bombardier from one of the other squadrons at Parsfield. The boy had neat, curly hair and was a year or two older than Reardon. His name was Otley, and Reardon knew that he had flown twenty missions or so, even though the numbers were not discussed—the axiom being that as soon as you uttered what number of missions you had behind you, whether it was five or twenty-five, you were somehow finished. Maybe even in a believer like Otley such superstition existed.

"Are you from Melbourne?" Otley asked him.

"No, Sydney."

"Ah, I have an aunt in Sydney," said Otley, without interest. It was obvious that he wanted Reardon to go away, so that he could talk to the Reverend Wraith as to an old friend.

Before the next meeting of the fellowship, a great force of bombers, including the two squadrons of Parsfield, were sent against the Ruhr city of Wuppertal. Wuppertal was in fact a twin industrial city, spread on either side of a river. It housed a number of German industries, both tank building and high-precision optics. The bombers' stream was to come in on a bearing of sixty-eight degrees to a large chalk-white parade ground on the western side of the town. The weather conditions were such that the parade ground ought to have been visible, but in any case, navigators would be using the wireless receiver called Oboe, which would bring them in accurately, given the excellent conditions for radio transmission. At the parade ground the Parsfield squadrons were to bank five degrees to starboard. Their task was to obliterate the suburb of Wuppertal-Barmen.

As the group commander instructed the Parsfield squadrons in the large ops room, he referred to a great map of Europe on which ribbons had been tied to show the dogleg route the bombers would follow, a route that would bring them in over Wuppertal at the last possible moment—a stratagem aimed at creating in the defenders' minds the idea that three or four industrial cities other than Wuppertal might be the target.

There was some surprise in the room, Reardon noticed, when the maps given out to the pilots, navigators, and bombardiers appeared different from all the maps they were used to seeing, the standard ordnance maps with their sprinkling of Maltese crosses marking hospitals, which were under no circumstances to be attacked. This one was in orange and gray. Looking over Punch's shoulder, Reardon saw concentric circles marked on it in blue and orange, and in the midst of the inner circle, a blue cross, supposedly the aiming point. But then the group commander asked the bombardiers to add another cross to the east, in the middle of the city.

Reardon and the others believed that this was to prevent what was called "creep back," which happened when bombardiers dropped their load early, on the home side of the target, rather than face the full fury of flak and searchlights at the center of the aiming point. Reardon knew that Punch, for all his apparently panicky speech, had never, would never, be consciously guilty of "creep back." There was Australian stubbornness in Punch too. He would rather die than be thought "windy," scared. He would rather die also than ask a question of the group commander.

One other, more senior Australian pilot did ask a question. "Sir, is this the real center of the target or just the point we're to be sure we go as far as?"

The group captain was a little petulant. "It's your aiming point. Have no doubt about it. What I've just asked the bombardiers to pencil in is the true aiming point for your squadron."

There was a mutter amongst the men. Each group would have a different aiming point, and bombs would fall continually along the line they would follow into Wuppertal that night. This should generate extraordinary destruction! They felt both amazed and chastened by the idea.

Then the group captain broke more strange news to them. The target would be marked by a force of Mosquitoes. They would drop red markers and incendiaries all around the group's aiming point. The bomber crews would be attracted by the red markers and by a concentration of incendiary flares.

The navigator nonetheless pointed to a large power plant in the suburb of Wuppertal-Elberfeld. "I bet that's the target they want us to hit," he murmured to Punch. "But they're expecting us to rabbit it a bit, to creep back."

"Bugger that. I'm not a rabbit."

A rabbit was someone who did not go the full distance, who dropped bombs short.

Reardon was very pleased that he did not have to indulge in these discussions of creep back and aiming points.

So the briefing concluded, and the crews went to eat their operational meal of bacon and eggs, knowing that some of them would die with the faint redolence of bacon on their tongues. And then they packed up and received their parachutes and the little perspex boxes containing a small amount of francs and marks, a map of Western Europe, what were whimsically called "wakey-wakey" pills, and a rudimentary compass.

The great bomber force of over seven hundred planes feinted

in the direction of Krefeld, Duisburg, and Essen, turning south to Wuppertal so suddenly that the towns' flak defenses were lulled into the belief that some other city was the chosen target. Reardon composedly watched the black silhouettes of bombs, dropped by Halifaxes above him, sinking past his turret without regard to his being there. But he did not particularly mind. He watched the great fire below, red markers glowing at its edges like coals of an especial brightness. Punch had irascibly come all the way.

The return from Wuppertal was a fairly benign business. Only once did Reardon see the black descent of a German night fighter from the starboard and have to scream, "Corkscrew port, go!"

After operations, the debriefing, the absorption of the loss of this or that plane, the fall of slightly or well-known men, the mug of tea spiked with rum, sleep was not always possible. But by nine A.M. a twitching, gray exhaustion would descend on the flight crews. The sergeants slept in rooms fitted out with iron bedsteads. Generally, even in summer, an orderly kept a stove going in the middle of the room, as if the fliers had brought with them from high altitude a coldness that could not easily be dispersed.

Reardon, Challenor, and the two other Australians who shared their dormitory were awakened a little after lunchtime by a commotion in the corridor. Challenor went to the door in his underwear and opened it. He looked quite middle-aged in his long johns.

Reardon, sitting up on his cot, saw a whey-faced Otley, barefoot, in shirt-sleeves and undress uniform pants, being pushed along by armed provosts. Various flight sergeants could be heard whistling the provosts, who would never know the things flight crew knew and who had therefore better have very good reasons for laying hands on Otley.

In the sergeants' mess that evening, when even the fens stretching away on either side of Parsfield aerodrome looked sweetly drugged in the late sun and butterflies flitted above the gorse, the rumor was that Otley had sent his operational map of Wuppertal to his local member of Parliament. Given the strict controls on mail leaving air bases, Reardon wondered how it could be true.

"Most of the time they move people who do silly things like that right away from the station," said a veteran Australian bombardier. "They're scared he'll pass the germs on, you know. But Otley's still in the guardhouse. They haven't finished questioning him."

"They haven't finished making arrests," said another bombardier, a policeman from Perth in Western Australia.

A red-haired nineteen-year-old New Zealander entered. "I just saw them marching the Reverend Wraith across to the guardhouse."

"Marching? Or accompanying?" someone asked.

But later in the evening Wraith appeared at the bar and ordered a pint. "Otley's just a little distressed," he said. It was a novelty to hear an officer, even a chaplain, refer to someone as "distressed." The fiction kept up by most officers, including surgeons, was that everyone was either a hero or vanished. That is, dead or as good as dead, in the limbo of L.M.F.—lack of moral fiber. "It's a misunderstanding," said Wraith, nodding soberly toward Reardon.

Sometime during that night Otley cut his throat and bled to death in the guardhouse. He had completed twenty-four missions. But he was not buried militarily, with the ceremonial his record perhaps justified. According to an orderly, his body was taken away after dark by an ambulance. Reardon had no doubt that he was as much a victim of Wuppertal as were the thirty-three crews Bomber Command admitted to having lost on the raid.

14

Chapter of Faults

WHEN you worked night shift at St. Bridie's, you got to the chapel in the morning only in time for Mass. You slept from nine in the morning until four in the afternoon—the monastic ration of sleep was always seven hours, one less than the secular norm. You meditated in the late afternoon, when the golden-colored glass in the chapel of St. Bridie's was at its richest. You had a number of companions, for St. Bridie's had a large company of nuns and kept a full operating theater and casualty crew on all night. Perpetua found meditation still the most difficult of all the spiritual exercises—to achieve that voiceless speech with the Divine, to avoid thinking of the patients awaiting you, or of what Paul or Brendan might say of you at the next Chapter of Faults after Fredericka's period of grace ran out. To let the mind go, floating like bread upon the seamless waters of the Godhead— that was hard for a girl from Rose Bay to manage.

Afterward, before going on night duty at a quarter past eight, she would study. Often it would be the notes of older nuns—Sister Agatha's neat, double-line-ruled notes on postoperative pain control, a subject Agatha had first taken an interest in as a young lay nurse in a military hospital in Mesopotamia in 1918. Or else Mother Augusta's compact but brilliant notes on obstetrical procedures. Perpetua loved to handle these pages, which were handed around from student nurse to student nurse. They signified for her the sisterhood, the family concern, she did not always glimpse at the order's most solemn moments.

One night in the winter of 1943, her meditation finished, she went to her cell to study. It was a mild but moist winter's night— if she stretched her neck, she could see through her window a string of lights disappearing toward Darlinghurst, a nimbus of moisture around each of them. She noticed the pub opposite the convent was closed now, according to the severe licensing laws of the New South Wales government, though you could bet the proprietor was selling liquor illegally by way of the back door. Drunken American and Australian soldiers and sailors, having done each other minor damage, would begin to appear in casualty from midnight on.

Looking at that other world of the pub, that alternative institution—Sister Agatha's notes on pain control lying on the little desk behind her—Perpetua was astonished to see a woman in a loose purple nightdress take flight from one of the second-floor windows of the hotel. She flew wide of the hotel balcony, as if she had been pushed instead of choosing to jump. Perpetua heard her horrifying wail as her arms reached to find purchase in the vacant night air. Whatever miracles and soft landings were claimed for thirteenth- or fourteenth-century sinners thrown out of buildings, clearly no miracle was going to help this girl. Perpetua saw her sharp, dark features and her stretched lips, and the thin arms opened in appeal from the wide-cuffed nightdress. She could not see, however, the impact of the girl against the pavement; the back wall of the convent blocked her view of the street. She left her cell at once, though she did not have her headdress on, and ran spiky-haired downstairs to the office occupied by the sister portress, the manager of all traffic in and out of the convent.

The portress looked up at her bare head with amazement.

"Forgive me, Sister Portress, but I have just seen a woman thrown over the balcony of the hotel behind us."

"A woman? Thrown?"

"Please. You must call an ambulance."

"Are you sure?" asked the sister portress.

"I saw it."

"Do you watch the pub a great deal, dear Sister?"

"I heard her scream, Sister," said Perpetua, appalled at herself for the lie. "But please, she is suffering now, outside there, on the pavement in Darlinghurst Road."

The portress, not taking her eyes off Perpetua, lifted the telephone and called the number. "We have had a report of . . ." That was how she stated it.

"Thank you, Sister," said the portress, putting down the telephone. And then she smiled genially, like the woman of no more than forty years that she was. "You can go back up and watch the hotel. And by all means, if there is anyone else thrown off the balcony, let me know."

Perpetua smiled and went to leave. But the portress had not yet finished speaking. "I suppose it's appropriate that young nuns should see a woman thrown out of a place like that. Despite what anyone tells you, we are all sisters in Christ."

When I am a senior nun, Perpetua thought, I hope I have the wit to talk to the young nuns like that.

When Perpetua went on night duty in the casualty ward twenty minutes later, the woman she had seen flying from the balcony was on a bed there. Her leg was fractured in a number of places and had been immobilized by being placed between sandbags. The rest of her body was a mash of grazes and violet cloth. Nurses and nuns cut the cloth away from the wounds while a young intern, Dr. MacMahon, sutured a gash above the girl's eye. A quarter grain of morphine had clearly been administered, but the girl kept asking, "Have the coppers got hold of the bastard yet? I hope they throw him in the deepest cell in fucking Darlinghurst!"

A voice full of hard masculine authority said, "Don't talk in front of the nuns like that!"

"Well, he's a fucker!" the girl said blearily.

"I'll warn you only once," said the voice from the wall. She looked and saw that a first constable from Darlinghurst Police Station sat there on a chair, clearly considering himself in charge. He had the sort of slab Irish face Perpetua, though Irish herself, mistrusted on sight. Piety was written all over it, but the venal features shone through. It was hard to look at a face like that and believe it wasn't fully engrossed in what they called sly grog and starting-price bookmaking.

"Don't you think you should sit outside, Constable," Perpetua suggested. "While the poor girl gets ready for X ray and surgery."

"If that's what you want, Sister," said the policeman, with bitter reverence. He got up and marched out of casualty.

"Good for you, Sister," said one of the lay nurses.

"You shut the bastard up well and truly," said the dazed and injured girl.

Perpetua helped move the girl to a trolley so that she could be X-rayed, and all the way the girl clung to her hand, for she had put the New South Wales Police Force to rout. The leg was multiple-fractured and splintered—her chances of walking properly again were not promising. An orthopedic surgeon would have to be called. Meanwhile more morphine was administered, and Perpetua injected atropine. She could have cut out the girl's heart and the girl would have trusted her.

Some hours later, about three A.M., when the orthopedic surgeon and the officious constable were both probably in bed, Perpetua crept up to the orthopedic ward to see how the girl was faring. Her eye where the sutures had gone in was very swollen, but the rest of her face was untouched. This, Perpetua assumed, could mean only that she'd been punched in the eye before being thrown, because if the pavement had made the impact, her entire face would have been destroyed. She was leaning over the girl, inspecting her face by torchlight, when Sister Brendan appeared.

Perpetua, who had been so commanding with the policeman and such a complete nurse with the damaged girl, was immediately at a loss to speak to Brendan.

"I saw this woman thrown over the hotel balcony. You know, the Clarendon."

"I don't particularly *know* it," said Brendan.

"Where is your station tonight?"

"I am in casualty, Sister."

"Well, this is not casualty," breathed Brendan with a half smile through those thin, cutting, but handsome lips. "This is orthopedics."

Perpetua nodded and turned to go. Brendan followed her to the door. "Sister Perpetua," she called.

Perpetua turned. "Yes, Sister?"

"That girl is not much older than you, is she?"

"It seems as if she's not," Perpetua conceded.

"Your compassion does you credit." Brendan stepped closer still and put a hand on Perpetua's elbow. "But as usual it is disordered. What is worse, it is seen by the rest of the community to be disordered, out of control. It takes you away from your usual post and has you following patients all over the hospital. For God's sake, I am sick of saying so in Chapter of Faults. Please get yourself under management. I don't want to have to keep on naming you for the next five years."

"Thank you, Sister Brendan," said Perpetua, unaware of what else she should say.

Brendan had not finished speaking. "I do not imply that we should be whitened sepulchers, all perfect nunlike composure outside and emotion within. It is just that a rigid external control is itself something of a triumph with a young, tender person like yourself. That is what I am trying to tell you."

And in fact at the next Chapter of Faults, it was the sister portress who raised the problem of Sister Perpetua's not keeping proper custody of the eyes and being concerned with what happened at the hotel. According to the rules of the Sisters of Compassion, as interpreted by minds like that of the sister portress, that Perpetua's lack of custody of the eyes and her curiosity about the Hotel Clarendon had helped bring aid to the woman who had hurtled from the balcony was barely a fact supporting leniency before punishment. In the Chapter of Faults rule was supreme. But this time Sister Brendan and Sister Paul had nothing to say in accusation of Perpetua. That pattern, Perpetua was pleased and yet strangely uneasy to see, had now changed.

Perpetua mumbled her thanks again. She wished that the declaration of good intent from Brendan could have made them friends, but it hadn't. Somehow, Perpetua felt, there was an unstated meaning to it, and Perpetua could not guess what it was. The networks, alliances, and innate mysteries of the community seemed so overwhelming that she believed she would never have a share in them no matter how long she stayed.

So Perpetua returned to casualty, and soon thereafter had her accident. Later, she would wonder if she had courted the accident as a means of getting further into the mysteries of the community.

She was working then on the obstetrical ward. One of the patients was a woman of about thirty years who had had seven children, all of them without complications, and who had developed as a result such a low blood count as to be near death from anemia.

Each night, when Perpetua came on duty, one of her tasks was to make up an iron-rich chocolate-flavored tonic for the woman, and feed it to her with her ferrous sulfate tablets. The tonic came in a large canister with a hard tinfoil lid which you had to puncture with a knife and tear back. One evening, after a day of inadequate sleep, some study, and a demoralizing attempt at meditation, Perpetua was making up the tonic for the woman when her right hand strayed and she felt the foil slice deeply into the meat of her hand between the forefinger and the thumb. Perpetua had a very inexact idea of what happened afterward. She remembered holding her hand as it rained blood down the white front of her habit, down the immaculate white of her sisterhood's cloth. She believed at once, on the edge of consciousness, that she was suffering this wound on behalf of her brother, Flight Sergeant Bernard Reardon. It was a wound he would be spared because she took it so willingly. She saw Sister Timothy's face, bigger than the sun, enter the room. There was a frown on the face. Then she fell a great distance, as if off a roof, falling and flailing like the woman in the purple nightdress.

She would have only the most hazy memory of lying on a trolley, one of the hospital's most senior surgeons frowning above her. The habit of the order, which she'd spilled so much blood on, had been cut away, or somehow taken from her. She wondered if they would give it back. In fact she asked the surgeon.

"Of course," he said. Because the damage was so deep, they gave her a general anesthetic.

She woke in the recovery room, but was soon moved to the small infirmary in the convent itself.

The hospital was quite twentieth century, with its newly installed sterilizing system and operating theaters, which were said to rival the best in the world. But the small clinic in the convent had a medieval look. First of all, of course, the convent section of the St. Bridie's complex was built in late nineteenth-century Gothic style, all its windows tall and pointed, as if to carry stained glass, or at least to allow a stone rose-shaped sconce to top each one when you saw the building from outside. These long windows, however, admitted very little of the Australian sun, since they were set deeply in the sandstone sills. In addition, the beds inside the clinic were low and flat, and harder than those in the hospital, the idea being that even in sickness a nun did her penance. One bed was screened off from the next by tall linen drapes, though the foot of the bed was open to the aisle to permit visits by the infirmary sister and, if necessary, by doctors.

Perpetua was, however, delighted with the place. She was able to pray at leisure, to make contact with higher realities at her own pace—that powerful world in which Christ healed the blind and halt, in which he honored his Mother and rose from the dead. She was permitted light reading, and so read James Hilton's *Lost Horizons* and William Makepeace Thackeray's *Vanity Fair* with great enjoyment. Three times a day her meals were brought to her. Sometimes in the evening Timothy would smuggle in a copy of *The Daily Telegraph* or even *The Women's Weekly*, full of contradictory appeals to women to be on the one hand fashionable and on the other sparing of cloth and all else that might be needed for the war. Around mid-morning, when she had finished her leisurely meditation and had had an hour of reading novels, Perpetua would turn guiltily to this secular reading, to the war news in the *Telegraph*, to the tips on love and housekeeping in *The Weekly*.

Each day while her wound healed, the infirmary sister, who looked in only occasionally and had other nursing work to do in the hospital, would help her get ready for a bath and encase her damaged hand and its arm in a sleeve of oilskin. All this was done according to the rule, and very modestly. The nightgown of the order was nearly a separate habit of its own. But the Sisters of Compassion considered themselves fairly modern in not requiring nuns to bathe in a chemise, as other orders did, the nuns never actually baring their skin to the water.

Perpetua was disappointed when another nun was moved into the infirmary, in this case Sister Brendan, sister-in-charge of the orthopedic ward.

The infirmary sister explained to Perpetua, "Brendan's got pneumonia. She's been treating it herself, struggling to and from work. Maybe the worst of the pneumonia's over, but she's very weak. We have her on sulfa drugs."

The narrow lips that had so often denounced Perpetua at Chapter of Faults hung partially open. Her eyes were closed, and the slick of sweat on her face, enclosed as it was in the order's night bonnet, showed that the fever had not yet quite passed. This face Perpetua would often sponge one-handed, working the cloth gently over the brow and deftly down both sides of the nose.

Brendan was often too tired or too feverish to know who was helping her, and that idea pleased Perpetua. She paid her small services to Brendan without regret. That Brendan was unaware of these kindnesses was something that gave Perpetua all the more the sense of being a friend to her.

Sometimes, especially at night, Brendan would cry out, or speak as if answering people she believed to be in the room.

"I don't want that, Ma!" she would say. Or, "Bless me, Father, for I have sinned." Or, "I don't want you altering the traction on the spinal cases. . . ." Perhaps the person she was chastising in her delirium was in fact Perpetua. If so, it only made it easier for Perpetua to nurse her. The sting of all the hard accusations at those Chapter of Faults had vanished.

Perpetua thought it a wonderful thing to see a fever break. It was like a rebirth. People emerged from the craziness of their dreams hollow-cheeked and with eyes full of a childlike bewilderment. Having sat at Brendan's bedside since the small hours, one-handedly tending her, Perpetua saw her sister emerge from the confusion of pneumonia at dawn. Brendan reached up and pushed Perpetua's hand, the cloth in it, away from her brow.

"You're not the infirmary sister," she said.

"No, Sister Brendan. I'm ill too. I have an injury to my hand."

"Where's the infirmary sister?" asked Brendan, still holding Perpetua weakly by the wrist.

"She'll be here after Mass. The priest will bring us communion. Let me set you up for that, Sister."

Perpetua organized Brendan's pillows, gave her a drink of water, since Brendan was not bound to keep the fast before taking communion, and went to a chest of drawers at the far end of the clinic. From it she took two fresh communion cloths. She arranged one over Brendan's chest. Then, hearing the tinkling bell rung by the sacristan sister and intended to tell the sick that the Sacrament of the Eucharist was approaching them, she went to her own cot and arranged the second communion cloth beneath her own chin

Afterward the infirmary sister fed a small amount of rice pudding to Sister Brendan. The long day stretched away then for Perpetua, full of the leisure that goes with being ill or damaged. But even though Perpetua had the privacy provided for her by the long drapes on either side of her cot, she suddenly felt more guarded in her movements, in her reading, and strangely embarrassed to be there, with her damaged hand which Brendan probably thought of as a minor injury.

Perpetua had barely started on her novel when she heard Brendan say, "I knew you were here, Sister. I was aware that you were performing little kindnesses for me. I am quite grateful to you."

Perpetua smiled. It was a large speech for Brendan to make—in fact it must have cost her something to utter it. There was a sort of submerged clause there, too, which said, "But don't expect any mercy from me!"

Perpetua said that it was good for *her* to have some nursing to do.

"When do your stitches come out?"

"In two days. Then I have to have an operation from Dr. Challis." Challis was an expert on the largest areas of skin grafting and what was known as "cosmetic surgery." Perpetua continued, "But I hope the operation mightn't be for some time. At least until after my exams."

Brendan could be heard laughing creakily. "You will pass your exams, from all I hear. Though I suppose you want to be first in the state?"

But, remarkably, it was not said with any disapproval.

These days Perpetua was allowed to move along the corridor and sit on a balcony that took the afternoon sun. While she sat there, reading on and off, she saw a figure, familiar around the hospital, reach the top of the steps and, without noticing her, pass on down the corridor toward the infirmary. It was Genevieve Langtry, a member of the congregation they called the Ladies of the Grail.

The Ladies of the Grail were not nuns, but they lived in community. They wore calf-length gray tunics and blue tops, long sleeved, with Peter Pan collars, and around their heads a veil. They could leave the congregation without anyone's permission, even without the Bishop's: they had taken promises, not vows. Some of them worked at St. Bridie's, either as nurses or else reading to, writing letters for, and saying the Rosary with patients.

Genevieve Langtry seemed even more elegant than Brendan in the way she moved. Since she was one of those who helped the patients at St. Bridie's in a range of ways on which no price could possibly have been put, Perpetua had often met her, and found she talked in the high, fey manner that involved the asking of a lot of rhetorical questions—"Don't you think?" or "Wouldn't you say a rational person would inquire?" She had always seemed very pleasant, but not quite practical enough to be a nurse. Of course, it was her very lack of practicality that the patients instinctively liked.

A natural shyness about intruding on any conversation Genevieve Langtry and Sister Brendan might be having kept Perpetua out on the veranda for more than an hour. By then she badly wanted to use a toilet—an irony, since when she'd been a child, like every other Catholic child, she had considered the nuns to be solid mahogany from the waist down.

Perpetua rose and walked down the balcony to the door of the infirmary. It had not been properly closed and hung about half an inch ajar. Even then she wouldn't have gone in except that she heard an extraordinary noise, as if Brendan were choking, or being throttled on her cot. She rushed into the room, but before she had gone far enough to pass the drapes that closed off Brendan's cot, she stopped. She could hear Genevieve Langtry's gasps as well and knew at once what they meant.

She was a girl of that age—she'd hardly heard the name of what she now heard. Girls had muttered about it at school, but she knew little enough about the physical realities between man and woman to be much interested in those between woman and woman. A flush broke out all over her body. She was concerned only with getting out of the room without being seen. A few inches at a time, backing away, she managed to do it, pulling the door nearly closed behind her and going back to the small balcony where she had spent most of the afternoon.

Above all, she was confused. Not so much shocked, as aware of the light that this threw on Brendan's accusations at Chapters of Faults and the way Paul took up the litany of accusation when Brendan ceased. That was really a particular friendship, a P.F., yet Fredericka seemed not to see it.

And what was her own responsibility now? Was she bound to say at the next Chapter of Faults, "It seems to me, dear Sister, that you fondle the bodies of other women?"

Twenty minutes later Perpetua saw Genevieve Langtry leave the infirmary, sway along the balcony in her distrait way, and descend the stairs. Again the Grail Lady did not notice Perpetua.

Perpetua waited a little longer and then returned to the infirmary herself, driven by desperation of the bladder.

She found it difficult to enter the infirmary. As she passed Brendan's cot, she heard her ask, "Did you enjoy it? In the sun?"

She muttered an answer and took refuge in the toilet. She was grateful that tomorrow her stitches would be removed, and if the wound were healed, she would be allowed back into the full life of the convent and of St. Bridie's.

What Perpetua was suffering that dusk, however, was the loss of her image of both the order and the hospital. She had not believed until this afternoon that such affections—if that's what they were—fitted into the system of the order. In fact, it was because of the danger of the very affections Brendan and Genevieve Langtry had been sharing that afternoon that Perpetua and Timothy had been pilloried at Chapter of Faults and made to eat their dinner off the floor. The accusations and the punishment were bearable if Brendan herself were pure. But as it was, they stank not only of the injustice Perpetua despised, but of a kind of mean vengeance.

The event had changed the view she had of herself as well. She thought that her girlhood had been worldly enough, at least by Australian standards. Now she could see how limited it had been. She had always taken for granted that if a nun was tempted, it would be by the image or presence of a man. The woman who had been thrown flailing in her purple nightdress over the balcony of the Clarendon Hotel had not been suffering from a cruel love of other women but from the cruel desire of men. Even by saying that a nun was "a bride of Christ," you were saying that potentially she could be someone else's bride and lover, and the someone else was, like Christ, a man.

Perpetua's world system therefore said that you could not be a nun and make love to a man. But where did the question of making love to a woman fit into the scheme? Was it a worse or a better sin for a nun to commit? It was simply so strange. She had not expected ever to meet such a thing in the order she had chosen to join in her girlhood, but it had demonstrated its existence to her. So what now?

Perpetua excused herself from the infirmary on the grounds that it was recreation time downstairs. She went in amongst the other nuns with her bandaged hand and played a game of checkers. She looked at Timothy, the country girl, and wondered if with her farmyard breadth of knowledge she guessed anything of Sister Brendan's strange passions. She looked in particular at Sister Paul, who had taken up the baton of accusation from Brendan at Chapters of Faults. The bitter suspicion had fallen on Paul as well. And again she was overtaken by a panic about what her responsibility was, what she was meant to do with her new knowledge. When recreation ended, she said good night to Timothy and Deidre and went back with dread to the infirmary.

She was relieved to find Brendan already asleep. She went to sleep herself, after hollowly, woodenly reciting the night prayers. She was wracked by an illogical fear that she was somehow connected with the crime she had stumbled on and that the crime in turn put both herself and, more importantly, Flight Sergeant Bernard Reardon, in peril.

She awoke at some hour of the night to see a shape standing above her. She presumed at first that it was the Brown Lady, and all her fear ran into her mouth and she uttered an animal cry. But then she saw by the stray light of Darlinghurst seeping in through the tall window that it was Brendan standing above her. In the order's nightdress, Brendan seemed thin still. She was only a few days recovered from her fever of pneumonia and should not have been standing there like a sentinel.

"What is it, Sister?" asked Perpetua, hoping that this appearance of Brendan had something to do with an emergency in the convent rather than what she suspected.

"May I sit on the end of your bed, Perpetua?" asked Brendan.

Perpetua had to say yes. Brendan sat painfully, as if the fever were still in her joints. She arranged herself so that one hand hung loosely across Perpetua's ankles. Since they were encased in a blanket, there was nothing wrong with this, Perpetua told herself. She had not known such a moment of supreme fear in her life up to now.

Brendan said, "I know you were here today, while Genevieve Langtry was also here. You came in. You crept out. You thought I hadn't noticed."

"It wasn't my affair," said Perpetua. Then she realized that this statement had a double meaning and might even encourage Brendan.

Brendan's hand moved more intimately to enclose itself around Perpetua's right ankle. It squeezed, adding emphasis to what Brendan said. "We have certain vows, I know, and within those vows we all depend on divine help to be the nuns we are. But isn't it possible for us to be loving sisters?"

Perpetua was too overcome with fear and a growing embarrassment to say anything. She thought: I might have to punch her, and how can that be explained in a community of nuns?

"I have watched you, Perpetua," said Brendan. "You're very flighty, and that has to be looked at, but it's mainly the product of your age and of the date you entered the convent. I came here in 1929, when the picture shows were still silent. But I know that now they've become talking. The newspapers have become full of photographs and scandals. In the decade you grew up, they have become more and more pagan and licentious, more and more devoted to the cult of individual . . . I think the term is 'glamour.' You have been affected by that. Addicted by glamour, perhaps. Even the lives of the saints are glamorized by those who make pictures. Do you know they're all Jews, the filmmakers? Of the race that killed our Divine Lord."

"Then what have you been affected by, Brendan?" Perpetua wanted to scream, but it came out as a pitiful, low question.

Brendan seemed unabashed. "I have been influenced by the aesire to be a good nun. Certainly we have foresworn men. Does not that mean of itself that we should sometimes depend for affection on a sister of ours. Does God want us to live in total isolation from all human comfort? I don't believe He asks it! It would be too cruel for Him to ask it!"

Perpetua remembered the day Wilhelmina had come to the novitiate and warned the whole order of the dangers of Japanese attack, of the physical peril the Japanese soldier might pose. Yet here she—Perpetua—was, in the infirmary of St. Bridie's at a time when the Allies were full of tentative hopes of victory, the Japanese peril had been thrown back, and the one she was threatened by was a sister of her own order!

Brendan abruptly leaned forward, putting her hands on either side of Perpetua's waist. Perpetua escaped her, pushing Brendan's still weak right arm aside, getting up from the bed, retreating out of her cubicle, backing toward the windows. The pursuing Brendan was between her and the door. A Brendan thin at the best of times, Perpetua told herself, lacking in weight, newly recovered from illness; a Brendan who was in one physical sense no threat, whom she could push aside, escape from with the greatest ease, as she'd just partially done.

Brendan said, "Don't you know it is possible to be a good nun and hold one of your sisters too?"

Perpetua shook her head. She was simply stumped to know how, with all the order's daily horror of particular friendships, Brendan could have come to that sort of conclusion. With this robust puzzlement, though, there came a sort of strength.

"If you don't go back to bed, Sister Brendan, if you don't leave me alone, I'll be forced to attack you." She raised her hand, open palmed. Even she could see it trembling in the dark.

"So you'd hit another nun?"

Perpetua uttered a sort of high-toned groan that indicated she would.

Brendan began to pant—her sickness seemed to be reclaiming her. "I could go to Fredericka and tell her you made indecent proposals to me. You are not highly respected in this convent, you know."

"Do it, if you have to!" Though Perpetua could not imagine what it would be like to be accused of this sort of thing at Chapter of Faults. Or to face Fredericka knowing that these things had been said of you. She would prefer to die.

To Perpetua's utter surprise, Brendan began to cry. In other circumstances Perpetua would have gone to her and put an arm around her. Hiccuping with sobs, Brendan went back inside her cubicle. Perpetua sat on the end of her own cot for all the rest of that miserable night. She was in the torment of those whose picture of the known world has been changed too much, beyond tolerance. How could she even look for advice on this whole business? How could she even utter what had been proposed between herself and Brendan?

The next morning Perpetua stayed in the infirmary—rather than going to the chapel, as she could have—to see how Brendan would face morning communion. She wanted to know by what mental gymnastics Brendan could fit what she had said last night into the sacramental routine of the convent. Would she tell the priest she did not want the Host? It was crucial to know that, Perpetua thought. It would indicate that Brendan had suffered some sort of temporary moral storm and would now repent of it, instead of taking the Sacrament unworthily.

The priest arrived, and Perpetua saw him carry into Brendan's cubicle the wafer of bread, transformed by the words of the Mass into the Body and Blood of Christ. Perpetua could not see—because of the drapes—exactly what happened, but it was obvious that Brendan did not refuse to take the bread.

When the priest brought the Host to Perpetua, she felt ill-at-ease about taking it into her mouth herself. And even as she swallowed it, she was putting new questions to herself. If Brendan had taken communion, did it mean that she considered any desire between herself and Genevieve Langtry absolutely right in the eyes of God? Did she consider her waking of Perpetua in the middle of the night to be the decent and sisterly thing? If she did, then according to the order's view of things, she must be mad.

Or if she knew it was all wrong, and was not mad, then it was sacrilege for her to take the Host without first having been to confession, without having made a firm resolve not to succumb to that peculiar lust again.

And underneath everything, *that* was the most compelling question of all.

Perpetua did not desire any nun, any patient. She could not remember having desired any other woman. But what she had briefly heard, the few carnal noises, had changed her. All day she kept suffering images of the hand of this or that boy she'd known in the Catholic Youth Organization. All day she felt restless with a sort of desire for them. It was as if Brendan had, by waking her in the middle of the night, at that dark hour, turned her soul grosser than yesterday.

She had her stitches out that day. The ragged wound had healed. She wept with gratitude—the doctor thought it was pain—when the bloodied lips of the wound sat firmly together. Her hand was bound again but she was ready for light duties. In the joy of escaping the infirmary, it came to her that perhaps others amongst the younger nuns had been approached by Brendan. But how could you ask them?

And then she thought, given the right moment, she could ask Timothy anything. For Timothy knew everything: how to make horses mate, the rutting habits of all animals and, if you could judge by her offhand remarks, even those of her parents.

That night her hand wandered, caressing her body in memory of boys who were, at that moment, far away in bombing crews in Europe or facing the Japanese on unimaginably humid Pacific islands.

The following Saturday was the next Chapter of Faults. Brendan wasn't there, but by now Perpetua's native common sense told her that even if she had been, she would have hesitated to make a false accusation of Perpetua. That is, unless she had become completely deranged. For there *must* be other nuns who had noticed this oddity in Brendan, unless it had only recently surfaced. But then, by Brendan's own behavior and almost by her confession, this did not seem to be the case.

Brendan's friend, Sister Paul, sat quietly through the Chapter and said nothing. A spottiness had come to the surface of her normally clear skin, as if she herself were sickening in some way. Were there jealousies in these things, the way there were amongst men and women? And if so, was Paul tortured by jealousy?

The Saturday afternoon walk in the garden was an institution. As you left the Chapter of Faults, you were supposed to pair off with whichever nun was closest and go strolling and conversing. Naturally, long-established friends hung back or maneuvered forward so they could find themselves outside, amongst the palm trees and the lilies of the valley, at the same time as their chosen walking mate. Perpetua was able to do this today, to find herself in the bright afternoon at the same time as Timothy. The garden walks were suddenly cluttered with pairs of nuns walking the paved path around the edge, crossing it diagonally, some of the older ones limiting themselves to laps around the central fountain. Timothy and Perpetua took to the outer periphery of the garden, though—a bigger space developed between each pair of nuns on this path, and so there was room for a little gossip and even levity.

Perpetua's hope of speaking frankly to Timothy was helped almost at once. Timothy's younger sister, no more than seventeen years old, was engaged now to an eighteen-year-old army conscript who, for reasons only the Department of Defense could understand, was being shipped to Western Australia, a remote and inactive theater of war. The news had come to Timothy by letter from her mother. Timothy seemed to be full of an earthy hilarity of the idea of her young sister and this coltish soldier nudging and hugging each other and then, as forlorn as pups, saying good-bye.

"Timothy, I—" Perpetua began, but Timothy rode over her with some other piece of information, about rains at Tyler's Arm and butter prices.

"Tim, have you ever known any women who didn't want to be touched by men?"

In despair, and without knowing she'd said it, Perpetua found that she'd uttered the right sentence.

Timothy balked and stared at her.

"Who'd—you know—rather be touched by women?"

Timothy frowned enormously and then her face relaxed. She had come quickly to a sensible answer, and she dealt with all hard questions that way—first the muscular frown, and then the simple smile that goes with an easy answer. It gave Perpetua the feeling she often got from Timothy—that things were simple in the bush, and if you looked at questions from a bush point of view, they just melted like meringue.

"There's two types of women who touch other women," said Timothy. She stated it as if it were a principle of mathematics. "There are the ones who touch other women because there are no men to touch. And then there's the ones who would rather touch women than men." Every child on Tyler's Arm, she implied, knew these things. "I wouldn't mind," said Tim, "being touched by a man. But you might have noticed that the Rule's against it."

They walked a little farther in silence. Perpetua looked at the other nuns and wondered what they would think if they knew the conversation that was going on. Where was Brendan's friend Paul in all this promenade?

Timothy said, "Did someone want to touch you, Perpetua?" Timothy's hand brushed Perpetua's as if the idea had sometimes occurred to her. Yet from Timothy it did not seem a sinister or shameful attempt at affection.

Perpetua could not answer, however.

"I'll bet it was that raving Brendan," said Timothy. "Come on, it was Brendan, wasn't it? I bet it was in the infirmary. Gosh, her friend Paul would be jealous as hell."

There was a flash of pain in Perpetua's head. Until yesterday the convent had been a convent, something like a failed version of that sisterhood she was always looking for. Now it was like a foreign village, full of unguessable resentments. Timothy seemed to understand them, to take them lightly. Perpetua wished she could do the same. But it wasn't possible. The pain continued behind her eyes.

"You know, you're lucky you came to the convent," said Timothy chattily. "Because you're quite good-looking, my friend Perpetua. I mean, if your good looks create this sort of ruckus in here, imagine what it would be like if you were outside!"

"What sort of ruckus do I create?" asked Perpetua. Even the healed wound in her hand was in pain.

"Well, those two, you know Brendan and Paul—they're so far into each other that Brendan denounces you at Chapter of Faults to stop Paul from being jealous of you, and then Paul decides it's all a good idea and starts accusing you too. They're good nurses, those two, but they're absolutely cracked when it comes to each other. And then, of course, I suppose because I come from the country and my manners aren't up to scratch, they accuse me of things. And I'm your friend. That's crime enough for them. I mean, something ought to be done about those two."

Perpetua was still staggered, even though she walked on in the seemly Saturday-afternoon way, her damaged right hand sheltering in the broad left cuff of her habit.

"I mean to say," Timothy went on, "we end up eating our dinner off the floor because we're supposed to be particular friends, and that's against the rules. But what about those two? What they get up to is a matter for the confessional, I'll tell you that. Or it ought to be a matter for the confessional. But that's between them and God. It's not my business. If Brendan wants to touch you, tell her to go and jump at herself."

Perpetua felt the stupid tears on her lids again. She bent her head. It was a matter of shame to be so openly emotional. If she were not careful, it could earn her a mention at the next Chapter of Faults. But she had lost everything, she felt, and Timothy had lost nothing, since Timothy already knew how things were.

Before she had gotten complete control over her tears, the walk period ended. Nuns went back to their cells to study or write letters, or to the hospital. It was an hour when those not on duty were allowed to visit patients, to be gracious and bring the clear light of compassion along the corridors to relatives of this or that nun of the order, or to the friends of relatives of this or that nun, or to the relations and friends from the country who had come down for the excellent surgery St. Bridie's offered, or to aunts of old school friends. In the sacristy of the chapel, the parish priest or one of the senior curates of Darlinghurst was available to hear the confessions of any nun who so decided.

For a while, as improper as it was for her to do, Perpetua sat in the back of the chapel, seeing if Brendan would arrive, or perhaps Genevieve Langtry, or Paul. What did they say to the priest when they did visit the confessional? How did they look going in or coming out?

The questions remained academic. None of them appeared. Deidre arrived, made tense preparation, went into the sacristy, made her confession, and came out with the same tense look on her face. Timothy, bringing up a little wind from that day's lunch of heavy lamb, made a blithe preparation, went in, came out looking happy and certain of the world. Perpetua did not go to confession at all. I've done nothing wrong, she told herself. The images of various young men had come to her without her asking for them. And it was not a crime, however much it felt like one, to be strangely desired by Brendan.

I must get out of here, Perpetua told herself. She thought of the hospital the order ran in the north of the state, at Rossclare. Surely there'd be nothing like Brendan at Rossclare. She thought of Brendan's malice or weakness or whatever it was as something that occurred perhaps a few times in a century in an order of the strictness of the Sisters of Compassion.

Fredericka, the Mother Superior, had been structured by bony Irish parents at some unimaginable point of history in some Irish county where only gusts of piety and clerical authority blew. Or that is the way it appeared both to the younger nuns in her community and even to the interns, registrars, and surgeons of St. Bridie's. At moments of extreme crisis in a nun's life, she could ask to see the large authoritative Mother Fredericka—it was known that Fredericka was available for such purposes between eight and nine o'clock on a Thursday night in her study on the ground floor of the convent. Fredericka's no doubt immaculate and bare cell lay beyond the study, but the bookshelves in the study held a library which various of the older, more dithery nuns liked to say was "better than anything a bishop could have had."

Fredericka seemed as ageless as the books on her shelves, but whenever anyone thought to guess at her age, they generally came up with a figure of not more than forty-five years.

Perpetua knew now that she must see Fredericka on the next Thursday night. What she should say she couldn't envision. What she wanted was to get out of St. Bridie's, that flagship of the order, to go to one of the quieter communities, perhaps Rossclare, if possible before Brendan left the infirmary, but at least at the end of her nurse's exams in the next few months.

By Tuesday she had still not finished preparing herself in either the mental or spiritual sense to face Fredericka. She could only escape St. Bridie's, which Brendan had made necessary for her to do, by at least being critical of the sisterhood and at most telling Fredericka exactly what had happened. She found it hard to imagine that Fredericka lived in the same world of furtive advances and caresses as Brendan, but then the week before, it would have been hard to believe that furtive caresses had anything to do with Brendan herself, either.

At morning meditation on Wednesday something very welcome happened to Perpetua. From being doubtful and tentative, from feeling guilty and foolish, she became all at once angry. It was a constructive anger, like the one that had come down on her father on the goldfields and led to the Illuminated Address on the living room wall at home. *St. Bridie's is my home, and I'm being driven out of it.* Then she decided she wouldn't go! Brendan was the stranger here, the liar, the pursuer of hidden and special purposes. I am at home!

I am a nun and a grown woman. I am not a child.

She felt sweetly the force of this new determination. The Reardons *were* just, by the grace of God, and God would protect them in history, in St. Bridie's and on the goldfields and in bombers. She had her tribe, and *this* was it, and she would not be driven out.

She was surprised, having reached this hard and just decision, to find the bursar, who amongst all her bill paying also acted as a sort of secretary to Fredericka, waiting for her in the corridor on the way to breakfast.

"Mother Fredericka wishes to see you, Sister, at four o'clock this afternoon in her office."

Perpetua felt thrown off-center by this summons. She had already decided it wasn't necessary—in her new certainty—to see the Mother Superior, yet now, as if Fredericka had picked up the

waves of Perpetua's intention, she had issued an order for a conference with Perpetua anyhow.

It was a winter's afternoon, and there was heavy rain, the water
running in long and continuous streams down the tall Gothic
windows of St. Bridie's convent. Perpetua loved the winter rains in
Sydney—they were so thoroughgoing. Fredericka was backed by
all the authority of her library, but Perpetua still felt some of the
strength of her new enlightenment with her as she was asked into
the office. Her hands were sweating. The interview she was about
to have could not be predicted or preimagined, and was all the
more frightening for that.

With a grave charity, Fredericka asked her to sit down. Perpetua obeyed. Fredericka said, "Sister, I want to discuss with you
matters of some seriousness. It would be a great help to me if you
joined me in a decade of the Rosary, asking for God's grace before
we speak any further."

Perpetua of course consented, reaching for the black thorn
beads that hung from her cincture. She was a little disturbed that
the decade of the Rosary Fredericka chose to invoke was the First
Sorrowful Mystery, the Agony in the Garden.

"The First Sorrowful Mystery, the Agony in the Garden," said
Fredericka. "Our Father . . ."

Perpetua recited the Our Father, the ten Hail Marys, and the
Glory-Be-to-the-Father all with earnestness, her eyes half closed.
She was certain that there was nothing to fear.

At the end of the prayers, Fredericka's eyes opened fully. "Is
your hand recovered?" she asked.

"It's completely healed," said Perpetua. "And the stitches are
out."

"If only," said Fredericka, "the soul was as efficient at these
things as the body."

Perpetua didn't know what this meant. She had thought till
then that, fueled by the divine wisdom that ran in orders like the
Sisters of Compassion, the soul had worked pretty well.

"You are not in any way a bad young woman. But there's an
impetuosity and a feverishness there. You've shown it often
enough. You've been in trouble for it often enough, while in the
area of your studies you show a lot of native talent."

It sounded like a lead up to some reprimand whose purpose
and content Perpetua couldn't guess at. She hoped she wasn't

going to be chastised. She actually thought with some defiance, Let the saints go looking for unjust accusation and unjust punishment. I'm not a saint.

"I don't see how I can have given any offense, Mother," said Perpetua. "I didn't leave the infirmary until last Saturday."

Fredericka's eyes took Perpetua's full on.

"Sister Brendan has been to see me. She is very concerned about your unfortunate infatuation with her."

Perpetua's mouth opened, but Fredericka spread her hands as if to advise silence.

"You are an ardent personality, and God does not oppose ardor. You have only to read the writings of St. John of the Cross or St. Theresa of Avila to know how close the ardent temperament is to what God desires. But there are dangers. You have been accused in the past a number of times of too much ardor and of particular friendship with Sister Timothy. Now every nun who has taught in a girls' school knows about girlhood crushes, the way a fierce friendship can develop between a girl and a nun. Sometimes, though it is pure silliness, the nun is able to influence the girl strongly through such a friendship. But in the convent this sort of passionate and particular attachment can be very dangerous."

All Perpetua could say was, "Sister Brendan?"

"She has been to see me, and she is acutely pained by this crush you have for her. It has to be recognized for what it is. A great danger to your vocation."

Perpetua could say nothing. She felt a great disappointment. St. Bridie's was uninhabitable after all. If Brendan was a liar, then were there other liars? And how many were there?

"I've done nothing wrong," Perpetua said. She felt her stomach turn and feared she would be sick in Fredericka's office.

"I know that. And it is possible for you to be a good nun—I know that, too, and I insist that it is so. But you are badly astray in this matter."

Timothy had said once, "When you're talking to the others, it's best to deal with them like other women instead of like other nuns." But Perpetua knew she couldn't do that, she could not tell Fredericka that Brendan was a liar. It was too large a thing to say about a Sister of Compassion in this office with the bare beeswaxed floor and the cliff of books. She herself found it astounding. She preferred not to utter it, even though it was the truth.

Instead of choosing justice for herself, as she had thought up to
now she would be able to, she chose the good name of the order,
the good name of the order even within the order. She chose not
to say that Sister Brendan lusted for her and tried to paw her. She
was back where she had started, after Brendan's approach in the
infirmary. She was shocked. She had lost her Eden. She wondered
where her home was.

Fredericka said, "I think it is best to separate the two of you.
You are an excellent nurse and should pass your exams with
honors, even if you sit for them away from St. Bridie's, in the
country. I am arranging for you to be transferred to St. John
Vianney's in the town of Rossclare. Do you know Rossclare?"

"I was once on a train," said Perpetua. "It stopped there."

"It is a grand town. It is a good Catholic town too. The seed of
the faith was planted there by Irish priests more than a hundred
years ago and has prospered. The cathedral is very modern, and
so is the hospital and the convent. When you arrive there, you are
to seek spiritual direction as a means of getting over this business.
I have a cousin there, a priest called Murphy, and I would say he
is an excellent spiritual director, though he's very worldly wise.
Above all, you are to try to overcome this foolishness. The atmosphere will be quieter there."

Perpetua was tempted to say, "Why not send Brendan, and
leave me here?" But somehow she sensed that if she said that, it
would be the end of her convent career.

Sometime late that night, when she was deep in a miserable
sleep, Perpetua was wakened by a rattling of her door latch. She
turned her lamp on and went to see what it was. There were a
number of elderly Irish nuns who might have come to her door in
confusion, seeking help for palpitations, a fit of nausea, or even a
less definable anguish.

She opened it to see Brendan there.

Perpetua would have liked to strike her, to insult her, to use
cruel names. But she could say nothing. She backed from the
door. Brendan stepped inside, closed the door behind her, and,
wearing the order's prescribed nightcap and gown, sank to her
knees. Perpetua could see her white heels, the flesh like beeswax.

"I must ask your forgiveness, Perpetua," said Brendan. "Do
you think I am a happy woman, accusing you like that? I do it
because I am damned. I've got nowhere to go. My parents are

dead, my sisters are married. You're young still, and you can move. You can leave the order if you want." Brendan raised her eyes—there was a sort of desperate humor in them. "Forgive me, please. God may not, but you can. You might be very pleased one day that I did this to you."

Perpetua was able to say, "I suppose you'll tell Fredericka I invited you to my cell at night?"

"No," said Brendan. "The telling is over. Listen, I might have been able to deceive my Mother Superior, as if that is something to be proud of! But there are three people I cannot deceive. I cannot deceive Paul, who despises me. I cannot deceive God, though I hope He pities me. And I cannot deceive you."

"Go back to your cell," said Perpetua. She gave way, in fact, to ordinary Reardon slang. "Get to hell!"

"You can be sure I will," said Brendan. She stood up. "I'd like to think that I am a good nurse," she said.

"Clear out!" said Perpetua, trembling.

And so Perpetua caught the train four hundred miles to Ross-clare, where within the limitations of the town and of the convent, she was to try to find her way of life again.

She hoped this Father Murphy gave exquisite guidance.

15

The Clothes of Others

O N their first long London leave, in the autumn of 1943, just when they needed one—the self-destruction of Otley still weighing on them—Challenor and Reardon, by accident, met Cannon in the Strand outside Australia House. Cannon was wearing Flying Officer's rank and had been serving with a squadron in Lincolnshire. He made a fuss over Challenor and Reardon and invited them to join him and a friend of his at an officers-only club with all the other codgers.

"But we're not officers," Challenor objected.

"I can take care of that," said the gunner-lawyer, with that peculiar rakish wisdom that had once so impressed the Reardon parents.

Reardon and Challenor went inside Australia House to find where they had been billeted for the night and to collect mail. There was a letter from Perpetua.

My dearest Bernard,
　　Your letter got to me quite torn by the censor, but at least I could tell from it that you were healthy and had not suffered any damage. I hope to God that as you read this the

same is the case. I see my life in large part as an offering for
your safety.

It has been very hot in Sydney, and the wards are very
crowded . . .

For the first time Reardon felt an impulse to write to his sister
and say, "No, no offerings. God is more complicated than that.
The world is more complicated than that." He wondered if the
virginal life of a nun in Sydney could influence the patterns of flak
over towns in the Ruhr, could so pitch the activities of the night
fighters that he could safely weave amongst them; or Flight Sergeant Punch, the pilot, could. Life seemed all at once so risky and
contingent and accidental that he wondered if he should write and
put his sister straight.

At six o'clock Cannon collected them from the reading room at
the RAAF Recreation Center in Leicester Street. He took them out
to a vehicle where a thin flight lieutenant lacking wings but with
staff patches on his collar leaned against the back door smoking a
cigarette.

"My Australian friends, Teddy," Cannon told the tall man.
"Bernie Reardon and Challenor. Challenor doesn't have a first
name. He's from South Australia."

"I talk in grunts, sir," said Challenor.

"Teddy," said Teddy in a vague and well-modulated voice.
"Hop in with us, chaps."

They followed Teddy into the back of the vehicle. Cannon sat
in the front with the driver, picked up two RAAF jackets from the
front seat, and passed them across to Reardon and Challenor.

"A flight lieutenant's uniform for you, Reardo, and the larger
one is for Challenor."

"But it's a bloody squadron leader's jacket."

"Well, we would have got you an air commodore's but there are
none of those left. Go on, put the bloody things on. You can leave
your flight sergeants' jackets in the back while we go to dinner."

Dubiously Challenor and Reardon did what they were told.
Reardon found his an excellent fit.

"Christ, if there's anyone who knows me in there, they'll have
me shot!"

"They won't recognize you," said Cannon. "Bomber Command
is a bloody big place."

Cannon winked at the Englishman, Teddy. "Very handsome," said Teddy.

Cannon said, "You blokes ought to consider yourselves lucky. Teddy generally charges uniform rental. But he'd do anything for me. I got his cousin off a charge of stealing gasoline."

"Bloody good lawyer, your friend," said Teddy offhandedly. "Actually, it's my cousin who does the uniform rental. Damn disreputable, but he's a favorite of my mother's. So what can I do?"

The car stopped in a narrow street in St. James's. The driver opened the back door for Teddy and the two gunners. Teddy pointed to Challenor.

"You go first, Squadron Leader. You have the senior rank."

"Well, bugger me," said Challenor, easing his way out of his seat and through the door and accepting a salute from the poker-faced driver.

"The table is in your name," Reardon heard Cannon tell Challenor, catching up to him on the pavement.

"Name of Challenor?" Challenor asked.

"No, you silly bugger. Squadron Leader Breville."

"And who's Breville?"

"Whoever he is, he's yours for the night, anyhow."

An aged doorman greeted them in the hallway, under a portrait of Pitt the Younger.

"Would you sign in, please, Squadron Leader?" he asked Challenor.

Challenor blinked and hesitated, the pen poised over the page.

"Squadron Leader Breville," whispered Cannon. "Spelled with a double L-E. Initials E.G." To Reardon he said, "And by the way, Flight Lieutenant, your name is Gordon, Ralph Edward."

Teddy was already warmly known to the old man, who smiled broadly at him. So was Cannon, who passed him a five-pound note which the old man grabbed prehensilely and stowed so rapidly in his pocket that no witness could have sworn with certainty that he ever had it. There was an air of excess about all this. Five pounds was a week's wages for a gunner. But then, Reardon decided, Cannon was a lawyer and probably had business and other interests back in Melbourne that made his weekly pay as a flying officer little more than pocket money.

The bar was crowded, and Reardon and Challenor quickly felt lost in the crush of officers of all services, including the Americans.

There were so many campaign and medal ribbons, so many epaulettes and stripes of braid, that you would have had to have been a Rear Admiral or an Air Vice-Marshal to have stood out.

"You'll just have to drink gin or whiskey, that's all," said Cannon to the two gunners. "It goes with your rank."

"Be buggered," said Challenor. "I'll have a pint and we can pretend that I'm a working-class boy promoted for raw bloody talent."

Teddy laughed. "And fair enough, too, old chap," he said.

As they got slightly tipsy, Reardon noticed that many officers would come to Teddy and speak softly and energetically with him.

"Teddy's big on the staff," said Cannon. "Matter of fact, he works for the committee that decides the targets."

"Shit," said Challenor. "Let's influence the bugger before he gets away."

Reardon remembered having a good dinner of lamb chops with a bottle of French wine called Nuit St. Georges. Cannon told stories of his station in Lincolnshire—how a group of them had stolen the wing commander's toilet seat and used it as a picture frame for the portrait of some Air Vice-Marshal which hung in the mess. How a friend of his had vanished when a stick of bombs, dropped from above, tore the entire turret assembly off the stern of one of the squadron's Halifaxes. How he'd seen another jumping without a parachute, since the parachutes were stored in a locker in the main fuselage and flame, funneling down the metal frame by Venturi effect, made it impossible for the gunner to open his turret doors and reach through for his particular parachute. A discussion began, to which Teddy patiently listened, on whether it was better to burn or jump.

"I reckon stick with the plane," said Challenor lightly, to Reardon's surprise.

"We wouldn't be talking like this," said Cannon, grinning, the lawyer-rogue of the Bar, "unless we were half pissed."

It was true, and seizing the opportunity offered by their condition, Reardon said, "A bloke from our squadron cut his throat in the guardhouse the other day. He'd done twenty-three missions too."

"Well, I reckon he was a bit of case," said Challenor, as if to end the subject. "Very pale kid. Always went to church."

"R.I.P.," said Teddy reverently, but at the same time winking.

Challenor said something about the case that Reardon had not heard before.

"He biked into little Parsfield after a mission and tried to post the map to someone."

"The mission map?"

"Tried to post the Wuppertal map. The gum came unstuck on the envelope and the postmaster reported him."

"Is that so?" asked Cannon, whistling. "Who was he posting it to?"

"The rumor is he was posting it to a bishop. The Bishop of Chester or somewhere."

"Chichester?" asked Teddy.

"That's it."

"Well," said Teddy, using the town for the bishop like a duke in a medieval melodrama, "Chichester's always disapproved of Bomber Command. We're the barbarians to Chichester. And His Lordship Chichester always knows so much about us, the bugger. What a spy network he must have. Devout young bombardiers."

"Otley *was* a bombardier," said Reardon. "How did you know?"

"Actually," said Teddy, "I *had* read a report of the poor boy's accident."

Challenor said, "Here's to Otley. He did what he thought was right."

"Now, Squadron Leader Breville," said Teddy, "let's not put it like that. He was a silly ass. What does he want this war to be? A medieval joust?"

Cannon cleverly dragged the conversation away from the subject of Otley, which he clearly considered unfruitful and morbid. He'll live forever, thought Reardon. There is not a mark death has made on his forehead. He'll end his life a whiskified and amusing judge, the sort of judge you encounter in plays and films.

As happens when a lot is drunk, it was eight P.M. at one second and near midnight the next. The dining room and the bar at the club were beginning to thin out. Officers had gone to look for women or to keep firm appointments they had with them.

"Come back to my place," said Teddy. "It's just a little flat near Kensington Church High Street."

On their way out, Reardon and Challenor visited the lavatory. Easing his bladder, Challenor said, "You don't reckon this Teddy's a fairy and going to give us a time of it, do you?"

"We'll tell him to get lost if he does," said Reardon.

But it became apparent that Teddy's intentions were purely based on having found someone to drink booze with. "His "little" flat seemed full of scotch and gin and cognac. Clearly, he knew someone in the black market—probably his cousin, whom Cannon had "got off."

A thought came to Challenor as he sat there, his squadron leader's jacket unbuttoned, drinking brandy as if it were beer.

"These jackets? I mean . . . do they come from blokes who got the chop?"

The inquiry made Reardon look down at his jacket, which hung loosely unbuttoned, the pilot's wings handsomely broad on its left breast.

"I mean," said Challenor, not wanting to seem ungrateful, "do these belong to blokes who've crashed or are kriegies?"

"Kriegie" was air-force talk for someone who'd bailed out over Europe and become a prisoner.

"If I bought it on a mission," said Cannon, "I'd like to think of some bugger wearing my uniform and my name for a good night out. Wouldn't you, Reardo?"

"And Teddy's cousin supplies these, too, I think I heard you say?"

"Teddy's cousin is a real, total provider," said Cannon. "He's one of those fellows who can find you anything."

Challenor took his jacket off right away, stood unsteadily, and made for the door.

"Where are you going?" asked Teddy from the cocktail cabinet.

"Appreciated and all that," said Challenor, "but I want to go to the car and get my proper jacket back."

"I told the driver to put them in the bedroom. First to the right. They're on coat hangers in the closet."

Reardon also stood and followed Challenor into the corridor. He found the closet, took his flight sergeant gunner's jacket off the hook and put it on again, regaining himself.

Cannon appeared in the doorway of the bedroom. "You mustn't think that some widow or mother is being deprived of what you've just been wearing. Sometimes a man's brothers and sisters tell the clean-up gangs, don't send us his jacket or else Mum or his wife will only dote on it."

"Teddy's got a funny bloody cousin," hissed Challenor.

But Reardon thought it was all right, a sort of immortality for the dead, the bailed-out, the captured. "God bless Flight Lieutenant Gordon," he said, reaching in and patting the empty jacket.

Challenor calmed down, took another drink to celebrate his return to the status of flight sergeant after the heavy duty of a night's dining as a squadron leader, and ended by accepting, as Reardon himself did, Teddy's invitation to bed down for the night. Teddy went to bed in the maid's room, Cannon took the sofa, and Challenor—used to sleeping rough on South Australian kangaroo hunting parties—rolled himself in an expensive rug, partly in vengeance on Teddy's cousin for recycling the clothes of the dead. Reardon, suddenly sick, was given the spaciousness of the double bed in the main bedroom. It smelled of a woman, the faint cosmetic redolence that comes from makeup that has stayed on a face all night and turned slightly sour.

When Reardon closed his eyes, he would feel the bed bank. "Corkscrew port, go!" he said once while swallowing bile.

He awoke dry to the core—sweating like an invalid, yet chilled and with a pain bigger than a football between his eyes—to the sound of an argument outside. Under the obligation that attaches to those who have drunk too much merely to prove that they can manage it, he found his shoes, looked at his crumpled flight sergeant's jacket, decided not to wear it, pulled up his suspenders, and, his bladder screaming, went out to the dining room. A plump woman with a copy of *The Times* in her hand was haranguing Teddy, Cannon, and Challenor, who sat around the table sipping cups of tea and looking hollow-eyed. It was an untoward sight, but he felt too nauseated to find it strange. Teddy nodded him to a chair, and with a gesture of his elbow and his index finger, indicated that he should pay attention to what the woman was saying.

"So I am always listening," the woman was saying—she pronounced her G's like a K. "Never do I hear Darmstadt mentioned. Never Darmstadt. All sorts of place get the bomb—Duisburg, Wuppertal yet."

"Well," Teddy rumbled, "of course, these cities you name have considerable industrial activity, Frau Vidler."

He paused to introduce Reardon to the woman. Mrs. Vidler was from the flat downstairs. She had got out of Germany in 1939 and now lived downstairs with her brother and sister-in-law. Her brother, said Teddy, was a distinguished businessman. "She is

wondering why we haven't bombed Darmstadt," said Teddy, winking at Reardon.

"Well, I mean," said Mrs. Vidler, "it has a big place—three-
and-a-half-thousand employees—making the finest optical lenses
for the submarines. You bomb that and the U-boat has no eyes!
Poof! I ask you, does that sound reasonable?"

"Sounds fair enough to me," said a bleary Flight Sergeant
Challenor, reaching for a cigarette.

"Not only that," said Frau Vidler, "but there is an I.G. Farben
gas and other chemical works in the city. You can look it up,
Teddy! Your superior officers would know it. Yet I listen and
listen on the BBC, and not a bomb drops on Darmstadt."

"There were a few bombs earlier in the war," pleaded Teddy.

"That was when the bombing was a joke. A cream puff here, a
torte there, no damage done. I mean, the Americans in the daytime and you boys in the night. But not you, Teddy. You should
stay tucked up here."

Teddy smiled. "Thank you very much, Frau Vidler."

"Well," said the insistent Frau Vidler, "are you going to arrange
it for us? Are you going to tell them what I say about the optics and
the I.G. Farben? Or does Darmstadt get off scotch free?"

"I think you'll find it's scot free," suggested Teddy. "But no, I
shall pass on what you say, definitely. However, don't necessarily
expect much to happen." He dropped his voice to a confidential
murmur. "Sometimes we hit targets but like to keep it secret."

"Secret? Secret?" asked Frau Vidler. "You should strike Darmstadt, hit I.G. Farben in the stomach, and hit the optics factory so
that the glass melts." She took on a reproving, guttural tone. "You
are kidding me, Teddy, about the secret."

Teddy at last got Frau Vidler to leave by promising that he
would press for Darmstadt. She excused herself and went off
contented. "Well, there's someone in Darmstadt Frau Vidler
doesn't like," remarked Cannon as Teddy returned from the door.

"There's a regime, old chap," said Teddy. "That's all. That
woman is the greatest student and critic of Bomber Command you
will ever find."

Teddy got together a breakfast of bacon and eggs, but before
they ate it, he excused himself. He had to go to the Ministry.
"Don't forget to put the lady's city on the list," Challenor called
after him.

"Dear chap," said Teddy, standing in the door a moment, "I'm such a junior in there that one word from me about bombing Berlin and they'd bomb Torquay!"

Reardon, feeling ill enough for medical attention, remembered to thank him for his hospitality.

"I'll send back my driver to take you to Australia House," said Teddy.

After he had gone, Challenor murmured, "I wonder how many poor bastards have to be shot down to keep Frau Vidler happy?"

The other two laughed, doubling over, hooting, coughing. Mrs. Vidler, they thought, was the girl for them.

16

Rossclare and Murphy

THE town of Rossclare had been founded by an Irish Protestant infantry officer who had come to Australia to guard convicts in the 1820s. Its location, in a fine valley where regular flooding enriched the mud flats, had been reported to him by convict escapees who had spent time in the wilderness but at last gone back to the convict settlement to the south, at Port Macquarie. They took with them news of the rich farming country and great stands of timber they'd encountered, in the hope that this intelligence would soften their sentence for having escaped in the first place.

The valley had become, and still was, a great source of native Australian cedar to the world, so that throughout the nineteenth century and virtually up to the time of Perpetua's arrival in Rossclare, the town served as a timber port and steamers from Sydney, or even from across the Pacific, could be seen in the river. The railroad and the operations of Japanese submarines off the coast had, however, diminished the shipping trade, so that Rossclare seemed to Perpetua to be dominated not by its river traffic but by the high, subtropical mountains that rose behind it, by logging and dairy farming. The romance of shipping lessening, Rossclare, thirty miles up river, seemed very much a landlocked town, low-slung on the river, subject still to occasional flooding and to heavy, humid summers.

The cathedral of the diocese of Rossclare rose on a slight hillock behind the main shopping street, and the Bishop's house and wide verandaed presbytery were set amongst palms behind it. A little farther up a slight slope stood the hospital and the hospital's convent. Diagonally across the town, about a mile away, was another convent, run by the Sisters of Mercy as a boarding school for the daughters of country worthies, pub owners, and the better-off dairy farmers. It had considerable reputation—its girls "married well," and a portion of them became in their turn members of the order of Mercy. But the greatest reputation and style attached to the Sisters of Compassion and the hospital of St. John Vianney, for it was regarded by the community as running across religious lines and catering to both Protestant and Catholic.

Perpetua saw Father Murphy for the first time when he said Mass in the convent one morning. There was nothing impressive about his movements or his enunciation. But after Brendan, she knew enough to understand that one should not proceed on appearances.

The Mother Superior at Rossclare, Felice, welcomed her warmly and said, "Mother Fredericka says you should seek out Father Murphy as your spiritual director. Perhaps that's so. I would like you to know, however, that there are other priests available."

It was the first time Perpetua got the impression that Felice did not like Murphy, and having given up so much, she made a stubborn vow not to be tricked out of Murphy. There was something she observed in the man as he turned to the nuns to say *"Dominus vobiscum,"* a whimsy at the corner of the mouth, which made her determined to have such a spiritual director.

She first approached Murphy on the second weekend after her arrival in Rossclare. The approach was through the confessional. The nuns confessed in the sacristy, where a structure consisting of two kneelers with a wooden barrier and a screen between them was hauled into the middle of the room by the sister sacristan. It was a Saturday afternoon in the spring of 1943. That is, the Australian spring, and so it was September. Sicily and most of Italy had fallen to the Allies, and the Italians were suddenly themselves allies. Perpetua did not understand that the air war followed its own dynamics and reasons and could be excused for being encouraged by the ground success of the forces of right to believe that it would now be the greatest of ill luck if her brother should perish.

She knew it was also time—for her own peace of mind—to be frank with someone about Brendan and the unjust, though welcome shift to Rossclare.

As she approached the confessional screen in the sacristy, she could see Murphy's square and rakishly handsome face beyond it, diffused by the screen wire. He did not seem passionately interested in what he was about to hear—the confession of a young nun. Perpetua was grateful for his lack of interest. Kneeling and blessing herself, she made the normal declaration. "Bless me, Father, for I have sinned. It is two weeks since my last confession."

Murphy did not actually yawn. But Perpetua saw that he was a particular kind of priest—a man of prosaic faith, of unimaginative spiritual life. Popular at the Monday get-togethers of other young or youngish priests throughout the diocese. A golfer and a tennis player who probably found one of the greatest hardships of the priesthood to be the fact that Saturday-afternoon confessions coincided with the Australian Broadcasting Commission broadcasts of the last races from Eagle Farm or Doomben in Brisbane or from Randwick or Canterbury in Sydney.

"I know that no one is just," Perpetua began, "except God." She believed it absolutely, not only as sound doctrine, but as sound history. Who had been just on their own merits? Napoleon? Caesar? Would they discover, when it came down to it, that Roosevelt was just, or Churchill? If they did, it would be through divine influence, not out of any innate virtue in the Roosevelt or Churchill families. "It will probably sound like mischief-making to you, Father, but I have to take that risk. I have to say I'm wracked not by something I've done, but something someone else has done. I just can't swallow it. I just can't forgive it. And there's no use pretending to myself or my superiors or anyone else that I can."

Father Murphy sat up in the chair he occupied and adjusted his stole. "Well," he said "'where did they get *you* from?"

She was amazed by the flippant answer, though she knew it was half caused by surprise. The priest himself seemed to regret it too.

"No, please, Sister," he said, "go on. It was a silly thing for me to say. Though I reckon you sound like a bit of a proud one to me. Are you a proud one?"

"People are meant to have a certain pride," Perpetua told him. She was already enjoying the debate in a funny way. She knew that with this priest she had room to speak.

"And to be able to swallow pride too," said the priest. "You think priests have it easy, with the laity bowing and scraping to us. But you have to remember that every priest has to fight that demon, pride, as well. So do ordinary people all the time, of course. Life is nothing except an education in the folly of pride. Well, now I've said all that, maybe you don't want to confide anything more in me. I'm not the world's champion confessor, so of course I would understand. Why don't you just tell me that you resent one or two of your fellow sisters, and make a sincere intention to try to like them, and I'll give you absolution, and we'll all be happier and not too dangerously wiser. How about that?"

Perpetua found herself panting, having not quite enough breath to answer. It was the most unorthodox confession she had ever made. He was the most unorthodox confessor. But what a man to talk to! You could tell this man anything.

"I was approached by another nun in my former convent to take part with her in certain carnal acts. I was very surprised, because I'd barely heard of that sort of thing."

"Are you telling me you said no? You . . . 'repulsed' her?"

"Yes, that's exactly right. I didn't know what was happening. I was astounded."

"It may have only been a momentary weakness," said Father Murphy. "I mean, on the part of the other one."

At least he did not now seem to be missing the race broadcasts from Brisbane. He was engrossed, but not in the way outsiders always said priests were, slavering over the sins of women. In fact, the confessions were always boring and repetitious. It was only in the motion pictures that priests heard fascinating things, like murders and really great infidelities. Mostly the races *were* more interesting. But Murphy was interested now, and it was a genial, humane interest, which made Perpetua feel instantly both more human and more of a nun.

"Had you by any chance had any affection of this sort for some other nun? A young nun, say? What they call a 'crush'?"

Perpetua was not offended by the question, since it seemed to be asked without either punishing malice or old-maidish interest.

"No. Not even at school. Of course, I had friendships. And they were very warm and loving. And I was accused of particular friendships at Chapters of Faults."

Murphy brushed this aside. "That particular friendship nonsense is one of the greatest red herrings. I had a mate in the seminary called Tim McCloud. We were always in trouble for particular friendships—we used to talk together all the time. He was a North Coast boy too. The whole thing is, half the rest of them were such boring buggers—I beg your pardon, Sister—such boring chaps, I should say. It doesn't matter now anyhow. McCloud left. He was killed last year in the crash of an Anson in South Australia. R.I.P. Rest well, Tim. I mean, particular friendships are only a problem when they cause bitterness and jealousy. But what no one ever says is that the main problem is that they cause an actual 'crush' sort of jealousy. So you never had anything physical with other women, then? I mean apart from embracing them, and if they cut that out, then they cut out being a human being, don't they?"

"The nun who approached me went to my Mother Superior and accused me of a crush. I felt I had a home there, and suddenly I was cast out."

"Do you feel cast out here?"

"No," said Perpetua with surprise. "No, I don't. I've been given an old nun to look after."

"Catherine," laughed Murphy. "She'll keep you busy." He tittered away about some private memory of Catherine. "You know, Superiors don't always botch things. Sometimes they do things that are wise. Mostly their wisdom is of the kind that you've got to be God to see. Sometimes I think—you can tell I'm an ordinary fellow—but sometimes I think that the wisdom of God is so hard to understand that only superiors are fit to impose it. Because to a lot of us ordinary infantrymen of the Church, it seems absolutely so strange that it must make sense. You see what I'm getting at? Let me tell you another thing. There are young fellows in the southwest Pacific at the moment, or in Europe, whose superiors seem to them as hard to interpret as ours do to us. Just remember that. At least our superiors aren't going to get us shot. It hasn't gone that far."

Perpetua said, "Everything you say is a great comfort to me." It sounded stilted to her, but it didn't seem to offend Murphy's down-to-earthness. "My former Superior was a cousin of yours."

Murphy hooted. "That one! What a hard case she is!"

"She said I should seek you out as my spiritual director."

"I'm already spiritual director to three of the nuns here," murmured Murphy. "I don't know if I'm any good. I'm very flattered my cousin recommends me. Or maybe it's God who ought to be very flattered. You can certainly come to me, Sister, if your Superior approves it. She'll be the first to tell you I'm a very fallible fellow. And now, if you feel you're finished blaming your sister for her Lesbian impulses"—it was the first time Perpetua had ever heard the word in her life, but she knew at once what it meant—"then I can give you absolution. And just remember, when you think of that sister of yours, that people don't always choose to be what they are. That's my experience, anyhow. I never met a man yet who chose to be a drunk. One thing before I give you the absolution, however. There's a young man in our diocese called Father Michael Proud. He says Mass like a priest should, and his piety is unquestioned. If, after you've met him, you would prefer to have him as your spiritual director, then of course I understand. There's no vanity in these things. Not for a boy from up the river!" And he pointed back over his shoulder toward the hinterland from which he came. And from which Fredericka, his older cousin, must have come! Perpetua wondered what sort of dairy farm it was that had produced something as Hapsburg as Mother Fredericka.

17

Chop Girl

CANNON, provider of high-ranking uniforms, did not come back from a trip to Dortmund. He was so well-known that the news spread quickly from his air station, Leconfield, to every field where Australians were part of bomber squadrons, and Reardon even heard English wireless operators mention the tragedy in the mess. He wondered how many airmen Cannon had put in contact with Teddy's cousin's uniform-hire service. Now Cannon's own uniform would possibly be included in Teddy's stock.

Cannon was believed to have fallen from his plane without a parachute. He had taken the option of many a rear gunner separated from his parachute by a blaze in the fuselage: he had swung his turret sideways, unlatched the doors behind him, and fallen out into the night.

The worst thing, Reardon thought, was that you were not allowed to discuss or analyze the extraordinary fact of Cannon's death. You were not allowed to say of Alf Hater, for example, "Cannon really had the air of someone who was going to get there, to fly the whole thirty and sign on again." The flak or the night fighters had been clever enough to get Cannon, and that meant that no one was safe. So even to raise the question, to compare Cannon and yourself, was forbidden. You caught the disease of "the chop"—of death over Europe—by talking about this man or that, particularly by letting it be known that you believed that this man or that would have still been flying long after the statistics had claimed *you*.

The evening of the day they heard about Cannon, Reardon's squadron was briefed to bomb the Hoechst Benzin Refinery near Dortmund. Even as the intelligence officer was informing the crews on the flak they could expect to encounter, rain flung itself against the windows and raised the stressful hope that perhaps the mission would be cancelled. A little after six P.M. the word came through on the teleprinter that indeed it was scrubbed. A liberty bus was arranged to take the airmen and any WAAF's who had passes into York for the evening. Reardon was delighted for obvious reasons, and also because, though no one would let him memorialize much about Cannon, this journey to York would permit him to observe his own informal wake for the man.

One of the favorite bomber crew drinking places was not far from the great Minster. The streets were narrow here, rather like the streets of all the *Nieumarkts* and *Altstadts* they had been bombing in the center of German cities. The pub in question, the White Stag, had a reputation for unadulterated beer, and the personnel of Bomber Command had rewarded its proprietor with photographs of bombers and crews. Some of the photographs were of Hampdens and Wellingtons, bombers now removed from commission or else lying as scrap in Europe. They were twin-engined and couldn't take the punishment a Halifax could. And where the faces were that beamed from the photographs, in the shadows of the wings—that was anyone's guess. You could safely bet that most of them were gone and unmentionable, the instantly forgotten dead whom Cannon had joined.

Perhaps God meant nothing, Reardon thought, or at least did not intervene. The ones who talked about "numbers coming up" were probably right. The numbers got you in the end. He had stuck to Challenor because Challenor had reeked of life and looked as if he couldn't be easily crossed off any list. But that appeared a naive illusion. How many completion-of-tour parties had he attended since last Easter—that is, how many crews at Parsfield had finished and gone off for their six-month rest at Operational Training Units? Was it two or was it three?

The thought, instead of making him despair, filled him with a manic gaiety. Substituting for Cannon, he guzzled the strong ale and looked around at the WAAF's. Alf Hater was in the bar, with his redheaded girlfriend from Parsfield, who had obviously got into York somehow, maybe on her bike, to meet up with him. She was game to hang on to Alf, given that everyone thought she wasn't worthy of such a gentle lad. She was using him, they said. But Reardon smiled across at her. Let her give Alf a little joy, especially in view of the matter of numbers. If Alf wanted a girl with a complexion like a brick, good luck to him. There wasn't any doubt he thought she was bloody marvelous.

Reardon noticed a small, neat-featured WAAF corporal drinking Pimm's with a group of other WAAF's and a few groundcrew—erks. He spoke to his captain, Ted Punch, newly promoted to pilot officer. "Who's that nice little creature over there?"

"Don't even ask the question," said Punch. "She's a chop girl. True! One kiss from her and you're finished. She came here from Leconfield to get away from her reputation. She knew Cannon." Pilot Officer Punch raised his eyebrows in a manner that asked "Need I say more?"

Another pint and Reardon began to move toward her. Punch called after him, "Don't bring yourself disaster, mate."

She was certainly the most perfect little woman Reardon had seen. In his slightly pint-sodden way, he wondered if she were Catholic. A remarkable number of the northerners were, and in view of his serious intentions, that would make things easier. But for her sake, he was willing to contemplate a mixed marriage. As long as the children were raised properly!

All that had been unilaterally decided by him before he reached the group in which she stood. He could tell that she had noticed him, but marginally, and was pretending she hadn't.

"Excuse me, ladies and gentlemen," he said to the group. "Do any of you need a refill?"

An erk fitter-corporal murmured jovially, "Here comes the flight pay talking."

The little woman said composedly, glancing into her glass of Pimms, "I think we're all right, thank you, flight."

Her voice did have traces of somewhere north in it—Yorkshire or Durham or Northumberland. It seemed very attractive to him.

"Oh, gee," said Reardon, grinning. "So much for the only time I've ever shouted!"

"You're from Parsfield?" the girl asked.

"Well, he didn't troop up here from Grimsby," said one of the erks, and everyone laughed.

"You're an Australian?" she asked.

"How did you guess?" he said in reply, tapping the Australia patches on his left shoulder.

"Just superior intelligence," she said.

One of the erks said, "I like the Aussie flight crew. They don't have the joystick up their arse, like our crowd."

"Let me buy you all a drink, just for that," said Reardon, and they relented, even the little WAAF.

Reardon looked over his shoulder, back at Punch and the others. It was a new thing for him to be a strolling romancer. He had no reputation for it, and he wanted them to be as amazed by his social success as he himself was.

One of the erks, an electrician, was telling them about dealing with a "hang up," a bomb that had failed to drop and which, suspended by one electrical switch, the crew had brought back all the way to Parsfield. Hang ups were not infrequent, so it was a prosaic conversation by the standards of Bomber Command, and particularly by the standards of ground crew, who were the ones who had to fulfill the dangerous business of releasing the bomb onto a cradle and storing it away for next time.

Under cover of this story Reardon leaned to the girl's extraordinarily neat ear.

"Sit next to me in the bus back?" he asked.

She looked at him sagely, without a smile. "Perhaps," she said. "Yes, just this once."

After drinking his round, Reardon went back to the crew giving the normal excuse, "My skipper just got commissioned. I've got to buy him a pint."

When the time came for the bus, and the proprietor closed the doors apologetically on them, Reardon moved in beside the small girl. When I say small, he told himself, I don't mean really small. Five foot three or two? Small by Aussie standards.

"What do you do on the station?" he asked.

"I'm in charge of a parachute-packing section."

"You must be doing a good job," he said, uttering an old, a lame joke, though it seemed passable in the glow of what he'd drunk.

"Why is that?" she asked.

"Bet you've never had any complaints," he said. "Sorry. Crook joke, that one. Never much liked it. I think I might have seen you in there. Been through that place a bit lately."

She led him far up the bus toward the back. They found a seat. All the smoochers went toward the back. Reardon felt both fear and exaltation that she would lead him so far. To his amazement he found he liked the rakishness of being one of the rear-of-bus Lotharios.

As soon as they sat, she took his hand.

"Now, what's the matter with you, flight? Your mates must have told you I'm a chop girl. That everyone I mix with gets the chop."

Reardon considered her perfect little face in the dim light. Was this the face of assured death? If she kissed you, did the lips leave a mark seen by God or Satan, the mark that meant your number, the number that came up in one of three dozen painful and horrifying ways?

For some reason he couldn't believe it. More than that, he refused to. Your number couldn't be a small-boned brunette. He didn't want to occupy a world where it was.

He said, "It must be murder to have a reputation like that. Totally undeserved, I reckon."

"They've got to be able to explain what happens to their friends haven't they? Well, I'm the explanation." And she squeezed his larger hand inside her small one. "Even so, I half believe it myself, flight. What's your name, anyhow?"

"Bernard Reardon."

"If I weren't a chop girl, I'd ask you how many missions you had up."

"Twenty-two. Eight to go to the end of the tour." The odds favored you at this stage of a tour. Everyone knew that they did. But if you had more than twenty missions up and said so, invoked the statistics, then they turned on you.

"I might be the chop girl, but I'll tell you what I'll do tonight. I shall drop on my knees by my bunk, in front of all the other tarts, and I shall pray to the god of gods that you finish the tour and go back to Australia and have as many children as you want, and die on the other side of the year 2000." She smiled at him. "You won't want to talk to me tomorrow, or the next day. And that's okay."

"But I will want to talk to you, Corporal . . ."

"Corporal Douglass," she said, "with a second S." She leaned her shoulder against his arms. "I'm telling you," she said jovially, "so you can remember who to avoid in the morning."

"I'm not superstitious," he told her. "In my religion superstition is a mortal sin."

"What religion is that?"

"The One True Faith. I have a sister who's a nun. God bless her. I bet she's praying hard for me tonight. Of course, in Australia it's not tonight at all. It's tomorrow. The land of tomorrow. It'll do me. A great place, you know. Blue sky, blue water. Blue bloody nose on the winter mornings."

He noticed that the bus was moving down misty country lanes, yet he realized with a shock that he hadn't even remembered it starting off.

"Did you know my mate Cannon at Leconfield?"

"The gunner? The lawyer? The Australian?"

"That just about sums him up, the bloody rogue. You knew him?"

"Of course I knew him. If you listened to what was said at Leconfield, I knew all of them. All of them who went."

"It isn't you, Miss Douglass. Believe me, I've been over there and I know what it is. It's the bloody searchlights, and when it's not them, it's the high flak, and when it's not them, it's the low flak, and when it's not them, it's the box defense of the fighters. And when it's not a 110 from behind, it's a 109 from above, or a bloody Heinkel. It's got nothing to do with you. You're just a kid. How can they put the whole blame on someone your size?"

She laughed at that and squeezed his hand again. "Nice of you to look at it in that light, Aussie," she said.

"Gee, I'm really raving on, aren't I? That's because you're such a good-looking girl, and I'm not good at talking to good-looking girls."

"Could have fooled me," said Corporal Douglass.

As they left the bus inside the gates of Parsfield Bomber Station, she put her arm round his waist. As many others were doing all around, he drew her into the shadow of administrative buildings and kissed her on the mouth. He was astounded what a delicious experience this was. This is genuine love, he told himself. I want her, I am prepared to wait a long time.

So was Corporal Douglass, though perhaps for other reasons.

"That's dangerous enough," she told him. He was leaden with beer, and did not have the coordination to follow her as she ran crisply away.

Two nights after Corporal Douglass kissed Reardon, Pilot Officer Punch took his crew on a frightful trip to the Ruhr. On the way in, and all down the path to Essen, there was continuous flak—the notorious Flak Alley of this great industrial province. The Halifax jolted up and down the sky. Reardon was continually thrown against the sights of his guns and the sides of his turret. Close to the target, he heard Punch turn command of the plane over to the bombardier, who was lying on his stomach in the forward section, watching the wire hairs of the bombsight creep toward the aiming point itself, the eastern side of the Krupp armaments complex, visible on this night of sparse cloud and marked by red and green target indicators dropped by the Pathfinders.

They were perhaps thirty seconds from bombing when a great blackness passed over Reardon's head. It was a Lancaster bomber. It began releasing its bombs perhaps sixty feet above them. Reardon saw a four-thousand-pound cookie fall away from the plane, a few braces of five-hundred-pound general purpose bombs, and sticks of little hexagonal incendiaries. All of them were released, it seemed to him, directly above his head. He heard Challenor in the mid-upper turret scream, "Shit!" He himself screamed, a matter of instinct rather than intelligence, "Corkscrew port, go!" Punch put the nose down and hit the left rudder. His profanities mingled with Challenor's screams. The Halifax fell, as Reardon could see in his side-on turret, toward the searchlights and the blazing streets. It was clear within two seconds that somehow the cookie, the general purpose bombs, and the incendiaries—all of them adequate to destroy Punch and his crew—had fallen past them. Reardon's order to Punch may indeed have saved them.

J-Judy, however, had nosed down to some four thousand feet, and all the light flak of the Ruhr was reaching for them now. Punch hauled the stick back and went corkscrewing upward into the night. The navigator was swearing as his instruments flew everywhere. The bombardier was thrown away from his sights and crashed his head against the main spar of the fuselage. Reardon, lurched forward over his guns as the bomber climbed, saw the yellow flashes of light flak pursuing him, bursting by his left knee, then his right. It was said that if a shell burst within twenty yards, the plane took damage. Yet these seemed to explode within a few feet of his nose, within inches of his left shoulder and his right. His night vision was gone, too, with all this explosive light, and it would take him time to get it back, and in that time the Halifax was utterly vulnerable from the rear.

Leveled out, Punch said, "All right, you blokes. With the permission of the fucking Lancasters, we're going 'round again. Bugger it!" For as Punch and all his crew knew, the level bombing run was the dangerous part, since it did not permit you to evade, and to do it twice was obscene.

As Punch yanked the Halifax around the heavens, Reardon felt the forces of the diving and turning on his masked face and bare eyes, ungoggled because goggles grew greasy and deceptive. Now he blinked and readjusted his features behind his oxygen mask and pointed his turret toward the darker segment of the sky, away from the searchlights, trying to get his night vision back. He heard the bombardier call out, "Right, level and steady, Punchy. To the left, to the left, steady, steady . . ."

Toward Reardon's left there was a great orange blast in the sky. "Bomber blown up on the starboard." Reardon reported.

"Sure of that, Reardo?"

"Sure, skip."

He knew it had been a bomber exploding, but you hesitated to tell the intelligence people back at base that it was. They said that these flashes, which rocked the Halifax off its steady bombing axis, were "scarecrow" shells, designed to convince the bomber crews that crews near them in the sky had just been destroyed. Experienced crews, though, were beginning to understand there were no scarecrow shells.

Because of the intensity of the exploding bomber/scarecrow shell, Reardon's night vision was again momentarily destroyed. Even so, he saw a flash above his head, in the direction of the front of the plane. He heard Challenor, calm this time, say into the intercom, "Bomber exploding high on the starboard, skip."

Punch said, "Got to be scarecrow. Not bomber."

"As you say, skip," murmured Challenor.

The bombardier was instructing Punch back on to his level run. "Starboard, starboard. Fine, steady, steady . . ."

An impossibly long ten seconds passed. Then Reardon heard the bombardier shout, "Bombs gone. None hung up. Let's piss off, Punchy!"

Lightened by some eight thousand pounds, the bomber rose nose up, and Punch accentuated the rise, climbing for height, banking back homeward.

Reardon could see with his peripheral vision the blaze below, but did not focus on it, instead swinging his turret, quartering the sky. Within twenty seconds of leveling out he saw what was possibly a Messerschmitt 110 rise into his line of sight out of the murky darkness behind and below the plane.

Even after he'd given the order to corkscrew, he tried to focus on the deeper darkness above his turret. The gunner was advised to do so anyhow. Perhaps this partially visible fighter was serving as a decoy, to cover the approach of perhaps a less visible one from above. Again they were plummeting from their desired height, again the navigator was cursing, and Reardon was forced back against the harsh edges of his turret. Punch dived for fifteen hundred feet, and Reardon saw the tracer from the fighter pass perhaps ten feet in front of his face. At the end of the spiral the Halifax began to climb again, this time to the right. The fighter had vanished entirely. "See him? See him, rear turret?" Punch asked. There was a reasonable frenzy in his voice.

"No sight, skip," said Reardon.

"Mid-upper?" Punch enquired of Challenor.

"Nothing here, skip," said Challenor, composed as a grandfather.

"He'll come again, wouldn't mind betting. Feel it in the water. Peeled eyes, blokes!"

In the crew rooms at Parsfield Station there was a large sign that said HEIGHT EQUALS SAFETY. Punch counted off the clicks in his altimeter as he reached for height. Ten thousand, ten thousand five hundred, eleven thousand, eleven thousand five hundred, twelve thousand, twelve thousand five hundred. Far behind the Halifax Reardon thought he saw a shape dropping fast. But no, it could have been a grease speck on perspex. Then it rose into his line of vision again, so close he could see the instrument light shining on the pilot's face. He did not have time to ask "Who is that fellow?" This time, and as it should according to both the theory of Bomber Command and of the night fighters, the attack was coming from Reardon's right, the port side of his aircraft.

He screamed now, "Corkscrew starboard, go!" As J-Judy swung away from the line of fire of the fighter, the circular bead of his gunsights passed it by and he pressed the two firing buttons, letting go a two-second burst. He thought he could hear, though there was no way he could, Challenor firing away from the mid-upper. And then they were gone from the fighter's sights and Punch was plummeting J-Judy down.

Eight times the night fighter, or a succession of night fighters, latched onto their tail and forced them down into wild corkscrews. Twice Reardon was able to fire, twice he was sure of inflicting damage. But the small-caliber guns and ammunition needed to strike something vital to cause much harm to the big night fighters, and perhaps nothing vital was struck. Or perhaps it was, and the face Reardon had seen by the light of its own instrument panels had gone blazing down and been replaced by one of his brothers.

The eighth approach was just like the second one—the suspicion of a distant plummet by the fighter, followed by a very close appearance. Reardon was sure he gave the command "Corkscrew" instantly, but perhaps by then the terror of it had slowed him, or more likely had slowed Punch, so that someone announced fire in the glycol tank of the inner-starboard engine.

Reardon could hear the flight engineer announcing that he was feathering the thing. Punch said nothing, but put the nose dangerously down now.

The velocity of this descent pinned Reardon to the back doors of his turret. He could certainly have swung the mechanism and slid out backward, but his parachute was in the rear of the fuselage, near the Nelson lavatory, and it would be almost impossible to retrieve it and make his way back to the turret with it. Besides, Punch kept calling now, "Stick with it! Stick with it!" It could be argued whether this was advice to the crew or an exhortation to the plummeting air frame, now traveling toward earth at a speed beyond the manufacturer's recommended specifications.

The dive contined, became an age in itself. You could hear the bombardier and the navigator, as well as Alf Hater the wireless operator, appealing to Punch for advice, but all he yelled in his manic way was, "Stick with it!"

Reardon remembered, with the nausea of this great fall from the sky, the chop girl's sweet little face. He began to recite the shorter Act of Contrition. "Oh my God, I'm heartily sorry for all my sins . . ."

Those in the forward section would later tell Reardon that Punch, having extinguished the engine fire by his dive, aimed J-Judy straight down toward the smokestacks of a large factory—the bombardier claimed that you could see the soot lining one of them and reaching down into the furnaces. They were only a little over a thousand feet when Punch pulled out, hit the rudders, opened the throttles, and strained uphill again on his three engines. He could be heard raving to himself: "Now find us, you bastard! Find us, go on, you prick! Come on down here, you poofter bastard!"

They were able to get to a little over ten thousand feet, but the Halifax would not go any higher without its fourth engine. Now it seemed a giddy and wonderful height. The navigator began praising the aircraft, its reliability, its friendliness, till Punch told him to shut up. Flak in Belgium bounced them around a little, and Punch cursed it, but they were not hit.

Over the North Sea they suffered a last assault from a flak ship, but Punch was feeling confident and deviated about the sky with great style.

But then, as they began to feel tentatively safe, the starboard outer died without warning. The flight engineer feathered it and wondered if it had been hit at some stage. Yet it didn't show anywhere on his instruments—oil pressure had been fine. It had simply died, that was all, a mysterious stroke had overtaken it.

They could feel themselves dropping belly first, a different, duller anguish than the dives. They could hear Punch arguing aloud with the controls. The air frame was juddering as if it intended to turn on them, and they were below six thousand feet.

There was an airfield in Kent called Manston—for the use of damaged planes that couldn't make it to their fields in Norfolk, the Midlands, or the North. Punch announced that they were going there. His decision was helped by Alf Hater reporting that he'd just received a notification on the radio that a belt of mist and fog had swept in from southwest England. Manston had FIDO, the method of marking an airstrip so that baffled pilots could find the place whatever the visibility and put down there. FIDO, according to those who admired it, burned a hole in the fog.

The navigator directed them straight in, and then they could see FIDO burning. It was a gracious system, gasoline running in long pipes down the runway and flaring up from nozzles spaced periodically. It burned with a constancy of life, with a tenderness of motherhood. So it seemed to Reardon as they began to circle and he saw it flaring beneath him.

Distinctly he heard ground control ask, "Calling damaged aircraft. State your situation. Over."

Punch immediately spoke. "J-Judy. Two engines gone. Over."

"Wounded? Over."

"J-Judy. No wounded. Over."

"J-Judy. Approach from the northeast," said the calm, brotherly voice. "You'll be landing behind Lancaster F for Freddy. Keep your distance. Over."

Punch heard a breathy, happy grunt from Punch as he saw the Lancaster. The Halifax swung in behind it. Reardon could see the glow of FIDO in the banks of fog around his turret. He heard the ground controller yell, "F-Freddy, you have a problem. Veer off! Veer off!"

Reardon did not see the disaster that now overtook the Lancaster. He felt its reverberations, a jolt as of heavy flak exploding beneath his turret.

He heard later from Punch what had happened. The Lancaster nad, it seemed, been leaking fuel. All Punch saw was a thread of fire rise from FIDO to the wing of the plane in front of him. There was a blue glow beneath the Lancaster and then, perhaps a hundred feet up, it blew to pieces and cascaded onto the runway. Reardon heard the ground controller in a stricken voice ordering Punch to go around again.

They circled lumpily for another half hour. Reardon poured himself coffee from his thermos. It was succulent as life. Yet he knew its promise was an illusion, since all the time new and equally damaged aircraft were arriving in the cloud banks all around. At last they were given instructions to come in. Reardon heard the bombardier saying, "We're not leaking anything, are we?"

The flight engineer came in with reassurance. His gauges showed that all his gas tanks were intact.

"Your bloody gauges told us there was no reason for that starboard engine to bloody well die," the bombardier said.

"Nice night," said Challenor in the mid-upper turret.

When Punch got the word, he brought the Halifax down over the end of the runway. You had the feeling that the survival of the plane depended on the way he was able to hold it together with his gloved hands. From the rear turret, the flanking fires of FIDO that had destroyed the Lancaster still looked like home to Reardon. He could see that they were about twenty feet up and level, and the omens were good.

Given the lessened control he had, Punch simply dropped the plane from there, bounced it down. The jolt was enormous, yet like a welcome.

After they had taxied to a dispersal area on the rim of the airport, there were five seconds of silence. Then everyone began unlatching harnesses. Reardon was aware all at once of howling pain and cramps in his arms and legs and stomach. With a delicious painfulness he swung the hind doors of his turret open, stood up, and stepped into the long tube of the fuselage. Challenor had already come down from the small, hard seat of the mid-upper turret and was working his legs and arms and chatting quietly with Alf Hater. He saw Reardon stumbling forward.

"Beauty of a trip, eh, Reardo?"

Various fitters and mechanics they'd never seen before crawled up into the plane. They were chirpy. "Welcome back, boys," a warrant officer told them. "Any problems?"

"No worries," said Challenor.

"She's got a few holes in her," said the warrant officer.

"We go in for good ventilation," said the bombardier with flight-crew sangfroid. Whereas half an hour before he'd been screaming.

Some mechanics were talking to Punch and the flight engineer. But Punch saw Reardon farther down the plane, briskly excused himself, and came toward him as fast as the confined quarters of the air frame and the cramped fuselage permitted. He raised his forearm and pushed Reardon back against the ammunition racks.

"Listen, you little turd! Get rid of that fucking chop girl. Or else find yourself another bloody home!"

Reardon felt the rage mount in him. He pushed Punch's arm away and began pushing in return.

"Don't you bloody touch me!" he said. He felt that having seen the face of the 110 pilot, having seen the features of his own death, he did not now need to be pushed around by a brother. "You bloody well touch me and I'll murder you, Punchy!"

The pilot struck him with an elbow into the ribs. Reardon threw a cramped blow that hit Punch on the shoulder. The navigator, the bombardier, Alf Hater, and Challenor all moved in, forming a wall between the two of them. Challenor was saying, "Come on, fellows!" All the others were muttering conciliatory things, pushing the two of them apart.

"This little cunt," roared Punch, "gave us the trip we just had. You bastards want more trips like that? Bloody 110 on our arse for forty bloody minutes."

"We got away," said Reardon. "If she's a chop girl, why weren't we chopped? Eh? Tell me that, bastard-head!"

"Come on, mate," murmured Challenor. "You can't call a bastard-head officer a bastard-head. Take it easy."

Reardon said, "Then tell me, why did we come through if she's a chop girl? Just answer me that. Tell piss-features to answer that."

"Come on," said Alfie Hater. "We're all a bit edgy."

What had hurt Reardon was that it was entirely his skill and Punch's that had saved them. They were brothers in skill. Yet Punch was denying all that.

So they were separated. Reardon was eased out of the plane, down through the hatch, by Challenor and found the barely remembered earth of England beneath his feet. He was still calling on Challenor to explain how, if Corporal Douglass were a chop girl, they'd gotten back. Punch went back to talk to the awed mechanics. Then one by one he, the engineer, Alf, and the bombardier got down onto the ground where the bomber was parked. A truck was waiting for them. There was an embarrassed air amongst them. Both Reardon and Punch were calming down, and the others seemed chastened.

With a crew they'd never seen before, as was the case with the mechanics, they rode back to the Manston crew rooms for debriefing. There was comparing of notes in the back of the truck. Both crews were at their limit. Tea laced with rum revived them as they made their report to an intelligence officer, who suggested that Punch was exaggerating when he said that a fighter had been on their tail for forty minutes.

"Listen," Punch told him, "do you want me to leave the room so you can question the boys?"

The intelligence officer, who was used to pumping frazzled crews, backed away from the question and made his notes.

They ate the egg breakfast so envied by the erks and then dossed down in their flying clothes; the bulk of the crew in a Nissen hut for noncommissioned men, Punch—mercifully, in Reardon's opinion—in some room in the officers' quarters.

Late that afternoon, clammy, their eyes seemingly still full of grit, they were loaded aboard a Lancaster being flown north to a field near Grimsby. They were passengers, clustered together aft of the air frame. The pilot was combining some sort of training flight with delivering them to Parsfield, and clearly had orders not to rise much above five thousand feet, so Punch's crew did not even have the comfort of oxygen. Reardon thought, I'll *marry* Corporal Douglass. She'll be a wife and not a chop girl. Then she'll be safe from Punch's aspersions. But as the Lancaster bumped above low sunlit cloud, and as the noise of the engines leveled out, Challenor turned to him and said simply, "Listen, old mate. It's purely a matter of whether you want to go on flying with Punchy."

And instantly Reardon saw that Challenor might not come to a new crew with him, and grew afraid.

Their squadron was flying again that night, but they were too late to be briefed. Reardon, sick with exhaustion, let himself be bussed into Parsfield to the village pub. He was drinking a pint with Challenor when a loud group of erks entered, Corporal Douglass in their midst. She hung back from her group and looked at Reardon. Reardon himself could feel the wistful penetration of the gaze she sent toward him.

"Home again?" she asked.

Reardon couldn't answer.

"A bit delayed, but that's okay," Challenor told her.

"I'd heard you got back this morning. I was very pleased." She laughed. "Needless to say."

Reardon still could not speak to her. He burned with shame, but couldn't frame any words. Again it was left to Challenor.

"Buy you a pint, Corporal?" asked Challenor.

"Thanks. I don't think that's wise. Do you?"

"Maybe not," said Challenor. "It's a bloody shame."

"There are a lot of bloody shames around just now," said Corporal Douglass. "Wouldn't you agree, flight? I'm glad you two aren't yet another bloody shame. That's what I'm pleased about."

"We are too," said Reardon, finding a voice.

'Good-bye," said the chop girl.

That, Reardon knew, was the right word. "Good-bye," he said.

Two weeks later she was sent away to an officers' training school. It was about the time—certainly sinisterly close to it—that Reardon was called to the station commander's office. The commander was an old Australian professional, though no more advanced in years than Challenor. He was broad-jawed and had gentle eyes. "I've great pleasure in telling you," he said, "that your pilot recommended you for a Distinguished Flying Medal. The reasons he cited were that it was due to you that the plane got away after the Essen raid. Congratulations, lad."

There was a loud celebration in the sergeants' mess, for which Pilot Officer Punch arrived late and already drunk. "I never doubted," said Punch in a more or less coherent speech, "that this little bastard from Rose Bay brought our skins home."

Afterward Punch and Reardon embraced.

"Thanks for giving up that bloody sheila, mate," said Punch. And Reardon thought, so clearly that he nearly said it to Punch, You get a reward for being a warrior only if you reject beautiful chop girls. And as he flung his arm around Punch, tears appeared in his eyes, which everyone seemed to think was normal.

Then a flight sergeant rode his Harley Davidson motorbike up the steps and into the mess, amongst the tables and the aspidistras, in which various young flight crew were later sick. At some stage Reardon fell asleep on one of the couches, and woke up later in the night to find himself surrounded by other comatose young fliers. A bombardier from New Zealand who owned a clarinet was playing a soulful tune above all the prone figures, the clarity of his instrument rising high above the confused slumber of young men who did not know if they would sleep in women's arms ever again.

Amongst the officers who had come unofficially to his party, and who were still drinking when Reardon groggily revived, was the Reverend Flight Lieutenant Wraith.

18

A Sublime Sense of Ceremony

THE young priest, Father Proud, said Mass that Sunday morning. In the large community of St. Bridie's, Sunday Mass was always sung, but the community up here in Rossclare was too small and too busy to produce a practiced and reliable singing of the plainchant ceremony. Of course, there were some regulars, like the Requiem Mass, that any nun could sing and knew backward. But the more particular the feast day or the Sunday, the more the music differed from the norm.

In any case, young Father Proud walked with his hands exactly joined, more like Bing Crosby in *Going My Way* than like the inexactly prayerful Murphy. Perpetua noticed, though, that Proud's Mass got slower and slower as it went on, so that by the time of the prayers preceding the consecration of the Host, the changing of the bread into the Body and Blood of Christ, he seemed very much a priest, someone selected from amongst the people to go on to a dangerous, high place where no one else would venture and to utter words that changed everything, words the world needed uttered, but that might kill the utterer.

He took up to an hour and ten minutes to say Mass, whereas one of the nuns gave voice at recreation to the rumor that Murphy had once polished everything off in twenty-eight minutes.

"Father Proud is too scrupulous," said old Sister Catherine, the invalid who lived in a cell next to Perpetua's and whom Perpetua had been given charge of, perhaps as a penance. She was, in fact, a delight. Catherine said what she liked—her years of service to the order, her venerability, ensured that she would not be disciplined for saying things—the idea was ridiculous. "Father Proud takes it all too seriously. Especially when he says, *'Hoc est enim corpus meum.'* For this is my body . . . There's a kind of priest who can get lost in the words and never find his way out except in a lunatic asylum. Let me tell you. I've seen it happen. It happens a lot in Ireland, where the sun doesn't shine like it does here."

At these pronouncements of Sister Catherine, the younger nuns would generally laugh, except Francis, the obsessive one, who would blink; she was, in a way, a lesser version of Father Proud himself. Oh, all the kinds of Catholics! thought Perpetua.

Father Michael Proud appeared frequently in the hospital, visiting patients, who seemed to love him. The Irish Catholic community on the north coast of the state was connected by old marriages and old friendships which dated back to the times when people drove thirty or forty miles by buggy just to attend Mass and affirm their faith. There had also been intermarriages with the general community, and Michael Proud seemed to be related in one way or another to most of the North Coast people who turned up at St. John Vianney's.

Because he was so often at the hospital, he met Perpetua soon after she arrived.

"Welcome to the jewel of the Tay, Sister Perpetua." The Tay was the river that snaked around the town and sometimes, in heavy rain, took a shortcut across the Rossclare showground and the lower stretch of railway line. "You aren't a North Coast woman, are you?"

"I am afraid I am a city woman," said Perpetua. She smiled. He was a great enthusiast for his part of the world. An intense and kindly young man. But Perpetua knew on sight that she did not want him as her spiritual director. There was even then something slightly out of control about him, as if he needed a spiritual director himself. So did Murphy, but in a different sense. There was nothing anyone could tell Murphy that would be news.

When the wife of a town councillor went over a cliff in her car on the snaking Pacific Highway south of Rossclare, Proud sat beside the comatose, hopelessly injured woman all night. Even her husband the councillor had to take an hour's sleep, which left him ill-prepared for his wife's death just before dawn.

There was an elderly patient, a farmer's wife from up the river and, like everyone else in the valley, a relative of Father Murphy's. She had shattered her hip and was in traction. Her lungs were considerably congested as well, and her heart history was such that all the nurses and doctors knew she would die within a few weeks, probably of congestive heart failure, or of pneumonia brought on by the shock of her fracture. Her lips parted slightly and ineffable hope entered her eyes whenever Father Proud visited her. One day when Perpetua was sponging her, wiping the sweat of pain out from between the flaps of breasts that had suckled a large family on a remote farm, the old woman said, "Will you tell Father Proud something, Sister? Something from me. When I start to slip, will *he* give me Extreme Unction?"

"I'm sure he will, Mrs. Rogan," said Perpetua.

"But I mean, whatever hour it is of the day or night. Will you ask him to come over from the presbytery? For me?"

"Either Father Proud or your relative, Father Murphy."

The old woman said, "Oh, save me from Murphy, Sister. He'll leave half of it out in his rush. I want Father Proud. You can hear every word. I might seem to you to be gone, but I promise you I'll be able to hear every word. And I don't want a mutterer! Will you promise me, Sister?"

Perpetua promised at once, for the long speech had already sapped probably as much as twenty percent of the strength the old farmer's wife had left for this world.

Proud sat with her the entire night of her death, as peaceful as it was, and a number of the nuns asked to be awakened so that they could come over from the convent and watch Proud anoint the forehead, eyes, ears, mouth, and feet of the old woman, and expunge them of any wrongdoing they may have been guilty of in a long life in the valley of Rossclare. No one could deny that Father Proud had a sublime ceremonial sense!

After saying Mass each morning, the priest—whoever it was, Murphy, Proud, Dr. Lawlor, the Bishop's secretary and canon lawyer, or even occasionally the Bishop himself—would return to the altar after unvesting, while the choir stalls were still full of the nuns of the community, and make his thanksgiving.

With Murphy it was a minute and a half—Murphy gave brusque thanks; with the Bishop and Dr. Lawlor it was a sedate ten minutes. But there were times when Father Proud spent more than an hour at the prie-dieu placed for him. And in that time his eyes were closed, his head bent, and he would occasionally raise and lower his clenched hands as if making an emphatic point to some spiritual being. The nuns, by and large, thought this length of time at thanksgiving and this clenching, lifting, and dropping of the hands to be pretty odd, and a sign of something not absolutely sound in Father Proud, even though he gave and performed the Sacraments as carefully as a saint. These women were Australians by and large, or if not, were Irish born, and neither race was comfortable with too intense a piety. That was Proud's problem— a piety like a minor madness. It wasn't that it was put on, assumed, a disguise. Then he could have been laughed off—he wouldn't have lasted the distance in the seminary, anyhow, and wouldn't have been ordained. It was more that he was burdened by the Mysteries.

And yet when you met him in the hospital, his pale, scrubbed face would be shining with happiness. Perpetua had never met anyone who so visibly loved serving people, or perhaps who so desperately needed to serve them.

One day in the hospital, Perpetua was stopped by Father Proud, who was carrying a slim, bound volume of poetry. He seemed very excited.

"I've just found the most beautiful line in the English language," he told Perpetua.

"Yes, Father." She smiled, used to his enthusiasms. "Are you going to share it with me?"

In St. Bridie's she would not have dared ask such a jovial, personal question for fear of being reported at Chapter of Faults. Fredericka was at least right in believing that here everything would be easier.

"This," said Father Proud, flourishing the book, "is the work of the Jesuit poet Gerard Manley Hopkins. He died fairly young in the last century, and had ordered that all his poems be destroyed. But God obviously didn't want them destroyed. A poet called

Bridges kept them against the wishes of the ghost of Father Hopkins, S.J. That's a pretty rough sort of defiance, isn't it? Except that I'm glad Mr. Bridges did it."

Somehow the treachery of Sister Brendan had made Perpetua a little cynical about the sorts of Catholics who believed that all the *best* lines had to be written *by* Catholics.

"And what is this glorious line, Father Proud?"

Proud opened the book to the start of the poetry, the poem called "The Wreck of the *Deutschland*." The first line read, "Thou mastering me, God."

" 'Thou mastering me, God,' " murmured Father Proud. "Have you encountered anything better?"

The line had its impact on Perpetua. "I have to admit," she said, "it's a hard one to beat."

"And it fits in superbly," Father Proud continued with an enthusiasm only an ounce excessive, "with Christ's description of himself as the servant of the servants of God."

Through this and other encounters, Perpetua began to wonder if Father Proud did not want to be her spiritual director, not out of any necessary vanity, but because he clearly saw her as someone he could talk to on his own level. It was not a true impression on his part, she knew. Perhaps one of the older nuns had described her as a bright student—she hoped they had, since it would be pleasant to have some background of approval within the order. But she was no mental giant. In any case, Father Proud began to loan her works of philosophy by Jacques Maritain, Etienne Gilson, Bloy, Henri Bergson, and by the English husband and wife theological team, Frank Sheed and Maisie Ward.

"Of course," Father Proud told her, "Frank Sheed is really an Australian. I had an uncle who knew his parents and grew up with them—just working-class people. They were fanatical about cricket. I believe Frank Sheed still is."

The idea of a theologian who liked cricket and had a wife intrigued Perpetua, and she found Sheed's books the easiest of all of them to read, other than the poetic. But between her nursing duties, her study, and her religious exercises, she had very little reading time. She was human enough to want to spend the recreation hour talking to one of the nuns instead of wrestling with Jacques Maritain. She ended up using her period of meditation in the mornings to acquaint herself with—and in theory, meditate on—some of the material in these books. But she found she could easily get Father Proud to give her a good rundown on the ideas of each writer—he had a keen and harmless intellectual vanity.

She saw, too, that other priests who came to the hospital had an ambiguous attitude toward Proud's cleverness. Although they approved of it, they came from the rugged tradition of the parish clergy—simple faith, a hard fist if it was needed to persuade the unbeliever or those who had attacked the sanctuary of the Lord, and perhaps more interest in the horse races than in the latest ideas from Paris or Louvain.

After Mother Felice put her in charge of getting aged Mother Catherine to the chapel, the dining room, the recreation room, and back, she had a good excuse for not taking every book Father Proud offered.

Old Mother Catherine liked having a young disciple to talk to. One night in the recreation room she had a game of dominoes with Perpetua and reflected on the connection between nursing nuns and surgeons.

"Sure it can't be the same as Ireland, where I come from. Doctors have great airs and think they're little gods run up by a tinker. You see, it's even worse in a town like this. There are no lords or ladies here, so people invent them, and the first one they invent is the doctor. They make him something like a duke, or an earl, or anything else as grand. They never ask themselves the question, 'If he's such a good doctor, why isn't he down in Sydney at St. Bridie's?' They just spend all their time thinking he's Christmas. Decent men and women, farmers and their wives, entrust themselves body and soul to these ordinary people, who behave like the pagan emperors of Rome.

"Well, I can tell you, a nursing nun has a place in pricking their bubbles for them. Because a nursing nun is greater than them. She is a bride of Christ. She will sit in glory, you see. They won't talk to us as if we're peasants, the way they talk to the lay nurses. We're like that feller who used to walk behind the pagan emperors whispering, 'Remember you are mortal.' That's our job, girl, and sometimes it's the fun of Cork doing it to the blackguards."

At first the Chapters of Faults at Rossclare were nothing beside those of St. Bridie's. Sister Francis, that scrupulous nun given to tormented and slightly hysteric devotions, would sometimes accuse Perpetua of minor faults, such as hearing her during the Great Silence. It was very hard for Perpetua not to be heard, since there was no way Mother Catherine would tolerate not being answered. All the others—Roberta, with her big bones; Calixta, with her efficiency and her concern for the correct forms—offered some tolerance, or at least an open mind, to the newcomer.

Father Murphy had a quarter to a half-hour interview with Perpetua every two weeks.

"I can tell from the way you move through the hospital," said Murphy at one of these conferences, "that you're forgetting that thing from down in Sydney. A good thing to forget too. It's also a good thing that you showed such an attitude. It means you're not what they choose to call 'unnatural.' No point in being a priest or a nun if you have the so-called 'unnatural' tendencies. Otherwise the seminary or the convent would become simply places to meet potential lovers."

The term "lovers" took Perpetua's breath for a second—it was not a normal theological term. She could not imagine the parish priest of Darlinghurst, spiritual director at St. Bridie's, using such a term, in spite of all the "unfortunate women" or prostitutes who inhabited the region around St. Bridie's and shared the same locality above which St. Bridie's rose, a Jerusalem amongst the rubbish, that cordon of human refuse through which the affluent of Sydney made their way to the surgical and medical mercies of the hospital of the Sisters of Compassion.

Then there was Murphy's use of *so-called*. Was he implying that calling that sort of thing "unnatural" was just a kind of convention?

One day, close to her final nursing exams, she was about to enter a room occupied by two wealthy farmer's wives. One had just suffered a hysterectomy and was delighted to have been put through the ordeal and to have emerged so strongly. The other had had gallstones taken out. They were both proud patients of Dr. Cormack and matriarchs of vast farming clans. And they were both now into a triumphant recuperation.

They were in the midst of some private conversation which made Perpetua hesitate at the door. Within a sentence she realized they were gossiping about some priest. It soon became clear which one.

"What I mean," one of them was saying, "is that he should go to his uncle's place for Sunday dinner after he's said Mass at Kolobbi." Kolobbi was a village far up the river. Father Murphy and Father Proud took turns to say Mass up there. But Father Proud had no uncles, aunts, or cousins in the region—all his people were farther south. So it wasn't Proud they were talking about.

"Well, it doesn't mean that anything is actually *happening*," said the farmer's wife who had been relieved of gallstones. "But I'd hate the news to get out to the Protestants and the Masons in town here."

"Well, that's exactly what I say," said the hysterectomy patient. "All the people up there know that as soon as he's done Mass—and that doesn't take him very long at all—and as soon as he's finished talking to the people at the front, he drives across the valley to her place, and of course nothing's happening on the other side."

"Well, I'm her cousin on the other side too. And her husband is a good friend of my son's. I mean, I believe you see it all over the place. Women in Sydney whose husbands are away in New Guinea, and they're carrying on with the Yanks, or even with other Australians. But when it's a priest involved—"

"The flesh is weak," said the one who had had the gallstones taken out, and who should have known.

"She has her younger brother there all the time—sixteen years, just left school."

"They could always send him away for an hour or two, I suppose."

"But nothing's happening."

"She's very good-looking."

"But nothing's happening."

"I don't think they train priests to deal with that sort of thing. And they're only human."

That seemed to be the recurrent platitude of this spate of gossip.

"It's not something you can train people to deal with."

Perpetua nearly walked in now, silencing the two women by her appearance. Yet she hesitated for a number of reasons—a certain nervousness these women created in her, a certain shock at the callousness that kept them attacking their kinsman Father Murphy, and an awful, immobilizing sadness at their willingness to draw a kind of blood out of genial Murphy.

"Someone should speak to her," said the hysterectomy. "Really, someone should. Because it will get back to her husband when he comes home."

"Maybe she's hoping that he won't ... or that he mightn't—"

"No, she's my cousin. She's a good woman."

"Then *she* should tell him not to have Sunday dinner there. And not to spend half his Monday there, either, when he's supposed to be visiting other farms."

"Or else one of us should speak to *her*."

"Or the Bishop should speak to him. Someone will break the silence soon and write to the Bishop."

Then they began to talk about other things, such as how he held the world record for saying Mass. That was ordinary gossip, and Perpetua rallied and went in to take their blood pressure, as she was supposed to.

There had been veiled rumors even amongst the nuns about this woman at Kolobbi who Father Murphy went to see. This again, in the convent as amongst the farmers' wives, was considered rashness rather than crime. Apparently the woman's husband had been away, with one short leave, since 1941. He had fought at the great battle of El Alamein in the Western Desert and was now a member of the forces reducing Japanese garrisons along the north coast of New Guinea. He had won the Military Cross somewhere and been promoted in the field. His wife was said to be very beautiful, though at some points of the gossip both nuns and ordinary people would begin to argue about whether she really was. She had gone on running the dairy farm with the help of her young brother. Obviously she did not have a record for flightiness, otherwise it would have been mentioned along with the other gossip.

A few nights after Perpetua heard this conversation, the farmer's wife who had had her gallstones out fell into a fever. Dr. Cormack diagnosed it as blockage of the lymphatic system. It happened often enough with her sort of surgery. Pneumonia developed and her respiratory system began to collapse. She asked for Father Proud to give her the last rites, Extreme Unction. Her grown and nearly grown sons and daughters gathered by her bed, including a tall soldier home on leave. They all wept softly, comforted her by the wrist and called her Mum, but she could barely hear them.

Father Murphy came in from the Bishop's house to kneel awhile dutifully beside his dying relative or relative-in-law—Perpetua could not quite remember which. Father Proud so precisely laid the chrism on the eyes and nostrils and mouth of the dying woman, and so beautifully uttered the Latin blessings, that the soft weeping of the womenfolk intensified. Then he, not Father Murphy, led the entire family in the Rosary, not rushing it. And Murphy patiently joined in, as did Francis and, at the invitation of Calixta, the senior ward sister who liked to work the night shift, Perpetua. It was a scene, and a series of prayers, that moved Perpetua to tears. It was the passing on of a woman of ordinary virtues and ordinary vices into the Communion of Saints.

When the Rosary was over, Murphy rose and went to the soon-to-be-widowed farmer—the man was probably his cousin—and squeezed his elbow. The man shook Murphy's hands. Then Murphy made in the air a none-too-exact blessing sign in the direction of his kinswoman and, nodding to everyone in general, left. Calixta, Francis, and Perpetua remained out of politeness until Father Proud was ready to go. They left one by one, Francis making off to her duty station at the head of the flight of stairs, Calixta to the office at the ground floor, Perpetua toward the general ward.

Father Proud caught up with Perpetua in the corridor. His eyes were brimming with tears.

" 'Felix Randall the farrier is dead then,' " he said to Perpetua.

"I beg your pardon, Father."

"It is a line from Father Gerard Manley Hopkins, the great Jesuit poet. It is about the death of a country person."

"It sounds superb," she said frankly, at the risk of encouraging him. And indeed it did have a sound. She found herself shocked by an impulse to put a hand around his shoulder. He seemed so affected by the coming death of the farmer's wife.

"You should go back to the presbytery now," she said. "And have your tea."

He turned without saying anything and walked away, as if

disappointed in her. Just as he disappeared around the corner of the room occupied by the farmer's wife, she heard Calixta call her.

"Sister Perpetua? Nothing is wrong?" It was a sort of order to her to get on with her work.

"No, Sister Calixta," she said, and, wondering if she might have to pay some of the price for Father Proud's strangeness, she walked toward the general ward.

Two weeks later she sat for her final nursing examination. She found herself unaccustomedly sitting, by morning light, in the recreation room with a sheaf of blank paper in front of her. Mother Felice would soon enter with the exam for that day in an envelope in her hand. The envelope would bear the letters OHMS—On His Majesty's Service—to show that it came from the state government, or had been manufactured with its consent.

First was the Medicine examination, the next day came Surgery, then General Nursing, then Operating Theater work. By the time she came to the oral examinations, or *vivas*, she was in a state of restrained confidence. Dr. Cormack and a few of his colleagues, including the anesthetist, quizzed her on Surgery. Felice and Cormack gave her tough questions on Operating Theater. But by now she knew the textbooks almost by heart. She had been straining, she suddenly realized, to attract their approval.

The result was that after the papers had been sent off to Sydney and corrected, she was informed by letter from the Department of Health that she had come second in the whole state overall and first in the state in Theater. The results were announced by Felice during recreation hour, where as an exceptional event a cake was produced, cut, and joyfully eaten by the nuns with tea. A photographer from *The Northern Catholic Leader* came and photographed her in the garden, surrounded by a group of smiling, congratulatory nuns. She was pleased to see when it was published that the photograph exuded sisterly joy. Looking at it, she felt that the malice of Sister Brendan was more remote than ever.

Occasionally she saw Father Proud in the corridors of the hospital. He seemed to be very pleased with her recent local fame. She feared that it confirmed him in his idea that she could understand or was really interested in the same sort of theological reasoning—

the largely French, intellectual Catholicism—he so liked to associate himself with and that the war had prevented him from pursuing during his studies in Louvain, the great Belgian center of Scholastic Philosophy to which Bishop Flannery had once intended to send him.

"Your brother must frequently pass over Louvain, and over Douai too," Father Proud said wistfully to her one day in the corridor. Douai was the Belgian town where a number of British Jesuits of the sixteenth century had made an English translation of the Bible.

Under the rule as it was practiced in Rossclare, she felt she could speak to Father Proud at perhaps greater length than she would have been free to speak to anyone at St. Bridie's. She knew enough about the muscular Irish-Australian clergy to understand that many friends of Father Murphy's—the muscular Aussies and Irishmen—would probably find Father Proud's interests and mental pretensions a bit high-toned for the diocese of Rossclare, New South Wales, Australia. Proud probably had very few close friends amongst the priests. Murphy himself, she was sure, was intelligent and kindly enough not to write Proud off. But then, Murphy was not quite like any other priest himself. The woman who had died of postoperative complications would have sworn to that.

Perpetua's certainty of being safe in talking to Proud vanished on a Saturday when she heard Sister Francis utter the by now morbidly feared words, "It seems to me, dear Sister Perpetua, that you have taken undue vanity in your examination results, and that you spend far too long talking about them in the corridor."

Felice imposed a nominal penance—some cleaning of candlesticks in the sacristy. But Perpetua, after she had taken Mother Catherine to her cell that night and left her there—tucked up, her eyes composed as much for death as for sleep beneath the night bonnet of the order—felt that Rossclare wasn't safe anymore. She cried herself to sleep that night.

Not long after that Perpetua heard Roberta and Francis talking in low voices at recreation about Father Murphy and the woman from "up the river." Her name was apparently Pauline Lacey. Her husband was away fighting in New Guinea as the two farmer's wives had said. Father Murphy visited her at some length on Mondays, the nuns were saying. They could only have heard it from patients.

The unfair thing was that Perpetua knew in theory that she could now accuse them at Chapter of Faults of gossip and back-biting, that they deserved it. But she knew she never would in practice. It would bring the venom of all the gossipers down on her. She saw that her aim of a simple and happy life at Rossclare was already defeated.

19

L.M.F.

CALLAGHAN was a dark, tall, and not very vocal pilot, a typical Queenslander, reliable and not too flamboyant. He was not a drinker, and when pressed to drink in the mess, always explained that there were too many drunks in his family already and he didn't want to get the taste. He had a crew of four Australians, an Englishman, and a Scot, and people talked about them as being close-knit, which was generally considered a good thing. Mutual trust—it was believed by everyone—saved seconds up there, especially the seconds that counted.

Callaghan's crew were also above average rank—some of them had been instructors, and their bombardier was on his second tour. Of this tour, they had flown more than twenty already. They had not shown any sign of suffering abnormal stress, at least in terms of stresses routinely borne in Bomber Command.

Their mutiny came at the end of their second Hamburg trip, one that had caused the squadron slightly more than average, but not astounding, casualties. It was a very quiet mutiny.

At debriefing they were one of many crews sitting around the trestle tables with their mugs of tea. Apparently they just told the intelligence officer, quite calmly, that they would not fly anymore. The intelligence officer argued with them for half an hour, and slowly men at other tables began to understand what was happening, mainly by observing the desperation of the intelligence officer who was trying to work on them individually, to separate the bombardier or the rear turret from the others, to break their solidarity.

At last, when the intelligence officer could find nothing else to do, the station commander was called in, a veteran Australian flier not so much older than Callaghan. He knew Callaghan, in fact, on first-name terms. This confrontation was acutely embarrassing to him.

Callaghan and his crew members went on insisting that they would not fly in pursuit of Bomber Command's present policies. They maintained this both when questioned separately and in a group. Now as always they showed a startling solidarity.

They were locked away, of course, before breakfast time that morning. That was how group headquarters wanted these things handled. Stricter isolation than for cholera.

No one ever fully knew the Callaghan crew's reasons for not flying. Crews that claimed acquaintance with them said they weren't scared, that they didn't lack moral fiber, although now they'd be accused of it. L.M.F. would be all over their files. Moral and social death. A casting forth from the tribe.

Those who claimed to know them said Callaghan and the others just didn't believe it was worth it anymore. They thought the losses were stupidity; they thought the bombing they were doing was stupidity. Such were the uneasy rumors, which nonetheless gave every member of the aircrew of every bomber some pause for thought. Men had to make new inner adjustments. Most decided to go on into further operations with their crews. And if some decided to die instead, perhaps without knowing they'd done so, you and they would not find that out yet, not for a night or two, anyway.

It was rumored too that group headquarters wanted a public humiliation for Callaghan's crew, and that the station commander was resisting. Public humiliation would require the pretense that Callaghan and his men had run out of courage, whereas the question nearly everyone was asking inside himself was whether or not in fact they were the most courageous on the station. Nonetheless a number of men, having slept fitfully since they got back from Hamburg and feeling the demands of their next mission beginning to rise, said publicly, "Why should Callaghan's crew be allowed to bow out at will?"

The station commander must have understood that a public event, a stripping of rank, would only make the bitterness and the internal question resound more sharply in the minds of everyone at Parsfield.

But group won the argument, of course.

At four o'clock on a tranquil midsummer afternoon, the entire station was paraded in front of the control tower. Only some thirty-six hours had passed since Callaghan and his men had signified their unwillingness to fly, but Bomber Command always moved quickly in these matters. Drawn up in a square on the asphalt were all the armorers, fitters, mechanics; all the provosts and cooks; all the meteorological, transportation, parachute, clerical, pay, and nursing WAAF's; all the medical staff; every one of what Challenor called the shiny-arses; and all the flight crews.

A highly polished squad of provosts, their boots clicking madly on the cement, marched Callaghan's crew out across the pavement. They all wore full uniform—a few of them carried on their left breast the ribbon of the Distinguished Flying Medal. They were lined up in the square created by the ranks of the station personnel and were faced toward the station commander and his senior officers, who all wore ceremonial swords. The adjutant read out a statement about their having shamed themselves and forfeited the trust of their station commander. They were to be reduced immediately by command of Air Vice-Marshal Cochrane, to the rank of aircraftsmen, pending a court-martial. Everyone on parade that afternoon knew what would happen at the court-martial. They would receive a prison sentence—rebellious flight crews received the stiffest terms, because their rebellions were considered the worst, the most infectious. Callaghan, the core of the abscess, might be shot.

Over some six or seven painful minutes the adjutant marched from one to another, ripping their wings off, their stripes, or the braid and badges of rank. Chevrons, wings, and fragments of cloth fell to the tarmac and blew lazily in the breeze. Callaghan's crew looked straight ahead and did not drop their gaze. Then they were marched off by a drummer, sounding a mocking, terrible tattoo. It was the only ceremonial music that Reardon would ever hear on Parsfield.

Wraith had been there, at the disgracing of Callaghan's crew, that day in late July, 1943, which everyone who lived remembered. Reardon wondered if it was from Callaghan that Wraith had become concerned over bombing, leading Otley to devise the curious scheme of posting maps to his Labor member of Parliament.

After every mission there was a grim but automatic ritual. When you woke toward noon, you went along to the beds of those who had not gotten back and took whatever the corpse detail did not need. The corpse detail was a number of reverent officers and NCO's who moved in and, in five minutes, expunged every trace of the missing airman in case his lingering ghost influence the remaining fliers. But first you—the survivors—got there and grabbed whatever the family might not ask for, such things as mothers and widows did not need: a pair of flying boots bartered from the Americans at a nearby field, a shirt, or an impressive kind of thermal underwear, something the Canadians were particularly proficient at.

One morning, when a crew that included a Canadian friend of Reardon's did not return, Reardon went to his locker down the corridor and plundered his striking red fireman's suspenders. They had seemed to Reardon to be an effective and—if one ever had to take one's jacket off in a woman's presence—spectacular form of waistband maintenance. And they always got a laugh if you took your coat off in a pub.

Wearing the suspenders nearly every day, Reardon still sometimes attended the Reverend Flight Lieutenant Wraith's Christian fellowship. At one of these the Reverend Wraith made a devotional sermon that he would have been chastised for had it not been for the fact that the station command, and Bomber Command itself, took the functions of the padre without much seriousness.

All people were the children of God. A simple proposition, but it meant that before you unleashed bombs on them, you had to consider that you had God's family in your sights. You had to ask yourself whether such a course of action would diminish or enhance the chance of God's will being accomplished through what you did.

Reardon told himself he still believed in what he was aoing, particularly in view of the long haul home from Essen, the outrageous struggle it had been just to save Challenor in the mid-upper and Punch in the cockpit. Yet he felt that Wraith was questioning him again, raising the question of acceptable casualties, of proper casualties. As if you could tell the difference when you were on the bombing run! But there was no doubt that in Wraith's world, somehow, a Christian should be able to do so. He didn't understand what twenty-year-olds like Reardon knew: in the frightful, freshly minted, and always self-enhancing world of bomber technology, the Christian concept of the justifiable target hardly made sense. You were drawn to one of two unthinkable propositions: either all war was equally wrong, even what they called "just war," or all war was equally justified.

Afterward the congregation prayed together, and then there were tea and biscuits. A young member of a flight crew did not easily bypass the chance of biscuits, so Reardon stayed. Also he was still fascinated by the question of Flight Sergeant Otley and his suicide, and the question of maps. He felt in an obscure way that the Reverend Wraith could somehow enlighten him.

Suddenly Reardon found himself amongst the last remaining. He had drunk four cups of tea, eaten at least half a pound of biscuits and he wanted to urinate. He saw Flight Lieutenant Wraith approach him.

"I wonder if I can speak to you outside, after we've cleared away the tea things. Would that be all right?"

Reardon agreed, though he hoped he was not about to be asked to be a substitute Otley.

Wraith approached him as he waited outside the hut, talking to a wireless operator who had flown only three missions and therefore did not suit Wraith's purpose.

"I wonder if I could go for a stroll with you, Flight Sergeant Reardon?" the distinguished churchman asked. The wireless operator excused himself. It was, in fact, the last Reardon would ever see of him, since he would not come back from his fourth operation.

They strolled around the perimeter. In the remnants of the day's light two squadrons of enormous aircraft—according to the daily press, the vengeance of the British, of those of Anglo-Celtic descent, against the Reich—could be seen parked on their separate pads of hardtop. There was no mission that night, although the flying weather was good. Both Reardon's squadron and the other one that shared the station had suffered a savage fortnight, and some wise counselor must have told the people who arranged these things that to make them fly again tonight would strain their morale and their nerves. It was rumored that the German fliers could not be permitted such latitude—they flew night upon night upon night. Only madness and death set a limit to their performance. The thought made Reardon even more delighted that he fought in a cause of righteousness in which people set a limit to suffering.

Wraith said as they walked, "Can I talk to you friend to friend, flight?"

"I hope so," said Reardon defensively, using an Australian mode of speech to protect himself from this serpentine English clergyman.

Wraith said, "Your squadron has had a hard time. I mean, the figures on the Essen raid . . . not that you didn't target in! You certainly targeted in. The photographic record shows as much."

Reardon said, though he knew it might be bad luck to say it, "Well, half our crews are old crews now—fifteen missions and over. They know what in God's name they're doing."

"Exactly," said Wraith. " 'In God's name.' I sometimes wonder what in God's name we *are* doing. Do you ever wonder that, Flight?"

"Listen, I have to be honest, Padre. When I'm over the target, I never ask myself a question like that. Not in the sense you mean it."

"Then what questions do you ask yourself?"

"You know what sort of questions, Padre."

"I don't. Stop calling me that ridiculous name. What questions do you ask yourself?"

"I ask myself if I'll ever have grandchildren. That's what question I ask. What sort of question—honestly—did you think I asked myself?"

"I wondered if you ever asked yourself whether this was the right way to fight a war."

"If we don't get them, they'll get us. I'm sorry Reverend, I don't mean it to sound like that. But it's the only thing you know over the target."

"But is the voice you get over the target a clear voice? Is there a higher wisdom and a higher concern there, in your mind, even though you stifle it? I don't know. I've never been there myself, but I wonder about you. About all the young!"

Reardon did not answer. Wraith continued. "I mean, isn't it true that you're given maps with a printed aiming point for your bombing raids, but then that bombardiers, let alone all the rest of the crew, are asked to *pencil in* another bombing point, which is generally—as far as anyone can tell—in the midst of some residential area occupied by ordinary workers? Is that so? And if it's so, does it worry you, Flight Sergeant Reardon? Or is it fine according to your lights?"

"A war is a war," said Reardon, sounding to himself almost peevishly defensive. "And the last I heard, they started it. They marched into Austria and the Rhineland, they took Czechoslovakia over. And then they hit Poland. Did they expect a bed of roses?"

"The question is, Reardon, was it the grandmothers and the grandfathers who did this? Was it the grandchildren, and the barely born? Did they march forth in their swaddling clothes? That's the question."

Reardon felt a helpless anger. "You fellows don't know what it's like there. All a person wants to do is get the bomb load away and come home. All a person wants to do is save Punchy and Challenor. That might be the way they train us, I don't know, but it's a fact. I want Punchy to be a grandfather, I want Challenor to be if he wants to."

"And I'll tell you what I want," said the Reverend Wraith. "I want all of us to fight an honorable war. But I want no slaughter of the innocents. And where they tell you crews to pencil in a cross, that's where the slaughter of the innocents begins. It's Herod who tells you to pencil in that cross, Reardon. I want you all to do what works best—to attack the U-boats, to bomb the oil fields. But it seems that most of the work our two squadrons do is attack the center of towns, and with considerable loss of our crews. Let me tell you why I'm speaking to you, let me be frank. I need a copy of the bombing maps for my bishop. He's a great opponent of the sort of mission you are being made to fly. I want a map with a cross printed on it at the supposed aiming point, and a penciled mark at the real aiming point. And if I can get such a map, it's quite likely that we can persuade or even *shame* the government into desisting from making you fly the sort of flights you do now. And if that were so, the casualties would be less and the chances of seeing old age for all those gentlemen you mentioned—was it Punchy and Challenor?—so much the better."

Reardon considered this. To him it stank of the truth. But he could not explain to Wraith how there was this higher truth, the truth of the bombing crew organically bonded for survival no matter what the circumstances, whether it be vacant air over the sea or flak-filled air over the land, over the cities of the Ruhr, or over the Baltic.

"I'm sorry," said Reardon. "I can't provide you with any maps."

"You obviously need to have one fall out of the pocket of your flying kit. Wherever you let that happen—either in the crew rooms or the mess—I'd be there to pick it up."

"I don't think so," said Reardon.

"I hope you understand, for dear God's sake, that I require these maps for the purest purposes. That I am in no sense an agent of the enemy. I am—if you wish—God's agent."

"It's no good," said Reardon, remembering that he'd given up something immensely more precious than a map for Punch and Challenor; remembering, that is, the chop girl. "It's no good. I can't give you a map."

"Will you at least respect my confidence?" asked Wraith.

"You mean, you're going to ask someone else from the flight crews for a map, and I'm not to say anything?"

"I'll relieve your conscience by not saying yes or no to that, Reardon. But if you change your mind, please contact me. A war unjustly won—if I can say that to one who endangers himself sometimes two or three nights a week—is not worth winning."

Reardon did not answer. But he did not consider Wraith a danger to the security of Bomber Command—or at least no more a danger than most of the other folk involved in keeping secret the target of this or that raid. Alf Hater's redheaded girlfriend from Parsfield had told them one afternoon, after sneaking into the station to visit Alf, that she had been waiting for a bus back to the village when one of the village women who worked in some fringe occupation on the station had turned to her and said, "A big one tonight. Over seven hundred bombers to Duisburg." This was barely before the flight crews had been briefed. Duisburg had indeed turned out to be the target, and more than seven hundred bombers had been dispatched, of which six hundred and fifty dropped bombs and six hundred and sixty returned. Whether the unauthorized knowledge the village woman took back to Parsfield had any influence on the losses suffered by the bomber command in the Duisburg raid, it was impossible to say. But it was unlikely. Parsfield never seemed a great arena of espionage. What Reardon knew with certainty, however, was that neither Wraith nor his bishop would use anything they discovered to diminish the chances of any of the crew.

In any case, whomever it was Wraith approached, they reported him to the station commander. Reardon did not see him taken away. But suddenly there was a less learned, a less serious-minded, a more childlike chaplain in his place. Reardon stopped going to fellowship. One day an air-force lawyer from the Judge Advocate's corps came to Parsfield and interviewed everyone who had been a member of the Reverend Flight Lieutenant Wraith's fellowship. Reardon knew enough simply to lie when asked if Wraith had ever approached him seeking information about bombing raids and maps.

With the passing of the Reverend Wraith and the death, capture, or passing on to training units of almost all those who might remember the rebellion of Callaghan's crew, all echoes of dissent vanished from the station at Parsfield. To have heard any dissent at all, you would have needed to enter the souls of the flight crew, or to hear in the hours after ops and debriefing their mid-morning nightmare cries.

20

Finding a Path to Nuremberg

THE last bombing raid of the first tour of Punch's crew was to Dusseldorf. Despite the flak over the Belgian coast and around the Ruhr, Reardon and Challenor saw no night fighters, and their Halifax returned to Parsfield almost routinely and intact.

Their photographs were taken in the mess after debriefing—numberless Canadian, Rhodesian, Czechoslovak, English, Scottish, Irish, New Zealand, Australian flight sergeants devoted to various disciplines of bombing excellence, lined up to touch them for luck. They were the ordinary fellows who had finished a tour. They were the ones who showed that there was a life beyond Parsfield. They had flown above that poisonous nexus of names—Hamburg, Dusseldorf, Duisburg, Essen—and lived. They had been to the Führer's city and unleashed incendiaries. Behind their success lay dozens of lost crews and forgotten names, and smooth, anxious faces from which the eyes would never again gaze on the sun, the faces of relatives or girls. They, Punch's crew, knew that they had no superior merit, yet in the mess they drank rounds to the best bloody pilot, the best bloody flight engineer, the best bloody bombardier, the best bloody navigator, the best bloody wireless operator, the best mid-upper, and the best rear turret the station had ever seen. For if you pretended it wasn't extraordinary talent that brought you through, then you undermined all the oncoming crews.

The next day they slept late and were summoned to the station commander's office.

"The first Lancasters are arriving tomorrow. I can offer you a fairly easy conversion routine followed by another tour of ops. Do you want to take it?"

It was the same competent, ancient, and youthful face that had announced Reardon's D.F.M. If you expected him to urge you to heights of imperial patriotism and loyalty to the Crown, or even in the direction of showing the Brits what you were made of, it didn't happen. He just left the question hanging—did they want to fly Lancasters or didn't they?

There was this, though: if they were brought back to ops after their six-months rest, they were likely to come back to a Halifax. Unless they took this chance.

Before anyone else had his answer ready, Punch said, "Well, I've got a wife and a child back in Melbourne, sir. I want to see them again, so I'm out."

"As you wish, Pilot Officer Punch," said the station commander. "Any others?"

It was a point at which you knew that Punch—even the station commander knew it—was the bravest since he had found the courage to go home. He had an investment in the future, and there was nothing further about himself, his competence or manhood that he needed to demonstrate. Flight crews were flooding in from Canada, more than Bomber Command knew what to do with, more than they had the planes for. They might never have to fly ops again. The station commander did not try to keep that fact from them.

For some reason he could never explain—maybe it had something to do with the experience he'd had with the chop girl—Reardon said, "I'll be in it. I believe they have Bolton Paul turrets."

"Yes," said the young station commander. "They've got Bolton Paul turrets."

"Okay," said Reardon, and that was all.

"Well, that's me in," said Challenor.

"And me," said Alf Hater.

Reardon had a sudden panic that he had started a rush in favor of the Lancasters.

"Any more?" said the station commander.

And so Reardon acquired—apart from Hater, Challenor, and himself—a new crew.

The training in the Lancaster was a delight. It was a bomber of such technical superiority that flying in it gave everyone a new and false sense of immortality—all this despite the fact they had seen Lancasters explode around them, including the terrible but not entirely rare destruction of a Lancaster by FIDO. Their new captain was a tall, young accountant from Melbourne named Happy Thompson. He, too, had been inveigled into a second tour by the promise of a Lancaster. He behaved a little less emotionally than Punch. He gave orders with a sharp intensity, but without the apparent emotionalism that had characterized Punch toward the end of the tour. You could not imagine Thompson, for example, attacking a crew member who had fallen for an unlucky girl.

In their new bomber they flew triangulation courses over Scotland, which gleamed in the sunshine. The great, awesome, dome-shaped mountains were a radiant violet in the autumn gloaming. You saw nothing except an occasional farmer's cottage or an army or air-force outpost.

Over the Irish sea Reardon and Challenor had their gunnery practice, shooting at drogues towed by real bombers—old Sterlings or Wellingtons retired from Bomber Command. Both Challenor and Reardon praised excessively the directness and mobility of the Lancaster's Bolton Paul turret, its sights, its one firing button instead of two.

Occasionally you would hear a gunner in the mess say, "Why don't they increase the bloody caliber?" for the ammunition in the Lancaster was still the .303, the bullet used in the front-line trenches in World War One and hardly worthy armament by comparison with the cannonry of the night fighters. But to balance the gunners' concern over caliber, there were rumors of extraordinary electronic developments, of squadrons that traveled in the bombing streams and carried with them a special radio operator to block the German transmissions to their own night fighters, to spread confusion, to send night fighters off to rendezvous in entirely wrong areas. Also, news passed from the squadron of Halifaxes still operating at Parsfield that briefing officers were actually promising spoof attacks. That is, a squadron or two of bombers using Window, or perhaps a few fast Mosquitoes, would peel off from the mainstream and create doubt amongst the German offenders about which target was the intended one. So you headed for, say, Oldenburg, then doglegged to bomb Hanover, but before you were over the target, a certain number of bombers had veered away to bomb Oldenburg itself and to divide and delude the night fighters and even the radar-predicted flak. Everyone felt, in their shining new Lancasters, that the great slaughters in the air were over and most of the problems solved.

Reardon could not understand why, amongst all the casualties, the two he most remembered and even grieved for were the Reverend Wraith and the now vanished chop girl. Perhaps it was because he had had no part in the other disappearances—in Cannon's, for instance, or in the vanishing of the Canadian whose red suspenders he still sometimes wore. Yet he could not shake a suspicion that he had helped the Reverend Wraith and the chop girl to their separate tragedies. Though who knew? If he ever finished another tour, he might go to Leconfield and see how she was—not try to court her, for he knew he'd sacrificed all right to that, but see how she was getting on, whether she was still tough and still had that sharp, ironic humor. That is, if Leconfield hadn't forced her to move somewhere else, made her carry her reputation for death-dealing farther and farther, to more and more remote fields.

Thompson's crew began flying operations again in mid-December. There were a few abortive briefings and then an attack on Berlin. No one was lost from the squadron, and for a day or so all the misconceptions about being invulnerable which they had built up during their training were confirmed.

They returned three times to the German capital in the next two weeks. Again Reardon was struck by the irony of destroying great European cities whose names had been so redolent of culture in the textbooks of his Australian childhood.

But after this first scot-free success, one night over Schweinfurt the Lancaster was coned by searchlights. A terrible blue-white incandescence filled the entire plane. By berserk corkscrewing, Thompson was able to wrench the Lancaster out of that sinister blaze of light. The crew discovered that the Germans were getting

more cunning too. Messerschmitt 109's now dropped flares above
the bomber stream and attacked the aircraft they saw by the un-
earthly luminescence. Often one group of fighters used the flares
from above to distract crews, and particularly rear gunners, from
the *unter von hinten* attack of others from the rear. Challenor was,
at least, credited with the shooting down of one of the flare-drop-
ping attackers. But the sky grew busier and busier, the rest hours
seemed shorter and shorter to Reardon, and there was really no
time at all for the species of question the Reverend Wraith used to
ask.

He could not have said he loved Challenor, the occupant of the
mid-upper turret and the brother for whom he was willing to
perish. He did not even know Challenor properly. Challenor was
tall and portly and what Mrs. Reardon would have called "a perfect gentleman." He had a vague belief in a deity who looked after
Australian boys, but didn't seem to live under any strict religious
precepts. Yet he was no chaser of the local girls. He never gave you
a sense, when you were on leave with him, that he was anxious
either to get drunk or to get to bed with someone. It was an
education, therefore, to Reardon—perhaps a far more passionate
young man—to see Challenor behaving in so civilized a way without the restraints of religion. For sometimes Reardon wondered
himself if, without his beliefs, he could be the decent fellow Challenor was.

By Christmas the decent fellow and Reardon had ten missions
of their second tour completed. They got leave for New Year and
decided to spend it in a flight-crew hostel in London. Reardon
found that he was drinking perhaps half as much again as his
capacity of a year ago. Many nights, despite his best resolve, he
found himself looking blearily across tables in pubs or restaurants
or late-night tea houses at girls with whom Challenor was in earnest conversation. Who are these women? he'd ask himself. How
do we all come to be here?

Or else he would find himself dancing with a stranger at the
Australian Comforts Fund dance hall near Leicester Square. And
again he wondered, Who is this girl and what do we have to say to
each other?

Reardon and Challenor went to a West End revue called *Victory Girls of '44,* but Reardon fell asleep during the final numbers. "You're a tired, poor little bugger, aren't you, Reardo?" asked Challenor. But Reardon denied it.

What he feared was that he was developing what his old man called, "the fatal Irish immunity to liquor!" Because in the mornings he was clear-headed and suffered no headache. Hangovers expressed themselves only in a faint though piercing morning sadness, which was soon done away with by a rowdy breakfast downstairs in the hostel. On one or two mornings various other Australians on leave would call out, "Go home with that brunette last night, Challenor?" Challenor would look staid, and Reardon would grope back to remote memories of himself being helped home alone by some chattering and motherly London girl, who would deliver him chastely, after a hearty sisterly kiss, at the hostel door.

Reardon felt a little jealousy. "I wish Alf were here," he said without meaning to one morning when they were waiting for a tube at Aldwych to take them to the Tower of London.

"You won't lever Alf away from that redhead in Parsfield," said Challenor.

Reardon thought—knowing he was prudish about it, not pleased with himself for thinking it—that Alf would have been better off in the flight-crew hostel in London than sitting around the redhead's kitchen table, making conversation with Mrs. Redhead senior and her stolid farm-worker husband.

On their last day of leave they were walking along the Strand toward Australia House, to collect any mail that might have arrived for them, when they heard a cry behind them. "Reardon, you son of a bitch, where are my goddamn red suspenders?"

They turned to discover the missing Canadian fleshed out in front of them. He looked a little thin and pale, but was otherwise the same man. Later they would confess to each other that they'd forgotten his name, but that didn't matter.

"Didn't they tell you?" Reardon asked. "I've been keeping them safe for you back at Parsfield! Thought you might be back for them."

But he wondered if he might not burst out weeping and embarrass the lot of them.

They took the Canadian straight to a pub. There were parts of his story he was not permitted to tell, he said. He had jumped out of the hatch of his plummeting Halifax and had come down in a garden on the outskirts of Liege. Very soon, because the householder knew who should be contacted, he found himself protected by a cell of the Belgian resistance. There was a beautiful, young, blond communist, who would have given Karl Marx a turn or two. He was a month with her and her colleagues. He was always in somebody's attic or somebody else's cellar. But then they started moving him along the escape route with faked papers. Sure, he'd had his little perspex escape kit with him in his flying boots when he left the plane, but they'd been torn off by the wind. The resistance cell set him up with everything, anyhow, much better than the escape-kit stuff. He got papers and clothes, and in the end he was ready to travel. He'd caught a train to Paris and then south and so on. Over the hills into Spain and then by train to Portugal. Long waits, of course. For example, he'd had to wait two weeks in a southern French city he wouldn't name, and meanwhile he was being moved around. But you got out in the end, if you were just patient. Easy as pie.

They spent the rest of the day with this pared-down but calm young man. It was such a tonic for both of them to have met a man who had walked and ridden his way out of the inferno. They were as exhilarated by his story as by their early flights in the Lancaster, and though they knew it might not last them too long, they were grateful for the influence it had on them, as they were about to return to Parsfield.

The Canadian, as an escapee, had a longer leave than they and could even be seriously considered for return to an Operational Training Unit. He had his salvation in his hands. And that's why they drank with him and feasted on him all day. And he, having had a harder journey than he wished to admit, feasted on them, too, for during the period he'd been hiding and running, they had been in business. They had been to Berlin many times while he endured the slow pace of days in cellars.

Later, therefore, urinating in the hotel gents' room, they struck Reardon as being like the three poles of a tepee. They kept each other up.

And it was just as well. From mid-January onward, over a

period of six weeks, the Parsfield station lost the equivalent of a whole squadron of bombers, and the news was that the figures were even worse in other places. You saw that most of the deaths were kids with less than twelve missions. But it did not mean that anyone was immune. The station commander himself died over Leipzig late in January—that composed, twenty-eight-year-old Australian who had broken to Reardon the news of his D.F.M. And though the long nights enabled the bombers to penetrate Germany deeply, they also exposed them longer to attack from above and below. And bombing results were not perfect every time. Berlin showed up very badly on the H2S radar screen, and even the Pathfinders could not always accurately drop their flares to mark the target for the bomber stream. Yet fortunately, as if it were a gift from the Canadian with the red suspenders or from some other source, Reardon went through a period of certainty that lasted him until the end of March. It was a strange, contradictory, and, he thought, mad thing, a chimera for which he might have to pay later. There were no grounds for it. The German night fighters were meeting the bomber stream halfway over the Channel, were pursuing it all the way into Germany and all the way out again. There was no night you did not have to corkscrew, and the bomber was coned by searchlights twice in a week. Yet on the last great raid of that series of Berlin, the worst one of all that March, Reardon was credited with the destruction of a Focke-Wulf fighter falling on them from above.

For Reardon the charmed existence broke on the last night of March 1944. It had been a cold day, with heavy overcast. But in the late afternoon a strong wind began blowing, against everyone's wishes. Suddenly the sky was clear, with just a few streaky clouds which dropped a few icy showers across the Parsfield base.

There was a lot of talk in the mess at lunchtime that operations would be impossible that night. The moon would be what Alf Hater called, "just shy of full." Nonetheless, gasoline trucks had begun to roll around the perimeter, fueling bombers. The young truck drivers, many of them WAAF's, had what was called "the poop from group," the orders for that night. It was maximum-fuel load. Two thousand one hundred fifty gallons of fuel meant a long leg. And incredibly, with such a bright moon coming up, a long leg was intended. The news was also that all the bombers that hadn't flown last night because of weather—when already briefed for a raid against Brunswick—would go out too. So were they all to go to Brunswick tonight? The sight of ground crews spraying the Lancasters with anti-freeze every hour produced a kind of nausea in Reardon.

At a quarter past four, a little before dark, the station commander of Parsfield, a freshly appointed Australian veteran, entered the briefing room accompanied by his two squadron commanders. The commander of Reardon's squadron, a man of the unreachable age of twenty-six, a man from Western Australia as well—a state of the Commonwealth of Australia that had relevance to the Reardon family myth—rose on the platform and dragged the curtains back from the map. Picking up a schoolmasterly cane, he pointed at the map of Germany. He called them gentlemen and told them the target for that night was Nuremberg, the center of Nazi mythology.

It was a wonderful statement in morale terms. For some reason it terrified Reardon. Did a myth need 2150 gallons of fuel, did it need a four-thousand-pound cookie and assorted incendiaries?

This briefing officer from Western Australia indicated the assembly point in the North Sea thirty miles from the Belgian coast. They were to head in past the flak of Ghent and Brussels, then make a dogleg into the Cologne corridor between the defenses of Bonn and Coblenz. And then, to the north of Schweinfurt, to head south in over Nuremberg. There would be a number of spoof raids, one on Aachen, another on Cologne, another on Kassel. Aircraft would peel out of the mainstream all the way along, even east of the Rhine, confusing the defense. Two hundred thousand industrial workers lived in Nuremberg, said the briefing officer, and also, he repeated, it was the symbolic center of Nazism, where Albert Speer had built the architecture against which Hitler had postured throughout the thirties, uttering threats to the world. To the south of the aiming point, right on the bombers' track, lay the M.A.N. tank company, two Siemens electrical factories, and some marshalling yards. The aiming point was to be one of the electrical factories and a square on one of the railway yards. The briefing officer mentioned that the Altstadt—the old town north of the aiming point—was full of ancient buildings that would burn easily.

Everyone who had any experience knew that the corridor between the Ruhr and Frankfurt, through which the bombers were intended to pass, lay on an interception track with many night-fighter fields and two German radio towers the German fighters used to rendezvous on.

At last the meteorological officer came forward. He told them that on the long leg into Germany, before they turned for Nuremberg, there would be clouds at the operational height of nineteen thousand feet. But the target would be clear. It seemed such a perfect diagnosis of what a bomber crew would need on such a night that people began to clap slowly and catcall, disbelieving the weatherman.

At eight o'clock a bus took Thompson's crew and a number of others out to their parked Lancasters. They crawled through their aircraft, chatted to fitters, armorers, and riggers, and in Challenor's and Reardon's case made sure that their perspex was clean. The sky would be crowded enough tonight without mistaking an oil smear for a fighter. Then they all climbed out again onto the pavement—it wasn't one of those nights when you were tempted to go off onto the grass and loll about on it. A number of them urinated against the back wheel. This was a standard good-luck ritual.

Alf Hater predicted that before takeoff a red Very flare would be shot from the control tower, indicating that the operation had been scrubbed. Then there would be a bus into Parsfield and he would see his redhead.

In fact the flare they saw was green, arcing up under the three-quarter moon.

"All on board the Mallee express," said Thommo, calmly reeling off the names of country towns in Australia. "Putting in at Ballarat, Ararat, Stawell, Warracknabeal, and Patchewollock."

"That's the bloody funniest thing you've ever said," said Alf Hater. As indeed it was; an omen for a remarkable night.

They had a slow climb to twelve thousand feet, before crossing the Suffolk coast. Over the sea their oxygen was turned on. Reardon and Challenor tested their guns in two-second bursts. As they approached the assembly point, navigation lights were used because of the risk of a grotesque and futile collision. Yet they saw no one there, over the North Sea. It was axiomatic you did not see the plane you collided with, so they did not get much reassurance from the apparent emptiness of the sky. In theory they were in the second wave, and around them were Pathfinders that would mark the target for them if the other markers had burned out or blown away. There were also, somewhere in the apparent vacancy, a number of ABC Lancasters whose job it was to jam the German radio transmissions to their fighters. That is, supposedly one hundred fifty bombers shared the immediate sky with them. There was very little of the high cloud cover promised by the meteorological officer. It was a still, bright night, the moon high up to the north and shining on Reardon's turret as he swung it in its arc.

The bombardier from his observation post reported flak coming up from Ghent, but it did not trouble them. Yet still there was no cloud. Perhaps it would move in at their next turning point, southwest of Liège. Every half hour Alf Hater received news from base of a wind shift. Yet each report varied wildly from the one before it. A wind of 50 miles per hour and 300 degrees on the compass, a wind of 280 miles per hour from 208 degrees on the compass! The navigator began cursing over the intercom.

Seconds after the navigator announced the German frontier, Reardon saw a fighter appear below him. He gave the appropriate corkscrew orders. Fifteen minutes later another appeared. As Thommo dived, Reardon saw flashes to his right and his rear, great gouts of red flame which he knew not to be scarecrow shells but exploding Halifaxes and Lancasters. He reported them to Thommo.

"Holy shit!" he heard Challenor say reverently, and there were reports from the bombardier of aircraft exploding below them.

Thommo said, "Think we ought to get out of this bomber stream, don't you, fellows? They're really on to the poor bloody stream. Nav, give me a course to the south."

"That'll run us into bloody Frankfurt, skip!"

"Can't be as bad as bloody this. Give me a course."

Though they did not know it, a malign shift of wind had driven them to the north in any case, had driven most of the bomber stream, so that they had met whole groups of German fighters circling and in cozy contact with, a radio beacon called Ida, which accounted for the slaughter going on all around them. Thommo, by some instinct turning them starboard, took them safely between beacon Ida and beacon Otto, between the Ruhr and Frankfurt.

The relief from attack was merely temporary. Reardon saw a Lancaster astern and above him. It may have been only half a mile away. A fighter whose make Reardon could not quite discern attacked this Lancaster again and again from astern. It took no corkscrew action at all. The gunner is dead, Reardon thought. Maybe they're all dead. The bomber passed away to port, still flying levelly, still pursued by the tracer of the night fighter. Two minutes later a twin-engined night fighter appeared beneath the Lancaster, firing tracer upward. Reardon was tempted to fire his own guns, if for mere relief. But he knew that he was beyond range, and that to fire might draw attack onto *them*. Besides, he was aware of Challenor's similar and parallel restraint in the mid-upper turret.

Closer into the next turning point, Reardon saw a Lancaster below and astern to his left hit by tracer. A burning stream of gasoline rolled back from its engines. As men bailed out of the escape hatch and opened their parachutes, the streamer of flame touched each silk canopy with terrible accuracy. The men fell briefly under a blossom of flame and then merged with the lower darkness. This is appalling, Reardon told himself. This is extreme, beyond the limit. There was no safe path back through France and Spain and Portugal for those hit by the banner of flame. The bundles of Window, foil strips the bombardier dropped through the hatch at the rate of one a minute, were clearly no protection that night.

They turned in toward Nuremberg. Reardon could hear them arguing up front. There were two contradictory sets of target markers ahead, but the navigator wasn't happy with the image he got on H2S from the more obvious of the two plantings. It couldn't be Nuremberg, he said. The time was already twenty past one, ten minutes later than they should have been bombing. There were cries from the navigator such as, "We've been buggered up by the wind and the turn to starboard!" And then Reardon heard through the intercom that more flares began to fall on the up-till-now lesser marked of the two targets. The navigator directed Thommo to the starboard. He grew excited when he got a good image of Nuremberg on H2S. "This is it! This is it!" he cried.

They got their bombs away at last. Yet all the way back their path was surrounded by attackers. At Reardon's command they veered away from terrible white tracer, corkscrewing ceaselessly. No chop girl to blame tonight, Reardon thought as he tried not to puke in his oxygen mask. They caught flak over Belgium and were torn across the sky. Even out over the sea the flak did not relent. And though they were able to fly on all the way to Parsfield untouched, they knew that terrible things had happened that night, that the German fighters had bettered them, that the weathermen had lied or been stupid, that the Command had been benighted. Reardon, by his response to earlier challenges such as the Reverend Wraith and the chop girl, had already backed the Command, so where did that leave him?

The next day the crews that cleaned out the effects of missing fliers were busy around Parsfield. Visits Reardon made to the photographic hut showed that many of the squadron's bombers had attacked the town of Lauf to the east of Nuremberg. The two sets of markers had accounted for that, and the fact that Lauf, though much smaller, looked on the H2S screen like a model of Nuremberg itself. Other bombers had stumbled on to Schweinfurt, again a town like Nuremberg when seen on an H2S screen. This was such a ridiculous thing to do, and the shame of it hung over everyone. The afternoon in the mess was a chastening affair. One sixth of the squadron were missing, and Thompson's crew was one of the few who had dropped their bombs anywhere near the aiming point.

After Nuremberg Reardon shifted psychological gear again. He lived two existences and was aware that everyone around him, even Challenor, was doing the same. There was the public, confident, battle-hardened, riotous-in-the-mess person, and then the other man, the one who sat up in his sleep in the middle of the night for no reason. The one also whom Reardon heard whimpering in one of the three other cots in the room he shared at Parsfield. Did Challenor, the Quorn bank teller, whimper? Reardon wondered, for the cries were in no voice he recognized. Reardon saw himself and Challenor and Alf as permanent warriors. And for such beings there were only two equally unimaginable outcomes—extinction or a final peace more remote than the next century.

For weeks *The Yorkshire Post* and the London dailies, when they at last reached Parsfield, had been boasting of the damage the American Strategic Air Forces had been inflicting on the German aircraft industry in Regensburg and Augsburg. And there were stories of a new wonder plane, the Mustang, which accompanied the American bomber streams.

All at once, in the month following Nuremberg, it occurred to Reardon that the sky was not as complicated. You still kept the two existences, since you knew nothing was settled yet. You followed the Pathfinders in to various railway junctions in the Region Nord and dropped your four thousand pounders, and by early June the bomb bays had been adapted to take eight thousand pounders. Somewhere in Bomber Command there were Lancaster bomb bays adapted to carry twelve thousand pounders called Tallboys.

On an unpromising night in early June the Parsfield Lancasters and Halifaxes took off and bombed coastal batteries, already marked with burning red and green flares, on the coastline of Normandy. As Thommo swung the bomber back toward Britain in the pearly, post-storm first light, Reardon heard promises over the intercom from those forward that he would soon find himself floating above thousands of ships. All at once they were there, below his open turret, below his frozen face. An extraordinary fleet making for France. Behind his oxygen mask, through his clenched jaws, he laughed stiffly.

Later that day, after Thommo had landed them back at Parsfield, they got a message that the station commander wanted to see them all at three. When they got to his office after a fitful morning's rest, he made a speech about how there were lots of aircrew coming out of Canada now, or flooding in from the Operational Training Units. More than they had bombers for.

"Everyone wants to be a flying hero," said the station commander, a young Queenslander, laughing. (When it came to flight crew, the whole station was almost exclusively antipodean.) It seems, he said, that their fellow countryman, Air Vice-Marshal Bennett, was looking for experienced personnel for his Pathfinder Group. "It doesn't include you, Thommo. It's across to Canada for you."

Bennett particularly wanted bombardiers, wireless operators, gunners. "By and large, you'll get to the target first, and you're given a silver eagle to wear under your lapel. That's about it. Let me know what you think."

By nightfall Alf, Challenor, and Reardon had all, independently of each other, volunteered. In Reardon's case it was almost that the other two would anyhow, and then he'd find himself alone. That was it—they didn't have the energy left to work their way into a new crew unless it was an elite one, one certified by Air Vice-Marshal Bennett as full of skills and the gift for coming back from Europe.

21

Parramatta, Newhaven, and Wanganui

THEY found the Pathfinder squadron they were intended for on the edge of the village of Starkley, in the marshlands east of the beautiful old town of Huntingdon. When Alf and Challenor and Reardon arrived there by truck one rainy afternoon in midsummer, the air station didn't seem very different from what they had left behind at Parsfield. But the barracks were less transient than the Nissen huts of Parsfield, solid brick, with modern plumbing. At Parsfield the high-altitude cold which would pursue you all the way to Germany and back, seemed still to be there, nuzzling at your cheeks, as you slept. At Starkley you got a sense of thawing out.

In the sergeants' mess the silverware was good, the bar stewards crisp and attentive. The tables were full of newly arrived flight sergeants from all over Bomber Command, as well as from the Middle East, and there were former instructors from training units in Canada.

Someone said, "We're here to replace those who got the chop at Nuremberg."

And someone else said, "And not only them. But blokes, too, who made navigational mistakes or dropped their markers wrong

or were fringe merchants. The group commander's not very tol-
erant of imperfection, I believe."

In Pathfinder Group, it seemed, "fringe merchants" were those
who did not make it all the way to the aiming point, but dropped
their target indicators early.

Reardon was resting after lunch in their new and superbly
comfortable room when he was aroused from shallow sleep by
Challenor.

"Do you know, we've got a flight lieutenant for a skipper and a
bloody squadron leader for a navigator. Our plane's called D for
bloody Dog."

Evening gunnery class: a turret had been set up in a hangar,
and a gunnery officer operated a rude control panel that sent
models of the usual German night fighters swinging toward you.
The idea here in Pathfinders, said the gunnery officer, was to
shoot ahead of the path of the plane, instead of filling your sights
with it. You judged the thing's make and distance, and according
to that you shot ahead, or "laid off" a certain number of the sight
hairlines—radii or "rads." You pressed the firing button and called
out to the officer, as the fighter drew up on the turret, the number
of rads you were laying off. This was, said the gunnery officer, a
method invented by the group commander himself, Air Vice-
Marshal Don Bennett, a regular with enormous experience in all
areas of operations. "Few people know him, let alone like him,"
said the gunnery officer. "But every bastard's in awe of him."

Over dinner that night Alf Hater announced he was being
taught a method of radio transmission devised by Bennett. The
bombardiers said the same thing, and the navigators were studying the principles laid down in the textbook Bennett had written.

"And he's not as old as most of those senior buggers," said Alf.
"He's about thirty-three, which is bloody old but not absolutely
bloody old. And he's flown ops in this war, not in the War of the
bloody Roses. He was shot down in Norway a few years ago,
bombing the bloody *Tirpitz*. After which he walked across the
mountains into Sweden. I mean, he knows what blokes go
through."

A Canadian murmured, "Don't get excited. Friend of mine says
he pisses iron ingots."

"Another thing," said Alf, "we all get an upgrade in rank if they
like the look of us. It's automatic."

The increased pay and new rank had been an important consideration for Alf, given his belief in an Australian future graced by the Parsfield redhead. Reardon hoped that she would visit Alf now and then—it wasn't so hard once you got to York to catch the train down to Peterborough, where she and Alf could spend leaves away from Starkley.

Reardon, Challenor, and the others performed Air Vice-Marshal Bennett's gunnery exercises for another two days. After breakfast on the third day they took off for the first time with Winton, the Kentish journalist. It was a training flight to let Squadron Leader Stove test out his H2S set on Sheffield. The bombardier released imaginary incendiaries over the city. All procedures were calmly performed. Reardon had a real sense of belonging to an elite force.

That evening the legendary Bennett came all the way from Huntingdon to address the newcomers. In directness of manner he reminded Reardon of the famous cricketer, Don Bradman, an Australian national icon and wondrous being. And although Bennett was visibly young, he seemed immensely senior.

"The Pathfinder tour is forty-five operations," he said in a level voice, "but this includes any flown with another squadron before joining our group. So some of you have already reached that number. If you wish, you can go straight on, and in that case an extra fifteen operations with us count as a second tour, and you will be considered a fully paid-up hero and be free to abandon this exciting and highly technical life. You will be permitted, once you have flown on one of our operations, to wear the silver eagle on your lapel, and though that will give you glory amongst men, it is *our* eagle and becomes permanently yours only after you have finished your tour. If you fail us, if you fail the bomber stream, if you are a fringe merchant, you will never keep your eagle and you will be spat forth from the group."

Looking at him, his galvanic seriousness, you did not doubt for a second that you had only one chance to perform. This certainly bred a tremendous radiant excitement in the room. They all felt fortunate to have been chosen.

"There will be no Victoria Crosses awarded to any living member of Pathfinder Group," said Bennett. "This is not to be considered an encouragement to seek death."

The newcomers laughed, but Bennett didn't.

"Prior to your promotion," said the Air Vice-Marshal, "you will be personally interviewed by me."

"Shit!" murmured Alf Hater. "They didn't tell us that."

Winton's crew flew together for the first time on a raid to the outskirts of the Norman city of Caen, which was under attack from Montgomery's army. They found their way in, after a short leg across the Channel, to a target brightly lit by the Mosquito Illuminator flares they shared Starkley station with. Around the flares of the Illuminators they dropped their Visual Markers, red and green, and the eight thousand pounds of bombs they carried as well—the incendiaries, that is, and the four-thousand-pound cookie. Reardon did not see a night fighter.

Most of Bomber Command had to pass beyond four degrees east longitude to complete an operation. But because of the special skills Pathfinder Group had to use marking the target, this short raid on Normandy constituted one full operation. Winton's crew, returned to Starkley in the small hours, and sipping their tea laced with rum, were delighted with the arrangement.

And as Bennett had invented all Pathfinders techniques, he had also invented the target-making system. If the target was clear, the Mosquitoes dropped the Illuminators to light the aiming point, and the Lancasters, using H2S radar, dropped target indicators of whatever color, under the leadership and orders of a Pathfinder Master Bomber who circled the target throughout. This clear marking method was known as Newhaven.

The bomber crews, whether using Newhaven or some other method, were Visual Markers and Centerers—that is, they either marked the aiming point or else dropped corrective centering flares in mid-raid if the first flares burned out or the bombing had not been accurate. The more experienced of them sometimes had to stay in the area a long time—to re-mark, if necessary, for successive waves of bombers. Sometimes Pathfinder bombers were directed to go in with a particular wave, to re-mark the aiming point for them, but most of the time you were over the target early and stayed longer than others.

When there was a haze or fog or low clouds, the Illuminators could not guide anyone into the target, and so the aiming point had to be marked entirely by H2S. Some cities, as the Nuremberg raid had shown, had a better H2S image than others. Mistakes were plentiful and were not forgiven. This method for haze and patchy clouds was called Parramatta—after Bennett's birthplace, it was said, west of Sydney.

The most difficult method of all was the one devised for thick clouds. It was called Wanganui and meant finding the target by using H2S and then marking the clouds above it with sky markers—flares attached to parachutes. The individual Pathfinder crew could be ordered in twice or three times to replace flares which, H2S showed, had been blown off the target. They did so at the command of the Master Bomber, the controller in one of the Lancasters or else in a Mosquito, who gave orders to the entire bomber stream, to hundreds of aircraft. If his navigator told him that the red flares had been blown aside, then he would order some of his Pathfinder deputies in to replace them with green, and announce curtly, "Bomb the green, bomb the green!" Or else he would order yellow. He was the only one in all that sky who was permitted to break radio silence.

On most nights during a fairly rainy August, a summer of storms across Europe, Wanganui had to be used. Winton's crew came in with the second or third wave and backed up the sky marking, hundreds of candlepower supported by silk, following the orders of the Master Bomber, the master of ceremonies. This officer was sometimes a man of composure like Winton, and other times a man of passion like Punch, and used profanities which shocked the more staid boys from the congregations of Saskatchewan, from the chapels of the north island of New Zealand, or from the reverent valleys of Wales.

Reardon suspected the weather often made the difference between the tone of one Master Bomber and the next. The Mosquito captains, flying sometimes only a thousand or so feet above the target—and closest, therefore, to the inferno, buffeted by it, in fact—frequently sounded the calmest, the most commanding. Everyone—Winton, the scholarly and exacting Stove, and Reardon himself—knew that somewhere in one of the darker corners of the night, skimming the thick arcs of searchlight that rose through the clouds, skipping amongst the light flak, taking his notes, preparing his report, was Bennett, flying his own Mosquito.

His occupational hazard, like that of his bomber crews, was being hit by the bomb loads from above. Rear gunners were susceptible. There were times you saw a Lancaster land entirely without its turret, the hydraulic pipes and ammunition belts sticking out like veins protruding from a torn-off organ.

One night, over the besieged German garrison in Le Havre, a stick of incendiaries struck a Starkley Pathfinder Lancaster diagonally—from the tail, across the fuselage, to the port engines. Briefly and luxuriantly it blazed until its own bomb load and incendiaries tore it apart in molten red and dazzling green.

22

Masters in Israel

AN Epistle for the mass recited fast at Quinquagesima Sunday by Father Murphy, famous verses she had heard before but without particularly listening, now haunted her. As Murphy had rattled through them in Latin, she had read them in her missal in English. They were the verses that began, "*Si linguis hominum loquar, et angelorum* ..." "If I speak with the tongues of men and angels, and have not charity, then I have become like sounding brass and tinkling cymbals. . . ."

It had become the question of her life: was it possible to have charity inside the Sisters of Compassion? "And if I distribute all my resources in food for the poor, and if I offer up my body even unto the flames but have not charity, it will profit me nothing. . . ."

These word were the greatest challenge Perpetua could have imagined to the life of a Sister of Compassion. Charity had been drained from her by the Chapter of Faults, by the malice of Brendan. Who had taken the charity out of Francis, who brushed her teeth three times one way for One Person of the Holy Trinity, three ways the other for Another, yet was willing to gossip about Mrs. Lacey?

Was it enough to live without charity as an offering for her brother's life? If anything happened to Bernard, she knew, her parents would fall away into a bitter and bewildered old age. Was that enough justification for her to go on giving out the mercies of nursing and to go on living inside the order? Did Francis and others really have a form of charity which she couldn't see because of her own imperfection? Again it was the old question that she could not reasonably answer for herself. She wished someone would explain away for her Francis's apparent ill-feeling.

One night during her quarter of an hour's spiritual direction from Father Murphy, when she had raised this question yet again, he got brusque with her. "For sweet Jesus' sake, for His Blessed Mother's, don't expect everyone to be more perfect than people outside. The more I stay in the priesthood, the more I understand that we're just ordinary people. Nuns, priests, brothers. We can put on the garments of perfection, but it doesn't make us perfect!"

"Why go to the trouble, then?" Perpetua fought back. "Why put yourself through the hoops if you can't get a little further that way? Besides, we're all prepared to accept the respect of ordinary people who think we're looking for a sort of perfection. What's the sense of poverty, chastity, and obedience if it gets you nowhere and simply bamboozles the lay people?"

Murphy laughed, and it turned into a groan. "Fair enough, Perpetua. And the question does you credit."

"I don't want credit, Father Murphy. I fear I'm going mad looking for an answer."

"Look, I know it plays on your mind. But you have to stop worrying about it. I would say that for a good nun it's probably painful finding out the sad truth that everyone finds out in the end—that the only one you can trust, straight out, no questions, is God. If we could trust each other, we wouldn't need Him. We could just go away and open a bank or a pub."

For Perpetua there was a temporary comfort in what Murphy said. Murphy was an enormously, almost an outrageously sane priest. That was because he looked for a minimum of perfection. So his weakness seemed to be a kind of strength, even the confession inherent in his statement, "The longer I stay in the priesthood . . .", the idea that he perhaps sometimes thought of not staying! Even that seemed like a sort of vigor. She hoped it was not just some sort of trick he was pulling.

*   *   *

After breakfast one morning Mother Felice called her aside in the corridor. It was excellent news.

"Perpetua, I want you to go to the railway with Sister Calixta at eleven o'clock this morning and meet Sister Timothy, who is on the so-called express from Sydney. You'd have been going now except that the train is, as usual, more than two hours late. The war, you understand, and the coming and going of American troops! I suppose you know Timothy, do you?"

"We were in the novitiate together," Perpetua said, trying to control her smile. "And we were at St. Bridie's until I came here."

"Mother Fredericka thinks her country style might be more suited to a country hospital," said Felice, and smiled.

Perpetua understood that of course Felice knew she and Timothy were friends. She was granting Perpetua an excursion. Perpetua had a daughterly impulse to kiss her for this small act of motherly feeling. It was as if she'd proven she had earned the title Mother, with its capital M.

Timothy would be an ally. She knew how to laugh at the Chapter of Faults.

"You will walk to the station," said Felice, "but Sister Calixta will be given money for you to catch a taxi back to St. John Vianney's."

At ten to eleven Perpetua met Calixta at the gate that led through the garden and into the main wards of the hospital. Calixta seemed genial.

"Ready for a stroll through town, Sister?" she asked.

"Definitely, Calixta," said Perpetua. She would not be embarrassed by the earnest nods and bows of Catholic mothers and shopkeepers, as she would have been a week before.

They walked down the hill and turned left into the main street of Rossclare. There was some activity on the street, even though the normal shopping day for Rossclare, as for all country towns, was Friday. A certain number of leathery farmers, in town to see lawyers or stock and station agents about cattle or boundary disputes, chatted on the corners. Young mothers were carrying or towing children and wearing that slightly stricken young-mother look as they peered at merchandise in the windows and made mouths at the prices. There, thought Perpetua: that's the face of womanhood. They're worrying about whooping cough and making the money last, instead of perfection, but they're as vexed as I am.

She loved them. She would have liked to put money in their hands. Perhaps that's what lies behind anyone's desire to be a nun, she thought—the wish to be that ancient figure, the good fairy.

Perpetua and Calixta, supposedly keeping "custody of the eyes," as the Rule prescribed, managed to inspect every face, even the faces of the town worthies—O'Sullivan, the whiskified lawyer who had declared himself an atheist but whose wife went to Mass, and Aldridge, the owner/editor of the Rossclare *Chronicle*.

The Catholics nodded or raised their hats as the nuns went past. The nuns at her school had always told Perpetua that you could spot Catholics in a crowd by the light of sanctifying grace in their eyes. Perpetua thought it was something else, an indefinable Irishness—a kind of reddishness in some, a darkness of complexion and melancholy in others, a distinctive Celtic beauty in the young girls, a rakishness of manner in the men. All of them outrageously Australian but representing something else, the oppressed, boozy, whimsical, song-ridden masses of the Irish peasantry.

They passed Rendall's with its windows full of Northern Rivers high fashion. They passed Mr. Brosnan's cinema. Perpetua remembered painlessly this morning how crazy Brendan had blamed the decline of morals on the films, on the homely movie theaters of such as Brosnan.

At last they reached Dignan's Railway Hotel, turned right, and found themselves on the high platform of Rossclare station. Some of Rossclare's best families were waiting there for their children to return from boarding school in Sydney or Grafton or Armidale for the Christmas holidays. Australian soldiers from the valley, some of them with yellowed skin—the giveaway sign of having served in New Guinea or the islands—waited with their knapsacks. They talked quietly to mothers and wives.

Here Calixta, surrounded by fellow humans, was calmer and chatted knowledgeably to Perpetua about the war. She, too, must have borrowed a few newspapers from patients.

Perpetua remembered a sentence from Thomas à Kempis's *Imitation of Christ*. The monk Kempis had been a fifteenth-century mystic. Perpetua remembered, too, a horrifying story the nuns of her childhood had told her of the man. That the Vatican had thought of canonizing him, making him officially a saint, and so his remains had been exhumed from the Dutch soil. The officials appointed by the Vatican discovered that he had been buried alive—there were scratches on the inner side of his coffin lid where he had tried to claw his way out of the grave. Did these scratches mean that he had despaired at the last, had cursed God? Because they might have, Thomas was never made a saint. But that sentence of his which Perpetua remembered, which in fact he had borrowed from the Roman Emperor Marcus Aurelius, was: "As often as I go amongst humans, I come away less a human." Yet the opposite seemed to be true of Calixta. She seemed to expand in the crowded station's sunlight.

When the train came in, all its doors stood open and from them hung gum-chewing young Americans, looking at this new town in the endless trip north with a frank boredom.

Before the train stopped, hundreds of Americans had already jumped onto the platform and begun prowling, as if this little strip of concrete and gravel might yet offer them something. They crushed into the Refreshment Room, past its frosted-glass doors, where pies and tea could be had.

Timothy got down from the sleeping car. Sleeping berths were very scarce these days, reserved for government officials and generals. But Sisters of Compassion obviously had good friends in the New South Wales Government Railway.

Her face was full of the joy of travel. "Never traveled in a sleeper before," she said, taking hold of Perpetua by the elbows and giving her a robust kiss on the cheek. "It's so flash!"

Even Calixta laughed. It was impossible not to enjoy her childlike excitement.

"Listen, Perpetua, didn't you show them in the exams! A fair dinkum genius. I just scraped in myself. The examiners warned me to improve my spelling."

A number of young men, some of them Australian soldiers from the train, offered reverentially to carry Timothy's bags.

"God bless you, boys," she yelled at them as they struggled down the station steps to the waiting taxis.

"Well, Mother Fredericka got fed up with me at last," she said when the baggage carriers had saluted and left. "Because I've been chatting too much with patients and stealing their newspapers, you know. Golly, it's good to be back on the North Coast again. The whole air's different up here."

"Yes," smiled Calixta. "It's twice as humid."

Perpetua stood back to take in her friend. Timothy had got even plumper.

"I know, Perpetua! I've put on a bit of weight. Don't *you* make a fuss about it."

During the short taxi ride back to St. John Vianney's, Calixta let Timothy chatter on. Perpetua sat in the middle, crushed by Timothy's bulk but exuding toward the driver in the front seat a quiet pride in these sisters of hers, in being one of their company.

"How's your brother the pilot?" asked Timothy suddenly.

"My father tells me he's been decorated. The Distinguished Flying Medal."

"That shows the Poms what Aussie boys are made of, eh?"

"I think that's his idea," said Perpetua, laughing. But she thought, I wonder if he's having as much trouble with his big idea as I'm having with mine. Surely, there'd have to be a generous atmosphere in those squadrons, amongst all those young heroes. Because you never knew when the boy sitting next to you at breakfast would be gone. What an irony, what a frightful thing, thought Perpetua with a pulse of fear, if there were greater love amongst the bomber squadrons than under the Rule of the Sisters of Compassion.

As if to quell this return of anxiety in Perpetua, Timothy reached out and grabbed Perpetua's left hand. "It's good to see you, Reardon," she said.

Calixta smiled at that. The idea that she would mention at Chapter of Faults this familiarity of Timothy's, this reversion to Perpetua's worldly name, was—in the back of that Rossclare cab— unthinkable.

And she never did. It was as if going out on that December morning to the station, and watching the townsfolk and the soldiers, and driving in a cab with Timothy, was all safe ground, immune from the accusations normal under the Rule.

The mornings in the operating room were also times of less doubt, times of decent busyness with Timothy and big Roberta and Sister McGowan, with the surgeon Cormack and his pale anesthetist. Often when she emerged toward lunchtime, Perpetua would find Father Proud waiting for her with some new and often thick book he wished to recommend. She was grateful when one day it was a slim one.

"This is the poetry of Professor McAuley of Tasmania," he said. There was a rash around his hairline, the first sign of personal imperfection she had ever seen, and he seemed to her to be sweating with excitement. "It's brilliant, brilliant." And to her astonishment he began to read it aloud there in the corridor.

"Since all our keys are lost or broken,
Shall it be thought absurd
If for an art of words I turn
Discreetly to the Word?
Drawn inward by His love, we trace
Art to its secret springs:
What, are we masters in Israel
And do we know these things?"

He pressed the book into her scrubbed hands. "You must read it. You must read it in full. Triumphant faith in verse. And the man is still alive. Working in the army—some job in intelligence. It would be a cruel war which destroyed his voice!"

Perpetua thanked him and dutifully accepted the book. But he walked the entire length of the corridor with her, too innocent or else too self-absorbed to know how he put her in danger of accusation by her sisters.

"Whence that deep longing for an exorcizer," he recited from memory, walking beside her,

"For Christ descending as a thaumaturge,
Into His saints, as formerly in the desert,
Warring with demons on the outer verge."

It was the sort of behavior, fine in itself but out of place in the corridor outside the operating room, which caused some of the nuns to mutter amongst themselves that Proud needed a holiday.

There were plenty of similar Proud incidents. In the main entry hall of the hospital hung a painting of St. Justin, the second-century martyr and wandering philosopher. In the picture Justin half knelt, bare-chested in his philosopher's cloak, and was about to pound and mortify the flesh of his chest with a rock he held in his right hand.

Father Proud increasingly found this painting worthy of great study. He would stand for twenty minutes at a time, completely immobile, staring at it. A number of nuns said that they were stopped by him occasionally and asked to look closely at the stone. "You see, there's a pattern on it. It coincides with the coastline of Australia as portrayed in the Dieppe map of the sixteenth century." He thought it was very important to prove that men of Catholic nations—Portuguese or Spanish—had been the first Europeans to encounter Australia. "That would make the continent holy and Catholic."

Discussing this proposition in recreation one night, Sister Timothy said pithily, "Maybe the Aboes would have something to say about that!" For her family farmed in a valley that was thick with displaced Aboriginal people.

But when Father Proud urged and orated at greatest length, it was always to Perpetua. To her relief, even Francis gave up accusing her of the vanity of discussion with the intellectual priest. Francis latched on to the idea at last that Perpetua could hardly help it, that she was bound by the rules of politeness toward God's anointed, the clergy.

That winter, with Timothy working in the hospital, Perpetua did not need quite as much information from Nurse McGowan. Timothy seemed to know everything. The war in Europe was rolling, according to everyone, toward a successful end. Victory might come by Christmas. Terms like "the final thrust" were entering front-page stories of the newspapers Timothy jovially plundered from patients. Of course, the newspapers that reached Rossclare might be two days old, but the idea of some terrible reversal of Allied success didn't plague Perpetua. The tide of reported victories was too strong. The Russians were over the Vistula. The acknowledged losses of bombers was much less than even three months before. Mrs. Teresa Reardon confided to her daughter Perpetua in the monthly letter Perpetua was allowed to receive that, when the telegram announcing Bernard's Distinguished Flying Medal came, she had not been able to open it. She had put it under her wedding photograph on the radio and circled it as one circles a beast on a leash. When Mr. Reardon arrived home from work, it was he who opened it. He had been sure what was in it—the announcement of his son's death. Instead there was this statement that his son was an accredited warrior. He had wept uncontrollably.

Now, Mrs. Reardon went on, Bernard had been commissioned and had joined another, special kind of squadron where, according to what he said, the risks were less, though she couldn't be sure he was telling the truth. So Perpetua herself should go on praying for him.

23

How many Rads?

ONE dawn back at Starkley, when they were being debriefed after a raid on one of the Channel ports, Bennett himself appeared in the crew rooms. The volume of conversation immediately decreased. He walked over to a crew who were sitting in at the end of the hall, sipping their rum tea.

He spoke without apparent passion, yet everyone in the room could hear.

"You pilot F-Freddy, don't you, Flight Lieutenant?"

The pilot stood and admitted it.

"The wind was from the northwest, you came in on a northeasterly bearing. The aiming point was the marshalling yards to the west of the town center, to allow for creep back. You dropped your bombs to the east of the town hall. I saw it absolutely clearly, and I saw your markings."

"I was on the advice of my navigator," the pilot pleaded.

Bennett seemed to ignore him. "You had no excuses at all. You not only had H2S, but Gee and Oboe, unjammed so close to base. We don't have room for you and your crew. You're all to hand in your eagle wings and be off this station by ten o'clock this morning."

Reardon was particularly aware of the ghastly despair on the faces of the two gunners, who could not be blamed for the crew's navigational and bomb-aiming errors.

The morning after this dismissal, Challenor, Alf Hater, and Reardon were to go to Huntingdon and face the Air Vice-Marshal for their promotion interviews. They had agreed to meet afterward at the bar of the George Hotel. There would be possible celebrations, and stories to tell. For they would by then be at least warrant officers or—with a little luck—commissioned gentlemen, with a new status, and access to the officers' mess.

As if to foreshadow their possible new status, they were driven into town by an erk in a staff car.

Air Vice-Marshal Bennett's headquarters at Huntingdon was quite civilized. The outer office was paneled, and a low table was covered with copies of *The London Illustrated News, The Tatler,* and *Life.* A young officer with an obviously glass eye came out from an inner office to greet them.

"I am sure, gentlemen," he told them, "you will understand that the Air Vice-Marshal does not want his outer office cluttered with air crew congratulating each other or otherwise. I would like each of you to depart in silence immediately after your interview and keep your news for the pub you are indubitably headed for. I'd say at a guess, the bar at the George.

"You're a bloody wizard, sir," said Alf Hater.

"Everyone's got to be a bloody wizard, flight, to work in this group."

They went in according to some bureaucratic idea of seniority. Challenor was first. He emerged after a quarter of an hour, cast his eyes upward, smiled broadly, and went through to the hallway. For some reason it was a performance that made Alf Hater more frightened still. "Jesus, I'll have to baffle this old bastard with bullshit," he murmured to Reardon, and nodded toward the inner rooms where the Air Vice-Marshal awaited him.

He was at last asked in by the young man with the glass eye. Reardon was alone with the copies of *The Tatler* and *The London Illustrated News.* From the former smiled couples emerging beneath archways of officers' swords into marriage. Some of the poor brides had married air-force men and might already be widows. All the young heroes smiled bravely out of the retouched fuzziness of the glossy pages.

Reardon now understood how profoundly he wanted—urgently enough to make his palms sweat—the paternal approval of the Air Vice-Marshal. Yet he knew it was ridiculous, to want to be patted on the head by Bennett whom he didn't know except as a gifted tyrant. And what did Bennett's approval matter? Would it make it easier to avoid being coned by lights, smashed by friendly bombs, or hit by low, medium, or high flak?

Poker-faced as a church warden, Alf appeared again, crossed the waiting room without looking at Reardon, and went out of the door. Reardon thought, There goes an officer.

Suddenly the man with the glass eye was waiting for him. He rose dry-mouthed. He wiped the sweat from his palms on the tails of his uniform jacket and followed the man into a small room occupied by a desk, a typewriter, and a WAAF secretary, and then to a large door at which the glass-eyed man knocked and, without waiting for an answer, grabbed the door handle, opened the door a few inches, and indicated that Reardon should find his way through.

Inside, Bennett sat behind his desk looking at a file. He did not go on with any nonsense, however, about making Reardon wait. He glanced up and indicated a chair beside the desk.

"Flight Sergeant Reardon," he said. Again Reardon, for some reason, felt an analogy with cricket. Bennett was opening batsman, had the steely, hooded look of a good opener. And he himself, of course, was the underpaced starting bowler.

"I see you have an enviable record," murmured the Air Vice-Marshal, still looking at the file. "And you're in a fair crew there, Winton's crew."

Bennett closed the folder and glinted up at Reardon. "Where are you from, flight?"

"Sydney, sir."

"So am I. Fellow Sydney-siders, eh? But Sydney's a big place, isn't it? There's Sydney and there's Sydney! Where are you from in Sydney?"

"Rose Bay."

"Ah, harborside."

"We were lucky, my family," said Reardon. "Not well off, but ... that's where we ended up, anyhow."

"I'm from Parramatta," said Bennett. "Western suburbs. Not as glamorous, eh?"

"More like out in the country, I suppose, sir."

"Yes, I suppose. If you were going to bomb Sydney, you wouldn't make the aiming point Parramatta, would you?"

Reardon said, "Unless you were coming in from the east and wanted to account for creep back."

Bennett laughed. "Too true," he said.

Reardon was nearly enjoying himself, but wondered if he wasn't being skillfully lulled, tickled into a stance where all his callowness would be clearly displayed.

"Do you have a religion, Flight Sergeant?" Bennett asked unexpectedly.

"Yes, sir," Reardon told the Air Vice-Marshal, thinking, Here we go. It was not always a fashionable thing in Australia to be a Catholic of Irish descent. There were companies that would not employ such people. Maybe Pathfinder Group was one of them.

But equally, Catholics learned from childhood bravely to declare themselves. "I am a Catholic," said Reardon.

Bennett frowned down at the file and found it recorded there. "Oh yes. Here it is. Well, is it important to you? I mean, is it there when you're over Germany?"

"Yes, it is. Or at least it is when I land."

Bennett smiled marginally. "Yes, we're all of the one religion over the target, aren't we?" It was a remarkable admission from the Renaissance man of Bomber Command. "Well, it doesn't seem to have affected your night vision. You're not a convert to your religion?"

"No. My father and mother are Irish." Some impulse told him to go the whole hog. "My elder sister is a nun. There are only two of us."

"A gunner and a nun," said Bennett, apparently approving.

"That's right, sir."

There was a model of a Messerschmitt 110 on the Air Vice-Marshal's desk. With a quick movement he picked it up and drew it back over his shoulder as if he would fling it at Reardon. "This night fighter is attacking your aircraft by the *unter von hinten* method, from behind and below. You are, of course, in the rear turret and at your sights. I want you to tell me, as it approaches, how many rads you lay off."

The Air Vice-Marshal brought the night fighter in from Reardon's starboard. It swayed in Bennett's hand—he had clearly seen such attackers make their subtle approaches. With his hand and his small model, he perfectly mimicked the way it was at night at nineteen thousand feet. So perfectly, in fact, that Reardon remembered the glow of the instrument panel on a young face the night Punch's crew had been chased for nearly an hour.

"How many rads?" asked Bennett as the fighter swung in. Reardon answered, barely with time to think. Then the fighter would change its angle of attack. "How many rads? How many rads? How many rads?" Bennett kept asking, and Reardon called the answers.

Next the fighter swung around to the port of Reardon's turret and made a long, swerving approach. "How many rads? How many rads?"

Reardon rattled off his answers, desperate, as in a real combat. Suddenly the night fighter swung away and landed on Bennett's desk.

"By my calculations," said the Air Vice-Marshal, "you got him, Flight."

"Thank you, sir."

"Do you know the marking method known as Parramatta? The name of my birthplace?"

"Of course, sir."

"*Of course?* I thought most gunners only understood the turret. Explain Parramatta to me."

Reardon did. After which, at the Air Vice-Marshal's request, he explained Oboe and H2S.

Bennett said, "You've done well for a gunner, Flight Sergeant Reardon. Or else your sister has been praying for you very hard. I'm not going to keep you in suspense. I think there's enough suspense in our trade. I am recommending that you be commissioned to the rank of pilot officer."

The Air Vice-Marshal pushed his tough, small fist across the table and shook Reardon's hand. "Thank you, Pilot Officer Reardon, and good morning."

Reardon stood up. Dazed, and feeling ridiculously honored, he saluted the Air Vice-Marshal and, as far as he knew, staggered out, even though some automatic impulse probably looked after his gait and made it look a bit martial. What he thought was, They've paid me back for all the terror I've felt.

* * *

They were waiting for him in the hotel bar. Alf Hater was smoking and shaking his head and looking wry. Challenor was simply enjoying his beer. Seeing Reardon come, he called for the ancient waiter.

Reardon sat. He did not want to speak first, so he said, "Well!"

"Well," said Alf Hater, "I'm going to be a warrant officer. Could have done with commissioned pay, but never bloody mind. My own bloody fault. Do you know what the old bastard did? I go in and he asked me where I come from, and I tell him Melbourne, and he says someone has to come from Melbourne, and I laugh along with him, typical Sydney-Melbourne bullshit, you know. And then he asked me how many words a minute I can receive. And I decide I'll pitch it a little high, so I say eighteen."

"You've never received eighteen a minute in your bloody life, Alfie," said Challenor.

"I've received enough to keep up in the air, you bloody old crow eater. Anyhow, to my astonishment, the bugger opens a drawer in his desk, and there's a transmission set and earphones. And he asks me to open a drawer on my side of the desk, and there's one for me, too, a receiver. And he gives me a pad and a pencil, gets me to put on the headphones, asks me if I'm ready, and starts transmitting, keeping time with a stopwatch he's got."

Challenor and Reardon laughed. "And how many did you do in the minute?"

"I got fourteen, and the old bastard says, 'Flight Sergeant, do you feel you're under a disadvantage? Do you want to do another minute's worth, or was eighteen a sort of excusable exaggeration?' "

For some reason Reardon was nearly weeping with laughter.

"So I told him, 'I might have been exaggerating a bit, sir.' And so he said, 'Well, fourteen a minute isn't bad in anyone's language, especially a radio man's language. I think it's good enough for me to make you a warrant officer.' Jesus, I would have loved to have gone back to Parsfield and gone into Lillie's parlor and seen the look on her old man's face when he saw the ring of braid around my sleeve. As it is, it won't be a ring of bloody braid. It'll be a crown on the shoulder. Still, not too bad. I'll just never be a bloody gentleman. It would have been nice for my mother if I'd been made a bloody gentleman."

"It's nice for all of us," said Challenor. "On occasion."

Reardon jumped in at the end of the sentence. "And what about you?" he asked Challenor. "Did he use the little model 110 with you? 'How many rads? How many rads?' "

Challenor nodded. "He shot me down a few times."

"And . . ."

"Well, at least he didn't throw me out of the group, though he seemed a bit doubtful. I'm a warrant officer, too, like Alfie."

"But you can do that aiming method to a T," Reardon accused him.

"Not me, mate. I'm just mid-upper. They put all the old folk in the mid-upper."

"You let him get you," said Reardon. He was certain of it—that Challenor's strange pride somehow wouldn't allow him to seek praise from such an exalted officer. It was a perverse Australian impulse—to stay obscure, one of the mob; perhaps a convict lost amongst other convicts in the great prison yard that Australia had once been.

Reardon said, "I was sure he'd given you a commission! Absolutely bloody sure! You walked out of that office like a bloody air commodore."

"Well, he did offer me that, but I told him you met a better class of people amongst the warrant bloody officers."

Both Challenor and Hater were looking keenly at Reardon now. "He commissioned you, didn't he?" asked Alf.

Fortunately, at that second, the waiter brought Reardon's pint. But it was only a brief lull. Challenor said, "I think if there's any officers present, they'd better bloody well buy a round."

Reardon pulled a pound note out of his pocket and gave it to the old waiter. "And could we order another pint all 'round?" he said.

The waiter nodded and went away. Hater said, "You bastard, Reardon! He commissioned you, didn't he?"

"Well, he said it was because we both came from Sydney, him and me."

Challenor was laughing, a deep, delightful laugh. "Jesus, you've done it now. You'll have to eat all your meals with strangers." This chastened Reardon. He hadn't thought about that.

Alf said, "There used to be a time when it was hard for bloody tykes to get promotion in the armed forces. Just shows you how bad we must have been, Challenor, if this bloody R.C. got promoted over us."

They both languidly extended their hands over the table and shook Reardon's.

"Mind if we don't call you sir till we get back to Starkley?" Challenor asked.

24

Stirhanger Christmas

THE listing at Australia House for possible Christmas lodging, Royal Australian Air Force flying personnel, 1944, included the following: "Stirhanger Farmhouse, charming eighteenth century building, good farm food, within easy walking distance of village. Train to Exeter, then spur rail to Callthorpe."

The duty officer at Australia House telephoned Stirhanger Farmhouse for them. He conversed pleasantly—and dimly through the receiver you could hear a well-modulated and young female voice. When he hung up, he said, "That's not the proprietor. That's the proprietress. Sounds like good company. She says there's room for the two of you."

Walking to the Leicester Square train stop they heard high above them the whine of a V-2 rocket. Everyone in the street stopped as if the sound might be attracted to them by movement. Reardon and Challenor stopped too. It was a primitive matter, this standing still as the rockets whined over. And then stopped whinning.

They waited half a minute. People began to move. The curse had not come down on them.

"I thought we'd finished off those bastards when we bombed Peenemünde," said Challenor, seeming a little ashamed at having stood still, of having been persuaded to stop in his tracks by anything that whined like that, like a mean-minded dog.

Reardon, given his fresh officer status, was entitled to a reserved first-class seat. But he had not asked for it. The air force was the only service where you saw friendships that crossed that ancient barrier between the officer and NCO. The division had been eroded by the night life of Bomber Command, where the skipper might be outranked by other members of the crew. The British reacted to this fact of combat by enforcing rigid class distinction on the ground. The Canadians dealt with it more democratically, by arguing that all flight crew should be commissioned. Frankly, they said, they didn't want British officers refusing under attack or during the bombing run to disobey Canadian NCO's, bombardiers or gunners, just because they didn't use the proper form of address. Finally, the Australians' and New Zealanders' answer, one that suited the informality of their upbringing, was to ignore the existence of the line, especially in the air. Any fool, as Challenor had already said, could be a pilot officer. You found commissioned idiots who hadn't yet flown their first operation, but you couldn't be a warrant officer, the highest noncommissioned rank, without having been through the grinder, up every barrel in the organ.

He and Reardon bore for four hours the cramped, steamy companionship of the corridors of a second-class coach. Some of the young soldiers around them had come back from France for Christmas. They spoke with West Country accents, the same broad vowels Reardon and Challenor identified with America. "Now we know where the bloody Yanks got their accent from," said Challenor.

These young soldiers seemed to be mainly support troops—they didn't have the fixed stare that went with those who had been in battle. They were also full of tales—Cherbourg, Caen, Paris. They were country boys who had seen extraordinary things for the first time in their lives.

There was also a good-looking young nurse who had less to say. The young warriors tried to engage her in conversation. It became apparent, during the more than three hours to Exeter, that she had been nursing her way across France and into Belgium.

During a wait of one hour at the Exeter station for the train to Callthorpe, sleet began to fall and soon turned to light snow. They were pleased they had worn their flying underwear and had their flying jackets in their kitbags.

A car with TAXI—HIRE OR WEDDINGS on its door was waiting for them at the rustic station in Callthorpe. An old man with an impenetrable accent drove them to Stirhanger in it. At last they found they could understand him if he spoke slowly. He told them it was the same with them. "You must be speaking slower, boys," he told them. "If I be understandin' thee."

It was slow going in muddy lanes, and the old gentleman amused them with gossip. In a knowing way he described Stirhanger Farm as "the Canadian Social Club." "That's what it be, a social club for them Canadians!"

"How do you mean?" Challenor asked him.

"There always be Canadian officers up there. One in particular. Missus—she's a widow. She be one of them widows young men go a long way to meet."

Stirhanger Farm had, as promised at Australia House, an eighteenth-century farmhouse. The ground in front of it looked bare and wintry hard, and a pig nudged the frozen earth disconsolately. The old cabdriver wanted to carry their kitbags "You boys is helping me. I don't see why I can't help thee."

He led them to the kitchen door off to the side of the house. He hammered on it jovially. "Come on, come on, some of us don't have all day, you know." The door was opened by an army officer. He was dark and lean and didn't seem very friendly. His shoulder patches said Canada. He was smoking, and he seemed to concentrate on that and give only a corner of his attention to Reardon and Challenor.

"Oh," he murmured, "you're the new guys. Come in, come in. Mrs. Bryant would have rather you went in the front door, she's very particular about that. Anyhow . . ." He indicated the interior of the warm kitchen.

A fuel stove was radiating heat right across the room. They walked in, took off leather gloves and flexed their hands in front of the stove. Challenor winked at Reardon. "Would you pay the gentleman, sir?" Reardon found seven shillings in his pocket.

"I likes Australians," said the old man, probably lying. "You have the generous streak. A happy Christmas."

He closed the door, and soon they heard his old taxi start up. The Canadian officer had gone back to reading the newspaper at the kitchen table. He would read a few paragraphs and then tap the page with the knuckle of his right hand. He smoked desperately, sucking furiously, like an asthmatic.

At last, his eyes still on the newspaper, he said, "Perhaps you guys better go and see the missus. She's through there with Major Samson."

They nodded and went through into the corridor. It was cold there. This was clearly the sort of house in which only pockets of warmth could be found. They could hear laughter from the front parlor, a man and a woman sharing a joke, and they followed the sound. It took them to a closed door at which they knocked. A female voice told them to come in.

They walked in and saw, outlined by wintry light from the parlor front window, a dark young woman and sandy-haired officer standing close together, as if they'd just been sharing an embrace or a secret.

"It's our Australians," said the woman, not to Reardon and Challenor but rather, privately, to the sandy-haired officer. He turned to face the airmen.

They saw that he, too, had Canada patches on his shoulders. His uniform was tailor-made and not as carelessly worn as that of the man in the kitchen. He didn't have a paratrooper's badge either.

"Welcome, gentlemen," said Mrs. Bryant. "Would you care to introduce yourselves? This, by the way is Major Samson of the Canadian Army."

"I'm Warrant Officer Challenor," Challenor supplied. "And this is my friend Pilot Officer Reardon."

"Merry Christmas, boys," said the major. He was entitled to call them boys, both by his rank and by the fact that he must have been in his late thirties.

"Would you like something?" asked Mrs. Bryant. "Tea? A beer? Even—if you're very good—some of Major Samson's scotch?"

There was an edge to the way she said it that made Challenor and Reardon feel awkward about asking for anything. Challenor said, "Maybe a cup of tea. But we can get it ourselves out in the kitchen."

Mrs. Bryant looked at Major Samson. "We're going to have a jolly Christmas," she said.

Out in the kitchen the intense young Canadian lieutenant was still reading the paper. It was the same page he had been reading when they went to see Mrs. Bryant. He looked up at them, gasped in some cigarette smoke, and said, "See Mrs. Bryant?"

"Yes," said Reardon. "We said g'day to her."

"Lucky she had time to talk to you."

Challenor said to the man, whose gaze had returned to the same page of newspaper, "You've been in France, haven't you?"

"No. Holland."

"Arnhem?"

"That's right."

The paratroop landing in Arnhem had been a disaster, though the newspapers had pretended that it was just another manifestation of British spunk. A minority of paratroopers had fought their way out. What an astoundingly different sort of warrior this man was to Reardon and Challenor. They could not, from their own experience, imagine what this Canadian's excursion to Holland had been like. Obviously, however, in the desperate way he smoked and dealt with the newsprint in front of him, it had brought him to a pitch of tension.

Challenor said, "How far to the nearest pub?"

"Mile and a half through the bloody snow," said the Canadian lieutenant. But he slammed his newspaper shut. "Let's go, guys!"

Reardon went through to the front of the house and told Mrs. Bryant that they'd decided to go for a walk and see the countryside. Offhandedly she gave them directions. It had already become clear that the party in the front parlor was mainly meant for herself and Major Samson.

Reardon and Challenor, muffled up in their overcoats, stamped their feet in the half-muddy, half-icy farmyard and waited for the Canadian to emerge. When he did, Challenor said, "Bloody cold, mate, wouldn't you say?"

"I'm from Alberta," said the lieutenant. "It's a summer's day to us." He extended his hand to both of them. "I think I'll like you guys. It's been goddamn miserable till you turned up. My name's Regan."

Challenor remembered rank and said, "Pleased to meet you, sir."

"Call me Regan and cut the bullshit."

They walked down country lanes fringed by hedges so high that what sun there was at this hour of the day did not reach or melt the ice pools. The pub, when they arrived, sat under the hill and looked sullen, but there was a smiling landlord inside with a broad West Country accent, and his wife made them Spam sandwiches. After the cold Devon lanes, this plain food seemed first class. "Thou hast a strange manner of speech," the pub owner's wife told Reardon. "All ye boys. What country are you from, my darlin'?"

Regan persuaded them to drink cider instead of beer, and already they were pleased at that choice. It sat in their stomachs like a gentle pool of warmth.

"Do you know this Major Samson who's back there at the farmhouse?" Reardon asked the Canadian lieutenant.

"Only since yesterday. He was already there when I arrived. He's a big-timer in Canada. Used to hear him on the radio. Canadian Broadcasting Commission. He works for headquarters in London. Press relations. Been to Europe and so on. He's been down here before too." Regan seemed to have no irony in his voice as he said, "Seems to know the missus already. One thing I'll say for the missus—she dishes up a good dinner. No shortage of eggs, butter, ham. So I just ignore the rest and get on with what I'm doing."

His hand reached, shaking, for his pint of cider.

The proprietor let them stay on after closing hours, drinking in the snug. It was quite late and the sun was low when they set out for the farmhouse again. As Regan had promised, dinner was superb—some beef and vegetable soup, pork cutlets, potatoes, a sponge cake.

Yet as fine as the food was and as ungrudgingly as Mrs. Bryant brought it to the table, the main conversation during meals was between her and Major Samson. They seemed to Reardon to be like two kids who considered themselves both very lucky and very clever to have found each other out of all the mass of humans. Later, in the cold upstairs bedroom the two airmen were assigned to, Challenor would say to Reardon, "It's like she wants us 'round just to watch her getting on so hot and strong with the major."

Occasionally during dinner Major Samson would ask Challenor

or Reardon a question. But mostly he would tell them what they had been doing in the past three months, and grin when they showed polite amazement at the breadth of his knowledge.

The next day, Christmas Eve, was even colder, but the people at the pub had a bowl of punch set in front of the fire. Regan loosened up. They found out that he was an engineer from Calgary. After a few large glasses of punch he told them funny stories about the building of a sewage works in Moose Jaw.

Later in the afternoon lots of Land Army girls arrived, left their Wellington boots out on the porch and walked around the bar in their socks. His head dislocated with the strong punch, Reardon saw Regan disappearing with one of them. He remembered deliciously kissing a number of them himself. Then he, Regan, and Challenor were rolling home down country lanes, following the choir of the village church. They joined with them for a visit to a few farmhouses, sang the carols with them, and were rewarded with a few more nips of whiskey.

In a way Reardon was never quite sure of, they peeled off from the choir and, when it was already dark, reached Stirhanger Farmhouse.

Reardon could remember sitting at the table, in front of a meal almost identical to the one he'd eaten the night before. And again Major Samson and Mrs. Bryant were engaged in their love affair, and Regan, Challenor, and he were mere witnesses, extras, picturesque uniforms from far away to add color to the infatuation. Reardon was angry enough to try to say something about it, but could not succeed. The next he knew he was waking up at his place at the table and Mrs. Bryant was laughing at him behind her hand. Challenor helped him up to bed and he slept profoundly but not without inevitable dreams, of fire, of falling, of the terrible luminescense, the unique light quality of a bomber fuselage when it is coned by searchlight.

Next morning, soreheaded but at peace, he gave Mrs. Bryant the bottle of Eau de Cologne he had bought in London before coming down to the farmhouse. "Now, Mr. Reardon," said Major Samson, "can you guarantee it comes from Cologne? After what Bomber Command has done to that city?"

Mrs. Bryant went off to fry eggs, and Reardon felt guilty for the unkind things that had nearly risen to his lips last night. He went to visit her in the kitchen.

"I wondered if there was a Christmas Mass anywhere in the village," he asked.

"My God, no," she cried, ladling molten lard over a rich-colored egg yolk. "I mean, there used to be a chapel and a priest over at Doonside House, but old Lady Trevor died and the war began. . . ."

She looked across the kitchen to where the chicken sat ready for roasting. Eggs for breakfast, chicken for lunch—it should have been a delightful day, but somehow it wasn't.

Reardon walked alone into the village and heard singing coming from the village church. In Sydney, where religious lines were drawn to resemble battle lines, you had to get permission from your parish priest to attend a Protestant service, even a wedding or a christening. But the world was upside down now. He went in and stood at the back. They sang "O Come All Ye Faithful" instead of "Adeste Fideles." But it was the same tune. There was a rich breadth in the way these West Country people sang on this Christmas morning.

Without warning, tears came to his eyes. They were peculiar tears. They were for these people. They were especially because these decent people in the pews didn't know about fire and Hamburg, about Cannon and Nuremberg, about the chop girl or the bomber claimed and consumed by FIDO. Their Christmas was therefore worlds removed from his.

When he felt the tears were getting to be too much, he left the church and sat on somebody's old tombstone outside. There, gasping, he got control of himself and turned back toward the farm. He wondered what was wrong with him. He remembered that only two days before he had thought Lieutenant Regan pretty strange.

At the farmhouse everyone was in the dining room, standing about with glasses in their hand. Regan and Challenor were drinking porter, and the Major and Mrs. Bryant whiskey.

"Pilot Officer Reardon," said Mrs. Bryant, saluting him a little tipsily. "We shall attack the chicken and ham in a little over half an hour."

He poured himself some porter and toasted her. Lieutenant Regan dragged on his cigarette and muttered every few seconds, "Merry Christmas. Merry Christmas."

The dinner arrived about the time Mrs. Bryant had promised. It was rich and plentiful, and as he ate, Reardon chided himself for thinking unkind thoughts about his hostess. Plum pudding arrived and was flamed in Major Samson's brandy. Tumblers of brandy were then passed around the table to celebrate the end of such a grand meal. The major, who was by now well-liquored, rose to his feet and made a little speech. "Gentlemen, I ask you to drink to our beautiful hostess."

They all obeyed. Then he went on in fairly sentimental fashion. Here was an English rose, he said, surrounded by men from the farthest reaches of Empire. The Empire, in the person of the elegant Mrs. Bryant, showed its gratitude, especially in gatherings such as this one. This might be the last winter of the war in Europe—in twelve months time they might all, as soldiers and airmen, be spending Christmas in the Pacific, in Singapore or in some camp in Japan. Or they might be home again, in the farthest provinces of Canada or Australia. Wherever they were, they would always remember this very special Christmas dinner and Mrs. Bryant's hospitality.

Two thirds of the way through this speech, Challenor winked at Reardon, a blank-faced, unsmiling wink. For some reason, instead of having to suppress a smile, Reardon had urgently to stop the flowing of tears again, tears from the same well—it seemed to him—that this morning's had come from.

The speech over, Samson sat down. What he had said was solemnly approved by Lieutenant Regan, and out of politeness by Challenor and Reardon.

Mrs. Bryant said that if they now went into the parlor, they would be just in time for the King's Christmas broadcast.

She stood suddenly, wiped her lips, put the cloth down, picked up her glass of brandy, and turned immediately to the door. Major Samson ran to open it for her. Regan and Challenor stood up, but a terrible gravity kept Reardon in his seat. He felt offended all at once that she should presume that he had been fighting for the British monarchy. He was desperate to let her know that it was something more—something mysterious. Perhaps it was the style that lay behind the Illuminated Address the union and the miners of Coolgardie had given his father. Perhaps it was some barely digested idea of Australia. Perhaps his staying in his seat was partially caused by the solid tumbler of brandy he had just drunk. In any case, he didn't move. And whatever it was that caused him to stay still, he himself was appalled at it, by its disregard for good manners.

"Aren't you coming, Mr. Reardon?" asked Mrs. Bryant from the door. Everyone had stopped, had noticed his inability to move and no doubt considered it unwillingness.

"I don't think I'll come," Reardon murmured.

"I think you should. After all, it's the King, and he's such a nice man."

"I don't particularly think much of him," said Reardon, astonished at himself, at the ungracious child who had control of his muscles and his tongue. "I've seen a lot of better blokes than him go down in flames in the last few years."

"Are you a communist, Pilot Officer?" asked Mrs. Bryant.

"No, I just don't want to listen to the King on the radio, that's all."

Mrs. Bryant was enraged. She inhaled, and blood came up behind the fine skin of her cheeks. "My husband died for him," she said. "You could at least listen to him."

But instead of politely agreeing, he felt to his bemusement an answering rage rise in him. He realized he'd been enraged since he got here. He liked to think it was Mrs. Bryant's fault and Major Samson's—all that sexual boasting of theirs. But he wasn't absolutely sure. All he knew was that he felt an enormous anger. And as if all his submerged Celtic ancestors had risen to the top of his soul, he resented lunatically being accused of risking his life for the King.

Mrs. Bryant stamped over to his place at the table. "I insist you come! It's only good manners!"

"I'm sorry," said Reardon. It was all he could say, otherwise this morning's tears would return.

Mrs. Bryant wheeled, the sort of movement that's called "turning on your heel." She led the other three men out of the room. Challenor, last to go, winked again, confused between loyalty and his duty as a guest. Challenor did not normally show any confusion. That's what I've reduced him to, thought Reardon.

Reardon continued to sit on the vacated table. The idea that he might appease Mrs. Bryant by gathering up the dishes and taking them to the kitchen occurred to him. But when he tried to stand, a sort of weariness pulled him down.

When the widow and the others returned, Challenor walked up to where Reardon was still sitting. "You all right, tiger?"

Reardon nodded. Mrs. Bryant was briskly gathering dishes and ignoring him. He stood up—he managed it all at once.

"I think I ought to go in the morning," he said.

"Yes," said Mrs. Bryant. "I think you had better."

"All right," said Reardon. He began to walk out of the room. But he paused by the door. "I wanted to thank you for the really lovely dinner."

"Oh," said Mrs. Bryant, and she was being ironic, "you mustn't even think of mentioning it!"

Challenor walked up the stairs with him, in case it was liquor that had caused his rebellion and might now make him slip and fall on the staircase built for the smaller people of two hundred years ago.

"I've got to stay, Reardo," said Challenor. "I mean . . . politeness . . ."

Reardon could see that. "Of course you've got to," he said.

"So you're okay, are you? You aren't pissed or anything?"

"No." Reardon found himself laughing. "I don't mind the King. I just don't like people telling me to listen to him. I suppose it's the bloody Irish."

"You should have come and listened," said Challenor. "You've done enough for the bugger."

"I have, haven't I?"

"You'll go to the Officers' Club in London, will you? The Strand?"

Reardon said, "Yes. I believe it's pretty good."

"Listen, I'd come with you except—"

"No, I know how well-bred all you bloody South Australians are."

Challenor suddenly paused near the head of the steps. Reardon had to turn back to hear what he said.

"I mean, we must have just about bombed every bloody thing standing," Challenor said. "I mean, we must have at least aimed something at every bloody structure. Wouldn't you think?"

Reardon said, "You're a bit tired?"

Challenor said, "No, I'm right as rain." He paused. "Yes, I'm a bit tired."

He had said the right thing. He had put Reardon's dismay into words, he had let Reardon know that he, too, was feeling the strain.

Within ten minutes Reardon had sunk into a profound sleep that lasted the whole night. This meant that he did not have to face Mrs. Bryant or Major Samson, or even the manically smoking and reading Lieutenant Regan. As well, he woke around the time he intended to—five o'clock on a bitter morning. Across the room Challenor was asleep beneath quilts and an air-force greatcoat. Reardon got into his pants, shirt, and uniform jacket, hauled on his own overcoat and found his cap. Thus, fully dressed, he began packing his kit. It did not take him long.

On the top landing he crept past the room where Mrs. Bryant and Major Samson lay—he supposed—in each other's embrace. You could be sure, given Major Samson's fondness for whiskey, that the sleep was profound. Cold rose up the stairwell to meet him. He got to the front door and found that it was not only bolted and locked, but that the key had been taken out. The same was true of the kitchen door. He tried windows, but they were nailed up to prevent the cold getting in. He moved across the kitchen, past the stove, which gave out no heat, past the table where Lieutenant Regan read newspapers, and into the pantry. Here he found that the window had not been nailed permanently shut. He struggled to lift it—it had clearly not been raised in decades. It gave a fraction of an inch at a time. The savagely cold predawn struck his face. He could see nowhere in the farmyard dry enough for him to toss his kitbag onto. So he hung it from the window latch—he would climb through first himself, and drag the kitbag after him.

The window was high, so he had to take the risk of launching himself through it head and shoulders first. As he wriggled to get his lower stomach and hips across the windowsill, he saw too late that directly below him in the farmyard sat a trough of watery, iced-over swill. He extended his hands. They broke through the ice and into the unspeakable sediment at the bottom of the trough. Yet he was able now to vault the rest of his body clear of the frozen swill. He landed on his right side in mud. Getting up swearing, he began the futile business of brushing the muck off the sleeves of his greatcoat and the mud off his blue pants.

He fetched his kit from the window, which he left open for the sake of revenge. At the gate he turned and cursed the house, feeling an ancient Celtic-Australian malice rising in him, and drawing heavily on a curse he'd once heard his father utter: " 'May all your hours be bitter, and all your wakings frightful. May you never know an hour of peace!' Fuck you and your fancy man!"

It was late in the morning before the small local train got him to Exeter. There, in the railway station, was an officers' canteen with lavatory and bathhouse attached. He gave his greatcoat, uniform jacket, trousers, and shoes—which were in so disgusting a state that a number of naval officers had stared at him on his way in—to an elderly orderly, who worked on them scrupulously and, now that the mud and swill were dry, got them remarkably clean. He washed himself thoroughly and shaved, and was presentable again by the time the London train came in, a little after one o'clock.

This time he had been to the booking officer and exercised his prerogative to a first-class seat. As soon as he got into his compartment, sat in his window seat, and nodded to the four naval officers who shared the compartment with him, he fell asleep again. He awoke just as the train was pulling in to the sooty splendor of Bath. He was at once struck by a terrible fear for his sanity, for he saw sitting opposite him a clearly defined image of Enid Hadgraft, whom he had met a year and a half before. She was smiling faintly but knowingly at him. He looked around in a panic. The four naval officers were still in the compartment. Clearly one of them had changed places to allow Enid the window seat opposite him. She was wearing the pips of a first lieutenant on her shoulders.

"Well," she said, "we've both been commissioned since we last met. Isn't it wonderful what a war will do for people?"

He must have made some sound, because she began to explain herself. "I boarded the train in Taunton. I work in a motor pool there—it was very busy before Normandy, but business has tailed off now. Are you still flying, Pilot Officer Reardon?"

"Challenor and I are still flying," said Reardon. He made no further comment. Even to say "still flying" was pushing your luck, more or less provoking the odds to turn against you. "Have you heard from your brother?"

"We got a Red Cross postcard. No news on it, of course."

"And your mother and father?"

"Mother's well. Father's not so well."

It struck him all at once that she looked handsome in her new uniform, and that she had none of the sharp-edged quality of Mrs. Bryant. Mrs. Bryant had so dominated Christmas that she was still, in his dazed mind, the yardstick.

Enid asked him if he had he spent Christmas down in the country. He nodded, and lied about how enjoyable it had been.

"And now you're going back to base?"

He shook his head. "I've got a few more days in London. I'm going up to the Strand."

"Good, is it?"

"It's really good. They look after you well. Are you going home to see your parents?"

"No," said Enid Hadgraft, and looked out of the window. They were just entering the railway station at Bath Central. "My parents are away, I'll be staying in our flat at Knightsbridge. I'm having a party, in fact. I mean, tonight. To make up for spending yesterday at the depot. Could you come?"

It was settled that he would. At Euston they waited in line for a cab. The idea was that it would take her to Knightsbridge and then drop him in the West End. But when they pulled up outside a block of flats near Harrods, Lieutenant Enid Hadgraft said, "Go to the Officers' Club later, Reardon. You can call them from upstairs. Be a dear and help me get the party ready."

It wasn't a bad building they entered, though the elevator seemed to be out of order. Four flights up she opened a door to what passed in London for a fairly spacious flat. The living room table was covered with dirty glasses and full ashtrays.

"Sorry to bring you to such squalor, Pilot Officer. This was a party in mid-December. I couldn't get rid of the blighters till nearly dawn, and then I had to catch the train to Yeovil. I assure you, I'm not generally as mucky as this."

Helping her clean up, carrying glasses to the kitchen and emptying ashtrays, he began to feel that he was enjoying his leave, a feeling he hadn't had since two days before Christmas when he arrived at Stirhanger Farm. Soon the sun had gone down and she turned on the lights. The furniture in the flat was quite elegant—there was a comfortableness here that he had not found at Mrs. Bryant's severe farmhouse.

While he washed the glasses, Enid Hadgraft moved briskly around the flat, polishing things. The first of her friends arrived—old school friends and girls she had met since, some of them in uniform, some dressed in the broad-shouldered fashions of the season. Enid excused herself, went to the bedroom, and came out again wearing a gown similar to those some of the others wore—this one however a vivid blue which beguiled Reardon. "I'm wearing your colors," she confided to him in a way he found exciting.

Many of the officers Enid's girlfriends brought were American and carried bottles of scotch with them. Reardon refused the early offers of liquor. He wanted to get the heavy drinking of the last two days, which had helped lead him to tears and wild behavior, out of his system. It was well after nine o'clock when he had his first drink, and even that was a pale ale. He found himself discussing beers with an American engineer. Both of them agreed that they thought British beer was slops, but what could a man do? About half past ten he began to feel very tired—besides, if he was going to appear at the Officers' Club, it had better not be too late. He went to see Enid, who was engaged in a passionate conversation with two of her girlfriends. Seeing him coming, she excused herself and stood up, moving to one side to meet him.

He told her he had to go soon. She said that there were probably people here who could give him a lift to the vicinity of Leicester Square. He looked around at the party-goers. None of them seemed ready to move. Abruptly she said, "Stay here, Reardon." She had her hand on his sleeve.

"It'd be nice," he said.

"Then stay here, Reardon."

He laughed. "I'm not supposed to do that sort of thing."

"Oh my God, Reardon. It's exactly because you feel like that that I want you to stay."

The prospect was so luscious that he felt the beginnings of a stupid erection, right there in the living room, surrounded by polished Americans and girls in wide-shouldered dresses. He could not remember having had one in broad daylight recently. Flying had inhibited all that.

"If God gave a shit," said Enid Hadgraft, "would He let the world burn like this?"

"Well," said Reardon, shaking his head, searching for a counterargument, "it's us who's sort of ignited the world, isn't it? It's our doing."

"*Ours?*" asked Enid Hadgraft. "Not bloody well mine, Reardon. Not yours."

Reardon suddenly felt as if he had no arguments left.

"You remember that talk we had when you were at our place?" she murmured. "It was really such a pleasure. I have to say the atmosphere at home that time was pretty claustrophobic. It was always pretty claustrophobic."

"I didn't think so," Reardon said, for politeness' sake. "Your mother and father were very hospitable."

She looked away, across the room, at the grinning faces of the Americans wrapped up in conversations. "My father killed himself," she told Reardon. "Last February. Last winter was a long one for a man of his beliefs."

Reardon didn't know what to say. He felt the girl's grief like an aura. But also he was astonished by the idea of death being so hard to come by that a man had to go seeking it.

Enid Hadgraft said, "He left us a long letter. He wanted to make it clear that it had nothing to do with us—it was just the way the world was going, that was all." She laughed, a sort of affectionate chuckle. "You have to admit he was a little eccentric. Taking us all to see goats get blown up."

"Look," said Reardon, "will you please accept my greatest sympathy?"

"Of course I do. Just hang around, Reardon, will you?"

At last, at one o'clock, they got rid of the last tipsy American and his barely conscious girlfriend. Again, with a casualness of accustomed lovers, they cleaned up, Reardon washing the glasses. Then they went to the bedroom—Reardon presumed it was the bed of the Hadgraft senior, in which the late professor had had his troubled sleep. Reardon was amazed at the grace with which he and Enid embraced. When, by the first light of dawn, he awoke to urinate, he felt that he'd been renewed, reconnected to the living.

Despite the war and what he had learned, in Reardon's world view if you slept with a girl you married her. As he reached the bathroom, he had that intention in mind. Hadn't her father so energetically praised the New World? What a wonderful girl she would be—an elegant, worldly girl—to take home to Rose Bay. When he had finished in the bathroom, he went to the kitchen for water. There was a picture he hadn't noticed the night before, hanging over the kitchen bench. It showed Enid and an army officer, laughing together. In the photograph Enid was dressed in white, though her dress did not come to her ankles but stopped at the calves. She was wearing a pillbox hat that had a lace veil pulled back to show her eyes. The officer was an older man—in his mid-thirties. Reardon looked closely to see his rank. He was a major.

What did this man in the photograph in the kitchen mean? What did it mean that the photograph *was* in the kitchen? Was that meant to be a comment on the fact that the man meant nothing to her? Yet if the man meant nothing, what was he doing on the walls at all?

Reardon was sitting in a chair beside her bed when she woke at about eight o'clock. "Good morning," she told him. "What are you doing there?"

"Who's the man in the picture in the kitchen?"

"My husband," she said.

"Hell," said Reardon. He thought awhile. "What's he doing in the kitchen? If he's your husband . . . ?"

"I married him after Daddy died. It's one of those things you do. Your father shoots himself. And so you look for the nearest man. An affirmation of life, you know, Reardon. Except it's not the best conditions in which to choose the right chap. I'm sure you understand that."

Reardon shook his head. This wasn't his idea of marriage. "Where is he?"

"I believe he's in Brussels at the moment."

"Bloody hell!" said Reardon. "On active service?"

"Not too active. Postwar reconstruction plans. The greatest danger he's in is if the lift cable breaks or if the smoked salmon isn't fresh."

"How can you talk about him like that? Don't you respect him?"

"Not—I have to admit—a great deal."

Reardon felt an acrid disappointment. He stood up and looked around for his uniform jacket. It was time he went to the Officers' Club.

"Do you think I'm beautiful, Reardon?" she asked him from the bed.

"Yes. I think you're very, very beautiful."

"And do you love me?"

In Reardon's world view he had just given the most remarkable demonstration of loving her. "You're a woman there isn't much trouble loving," said Reardon. "But your husband . . ."

"Are they all like you in the New World?" she asked. "In Australia?"

"I don't know. I just know that I couldn't have stayed if I'd known you were married."

"Well, for God's sake, Reardon, I'm the same woman, married or not!"

He did not rush away in moral outrage. In fact he found her too hard to leave. That night he slept with her yet again, even though he now knew that it was adultery. At some stage, because it was required of him, he would have to take this to the confessional, but he felt a sinister lack of guilt. He wondered what was more dangerous—to sleep with a married woman and know it was wrong, or to do the same thing and feel it was right.

That night they went to the theater together. He was very pleased that there was too much happening for him to think.

The next morning they walked down to Harrods to drink tea. He was to catch the three o'clock train back to Huntingdon that afternoon. A little after dark it would get him to the village of Starkley. His consciousness was by now pervaded with Enid Hadgraft—for another night with her, he might almost have sacrificed the chances of coming through, and the moral technicalities in which the Brothers at Rose Bay had raised him seemed nearly irrelevant in the light Enid Hadgraft gave off.

He talked a lot on subjects he could not later remember. The tea came and was drunk. Suddenly Enid put a hand over his. It was a normal movement you saw a hundred times a day in this London of quickly grabbed joys and contacts.

"This is all you're going to see of me, Reardon." He must have frowned, because she said then, "I'm a married woman. And I'm English. So I don't want you having any little fantasies about a future. Yet I fear I see that developing in you."

He pretended to take this lightly. They walked back from Harrods to her flat. The streets that had looked translucent on their way, now seemed their drab selves. He did not particularly argue. There was a finality in her voice you couldn't argue with. He had been making up his mind that she was worth the risk of hell, but here she was, braking well before the cliff for the sake of mere respectability. He already felt in his body the peculiar ache of the coming weeks without her.

"I wasn't being cruel, was I, Reardon?" she asked. "Seducing you like that? I assure you, I do not go in for that sort of exercise."

He thought, But you've made a vacuum where my guts used to be.

Back at Starkley Challenor said he had been looking for Reardon in London. He had left Stirhanger Farm two days after Christmas. Reardon's escape had created some comment, so that Challenor said he had had to make a speech warning them off the subject on the grounds of his friendship with Reardon.

Though Challenor guessed that Reardon had been with a woman, he didn't share his speculation with any of the bomber crew. So there was no low mockery. Reardon eked out a quiet grief for a week or so. Bad weather kept the squadron grounded, and he had plenty of time to work out whether he was really contrite or penitent about his adventure with Lieutenant Enid Hadgraft—his one willing fornication and his subsequent adultery.

A week passed before they went on a mission. They were briefed to be deputy Master Bomber over Bochum. They directed bombers in to the target by means of H2S, for there were thick clouds. So they used the marking method called Wanganui, parachute flares. This was the peak of their bombing career, they decided the following day, when the reconnaissance photos came in.

25

Brosnan's Beach House

FOR Perpetua the spring and early summer approached at confusing speed. She was still beset by the questions her year at Rossclare had brought up. Whether she was sleeping or waking, they teased her mind and gave her dreams their awesome flavor.

But there were some bright prospects. A prosperous Rossclare layman and church pillar, Mr. Brosnan, owner of the Victoria Cinema and sundry other Rossclare businesses, including an agricultural and milking equipment agency, owned a large cottage down at Polly Heads on the coast. The beach there, said Sister Calixta, who had visited it once before, was twelve miles long. There was a general store, a few houses, wide paperbark swamps, and a great stretch of Pacific coast.

As the spring began, the sisters were offered the use of the place for a short vacation. Negotiations took weeks, but in the end it was decided that half the community would go in the next to last week in January, the rest in the last week. Being high summer in Rossclare's humid valley, fewer people got ill, and if people could postpone surgery, they tended to do so, at least until after the year started properly.

Perpetua concentrated throughout the early months of summer on that promise of the sea. And because of the daily regimen the sisters lived, the sort of routine that consumed days whole, consumed Christmas and New Year; because of the pace of even a questioning life, the vacation approached with astounding speed.

To begin the transfer of the first five nuns—Felice and one of the other nuns would not take a vacation but would instead attend a conference in Sydney—Father Murphy drove his large black Chevrolet, its gas-saving methane bag on top, to the garden gates. He transported the five nuns to the beach—Calixta, old Mother Catherine, Francis, Timothy, and Perpetua. He put their baggage in the Chevrolet's vast trunk. Both Perpetua and Timothy, the two youngest, crushed into the front with Francis and with Murphy so that old Mother Catherine in the back with only Calixta, would have room to stretch. Murphy had to drive in a sideways posture, but that was all right, said Catherine. God would protect them.

As they rolled down the valley, following the river, fields of cane, bananas, and maize along its banks, Mother Catherine would give her Irish chortle and say, "This is God's country indeed, indeed! No wonder so many of God's children can be found here! Their reward for centuries of British tyranny!"

By "God's children," of course, she meant the Irish. And my brother is a hero amongst those British Catherine denounces, Perpetua thought, and has somehow redeemed this glorious land.

"You can do your meditation on the beach in the mornings," Father Murphy told them. "Not that I was ever a champion meditator." He would be staying the day and then returning to Rossclare. They would not have Mass each morning, and it would be up to each of them to get through their daily roster of prayers and meditation. Apart from that, these limitless summer days were their own. But it was not just the lack of the normal convent regimen that excited Perpetua. It was the lack of Father Proud asking her to see the ancient coastline of Australia in the stone St. Justin held.

From one of the coastal hills they saw the long stretch of Polly Heads beach, and waves rolling ashore in perfectly formed crescents.

"I'll show you where it's safe to swim," said Murphy. "It's not safe just anywhere, you know. I don't want my old mate Catherine to be swept to New Zealand."

The Brosnan house was a bungalow in the sand dunes. Its long verandas were covered with lattice. There were beds on it, and as long as you used mosquito coils, it would be comfortable to sleep there at night. Amongst the cane brake behind the house stood a spidery and snaky-looking outhouse which Perpetua promised herself to use only by day. The view from the veranda itself was paradisal, and so wide open and empty of other humans that it was hard to believe it was specifically for this ocean that tens of thousands of Japanese, Americans, and Australians had perished.

Mother Catherine was placed on a chair in the shade of a pandanus tree. Father Murphy had brought one of the Sydney newspapers for her to read. The other four nuns and Father Murphy himself unpacked food from the car. He would pause on the veranda and nod toward where he and Mr. Brosnan had always found the best fishing holes, the pockets in the sand where the bream and whiting were, the sun-drenched shallows where the flathead lazed. Four black and highly modest swimsuits had been bought from Rendall's store. Perpetua, Timothy, Francis, and Calixta changed into them inside. Then they put on the loose but voluminous wraps which generally went over their nightgowns. They emerged one by one onto the lawn to see Father Murphy, wearing a white shirt over his shoulders and his paunch, looking strange in a black woollen pair of swimming shorts with a chromium buckle.

"Well now, sisters," he said. "You don't swim too close to the mouth of the lagoon, because sharks sometimes feed there. Right in front of the bungalow here is always safe. In heavy weather there's generally a rip down there, about a hundred yards north. Beyond it is the best place for fishing. Last one in's a heretic!" And he went jogging out onto the sand, slewing and crookedly dancing as the heat of the beach attacked the soles of his feet.

The nuns dropped their wraps and took off their sand shoes above the high-tide mark, where the sand was cooler to the tread. They stole glances at each other in their unfamiliar swimming suits. Calixta was a little narrower in the shoulders than in the hips. Timothy showed herself, as you'd expect, pale-skinned and hefty. Francis was lean and small-breasted. Perpetua wondered how they would define her. It was astounding that you could live for years and depend on these women, yet never—except in obvious cases like Timothy's—understand their true shape.

They all followed Father Murphy at a jog into the surf. There was the first shock as surf hit Perpetua between the legs, and then her breasts. She dived beneath. Timothy, who was unfamiliar with the sea, and in fact had not been introduced to it until she came to Sydney to become a novice, gamboled, deliberately comic, in the shallows. Francis and Calixta were content to reach waist depth and to jump as each wave struck them. Perpetua and Murphy found themselves out beyond the broken water looking for a wave to catch back to the beach.

"Obviously a surfer," commented Murphy, bobbing in the water some ten feet from Perpetua.

"My brother and I swam nearly every afternoon, and certainly on Saturdays and Sundays."

"And it seems better now, doesn't it?" he asked. "All the questions you have. They seem better now, here, don't they?"

She laughed at the truth of that.

"Dear old Brosnan—he might be a bit of a windbag, and he certainly drinks too much, but thank God for his generosity. I'd go mad if I didn't get down here every few weeks."

Father Murphy swam a little way away from her and then back. "I wonder if there is a Japanese sub out here? There've been plenty of ships sunk along the coast, you know. More than the government lets on. We were brought down here one weekend to give the last rites to what was left of some sailors from a freighter taking butter and shells to New Guinea. It was terrible—Mickey Proud was sick when he saw them. I wasn't much better. I still get nightmares. It's not like it is at the pictures, when the hero gets washed up in one piece."

They bobbed a little more. The other three sisters, as remote as children on the edges of the sea, were continually being thumped and clouted by the breaking waves. Out here it was tranquil. The fear of sharks lurked only remotely in the corner of the mind and actually made the swim more delicious.

"You know there are people in town who say that Michael Proud and I are priests only so that we can avoid the war."

"Catholics wouldn't say that," said Perpetua.

"You'd be surprised. As if I knew there'd be a damned war."

He dived for the bottom and appeared again a little closer to her. "I applied to be a chaplain, but everyone wants to be a chaplain, of course. I might have made a good chaplain. People are always telling me I've got the common touch, whatever in the hell that is. Listen, you're a game little woman, Perpetua Reardon. Don't take any risks with the surf. I don't think those three will be able to do much to help you if you got into trouble." And he nodded back to the shore. "You may find that Brosnan comes down to visit you one day. Just to have the gratification of seeing nuns enjoy themselves. It'll make him feel as if he'll go straight from Rossclare to the mansions above. So be patient with him, eh?"

The Rule was, no sunbathing. Sunbathing was vanity and was correctly seen as not far from sun worship. And in any case, as old Mother Catherine said, still sitting gratefully in the shade of the pandanus, "In my day girls would have sold their souls to the divil to look milk-white and pale. Because only farm girls looked red or brown. These heathen days, for no good reason, it's the other way 'round."

Rather than sit on the beach wrapped in her gown, Perpetua stayed in the water longer. Calixta timed her one morning—two and a half hours. Timothy, who was uncomfortable with the turmoil and noise of the surf, sat on the veranda playing dice games like Ludo with Sister Francis. Calixta fussed in the shallows while Perpetua bobbed farther out.

In the late afternoons, stinging with sunburn, her cap pinned into her half-dried hair and her gown belted up to leave her legs bare from the knees down, she would go fishing with whoever wished to join her—generally Calixta and Timothy. Timothy, with her bush background and unsentimental view of the death of animals, enjoyed fishing. It was Perpetua who felt some minor uneasiness. The whiting she caught were such beautiful and subtly colored creatures, and their eyes were as perfect as jewelry.

Mid-to-late afternoon there would usually be a thunderstorm—great cauliflower heads of cumulus would appear over the mountains behind the house, and then the sunburn would sting more joyously still.

Out of the money the sister bursar had allowed them, there was enough for an occasional ice cream cone which they bought at the general store. By the time they got Sister Catherine's back to her, it would be half soggy in the persistent late afternoon heat.

Their first visitor was not Mr. Brosnan. They saw Father Murphy's big black Chevrolet rolling along amongst the paperbarks, and when it stopped, an unsteady Father Proud, laden with books, opened the door and stepped out of the driver's seat.

"Sisters, sisters!" he intoned. "Some reading matter!"

As he reeled around Brosnan's great veranda, they could smell the liquor on him, emerging in his innocent and normally teetotal sweat. Maybe he had gone to a lunch somewhere, maybe at one of the hotels in Rossclare, and some admiring layman, pitying him for his seriousness, had given him too much to drink. And then he had done the first thing that came into his mind. Got into Murphy's car and driven down to Polly Heads to see his friend Perpetua and to bring her books. "A bit of light reading," Timothy would say without malice that night, turning the books over and looking at their titles. Maritain again, and Frank Sheed, and Etienne Gilson, and various poets, including Hopkins and McAuley.

"Wish he'd stayed home," Timothy murmured at one stage. And certainly, it was as if he'd brought Rossclare and the complications of the convent with him. They simply had not needed him, yet here he was, imposing himself.

Calixta cooked some extra food for him—lamb chops and potatoes—and set a special place for him on the veranda. He was not so far gone that he did not understand that the Rule made it impossible for him to eat with the nuns, even under the relaxed conditions of a vacation at the beach.

He left his meal half-eaten however. Joining the women afterward as they sat around the big table dutifully looking at the books he'd brought with him, but actually reading others specially borrowed from various nurses for their holiday—murder mysteries mainly, and an occasional Georgette Heyer—he began to talk manically about Louvain again. The occupation of Belgium by the Germans in 1940 had made it impossible for him to study there, he explained anew, even though His Lordship Bishop Flannery had already approved him to go and attempt to get his doctorate. "But now it's been liberated, you know," he said. "So in theory I could go any day. However, there are restrictions on travel, you see . . ."

It was ironic that Europe was full of young Australians, like her brother, who really wanted to be home, and here was a young Australian who wanted to be in Europe. Father Proud would always be the sort of Australian who looked upon Europe—rather than the coast of New South Wales, with its tough-minded dairy farmers and wistful green mountains—as home.

As the evening went on, the nuns realized collectively and as individual women that they were not at ease. Perpetua went to the kitchen with Calixta to make a pot of tea. The Rule could be waved to that extent, at least at Brosnan's beach house. The nuns could at least drink tea with Father Proud!

"He isn't fit to drive home," said Calixta, putting the kettle on the fuel stove. "We can't telephone the Bishop's house because there's no telephone, even at the general store. It's a mercy that on the way down here he didn't hit a cow or a Protestant." And even she began to laugh nervously at the problem Father Proud had set them. "I'm glad *The Rock* isn't around to see the car parked outside all night."

The Rock was a newly famous sectarian paper, produced in Sydney—even though newsprint was supposed to be rationed—which accused nuns of love affairs with priests, of secret pregnancies, and so on.

Francis and Timothy were meanwhile making up a bed for him in the front room, which Mother Catherine was willing to vacate. She had a lifetime's experience in letting the clergy have the best of everything. As they put the tea in front of him, he was still maundering on to Catherine about Louvain. Perhaps encouraged by Calixta's earlier remark, Perpetua found him sinisterly like a young suitor trying to impress a mother-in-law.

The other two nuns, their task of setting up the front bedroom for him finished, returned. He took a few sips of his tea and then fell asleep noisily in his chair. It was time for them to treat him as a patient. Timothy went ahead to pull the sheet on his bed down. Perpetua, Calixta, and Francis, in their practiced way, moved him upright. His eyes snapped open. He looked at them with a terror in his eyes, as if he had forgotten everything and was indeed just another patient, confused by ether, not fully conscious. Then his gaze softened. Perpetua had him by the wrist, but he pulled his arm out of her grasp and then sought her hand, as if he wanted to shake it. His eyes focused on her, and he gripped her fingers. The others did not seem to notice, and Perpetua thanked God for that. All the way down the dimly lit corridor and into the bedroom he kept his eyes on her, and she would have struggled to release her hand except that the others would have noticed. Yet letting him grasp her like that while he stared so frankly at her made her feel as if she were giving him a promise she had no right to give. Even when they had forced him down on his bed, he still gripped her, and in the end she had to forcibly wrench her hand away from his fist.

"Perpetua?" he said.

Thinking quickly, she nodded and said "Yes. And Calixta and Francis and Timothy." Which made the others titter indulgently.

"All right," he said. "All right." He belched—it was a little like retching, and quite uncharacteristic of his normal delicacy. Then he turned on his side and fell instantly and profoundly asleep.

The innocence of the vacation was marred now. His stare and his grip had altered things. She felt vaguely but painfully ashamed that she knew, on the basis of her limited experience but with absolute certainty, Father Proud wanted her as men want women. She could imagine herself in other circumstances being happy with a world where desire was not suppressed for supposed higher purposes. But in places where she thought it was safely at bay, at St. Bridie's and now at Brosnan's beach house, it had shown its rawest face.

Perpetua was awakened at first light by the snarl of a car's engine. It did not rouse Timothy, who shared the room, but when she got to the veranda she found Calixta and Francis both already there. Father Proud's car was vanishing down the sandy track amongst the paperbarks. He would be back in Rossclare to say a troubled morning Mass either in the glorified parish church they called the Cathedral of Rossclare, at the convent, or even down the hill at the boarding school.

He had left the books he had brought scattered across the dining room table.

Sister Perpetua and her four companions were collected from Brosnan's beach house in the last days of January and returned to the convent. Five other nuns then spent a week at Brosnan's, enjoying it all the more because of the coming fasts of the Lenten season, which this year began very early.

As it was, Perpetua both dreaded to see and very much wanted to see Father Proud in the corridors of St. John Vianney's. But he was not around the hospital much. Occasionally he said Mass in the convent, and then his thanksgiving afterward made the nuns later than ever for breakfast.

Perpetua wondered if he'd gone back to being his slightly obsessed self again and already forgotten his stare and the way he'd held on to her. But she had no way of telling, because she did not see him.

On Shrove Tuesday—that is, the eve of Ash Wednesday—she was woken very early in the morning by Calixta. The day was already so hot, bright, and still, that she thought she was in trouble for oversleeping when she saw Calixta fully dressed standing in her open doorway. "An emergency, Sister Perpetua," said Calixta very solemnly. "Mother Felice wants you to report to the operating room at once."

Perpetua, going briefly to the lavatory and the hand basin, was surprised to see a number of other nuns there, brushing their teeth and washing—Timothy sponging herself beneath her white and freckled shoulders. "What's all the fuss?" Timothy asked.

Perpetua shrugged in a way that said she had no idea. Mother Felice entered the washbasin area. "Hurry, sisters, please."

When Perpetua got across to the hospital, Felice was waiting for her in the downstairs corridor. Other nuns, including Calixta and Timothy, arrived. Felice spoke to them in a low but reverberating voice.

"Father Proud has suffered a serious injury. It is the sort of injury about which there must be no gossip at all, not even amongst yourselves. I must say that again—not even amongst yourselves. Because if people heard about it, it could put the Church in a position of mockery. You understand that, don't you? There will be no lay sisters at all on the operating team, because the Church *must* depend for its reputation on you. I do trust that it can, with confidence, do so."

As they scrubbed up, and then as they waited in the operating room, nothing further was said. But when Father Proud was wheeled in sedated, a canopy over his lower abdomen, and when—the canopy having been taken away—they saw the nature of his injuries, an explanation had to be made to them. Perpetua heard the details from Felice with horror and with a fearful sense of responsibility. She could have spoken to Father Murphy about the way Father Proud pursued her with books and ideas, but she was frightened that Murphy might think she fancied herself, somehow, as a girl, or was deluded. And so out of vanity she had not, and this was the result. The housekeeper at the Bishop's house had gone to awaken Father Proud at five o'clock and found him in a coma on the floor of his room. He had driven a pencil squarely and savagely into his penis, along the urethra and through it into the abdominal sac, where he had punctured the peritoneum.

Dr. Cormack's remarks, when he arrived and during the operation, were an indication that he believed it to have happened early in the night, rather than in the small hours. He was worried that fragments of lead might cause septicemia.

As she had been for some months, Perpetua was operating-room sister to good Dr. Cormack, the only Protestant who was to be let into this terrible Catholic secret. She found herself working with a remote efficiency. No one seemed to blame her. Perhaps she could have more easily come to a decision if they had.

26

Firestorm

THERE were groans on Shrove Tuesday, 1945, when the station commander said it would be Dresden. Not from Squadron Leader Stove, however, who calculated in a notebook on his lap and murmured quietly to Winton that it was about ten hours' round trip.

The station commander argued down the noises of dissent. He told the crews that Dresden had become a crucial supply dump and transit center now that the Russians were on the borders of Saxony. There were ammunition works there, I.G. Farben's petrochemical plants, Zeiss precision-instrument plants. The Russians wanted it bombed, he concluded.

"Then why don't they do it?" asked Alf Hater of Reardon and Challenor. "They're only ninety miles away."

The station commander was followed by the intelligence officer. Though the Russians wanted Dresden bombed, bomber crews were to be very careful to head back west if they got into trouble on the way in. Navigators were to look for the distinctive H2S image of Dresden. In some ways it was like the image of any old German town on the banks of a river, so navigators and set operators were to look for the distinctive S bend the Elbe traveled at Dresden. Unfortunately, there were no radar comparison photographs of Dresden for the navigators to use, so everyone had to be very careful.

A woman corporal went around the room distributing little perspex packages to every crew member. You could see, inside the perspex, a union jack. "What you are being given is a British flag in case you come down behind the Russian lines. Be sure to show it to our Russian brothers. It has, printed on it in their language, 'I am an Englishman.' Those of you who aren't Englishmen, like our Australian friends, will simply have to do their best."

Beneath the cover of some booing from the Canadians and Australians, Reardon thought, I don't want to make any more fires. As well as that, ten hours was too long for him. He didn't know if he had the internal fuel for it.

Unfortunately, the intelligence officer continued, as was the case with the radar comparison pictures, so it was with the maps. They didn't have the usual maps for them—the high definition blue and gray maps with the target marked in orange. The map for tonight was an older map made up from aerial photographs.

How old were the photographs? one of the pilots asked.

The intelligence officer said airily, "A year? Eighteen months? Something like that."

The station commander took over again. He traced their route in—across the south coast of England, over the French coast near the Seine estuary, then a dogleg ten miles north of Aachen to tease but avoid the Ruhr flak defenses, then north of Cologne, north of Nuremberg, a feint toward Leipzig and straight on to Dresden, following the curve of the Elbe. The homeward course was away to the southwest, south of Nuremberg, Stuttgart, and Strasbourg.

The maps that were given out now had no flak positions marked on them, nor any warnings as to the decoy sites the Germans generally prepared and then lit on the outskirts of cities to deceive bombardiers. Reardon began to taste the ashes of death on his tongue. He had had his joy with Enid Hadgraft, and now it was time for the worst of things. If they had not marked the flak positions, it was because they must know the flak was too massive to tell crews about.

Reardon, having reached this conclusion, looked around to see if the others had. There was the usual tautness in their faces, nothing more. He must not, of course, mention it.

Call sign to the Master Bomber was "Cheesecake," an echo of

"Piece of Cake," a term which Reardon had not heard for some months now and which he despised. Winton's crew and eleven others in the squadron were to act as Visual Centerers—that is, they were to find Dresden by H2S and then, when they were in visual contact, drop their red and green target indicators on either side of the aiming point. They would be backed up if necessary, and in case cloud drifted over their target indicators, by Blind Sky markers with the Wanganui-style parachute flares. Their call sign was to be "Press On." Reardon could hear men swearing around him. It was such a childish call sign. But if you looked at it, it was full of the warning of fierce enemy defenses.

The meteorologist was gesturing at the route map on the wall and talking of the weather. Ten-tenths cloud was covering most of Western Europe. There was a danger of icing, and there were electrical storms over France and western and central Germany. All this would keep the fighters down, said the weatherman. As for the target itself, a gap in the cloud would edge up from the southwest and display Dresden to view for five hours from about nine in the evening until two in the morning. That window in the cloud would make the attack possible.

Outside, on his way to the crew rooms, Reardon eyed the chained and sealed public telephone. He had an impulse to call London, to speak with her. He even began to feel the coins in his pocket, the coins he would not be permitted to take on the operation. This futile impulse scared him. It's not like me, he thought.

The attack on Dresden was to be in two waves. The first one would get the city burning and draw in fire brigades and other resources from all over Saxony. The second blow, some three hours later, would attack the city just as the gauleiter was getting things under control, just as the fire fighters were beginning to think they might have a chance of controlling events.

In trying to reassure the crews, the station commander let it slip that he wondered how their red markers were to show up against the fires generated by the first wave.

Over parts of France that now lay in Allied hands, the bombardier, helped by Alf Hater, began tearing the brown paper off the stacks of tinfoil called Window and dropping it through the hatch. Alf was always grateful for something to do—time pooled heavily between the half-hourly wind direction and weather forecasts that came in over his radio. There were times when he had even brought a book aboard, though the others who were forward in the aircraft mocked him for it and said he'd never finished a paragraph. Reardon, who had nothing to do except go on quartering the sky, would have welcomed such a regular task as dropping Window every minute down through the blast of cold air from the hatch. As the Lancasters from Reardon's squadron crossed the front line twenty miles north of Luxembourg, the pace of Windowing increased to once every thirty seconds.

Winton was climbing now, for the parachute flares they would have to release were timed to explode at a high altitude. The sky was empty, but sometimes Reardon would see another bomber appear for an instant as St. Elmo's blue fire defined its engine cowlings or its wings in the distance. The cloud was high and thick, but Reardon did not let that lull him. Already he felt in his brain the jolting of the terrible Dresden flak that Bomber Command had not dared mark on the maps. Behind him he saw a flak barrage rising into the sky—it must have been radar-directed flak from the cities of the Ruhr. That was probably a spoof attack, Reardon knew, a fake assault by a light force with a few bombs, just enough to confuse the German defenses.

It was one o'clock, then. A yellow gout of flame pushed Reardon's turret sideways. To his port he saw a Lancaster explode. It was known now that there was no such thing as scarecrow shells. He reported the loss to Winton. Then he switched off and began to whimper. Oh God, do not sunder this body beloved of Enid Hadgraft. Well, it wasn't beloved. Not on a permanent basis. Oh God, do not sunder this body beloved temporarily by Enid Hadgraft. Another Lancaster exploded to his left, which was the starboard of the bomber. Was there a city down there? The air was full of flame. Over the intercom he heard Winton screaming, "What in the bloody hell is happening? That's not Dresden, for God's sake, is it?"

"No, it must be something else," said Stove. "My God, it must be the batteries at Chemnitz."

"Why didn't you take us 'round them?" asked Winton. For

once, the characteristic petulance of pilots, with all their manhood and reputation invested in their aircraft, was palpable in his voice.

"Actually," Reardon heard Stove answer, "it's not on the map we were given."

"For Christ's sake!" said Winton. And then you could hear him bite off further reproaches of Stove. He growled, "Bloody Bomber Command's not getting more efficient, it's getting more amateurish!"

For some reason this remark sent odd waves of comfort throughout the plane. An instant later the craft was madly rocked. On the intercom Reardon heard, "Holy shit!" from Alf.

And yet whatever it was permitted Winton time to ask, "What is it?"

"A bloody eighty-eight-millimeter shell," Alf said. "It came in through the floor and out through the bloody roof. Bloody hell!"

Reardon sat in his turret moaning and bewailing, quartering the sky as he had been told to do. He saw a Lancaster close behind, four hundred yards, maybe—one of their own squadron, you could bet—blown to pieces in an excess of red and yellow flame. Its parachute flares went zipping toward earth and its green indicators exploded as it fell through twenty thousand feet. All the crew's experience was torn apart and sent glowing and burning through the night.

Reardon reported it numbly, "Lancaster hit to starboard. No parachutes."

He thought, If it's like this over Chemnitz, what will it be like over Dresden?

Perhaps ten seconds after the Chemnitz barrage stopped, he heard someone in the crew say, "Oh my God!"

Inch's Ulster accent asked, "Is that Dresden?"

Stove murmured, "There *is* a gap in the cloud."

"And if there weren't," said Alf Hater, "*that* would have burned one in it."

They all sounded reverent.

Winton muttered, "The bloody Lincolnshire Poachers." For the marking of the target during the first raid had been done by Mosquitoes and Lancasters from Number Five Group, based in Lincolnshire. Reardon marveled yet was also grateful that his captain could, in this deepest hour of the night, feel a professional jealousy.

Reardon heard Challenor say from the mid-upper turret, "No flak at all."

Winton heard this and called to Reardon, "Fighters, Reardon?"

Reardon quartered the increasingly bright sky. "Nothing, skip," he said in his deliberately constructed normal voice.

They heard for the first time the excellent modulation of the Master Bomber—they sent Master Bombers to a special radio announcer's course.

"Cheesecake to Press On force, Cheesecake to Press On. Aiming point obscured by fire and smoke. Drop Target Indicators either side of fire storm. Two runs, three T.I.'s per run. Press On number one T.I.'s to right, number two to left, and so on. Over."

Reardon saw the sky full of Lancasters, lit as by late afternoon summer light. He could see the vapor trails of the engines. There were still no flak bursts, still no fighters. Were they waiting to make a hell of the way out?

He heard Winton say at last, "Press On number two dropping T.I.'s to left of fire storm. Tally-ho!"

Their bombing run was straight and level at twenty thousand feet, but through the perspex of his turret Reardon could feel the city's astounding heat. For the first time ever on a mission he closed his eyes for a conscious second. The bombardier announced that three T.I.'s and a two-thousand-pound cookie had been released. He heard the Master Bomber announce, "Cheesecake to Press On force, nice placement number one and two. Imitate, numbers three and four, etcetera."

Reardon watched the sight below with an astonishment and a terror not muted at all by his earlier experience of fire storms. From end to end, it seemed, the town blazed incandescently. Medieval streets and alleys showed up like wires in an electrical fire. You could see the headlights of trucks approaching the city—fire brigades, rescue workers, bringing succor into the inferno. Down there, something quite inhuman had been released. Anyone writing of hell who had not seen *this* fire lacked authority.

"I didn't want to make this sort of thing," he announced, hoping that he'd switched off his intercom but not remembering if he had.

Winton took the bomber away from the great visibility the fire gave. Yet in the edges of the night, where they circled for a quarter of an hour, waiting for the order to re-mark the target, it was still a vivid twilight.

Winton must have found the silence over Dresden astounding, for he asked the crew if they could see anything, and banked the plane so Reardon could see beneath the fuselage. Any Messerschmitt beneath them would have been delineated—brighter than most European days—by the furnace below.

As D-Dog circled the eastern outskirts of Dresden, Reardon saw the main bomber force arrive——under the Master Bomber's request—at a lower altitude. The Master Bomber had decided there would be no flak, and he probably had the experience of the first wave, relayed to him from base, to go on.

There wasn't even the danger of being struck from above, Reardon thought, and for some lunatic reason he began to feel ashamed. You could see the racks of hexagonal incendiaries, the canisters of high explosives, and the general purpose bombs descend individually, marked out by the blaze. Almost unnecessarily the Master Bomber ordered D-Dog in again to drop the rest of their target indicators to the left of the enormous fire.

Cringing but alert behind his guns, Reardon felt the radiance of the ball of fire enter through the opening of the perspex and strike his eyelids, which at this altitude were generally frozen. In that heat, he believed he could feel, each strand of pain absolutely separate, the consuming of everything—the wooden Virgins in the medieval churches, the marriage beds and the cradles and the dining room tables. There was a breath of exploding gas mains, the puzzlement of citizens in cellars down there, the cries of children appealing to Deity and Mother, the cries whose oxygen went to feed the fire. "It's terrible, terrible," he informed himself. And then, since he could not speak normally, he decided not to speak at all. He rehearsed the only words he wanted to utter. They were, "All clear, skip"; "Corkscrew hard port!"; "Corkscrew hard starboard!" That was all the vocabulary he now had left in him.

The Master Bomber said, "Cheesecake to Press On force. Nice backup marking. Go home, repeat, go home!"

He heard Winton acknowledge, and with a fake laziness, announce that they were turning home. In his turret Reardon could not escape the sight of the fire. A hundred miles away, even though Winton was beginning to dive so that he would get under the German panorama radar, the blaze still remained a molten clot in Reardon's night sight. It remained there when he blinked. He knew it would always be there whenever he closed his eyes. He would not be relieved of it by the passing of time.

He did not have to tell Winton to corkscrew, for soon they were over occupied ground in France and their only anxiety was whether Alf Hater had remembered to turn on the Identification Friend or Foe device, or whether some exceptionally rugged night fighters might be operating here, over these skies which now seemed to belong exclusively to the Allied bomber and the Mustang fighter. A few times he had the honor of reporting to Winton that everything was clear.

When they landed at Starkley, he could say nothing more. He stayed in his turret. His armorer turned up, unlatched the doors from the inside of the fuselage, and said, "Any problems, sir?"

When he could not get Reardon to answer or even to turn his head, he fled from the plane in awe and reported to Winton and Challenor. In the cold fumes of expended gasoline, and above the whining of trucks taking crews back from dispersal for debriefing, he heard the erk saying, "He doesn't move, sir."

At last, as he had hoped, Challenor appeared. "Come on, mate," Challenor told him in a low voice. He stood him up by the shoulders and folded down the metal seat to allow Reardon to back out of the turret. "Hey, that wasn't a bad one, was it?"

Reardon could not answer. He was aware of the extraordinary, aged stiffness of his limbs. Challenor helped him down through the hatch, expecting of him something of the normal agility of an undamaged member of an aircrew. In fact Reardon fell forward onto the pavement and landed with his nose in a pool of oil. He could not move. The great fire of Dresden had burned out of him all juice and all the liquid electric energy. He could hear from behind the other crew members, Challenor and Alf, Stove and Winton, discussing his case, speculating whether he was wounded. They did that as an act of grace to him, he thought, even though they knew he wasn't wounded. They knew what had happened to him. What had happened to him, he understood at once, had very nearly happened to them. Some orderlies put him on a stretcher and he traveled by ambulance with Challenor. No matter how he tried, he still could not find anything to say. What did Challenor think? he asked himself. But then he remembered that, compared to the size of the fire, what Challenor or anyone thought didn't count.

He was taken to a room of his own in the station hospital. Challenor refused to leave him. Yet as he lay on the bed, still in his flight suit, a great fear overcame him, fear that had risen from the Saxons of Dresden and entered his chest. Again he felt a child's panic. He said, "Mother!" He could feel his face dancing, frantic nerves jumping under the hollows of his eyes. Challenor stood up, had spotted the crisis, and held Reardon's hand. "Hang on, sport. I'll get the medico."

A doctor came and instructed an orderly to issue Reardon with certain pills. Within ten minutes Pilot Officer Reardon was unconscious.

27

Flannery's Council

THE day after Father Proud's operation, he was still confused and half conscious, and Dr. Cormack chose to keep him in a state where he rarely emerged from unconsciousness. This was for the young priest's own sake and also, perhaps, to allow the Bishop time to decide what to do with the boy and his mad act.

At mid-morning Perpetua and Timothy were given the task of serving tea to Bishop Flannery, His Vicar General Monsignor Curran, his secretary, Dr. Lawlor, and his Privy Council. The most junior member of this Privy Council of seven priests was Father Murphy.

Timothy opened the door to the front parlor where the Council was meeting, and Perpetua wheeled in the tea trolley. Half a week's ration of eggs for the whole convent had gone into the sumptuous cake that lay under a cloth amongst the tea things. Perpetua expected the appearance of this phenomenon to cause a lull in the discussions about what to do with Father Proud, but the Bishop and the others went on discussing the question as intently as ever and as if she and Timothy weren't there.

Monsignor Curran was talking as Perpetua brought the tea trolley to a halt behind Bishop Flannery.

"So," said the Monsignor, "one thing's certain—the boy has to be got out of the diocese as soon as possible, before gossip spreads. If he's out, there might be rumors about that, certainly, but they won't be able to be checked—as it were—against the man himself, since the man himself will be gone."

"This is if the poor little fellow lives," said one of the priests from farther down the coast.

"Please God," said the Monsignor, "he *will* live."

"The new drugs make that a more and more likely outcome," said Father Lawlor.

"Praise be to God!" said the Irishman from down the coast.

A bottle of whiskey sat in the middle of the parlor table, and some of the priests reached for it and unselfconsciously poured a slug into their black tea as Perpetua and Timothy served it.

"Have you heard of this new treatment called psychiatry?" said one of the priests. "Much in prominence because of the war—all the boys who've gone troppo or shell-shocked?"

There was a growl from the Bishop. "Just a modern version of exorcism, isn't it?" he asked. "I mean, it comes down to the same thing. Getting rid of the spirits that are preying on a person, making his soul sour, holding it captive?"

"The finest exorcist is Monsignor Cleary in Sydney," said the priest from down the coast. "Spent years driving out demons in China."

As if he thought the conversation was getting too speculative, Murphy interrupted. "Surely it's not a matter of driving out devils! I mean, the poor boy's driven by some impossible idea of achieving perfection. They could never say that about me, maybe. But everything about Michael Proud showed you he was crazy for perfection—perfection in saying Mass, perfection of ideas. Please, Your Lordship, don't do him the wrong of considering it a matter of demonic possession! Unless you can consider the flesh itself a demon! And if his flesh is a demon, then as God knows, the poor little bugger paid it off pretty savagely."

The Bishop coughed and exchanged a glance with dapper Dr. Lawlor, his canon lawyer. One of the priests said, "What if we sent him home to his parents for a year? When he can walk, that is. When he's up again."

Murphy shook his head. "Your Lordship, it's too small a town where he comes from. It's a village. He'd go mad there."

"Well, Father Murphy," groaned Bishop Flannery, "you're his closest friend. Although, did he had any *close* friends amongst us? Maybe that was his problem."

Perpetua heard the rumble of matey assent around the table.

"What would you suggest?" the Bishop asked Murphy.

Murphy frowned and spoke carefully. "If he'd been able to go to Louvain and live the intellectual life that was so dear to his heart, he might have been all right. He could have taught in the seminary in Sydney, which is a sight easier than working in a parish." Again there was a rumble of agreement. "May I suggest, Your Lordship, 'kissing the sacred purple,' as the old phrase has it, that Dr. Lawlor should apply to Rome to release Father Proud from his vows." He raised his hand as if to still the inevitable dissent. In fact, Perpetua noticed, her own face burning, Father Lawlor had inhaled sharply, intending to disagree to the limit.

Murphy argued on. "The life of a priest is absolutely impossible for him now. He needs a different sort of care than any of us can give him."

"You mean marriage, I suppose," said one of the Irishmen. "But how can we be sure he hasn't neutered himself?"

Perpetua spilled some of the tea she was serving to the Irishman from down the coast. "Sorry, Father," she muttered, and began to ply a cloth across the surface of the mahogany table.

"Don't fuss yourself, Sister," said the priest.

His Lordship said, "We can't make decisions for the poor fellow, even though he's not fit to make them for himself just now. We've had a number of suggestions. One, get the boy a dispensation from the priesthood. Now that, if I might point out, Father Murphy, is a choice full of potential scandal in itself. It might unbalance the boy further still, you understand."

Father Murphy lowered his head and shook it a little.

"Then," continued His Lordship, "we could send him home to his parents. What would he do, poor little fellow, in a village like that? You're quite right there, Father Murphy. It isn't the sort of place where the faintly tetched get better. It's more a place where the definitely sane get faintly tetched."

There was laughter, and one of the Irishmen took an extra slug of scotch in yet another cup of tea, and around the table the healthy, whole priests of the diocese bit into the wedges of sponge cake Timothy was now serving.

"There's another thing we could do, and I wonder what you think of it. I have a brother who is provincial of the Missionaries of the Sacred Heart in Sydney. They've got a big place, a monastery, on a hill near the race course. A few days at the races would do young Michael Proud a wealth of good. I'd give him a dispensation to go."

"Most of the priests in Sydney don't need a dispensation," said one of the Irish. "They're there every Saturday."

Again there was laughter and good humor—the sugar and eggs of the cake, and the drops of "the crater" in the tea, all helped ensure that.

"He could have a room at the monastery, and the good monks could keep an eye on him. And then, of course, if anything went wrong, he'd be close to clever men down there—even to psychiatrists. He could study if he wanted; he could write a book. Well, what do you think, gentlemen?"

"That's the way to go," said the Vicar General. "Even Murphy would agree with that, wouldn't you, Brian?"

Some of the older priests dug each other in the ribs as if they knew what a character Murphy was.

"It might be the way to deal with it," said Murphy. And then he smiled himself, wanly, more wistfully than the others. "Perhaps His Lordship could send me down there to take young Mike to the races now and then. Perhaps I could be the horse-flesh chaplain. . . ."

None of the priests went home for another two days. Their time in Rossclare was spent mainly in the parlor or the Bishop's house. There was much tea and, you could judge from the increasing joviality of the Privy Council, some quantities of whiskey. Dr. Cormack continued to keep Father Proud heavily sedated, and yet one afternoon Perpetua and Timothy, entering Father Proud's room, saw one of the priests with his pants unzipped and unbuckled and fallen to about thigh level. While dazed Father Proud tried to focus on this amazing spectacle, the priest was pointing to the red dots on his underwear. "What do you think of these, Michael, my boy?" the priest was asking. "Sure, it's my sister in Philadelphia sent them to me by ship."

The priest did not seem panicked by the arrival of the two young nuns, but calmly belted and buttoned himself up again with such innocence that you did not doubt for a second that all he was doing was showing off his comic underwear in the hope of cheering his overserious colleague, Proud.

28

Dow

REARDON revived in a wintry dusk. All he knew was that he was being carried like a baby up a long stone staircase from a gravel drive. There was a smell of salt and a cawing of sea gulls. He was in his uniform—even in his greatcoat, he understood—yet an enormous middle-aged warrant officer held him like that, hunched and fetal, in his arms.

"It'll be all right, son," said the warrant officer. "You just need to sleep."

The warrant officer bore him along a corridor and into a room where two beds stood beneath a high, molded ceiling. From his infantlike vantage point he saw over the warrant officer's shoulder a glint of last light on a gray sea.

"Where is this?" asked Reardon, finding to his amazement that his mouth was drier than a bone and that he couldn't use it properly.

"This is RAF Hospital, Torquay. Bit of sea air will set you up, eh? Your roommate is Flight Lieutenant Mulray. An old hand. You'll see him come and go. You don't have to say anything to him. He's a good fellow."

"What's your name?" asked Reardon with a mouth that seemed

to be constructed with steel wool. Yet it was all at once an urgent matter to find out what the warrant officer's name was.

"I'm Warrant Officer Dow, son. I'm an old bugger. I'm not a young hero, like you."

Reardon sat woodenly as Warrant Officer Dow changed him into pajamas and showed him where the pot was under the bed. The pot was in case he could not manage the journey down the corridor to the toilet.

Over the next drugged week Reardon was aware of Mulray coming and going. He was a solid young man who sang tunes to himself and smoked an aromatic pipe. He wore his uniform and hung a picture of a country house, his or somebody else's, above his bedside table. He had quite a pile of books there, too, so that his side of the room looked well lived in.

Reardon could tell in a confused way that Mulray was also used to having barely conscious roommates. He accepted Reardon as part of the furniture. You knew that you ran no risk of waking and finding him standing above you, and that was a comfort. Sometimes Reardon woke, however, and Warrant Officer Dow was there, standing as if he'd been waiting awhile for this brief contact. But that was all right. Dow would generally wink and say something like, "Feeling better, son?"

It was eight days before Reardon left his bed. He could not remember in that time having eaten a meal, yet he had no appetite. He put on his uniform now to go to the toilet—in hospital pajamas he felt vulnerable. Mulray came into the room one day when Reardon had just returned from the lavatory and was sitting, groggily staring at his own unoccupied chair, on the edge of his bed.

Mulray said, "Want a turn in the garden before dinner, old man?" An observer might had thought that Mulray and Reardon were intimately connected with each other. "Does chaps a world of good, a bit of a turn through the shrubbery. And I must say, not a bad day today, sun sinking to the west, a little light on the sea."

Reardon got up to follow him, not knowing why. He couldn't think of anyone else in the world for whom he'd go strolling in some meaningless garden. Mulray was leading him out through French doors. But Reardon stopped a few paces from them. It was simply that he had no fuel left. He stopped and said nothing. Mulray said, "Oh, I can see you're a bit dusted, old man. Why don't you go back to bed for the nonce? Perhaps we'll go for a garden hike tomorrow."

Mulray, Reardon was very pleased to find, did not try to bully him into curative strolls. The flight lieutenant's politeness in the matter showed one thing. He had thought and felt at one stage the way Reardon thought and felt now. So, though it did not seem possible, perhaps there was still a future in which a person could hang pictures and enjoy a constitutional walk.

He found the air-force doctors brisk, but they were allowed to be compassionate in a way not permitted to flight surgeons at bomber stations. They, too, seemed to understand precisely Reardon's condition. They were cheery and practical. They did not probe. All they did was write orders for medicines that gave you oblivion.

In his third week in Torquay Reardon remembered that the war was still on. He had more or less remembered during his long slumber, but did not want to know anything, for after the great blaze of Dresden, who won or lost didn't mean anything. One of the things he wondered, however, was whether any new rockets had come from the German arsenals, and whether, too, the Luftwaffe jet planes had become more apparent. It was no more than a glimmer of interest.

He found out from a copy of *The Express* that the corridor of German-held territory between the Russians and the Allies had narrowed to less than two hundred miles in places. There were cartoons of the German leaders sitting in rubble, amongst broken chancellery columns. The captions read, "Masters of their own Empire!" The broken rubble reminded him too vividly, though, of the damage Winton's crew had done to Europe, and so he turned the page, looking for the comics. He did not want to become riveted and hypnotized by war news the way Lieutenant Regan had.

Very soon afterward Reardon went on a stroll with Mulray along the clifftops.

"I believe that you're quite a veteran," said Mulray. "Warrant Officer Dow is very impressed, and you've got to be pretty good to impress that old sod."

Reardon said nothing.

"How many missions?" said Mulray, obviously giving way to an impulse.

"Seventy-two, I think. Yes, seventy-two."

"My God," said Mulray. "I've been far too long here. Nearly eighteen months in fact. I mean, I want to fly ops—I'm a regular, after all. Just a few problems left now, nearly everything fixed. I'm really looking forward to getting back. I mean, I'm a regular. I was one of those who actually *enjoyed* it. Ops, I mean. That's what I can't understand. The medicos told me not to try. They say that will hold things up."

"You wouldn't want to fly ops," said Reardon. "It's not like you remember."

"Funny. A number of chaps have said that. Of course, I don't meet them when they're on the top of their game. Tell me, what did you do in the big world? Before all this, I mean?" He gestured at the hospital. It was in fact a commandeered spa hotel of Victorian vintage. You could imagine girls in summer dresses running down the terraces, drawing the vitriol of elderly uncles and maiden aunts.

"I was a student," said Reardon.

"Oxford? Cambridge?"

"No. I was at school. At Rose Bay. In Australia."

"That's right. You *are* Australian. I think it's jolly decent of you to fly seventy-two missions. Mind you, I desperately want to get back myself. As I told you, I'm a regular."

"Yes."

It was only after they finished walking that Reardon realized that he had said more words in ten minutes with Mulray than he had in the past month.

The Allies were parked now on the Elbe, and the Soviets were over the Oder. There was a hope in the streets of Torquay of a coming old-fashioned English summer by the sea, and it reached even the patients in the gardens of the spa hospital.

As the first spring sun manifested itself, Warrant Officer Dow invited Mulray, Reardon, and two other patients home to his suburban villa for tea. It was a fine evening, and Mrs. Dow, a woman of comfortable proportions and a pleasant face, made conversation, about how this was the beginning of spring in early March, as she put the tea things out on the table in the parlor. The Dows had a much doted-on daughter of nine. Her name was Daphne. She was encouraged to be clever, and had no trouble speaking to adults. Reardon noticed that she did not ask awkward questions of the airmen, even though one of them had a hectic facial tic, another was permanently silent, and Mulray might at any time go off absentmindedly into humming a tune. Reardon wondered what peculiarities he himself was showing.

Dow cunningly encouraged his daughter to ask Reardon questions about Australia, the standard questions about natives and kangaroos and sheep farms. Reardon would not have dreamed of giving way to the silences he had recently been choosing to keep. Not in front of the child.

They were eating Mrs. Dow's fine sponge cake on floral plates with proper cake forks. Suddenly Mulray dropped his fork to the ground. Reardon could see it on the floor, quite close to Mulray's shoe. Mulray's hand began to tremble. He looked at the floor and could see the fork himself. Yet he did nothing. A terrible, child-like, appealing cry came from him. He cringed, covered his eyes, and began to weep.

The child got up from her place, picked up the fork and put it back on the table, but was gracious enough not to say anything. I would like my children to have as much humane skill as that, Reardon thought. But then there's no sense to having children in a world of fire balls.

The officer who did not speak left the room and began pacing the hallway and smoking. Warrant Officer Dow knew that the tea party was over, and very soon afterward a taxi arrived at the front door for them. As he got into it, Reardon said to Dow out of a drug-dried mouth, "You're very kind." He meant it, too, and he hoped Dow knew that.

On the way back to the hospital in the cab, Mulray was silent for the first half of the short journey. Occasionally he would scratch, rather than wipe, his tearstained face. At last he said, "A chap got a little bit carried away. I mean, that's been the problem for some time. Damn it . . ."

"It wasn't anything to take notice of," said Reardon. "I'd forget it if I were you."

"Would you really?" asked Mulray. "Would you be able to forget it?"

"Of course I would."

"You know what I'd like, Reardon. I'd like to buy you a pint."

But the patients were not supposed to go to pubs.

"Wouldn't mix with the medicine," said Reardon.

I am getting better, Reardon thought. I am better than these men. In spite of the fire, I did think of children.

Then, from nowhere, these words came to his lips. "I have a sister who's a nun."

Mulray stared at him.

"No," said Reardon. "It's the truth, and until now I'd forgotten it."

29

Murphy's Conference

WHAT she had overheard of the Privy Council meeting, what they had after all let her hear, had changed Perpetua for good. She knew that, but was too busy with her daily life to inspect what the change was, to ask the question. It might in fact take years before she was ready to examine the new being she'd become. It was, she could tell by instinct, a lesser being than she'd been before, a being of diminished horizons.

Whenever the dazed Proud saw her enter his room, he would try to hide his face and weep creakily, like a scared child. Felice saw this too. "It isn't your fault," she told Perpetua, "but I think we should keep you away from him. For some reason you represent an ideal he believes he's let down through his attack on himself." It was a kindly reading of the relationship between herself and Father Proud, and not for the first time Perpetua was grateful for Felice's convent-style savoir-faire.

There were fevers and other signs of Proud's peritoneal damage, and even a week after his operation no one would predict his survival, though everyone said his youth would be a critical factor. Just how much that positive advantage would be cancelled by his obvious despair and shame, no one could predict.

*   *   *

Mother Catherine was exempt in view of her age both from Chapters of Faults and from the burden of knowing about Father Proud in too greater detail. It was clear to Perpetua, however, that she was not ignorant of what had befallen young Michael Proud. At recreation she asked the young nuns penetrating questions about it.

"It's getting to be a dangerous world," she said. "Sure, I hope I get out of it before anything worse happens."

The old nun was alone in the convent one afternoon when one of the characteristic summer storms unleashed itself above Ross-clare. At such times, she often tottered around seeing if windows were shut. She found her way down the corridor to the bathroom. Above the bath an open window let in a torrent.

Catherine felt very much in command of this bathroom. She never let Perpetua, the most junior of the nuns and her kindly right hand, fuss around her in here. She put herself into the bath, she took herself out. Everyone, even Felice, knew that she would not tolerate it any other way. So this was ground on which she had some practiced skills.

She found a wooden stool, dragged it over under the window, hoisted herself on it and reached up to close the window. Great stinging drops of rain blinded her. The stool shifted beneath her feet. She grabbed for where she believed there was a railing. There was none. She found herself hurtling sideways into the bath. Through her efforts in midair, she fell back and landed in the tub. Her head cracked against the far enamel rim, and she thought that that would kill her. But though her head rang, she was still living. There was frightful pain in her hip. She could see her shoes, her white-stockinged legs, protruding from the far end of the bath. She called. Perhaps Callixta, recovering from night duty, might stir and visit the toilets and hear her. Otherwise it was unlikely she would be found in the near future. And she didn't want to be found—she didn't want doctors to see her with her legs in the air like this. And yet the pain was astounding. She felt the bath itself swimming through space.

No, she understood, it was her consciousness going. The bath was staying. It was she who was falling.

*   *   *

They found her a little after five o'clock in the afternoon. The storm had drenched her and she was unconscious. They moved her to the hospital, carried her on a litter into X ray, and discovered she had broken the head of the femur. Dr. Cormack put her in traction, or "on the rack," as patients called it. Ideally he would have operated on her and inserted a Smith-Peterson pin and plate, but Catherine was in shock, and aged, and therefore—for a start, anyway—traction was indicated.

She would wake in considerable pain to see that Perpetua, Timothy, and Bernadette Brady were in the room. A day had passed and another summer storm crackled over the town. Bernadette Brady was taking her pulse, Timothy and Perpetua inspecting and adjusting the traction in small ways. Their movements were the concerned movements of children who were not sure what they could do to help.

"Oh!" she said.

She seemed profoundly disappointed. The two young nuns approached the head of the bed.

"I wanted to die in the convent," said Catherine. She had, as Perpetua could see, begun to weep.

"You can go back to the convent very soon, Mother," said Perpetua, smiling, yet aware of the lie in her smile.

"No," said Catherine. "This is my sign. The femur is always a sign to old people. I'm not going to let it run me about, give me the fun of Cork. I know a sign when I see it. I am in pain now with my Crucified Lord. It's time to go to him."

Perpetua and Timothy exchanged glances. Will I ever be able to utter a sentence like that? Perpetua asked herself. Will I have the faith for it, the composure?

The other two went, but Perpetua stayed. This was appropriate, given that she was Catherine's attendant. Orphaned, she leaned over the bed, trying not to break into tears in front of the old nun. Catherine didn't approve of excesses of emotion.

"Where are my rosary beads?" asked Catherine.

Perpetua got them from the old nun's bedside table. "Here they are. Did you want to say the Rosary?"

"The Joyful Mysteries," said Catherine. "They're the ones for me now."

Perpetua recited two decades, that is, twenty Hail Marys, with Catherine. Then she noticed that the old nun had fallen unconscious or asleep. She let go of her own rosary beads, which hung from the belt of her habit. She rose. But the old nun instantly woke and raised a hand, grabbing Perpetua's right wrist.

"Perpetua, you're not a happy girl, are you? I can smell unhappiness. It reeks, you know. It's worse than swill or this body odor they talk about these days. If you want to be a good nun, you have to be at ease. And you're not at ease. If it stays like this, then you have to do something for it. That's my advice, mother to daughter, and it's serious advice because I won't be giving you much more. You can lose your soul in the convent. I've seen it happen. So do something, girl. Do something. Be brave and talk to your spiritual director. You will, won't you?"

"Yes," said Perpetua. "I'll do something."

The old lady smiled painfully. "You'll have a friend in Paradise," she murmured.

And on that last canny smile, she did become unconscious, and barely rallied over the next three days.

Perpetua sought permission to stay on night duty the evening they knew Catherine would die of congestion of the lungs.

She'd heard nuns speak of someone having "a sublime death." In fact it was looked upon as something worth both praying for and working toward. Yet she never thought it achievable.

Catherine, however, had a sublime death. As life diminished in her, and her face became more sculptured, a glow of expectation rose in her face. She expired in the classic way, emitting her soul in one long, well-modulated breath.

Perpetua did not weep. But she felt orphaned nonetheless. *She* was left to live with Catherine's last and crucial items of advice.

In that front downstairs room, the one for distinguished patients, Michael Proud was making a melancholy recovery. They were beginning to set dates when he could travel, so that the Church in Rossclare could be relieved of his scandalous presence. It was just as well he was making some sort of recovery, since he was not ready to die; his death would have been a tormented one. And if I stay here, Perpetua realized, mine will be intolerable too. A miserable death at the end of a miserable life. Just for the privilege of wearing the habit.

Cunningly, as if no special counsel had come to her from

Catherine, she tried not to show more than normal grief at the old nun's graveside. Catherine was buried in a section of Rossclare cemetery devoted entirely to nuns and brothers. Here the names of saints and the names of the Irish—for nearly all *these* dead were Irish—called from the gravestones. And now Catherine was joining them in their mansions, in a burial ceremony conducted by His Lordship Bishop Flannery and attended by the Privy Council of the diocese. In fact, since they had solved the Proud crisis, Catherine's funeral was the last thing to delay them in Rossclare, and they would now return to their parishes.

"God's daughter, Catherine, is now safely gathered in the beatific fold," said His Lordship, and the words very nearly drove Perpetua to frank howls of grief, to a primal keening that celebrated the greatness of the holy dead, but also declared how orphaned we are without their presence.

She had been putting off all decisions because she wanted to stay with Catherine, and because the sanest voice, the one she first heard in the mornings, was Catherine's.

Generally the nuns received their mail on Saturdays, except in the penitential season of Lent, when no mail was handed out except in the case of a member of a nun's family becoming ill or some other extraordinary event. Perpetua was handed a letter from her mother. Felice said Mrs. Reardon had called long distance and asked that Perpetua be given the news and the letter, which told that her brother, although whole, had finally been taken off operational flights and was receiving medical attention.

Perpetua felt the weight of Bernard's night terrors lift from her, an echo of the way they must be lifting from her parents and from Bernard Reardon himself. Yet the letter above all confirmed that now she was awesomely alone; that jubilant letter from Mrs. Reardon telling her that her brother was off operations. Catherine being with her Lord, the question of Perpetua herself, the nun, the woman, the—as Catherine would have said—*girl*, now had to be faced on its merits.

On the strength of the letter from her mother, she wrote one of her own to Father Murphy.

Dear Father,

I know you are very busy with the Privy Council, but I feel that after having delayed too long to see you, I must see you and seek your advice.

Yours sincerely,
Sister Perpetua

Murphy sent her a note in reply, saying that he would see her at quarter to six that evening in the sacristy of the convent chapel, the normal place for such conferences.

Her hands were sweating as she entered the sacristy from the direction of the chapel, right on time. Murphy generally entered from the outside, using the key Felice had issued him. He was already seated at the conference table as Perpetua came in, found the small font of holy water by the door, dipped her fingers and blessed herself. She was distressed to see that Murphy looked a little distracted and pale, as if he had stayed up too late talking, arguing, even gossiping with his fellow councillors.

"Well, Perpetua," he said. "Let us pray."

He half knelt, as if his muscles weren't up to a full-scale kneeling. Perpetua went to her knees. Murphy rattled through the first half of the Hail Mary. Perpetua supplied the second half at a somewhat more sedate speed, but not enough to offend him by implying that he'd rushed the first half. What did it matter anyhow? she asked herself.

He took to his seat again, and so did Perpetua.

"It hasn't been much of a week, has it?" he asked. "I suppose it's worse for some people on the battlefield. My cousin Frank Lacey, for example. Pauline Lacey just got a telegram from the army. He's been wounded on Bougainville by a sniper. What a bloody waste. But it seems he'll live—no worries about that."

Perpetua was chastened by this news. "Please, Father Murphy, if you'd rather—"

"No, no. It's now above all that a man would like to be of some use to someone. With poor Mickey Proud like he is. and Pauline Lacey demented." He laughed. "And the Privy bloody Council all gathered in Rossclare." He shook his head. "Tell me what's distressing you, Perpetua."

"Don't be angry with me," she said. "It won't be any use." She thought she knew him well enough to be able to tell him that. "I understand that I'm responsible for what happened to Father Proud."

He shook his head. "We're all responsible, Perpetua. Now come on, you're a good-looking girl, and everyone knows it, and you'd have to be an eed-jit not to know it yourself. But you're not as *fatale* a *femme* as all that. In fact, if I didn't know you better, I'd say you were indulging yourself with vain imaginings."

She felt angry blood in her face. "I've been deceived long enough with that sort of argument."

He looked closely at her. "Yes, I suppose you have. Sorry, Perpetua. Go on."

So she went back to Father Proud's visit to Brosnan's beach house, of the stare and the fierce grip which, if she had had the courage, she would have reported earlier to him, to Murphy.

"And what could I have done with it?" he asked. "Do you think I'm a wise man, some sort of a shaman? Do you think I could have read the signs?"

"I think you would have stopped him from hurting himself."

"You flatter me, Perpetua. I couldn't have stayed with him all night, could I? And if a man wants to do that to himself . . . then he will. No one's to blame directly, because what he did couldn't be predicted."

He wiped his forehead and then his eyes, and Perpetua could not tell if there were tears there or not.

"I want to leave the order," said Perpetua.

She knew he would always be her friend when he did not blink. Instead he said a little wearily, "Do you know, or are you able to say, why you want to leave?"

"I wanted to remain a nun to stay with Catherine as long as she lived. I'm sad to say that reason's gone now. I have to go. Because I cannot *save my soul* here, I can't be properly happy as I'm meant by my Maker to be. I wanted to be a member of a sisterhood. But the sisterhood keeps on breaking down into what is certainly meanness. There are great women here who can face that and continue joyfully. One of them is Felice. Another is my friend Timothy. But it's not possible for me, and I'm certain I won't be given the means to make it possible. I don't mind for a moment giving up the normal desires of the earth for the desires a nun should have—above all, the desire for sisterhood and compassion.

But desire of all kinds keeps breaking through too. It would be better to lead a normal life, with normal desire, than face the sort of thing that's happened in the last few days. That's what I'm certain of, anyhow—that God wants me to keep to the simple, the normal."

"You're not very impressed with the way we handled the Michael Proud business, are you?"

"I'd rather not say. It's hard enough to talk as I'm already talking."

"Come on, Perpetua," said Murphy. "You can be honest with me."

"We were all too concerned," said Perpetua, deciding to try telling him, "with keeping the matter secret than with asking why he'd done it."

"You're right," said Murphy, shifting in his chair. "Go on. Go on, for God's sake."

"No one worried about his happiness. Except, I have to say it, you."

He waved that aside. "So the Proud business wouldn't have improved things for you . . ."

"In some ways it brought the question to a head."

"You haven't lost what they call 'the Faith'?"

Perpetua had to pause. "I don't think so."

"And you can't forgive us our imperfections?"

"It's not a matter of forgiving. And it's not a matter of perfection or imperfection. I'm the most imperfect nun there is, and a lot of people rightly tell me so. It's meanness I can't live with. There isn't sense to living with meanness, to obeying the Rule and living this life, just for meanness. That's what I'm certain of, at least in my case."

Murphy looked away for a second. Then he said, "Well, I suppose you know what I'm going to say to you, don't you? I'm going to say that you should reflect about it, meditate on it, pray on it. You can't be certain that you're certain at any given moment." Then he stared at her. "Perpetua, you're always talking about your life being devoted to your brother's safety. I just mention that—"

"They've taken him off operations and promoted him again. And decorated him. He's safe from *that* kind of death now. But no matter what I do, I can't bring about his utter safety. I know that. Father Proud taught me that. By what he did."

"Indeed," murmured Murphy, and wandered off into reflection.

"I know I'll never be able to accept the meanness," said Perpetua. "That'll remain the same yesterday, today, and so on."

He said with a trace of irritation, "Don't be so certain about things. You had better be convinced before you face Mother Felice, and then I'll tell you the one you shouldn't face before you're absolutely certain. And that's Dr. Lawlor. I mean, it's not a simple matter for you—your order takes solemn vows. If you want to leave, it's going to have to go to Rome. Imagine that. The Congregation for Religious." He shook his head. "Wouldn't it be easier to stay and put up with this? No, I don't mean that. I agree with you. It *oughtn't* to be a compromise. But of course it is. In the end. Life is a compromise for all of us, God help us. For lay people too. They do the best they can with the cards they're dealt."

Perpetua knew this to be the truth. She'd seen her parents doing the best they could with their cards while attending to the accounts on Saturday afternoons in Rose Bay.

"It's hard being a nun, Father Murphy," she said. "It isn't worth it if you have to live meanly."

"Why do you keep using that word?" he asked with a little stutter of dismayed laughter. "Maybe you're right, Perpetua. But you know what I think? About myself, I mean. I think I wouldn't have joined the seminary, lasted throughout that training, and been here, if I wasn't meant to be here, the howling scandal that I am! Don't worry, I know how they talk about Mrs. Pauline Lacey and myself. Well, I'm not going to make any confessions in that regard, except to my confessor, under the seal of the Sacrament. And they can say what they damned well like. You see, I've accepted it all. They're all limited fellows, one way or another, the Privy Council. We were told when we were children that they were the receptacles of all wisdom. But we know they aren't, and my only concern is that the College of Cardinals mightn't be much bloody better, excuse the French. But you don't think that the Bishop doesn't get letters about me, my behavior, the way I rush Mass, above all the way I admit I'm just a poor wanderer, like every other miserable creature in the pews? For some reason people think it's heresy for a priest not to shine with some sort of narrow-minded certitude. It seems to me, Perpetua, that sins and all, faults and all, we are exalted by the Grace of Christ. Let me tell you what I also believe, since it may be of some small help to you in this puzzle of yours. I believe that all the suffering of all the boys—the suffering of your brother, for example, the suffering of my cousin Sergeant Lacey as the sniper got him—all that is a renewal of the suffering of Christ, it's working toward some ultimate perfection that we can't understand but that we have to believe in. I believe in it, anyhow. So the meannesses—my own included—don't worry me the way they worry you. It's what I expect."

"Please pass on my regrets to Mrs. Lacey," said Perpetua. "And my best wishes for her husband's recovery."

"Perhaps you could write her a letter," said Murphy. "I don't know how many letters a week the Rule allows. It doesn't matter a hoot anyhow." He smoothed the folds of his cassock across his knees energetically, as if he were trying to combine the fabric with his skin.

Murphy said, "Listen. Take my suggestion. Go out of here with a clear mind, please, Perpetua. Just let the weekly routine of the Sisters of Compassion carry you along. We'll meet here in a week's time. If you still feel like you do now, then we'll start taking steps. But we won't rush it. I *know* the Bishop, I know Lawlor. You'll need some coaching in how to deal with them. But for another week look on yourself as a nun. Imagine yourself an old nun, like Mother Catherine was. She'd seen everything, yet she still stayed a nun."

"She became a nun in a different world than I became a nun in," said Perpetua.

"It's always the same damn world, Perpetua. Always."

They ended the session with yet another Hail Mary. Perpetua was full of an unrushed certainty that she would be needing Murphy's coaching on how to deal with the Bishop and with everyone else.

30

Decrees

FATHER Proud left the diocese of Rossclare by train one morning nearly three weeks after his operation. A brother from the monastery in Sydney where he would be recuperating was sent up the coast to travel with him and make conversation during the journey. None of the nuns at the hospital was given the chance to say good-bye to him. Perhaps he was too confused and even abashed to say anything to them anyhow.

Yet his departure did not seem to have undermined the majesty of Bishop Flannery, who summoned Perpetua to his house one day in early March, a few hours after her brother had returned from Warrant Officer Dow's tea party, and while he dreamed, on a lighter dosage of drugs the doctors were trying to accustom him to, of the fire of Dresden. Sister Francis was assigned to travel with her the two hundred yards or so between the convent and cathedral. Francis would not be admitted to the Bishop's parlor, however, but was expected to wait outside while her sister in the community was interviewed. Nor did Francis know why Perpetua merited an interview with the exalted Bishop of Rossclare. Francis may have been chosen to go along to the Bishop's house with her, Perpetua thought, exactly because Francis wasn't really a gossip—denouncing you at Chapter of Faults was her passion. She could, however, be depended on not to start speculating aloud about Perpetua during the recreation hours in the convent.

With Perpetua in the Bishop's hallway, she sat without speaking at all. The house was paneled with cedars from up the river, cedars probably cut down and milled by relatives of Father Murphy's. Life's great circle, thought Perpetua.

They were there a quarter of an hour before Dr. Lawlor, the Bishop's secretary, appeared from the parlor door and said a little peevishly, "His Lordship is waiting for you inside, Sister Perpetua."

Perpetua got up trembling. She felt like a heretic about to face a medieval bishop. Perhaps that was what His Lordship Patrick Flannery was. Perhaps that was the trouble.

She suffered a sickening doubt about her strength to face this great dignitary, to keep on insisting to his face on what she knew was necessary for her survival. She could not see the man at first. His parlor was dark—the blinds were completely down to keep out the glare of the summer's day—and as well paneled as the hallway. An enormous reproduction of Da Vinci's *Last Supper* hung over the large sideboard. There were framed photographs of Popes Leo XIII, Pius X, Pius XI, and the rather clerkly features, in color, of Pius XII, who throughout the war had remained on his island of autonomy in the Vatican and was now surrounded by the genial armies of the Allies—just as a year past he had been surrounded by the German Army.

The Bishop of Rossclare could be seen now in the diminished light, sitting at the head of an enormous cedar table. He wore his purple-piped soutane and the pectoral cross he had received in 1938 from the hands of the Pope himself.

Absently he extended his hand, his Bishop's ring on it, inherited for centuries by one Irish Bishop after another, a fragment of the true cross contained in it. Perpetua walked up to the table, went down on her knees and kissed the ring. Then Lawlor led her back down the table to a chair set directly to face the Bishop down that long stretch of cedar. He had put a chair for himself to one side of the table, closer to Perpetua than to Bishop Flannery. She could smell Lawlor's scented brilliantine, and down the table the Bishop's ruddy face, his white scalp under his rakish white thatch of hair, shone with authority and seemed to her to have been polished by the same hand that had brought the table to a high gloss.

"We should pray," said Bishop Flannery. He began to recite— a Pater Noster, three Hail Marys, a Glory Be. Perpetua and Dr. Lawlor recited with him, leaving the first half of the Hail Marys to him, but reciting the second half. When it was all finished, he raised his head and stared down the table at her. She could not help but drop her eyes, but then she thought, If you drop your gaze now, how will it be in a quarter of an hour?

Bishop Flannery could, by pursing his lips, speak in a voice as thin yet as penetrating as a sharpened wire. "Sister Perpetua," he intoned, "your superior, Mother Felice, has asked me to speak to you, and of course I invited my secretary to be present, given his grasp of the canon law. I believe you've actually gone so far as to utter doubts about your sacred calling. You've gone so far as to be quite definite about it as well, definite with your spiritual director, definite with your Mother Superior. Some would say your entire convent career has been marked by a certain impetuosity. How old are you, Sister?"

"Twenty-four years old in April, Your Lordship." She swallowed. "A grown woman," she insisted.

"Twenty-four years. That's the age at which many a student for the priesthood takes inescapably, for life, for all eternity, the responsibilities of the priesthood. It's an age when people are supposed to be approaching mature judgment. People shouldn't be surrendering to impulses at such an age."

Perpetua said, "Your Lordship—" but her voice perniciously broke, so she coughed and began again. "Your Lordship, this is not a matter of impulse. I'm willing to admit that such a decision could in some cases be a matter of impulse, though I don't think anyone lightly takes on or lightly casts off a life like ours. But impetuosity doesn't apply in this case. I would very much like to be able to stay. It would be easier, it would create less turmoil. But I can tell it isn't God's will."

Bishop Flannery hit the table with his left, unringed hand. "There you go. You're telling me what is and what isn't a matter of impulse! You're telling me that you know what God's will is, as if He speaks to you. I've rarely had nuns twice your age talk up to me like this, do you realize that? The Pope's supposed to be the one who's infallible. Not junior nuns in the Australian bush, I'll tell you that much."

"Forgive me, Your Lordship," Perpetua insisted. "But we only have the conscience that we're given. And that conscience says that I am not meant to stay."

She was pleased to realize that the argument had become one between equals, even though in Church terms she and His Lordship were nothing like equal. In arguments waged as between unequals, she knew she'd be swamped.

"Vanity," said Bishop Flannery. "You *made* the vows, Sister. I presume you meant them when you took them, though I'm beginning to wonder. You can't run away from them just because there are little unpleasantnesses, or because someone treats you meanly at Chapter of Faults. If we all ran away for those sorts of reasons, the convents and the altars would be empty."

He thought for a while, and Perpetua could see that he didn't intend her to interrupt him. "This nonsense hasn't anything to do with Father Proud, has it? Answer me the truth!"

Perpetua's hands were sweating. How could she answer that? She could say yes, she was appalled at the solution they had arrived at, but then he would be able to flay her again and ask her what would she know about it. Or else she could lie and say it had nothing to do with that. Before she was ready to speak, she could hear her own voice in the room.

It said, "I am a member of the order called the Sisters of Compassion, Your Lordship. Perhaps I was expecting a different sort of community. I see compassion in what the order does, and I see it in Mother Felice. But I don't always see it in myself and in the others. And one part of me says, What is the sense of all this, of the habit and the Rule, if there isn't compassion? And another part of me says that if I can't find compassion here, I have to go and look for it somewhere else. Otherwise I'll lose my soul for the sake of staying a nun. I'm trying to be honest, Your Lordship."

Dr. Lawlor had made a sucking, skeptical noise with his teeth. Otherwise there was silence.

"What a folly!" said Bishop Flannery at last. "Do you expect perfection from everybody? Yourself excluded, of course. Let me tell you, girl, that's the worst arrogance. Jesus, Mary, and Joseph! Who gives you the right to expect perfect compassion from everyone around you? You won't find it out there, you know. Not in the world. You'll find only ruins, let me tell you. Dr. Lawlor, tell her the position in canon law."

Dr. Lawlor smoothed his eyebrows and began. "Well, the position is that the Sacred Congregation of Religious in Rome has more to do than discuss your vocation, Sister Perpetua. Your vows are made for eternity, like the vows of a priest. You must live with them. Are you going to shame your parents, and the faithful in your parish and here in Rossclare, by refusing to do so? If you did that, you'd be really lost and your name would be a matter of shame. . . ."

"And so, dear Sister Perpetua," said the Bishop, clapping his hands, "I'll say a Mass for you and you'll return to your convent and pray and meditate for the coming year, and you won't expect people to be absolute saints, because that is really the height of satanic pride. I am willing to bless you."

Indeed he stood and sketched a sign of the Cross in her direction.

"Your Lordship," said Perpetua. The words ground through her throat and over her clenched tongue. "I believe that there is a section of the canon law which deals with this sort of matter. I believe there is a chapter called 'About Leaving Religion.' I believe there is a decree of exclaustration for those who wish to leave the order temporarily, and a decree of secularization for those who want to leave permanently. I would be grateful for either of those decrees, but I think it is only fair to tell you that I know in my conscience that what is needed is a decree of secularization."

The Bishop had gone more ruddy still. "Who has been coaching you, girl?" he asked. "I can't believe this. Are you teaching Dr. Lawlor, a doctor of canon law from the Collegio di Propaganda Fide in Rome, how to suck eggs?"

I might as well speak while he's suffering shock, Perpetua thought. "Forgive me, Your Lordship," she said. "But the Church is merciful in its canon law." Though she wondered if it was so. "I want its mercy now. I beg you to apply for a decree of secularization."

She heard a silence all around her. Then Dr. Lawlor's precise voice. "It is a matter for Mother Felice. And for your ordinary, the Bishop of Rossclare. They will decide this between them. Speak to your spiritual director. We certainly shall."

The idea that they would speak to Felice and Father Murphy heartened her. She heard the Bishop say, "Do you have some grand scheme to do with marriage?"

A sudden rage rose from her stomach, trembled in her shoulders, yet came out cold and calm in her voice. "I have no grand scheme, Your Lordship. My only grand scheme is the demands of my conscience."

"And if let out, even temporarily, if 'exclaustrated,' I suppose you'd go and pester poor Michael Proud?"

"Your Lordship is very wrong to say that. I have never pestered Father Proud."

"Don't tell me I'm wrong!" said His Lordship, his voice trembling dangerously. He was not used even to his own priests standing up to him frontally.

"It would be a falsehood if that sort of thing were said about me," Perpetua insisted.

"You can get out, Sister Perpetua. You can leave. Get back to your convent. I can see the unsuitability that hides there behind the habit of nun."

Tears rose to her eyes. She fought them. "That is all I've been trying to talk to you about, Your Lordship. My unsuitability. I confess it. And if I do, then the canon law must take a certain direction. The decree of secularization."

"You can go," said Bishop Flannery again. "I mean, back to the convent. You are a most unfilial girl. If you wish to stay a nun, you'll need to improve. If you don't improve, the order's well quit of you."

"I've tried to be a good nun."

"You are a peevish child," said His Lordship. Yet somehow there was a streak of childlike peevishness in his own voice.

She rose, inclined her head, and left.

She found it easier to talk to Felice, who spoke to her over the next two days while she went on working in the hospital, hospital work being, she suspected, the main remnant of her vocation as a nun. She was aware that Felice was making complicated long distance calls south to St. Bridie's. "I am not convinced," said Felice, "that you're simply not being wrongheaded and deliberately strong-willed."

At five-thirty one morning it was Felice who woke Perpetua,

and not the normal rostered nun, and cried, *"Benedicamus Domino,* Perpetua."

"Deo gratias," sang Perpetua, struggling upright from her bed.

"This morning you are exempted from office and meditation," said Felice. "You are to pack your bags. You are going to our house at Potts Point in Sydney to do a retreat of three days. The train leaves, as you know, at half past eleven this morning." Felice turned, then paused. "Don't take everything with you, Perpetua. Dear Sister, I would like to see you come back. You're a good girl. You will make a good nun. I don't think you should talk to the other nuns. You can come back to your room straight after breakfast. I shall help you down to the side gate of the hospital when the time comes. Father Murphy will be driving you to the station."

Perpetua began packing. Books, nightdress, hairbrush to comb her spiky, cropped hair, notebooks, medical texts, her whole life. It fitted easily inside one big "port," as Australians called it—one large piece of luggage.

Perpetua wrote a note for Timothy.

My dearest Timothy,

I am being sent to Sydney, and I intend to leave the order. I hope this does not shock or scandalize you. I am happy for you that you have found a home here. I'll always remember you, and perhaps they will let me come and see you after I've been a lay person for a time.

Give my warmest love to Sister McGowan and Bernadette Brady. They are in my memories and my prayers.

Your sister in Christ,
Perpetua Reardon

This note she slipped to Timothy as they both left the chapel for breakfast. During the reading in the refectory, Timothy sought Perpetua's eyes. She looked stunned, Perpetua was unhappy to see. She tried to combine reassurance, encouragement, consola-tion, into the one returned look, but it wasn't possible.

Back in her room she had time to think. There was a future she had to deal with. There might be men in that future. She realized with surprise that she had thought of none of that up till now. All her care had been concentrated on the battle to achieve the decree that would be the beginning of her sanity.

At half past ten Felice knocked on her door again. Half embarrassed at each other, between them they carried her bag down the strange, vacant mid-morning corridor of the convent, downstairs to the garden, out of the side gate by outpatients, where a soldier, his wife, and a young child just arriving for treatment stood back and nodded to the two nuns. Beyond the fence waited Father Murphy's black car. Perpetua kissed Felice's hand and then got in the back of the car while Murphy held the door open. He closed it after her and threw her bag into the back. Felice was weeping now, Perpetua saw.

"Don't cry," Perpetua begged her. She wound the window down so Felice could hear her. "Don't cry."

"We'd better go," said Father Murphy. "They say the train is right on time." He got into the driver's seat and they drove away. Perpetua looked at the already strange and diminishing figure of Felice. The convent of Rossclare, which Perpetua had left only a few seconds before, was already shrinking in memory.

She and Father Murphy journeyed largely in silence, making only the most routine remarks, between the convent and the railway station. But as he carried her bag onto the platform for her, up the set of wooden steps beside which there was a stand for milk cans, he grew confidential. "You've faced Felice, and you've faced the Bishop. Don't let them persuade you against your will. If something changes inside you while you're on retreat and you feel that it's right to stay, then do so. But don't stay if you know in your blood that it's a mistake."

They emerged on the station amongst the farmers, the soldiers, the commercial travelers, and looked north into the sun to see if the train was coming.

"They think I'm willful, and arrogant," said Perpetua. "Perhaps I am."

"You're given an instinct for survival," said Father Murphy, "so that you can survive."

The train arrived, and long after he had helped her aboard and found her reserved seat, he stayed dolefully outside the window of her carriage, as if he, too, dreamed of some sort of escape. She felt unworthy as farmers and schoolboys, soldiers and occasional sailors and airmen passed in the corridor, chatting, looking for seats, speculating on whether they ought to risk grabbing a first-class seat. How she wished she wore their prosaic clothes, that she were not an impostor in a medieval habit.

As Murphy had predicted, nothing came out of the retreat except a greater certainty that she should go. Even Mother Fredericka, the provincial, became reconciled to that. Under the suspicion, though, that she was just being stubborn, Fredericka brought in the Novice Mistress to speak with her. But by now Perpetua was resolute. She dreaded only telling her parents, meeting them, looking for signs of disappointment in them. But she had the strength of someone who knows she is fighting for everything.

31

―――――――

Ordinary People

A T the end of her three days of silent reflection, she was allowed to write to the Reardons.

Dear Mother and Father,

I am very sad to have to tell you that it has become impossible for me to pursue the vocation of a Sister of Compassion. I regret very much the grief and even the expense this will cause you. I hope it will not give you too much social embarrassment, but if it will, I don't have to come home—I can live apart and visit you. I know that being the people you are, you will want to see me, and I am grateful for that. There are parents who would cast off a daughter who left the convent.

That is one of the reasons I am leaving—because I am your daughter, and I am aware of the danger of a religious vocation turned sour. Indeed, I have seen such vocations, occasionally, in the convent, though by and large I am full of admiration for my sisters.

I have applied to the Holy See through my superiors for a decree of exclaustration and secularization. When I receive it, I shall be able to pursue a normal life. In the

meantime, as long as I keep certain of my vows, excluding
the vow of poverty—I intend immediately to seek a job in a
hospital—I can live in the outside world until the decree is
granted. Apparently it is a matter of course, otherwise
Mother Fredericka would not be willing to let me go.

There is a stupid practical problem. I have no clothes—
the clothes I entered with in 1938 have been given to the
poor. I wonder could you approach one of my old school
friends, Kathleen Corrigan, say, and ask her would she
mind loaning me some clothes with which I could leave the
convent. I shall need a scarf, since we keep our hair cropped.
Again, I am sorry for the grief this will cause you. But our
main duty in life is the salvation of our souls, and I have
always taken this to mean happiness. You have taught me in
those terms. I thank God for the parents I have.

Your loving daughter,
Perpetua—Teresa

One morning in late March Fredericka took Perpetua straight
from the breakfast table into a dimly remembered part of this
convent where Perpetua had been a novice. She opened the door
into a room Perpetua had nearly forgotten, the room where she
had been presented by her parents years ago when she first applied to join the order. There was a redolence of beeswax and
polish, a table smaller than Bishop Flannery's, and, severely ar-
rayed around the walls, a series of chairs. A picture of the Sacred
Heart adorned one wall, a statue of the Virgin on a pedestal
backed onto another, and a photograph of the Supreme Pontiff,
for whose safe survival of the war all Christendom had prayed,
hung by the door.

A genial, freckled Irish nun called Helen, who looked after the
doors and did little else, entered with a bulky brown-paper parcel.
She put it on the table, nodded to Fredericka, then withdrew.

The elderly nun said, "Your worldly clothes are in that parcel.
I pray for your happiness, Perpetua. But I still believe that behind
all this is impetuosity."

"Mother, can I say without seeming impudent—our wills are
there to be exercised?"

"That's a glib answer, Sister Perpetua."

"I must go. I know it."

Fredericka uttered a great sigh. All at once Perpetua understood that Fredericka's own life as a nun was under threat, that it was the same with all of them. That every time somebody left, as rare as that was, the question of the wisdom of the convent life had to be asked; and that was not always a comfortable question.

Perpetua kissed her hand.

Fredericka said, "You will place your habit across the table as you take it off. When you are dressed in your street clothes, Sister Helen will let you out of the side door where your parents are waiting."

The old nun closed her eyes. "There is some time, Perpetua. It will be weeks before the decree comes from Rome."

Perpetua said, half embarrassed, that if she could return with a full heart and an easy conscience, then she would.

"What does 'full heart' mean?" asked Sister Fredericka. "God go with you, daughter."

Then she dipped her right hand in the holy water font by the door and left while crossing herself. Suspended between two worlds now, Perpetua had limitless time to change. She took off the veil, the hard-starched headpiece, the cap that held the veil together, the starched breastpiece. She was grateful there was no mirror in the room by which she could see herself. She did not want to be aware of herself half habited in this way, with her spiky hair above the main robes of the order. She took those off too. Suddenly she was just a girl in a slip.

She undid the bundle in the brown paper. Someone had put a sachet of lavender in with the clothing—it was probably Kathleen Corrigan, whom Perpetua remembered as a fastidious sort of girl. The suit her mother had brought for her from her old school friend was a light violet. Perpetua's stomach turned over at its beauty. Will I be allowed to wear such things? she wondered dazedly. But then, of course, she realized she was about to wear such things. There was also a plain white blouse and a blue scarf. Last of all, a black handbag, a pair of black shoes with very high heels, and some stockings. She knew enough about the outside world to understand that stockings were hard to come by. She wondered how her mother had acquired them—it was more likely that her mother had found them for her than that Kathleen Corrigan had donated a pair.

She hoped that her plain, convent-suitable slip would not show beneath the hemline of the fine violet suit.

Into the handbag she put her crucifix, which she had been allowed to bring with her. And she still wore on her right hand the narrow gold band she had been given at her profession as a nun.

It took her nearly half an hour to dress. Without a mirror, she had to check by look and feel. She was not accustomed to the business of getting her stocking seams straight, and even that took more than five minutes. She was not accustomed to high heels, either, and had to practice walking in them.

She tied the scarf around her spiky brown hair. She felt branded by the odd way the scarf felt, and wondered how she would pass as a normal modern girl on the street outside. But above all she had a terror of facing her aggrieved parents.

At last, when it could be avoided no longer, she opened the door into the corridor. The Irish nun who looked after the doors was in the corridor. "God bless you, Perpetua," she said in a singsong voice. She opened the door into the street. Perpetua stepped through slowly—she wanted this exit to take a little time. But the instant she was clear of the door, it shut behind her. She turned and looked at its wood. She heard a crunch of shoes behind her, turned and saw her father first, in a good suit, and then her mother in a large hat with a veil. Her father began weeping.

For a time she could not breathe, but at last she said, "Don't be sad. Please don't be sad."

He had not wanted her to be a nun at first, but she feared he may now have gotten used to it, to the especial pride and credit a man had in the Irish-Catholic community if his daughter belonged to such a famous order.

But he waved his hand. "I'm not sad," he said. "It's the twentieth century, after all, not the Middle Ages, no matter that some would like to pretend so. I'm glad, that's all, to have my son and daughter back."

She did not understand exactly what he meant.

Her mother swept her into her arms. "Your brother's coming home, Teresa. He's been decorated as well."

"Yet again," said Mr. Reardon, the weeping rebel. "He should have told them to keep it."

But he was laughing too. Bernard was flying home, they said, in a flying boat, all the way from London, by way of Egypt and South

Africa and across an ocean dotted by a series of island air fields built by war.

Their arms tentatively around her, or else occasionally holding and squeezing Perpetua's hand, the three of them walked like ordinary people up the corner and turned right to King's Cross, said to be the sin capital of the nation, whose violence fed patients directly into the casualty ward of St. Bridie's. Her father hailed a cab.

She sank into its backseat and looked at her parents on either side. "We've all come through the furnace," she said.

"Exactly right," breathed Tom Reardon.

32

The Girl Who
Dressed Like Nurses

SHE got herself a job in the casualty ward at the Prince of Wales. There was a young doctor named Foley there, a resident, who joked with her, yet she found she remained reserved because of the suspicion she might be taken to task at Chapter of Faults. But then she remembered that she would never face a Chapter of Faults again.

It was the best job she could have gotten, since it required her to wear the nursing sister's veil, which hid her not properly grown hair. She looked very handsome in her nurse's uniform, or so her father told her. And so Dr. Foley regularly implied.

One day as she left the hospital after duty, making her way toward the bus stop, a black car pulled up beside her. There was a frame on its roof which held a thick, squarish canvas balloon full of gas—that is, it was a typical, gas-saving, patriotic car. Foley jumped from it, from the backseat. He wore his white coat and the professional-looking array of pens he kept in his breast pocket. He approached Teresa Reardon.

"You'll have to get back into the car with me," he said with a rakish grin.

"Why?"

"I flagged that driver down and told him that one of our

psychiatric patients had escaped, one who steals nurses' costumes all the time and walks out in them. Now, if you don't get into the car, his faith in the medical profession will be undermined. You wouldn't want that to happen, I don't think."

"You're going to take me back to the hospital?"

"That's the idea."

"And what happens then?"

"I'm off duty in twenty minutes. I've got a little Austin, and I can take you home, or maybe out to tea and to the pictures. Have you seen *Song of Bernadette* or Errol Flynn in *Custer's Last Stand?*"

She couldn't tell him, in a suburban street, that she didn't think it right to go out with him or anyone else until her decree came through from Rome.

"No, I haven't. But I don't need to."

She had been worried about going out on her own, in this season of such full-blown fashions, when women wore their hair pendulously over their shoulders and in hair nets, while others, particularly blondes, wore it piled as profusely as a fancy cake on top of their heads.

"Well, we could see *Song of Bernadette* or *Custer's Last Stand.* And afterward we could go to Repins for coffee, like a couple of Bohemians. Or if you like, I could try to undermine your virtue with a bottle of wine. Listen, you should stick with me. When the Germans surrender—and it's got to be any day now—I'm going to stage the party all the glamorous nurses will want to be at. So don't give me any trouble. And get into the car."

The idea made her laugh. She decided to go with him to the car. The berserkness of it appealed to her.

"Am I supposed to behave madly?" she asked.

"It'd be better," said Foley, "if you acted catatonic."

He took her elbow and helped her into the car. She found to her astonishment that she was enjoying herself.

The driver was a thin, serious man of about forty. He wore his hat even inside the car and, from beneath its brim, looked at her with some fear and suspicion.

"Just back to the hospital, if you would be so kind," said Dr. Foley.

"But I'm Sister Reardon, from outpatients," said Perpetua in a version of a confused voice.

"Come on, Amy," said Dr. Foley. "You'll never get out if you keep saying that."

"But I have got out," said Teresa. That was a joke inside the larger joke; a joke of her own. It gave her an air of mental confusion that seemed to have convinced the driver.

"Listen," said Foley, outrageously enjoying himself. "You've been good lately, but this is very reprehensible. We're going to have to put you in the isolation ward if this goes on!"

When they were back at the front gate of the hospital, Foley roundly thanked the driver. Teresa Reardon left the car lightly, and dutifully waited on the pavement. She had an acute temptation to smile sanely at the man, to include him in the joke. I'm getting used to behaving like a normal woman, she thought with a little amazement.

She did not smile, though. The man deserved not to be mocked, and even now gas was precious, and Dr. Foley had used a little of it up flippantly. For all anyone knew, even that cupful might be needed for the invasion of Singapore and Malaya, the invasion of Japan itself. After the man had driven off, Sister Reardon said, "Do you mind if I catch my bus now?"

"Look," said Foley. He had a crooked smile that was characteristic of her father as well. "I'll make a deal with McMahon—he can take my last twenty minutes. Registrar will slit my throat if he knows."

"But I live at Rose Bay," said Teresa. "Won't it use up a lot of gas?"

"It's worth it."

"I was thinking of the war effort."

"I *did* spend two and a half years in the Middle East, in the infantry. I'm not just the handsome civilian wastrel you think I am. I'm entitled to a little indulgence, especially when I meet a girl like you."

"I'm not a girl like me," said Teresa. "At least, you don't know anything about me."

"Are you a Catholic or a Protestant?"

"Catholic. Why?"

"Well, Catholics are livelier. Once you get them past the venial sin part."

Soon she was sitting in the front of his Austin with him, heading toward the eastern suburbs, through the Cross to Rose Bay.

She evaded his questions about what her professional career had been. She asked him a number of questions about himself as a means of stopping too much inquiry from him. He said that he'd had some liver disease in the Middle East. They'd shipped him home. It had been a bit touch and go, but he'd been able to do his final year of Medicine in 1944—he took it up from where he'd left off in 1939. It was much easier now, he said. If you'd been a soldier, they were pretty soft on you.

"They didn't know what fools they were letting loose on the public! But there you are. Doctors aren't God, as much as people would like them to be. I don't know. I wouldn't really mind doing something else, now that I know how big the world is. Maybe go to Europe and paint pictures. Do you think that Australians can paint pictures? Or do you think we're only good for cricket?"

At last, quicker than she thought, they were turning out of Old South Head Road into the Reardons' street. Foley braked in front of the house she indicated. On the veranda three people were drinking tea. One of them was for some reason a thin RAAF officer. She jerked in the front seat. Something had happened to her brother. This man had come to break the news.

It was only an instant's terror. She realized that this thin man, chatting away, smiling shyly, staring at his teacup through hollow eyes, was her aged brother, the Australian hero.

"Who's the fellow with all the medals and campaign ribbons?" asked Dr. Foley. "Don't tell me you're a married woman."

"It's my brother," said Teresa Reardon.